THE RAVENING WOLVES

A NULL
&
BOYD NOIR

GARY S. KADET

For the Greater Boston Visionary Outpost — GBVO — that still exists somewhere in time and the multiverse and its members Link Yaco (Weasel), Anne Snodgrass (Snuffy), Me (Perfessor), Randy Winchester (Tubby), Erica Fox (Mrs. "T"), Meg Ormond (Spooky), the late Arnold Lelis (Bruiser) and the late Steve Campbell (Soapy).

And especially for Jeff Kadet, world-champion DX-er, TV Guide Specialist and my first bad influence.

"Beware of false prophets, which come to you in sheep's clothing, but inwardly they are ravening wolves."

— MATTHEW 7:15, KING JAMES BIBLE

"As long as the house of The Holy Spirit remains a haven for criminals the reputation of the Church will remain in ruins."

— SINEAD O'CONNOR

"Our work has made us realise once again that the gravity of the scourge of the sexual abuse of minors is, and historically has been, a widespread phenomenon in all cultures and societies. I am reminded of the cruel religious practice, once widespread in certain cultures, of sacrificing human beings – frequently children – in pagan rites."

THE GUARDIAN, SEPTEMBER 24, 2019, ANGELA GIUFFRIDA IN ROME

ONE

"You must have confessed *sometime,* my son."

"No. I mustn't."

"Just tell me how long it's been."

"I've never had the need."

"But you want the Lord Jesus Christ to absolve you of sin, which is why you're here, is it not?"

"No, Father. It's not."

"You're really not here to receive the sacrament of penance and reconciliation?"

"No, Father. We're long past that."

"Care to enlighten us as to why you seek confession my son?"

"I'll get to that."

"But you have sinned my son, is this not so?"

"Yes. In the Catholic faith, I have original sin, and all the sins I willingly heaped upon that after the fact."

"You can confess them to me now, if you like, my son."

"I don't care one way or the other."

"But we're talking about your immortal soul."

"Are we though? Is that really true?"

"Do you believe in God—are you even a *Catholic?*"

"I believe in nothing. But yes. I learned the Catechism and my mother had me baptized."

"I will hear your confession now, then, but you must first tell me your name, at least, so that I'll know who I'm talking to."

"If you're the voice of God, wouldn't you know already?"

"You must offer it."

"Joseph Xavier."

"Now confess."

"I was, I suppose, a good Catholic until Eamon Cuchulain—calling himself Uncle Jimmy—moved in with us. He beat my mother, pimped out my sister and had me arrested by cop cronies at age eleven. When I got out of juvie, he set me up to be a bagman for Winter Hill, then for the Family. I became a drug addict, a gambling addict, and then a low-level decoy snitch for Boston PD's Organized Crime Task Force, who ratted me out to the Family and their most deranged enforcer Ignazio "Cousin It" Cavilli, who tortured me for months, keeping me alive with medical care and a feeding tube while he mutilated me. He removed one of my testicles, sliced into my hamstring, applied an electric drill to my stomach—"

"There'll be enough of that, Joseph Xavier."

"Sorry, Father."

"Continue, please."

"After months of that, I lost my mind, and then some illegal therapy designed by a madman brought me back. But I wasn't the same. I was changed. Then I became…something."

"Became what, my son?"

"Something very different. Something…*strange.*"

"But none of this sounds as if it were your fault. And you're off the drugs and the gambling, yes?"

"That's right. They don't matter anymore."

"It hardly sounds like you're guilty of very much sin there, my son. And God has blessed your life by getting you off the drugs and the gambling. Your only sin is the sin of ingratitude. And for that, you must do penance. So, you shall pray the rosary—"

"I'm not done."

"How much more is there to confess, my son? It's growing quite late."

"I haven't gotten to the murders yet."

"You—haven't? *Murders?*"

"That's right, Father."

"Remember, Joseph Xavier: I'm not Father Mammock in the confessional. You must realize that I speak with the voice of the Lord. You'd do well to take that to heart, as penance has yet to be fully visited upon you by God."

"I killed them all. Every single member of the Family but one, and he'll be spending the rest of his life in the Lemuel Shattuck Hospital Correctional Unit."

"The sanitarium?"

"The laughing academy. Only he isn't laughing."

"You can't have done all that. You can't have gotten away with all *that.*"

"Why not? It's the one thing I do. And I'm really very good at it."

"That would make you a mass murderer. The newspapers reported the end of the Family years ago. Certainly, you'd have been apprehended by now."

"They think I'm dead."

"That's not possible."

"Yet, here I am."

"How can you survive?"

"I'm also the Meth King of Boston and, no longer only of Boston, but of all New England. I have heavy cash reserves. And the competition is...indisposed."

"And at the same time, they think you're dead."

"They *know* I'm dead. I've become an urban legend, a joke to the police. The bogeyman. A zombie. Except for one. She knows I'm alive. But wishes I were actually dead. And If I could wish for anything, I might wish that for myself, but I have no such feelings, impulses, yearnings, longings—even anxiety. They just don't exist for me. I don't even care in the most literal sense of the word."

"You blaspheme, Joseph Xavier."

"Of course, I do. Your religion is false, as all religions are false. I'm ecumenical in my blasphemy."

"And you sell poison to children. I'd like to turn you in myself—"

"But you can't. You believe in your medieval religion. You're bound by the confessional not to."

"There aren't enough "Hail Mary's" and "Our Fathers" in all the known world you could repeat that could begin to approach atonement for such crimes. The only thing you can do is turn yourself in, make a clean breast of it, pray the rosary, make offerings to your Lord and Savior Jesus Christ for forgiveness every remaining waking day of your life. And even then, God might still renounce you." A silence followed, broken only by the sound of the steam heat coming up and the low buzzing of something electrical like a far distant cicada.

"Would you like to pray with me now, my son?"

"I can't think of a bigger waste of time."

"But you're here to make your confession, to be cleansed and forgiven."

"No, I'm not here for any of those things."

"But God *put* you here to do all of those things, and so far, to my mind, you have already done most of them."

"It's an interesting idea that you think God brought me here. You could actually be right about that, you know. A minuscule of a percentage point, but the fact exists."

"I feel there's a glimmering of hope yet within you, my son."

"I think there's none of that, if I'm to be honest. I find it's best to be honest when you can help it, and I know you can't always be, so I don't fault you for that."

"How could you fault me for anything? I speak with the authority of Jesus Christ, your Lord and Savior."

"I suppose I don't fault you. Maybe I can't fault you, actually. I'm not here to judge you, so don't worry about that. I'm here for something else altogether."

"It's late, my son. I must get home. Perhaps you'd like to return and unburden yourself further at another time?"

"You and I have plenty of time together, Father Mammock. There's no place more important where you have to be right now. Besides, we both know you're staying even if I should leave. And I'm not going to leave. Neither of us is going to leave. For a while."

Temper rose in Father Mammock's throat. He had to get rid of this nutcase. He wasn't as young as he used to be, and he felt his energy and vigor waning. And he needed it for the long night to come. He nervously, almost reflexively, popped another bluish-looking pill from his secret pocket and resigned himself to be more direct in booting this deluded derelict out the door.

"I hate to disappoint you, Joseph Xavier. But the time to leave has come upon us. Come now. Busy lives require rest," he intoned with poor fake jollity. He slammed the panel down over the screen that allowed them to almost see each other's face with what little light interrupted the dim shadows of the partitioned box as they spoke. He left his part of the chamber only to find Joseph Xavier Null standing in front of him, distorted by the chiaroscuro of flickering neon votive candles and the soft, golden aureole from gas jets long ago converted to hold flame-shaped low wattage lightbulbs.

"You'll get your rest soon enough," said Null.

Father Mammock, short, blocky and ungainly looking even in his black cassock, with close-cropped salt-and-pepper hair and a nose resembling that of a drunken proboscis monkey, inflated his cheeks with suppressed rage. Who the hell was this pipsqueak wasting his time and ruining his evening? Even in his current dotage, he was certain he could take this poor twisted little man. He couldn't help but smirk as he let his cheeks deflate.

Null stood there, stiff, slope-shouldered, without the slightest movement. Father Mammock was uncertain that he was even breathing. He nodded so that Null could see it, even with eyes shadowed under the fedora. He was a slight man, his posture slightly off, favoring his left side possibly due to a leg injury. Built as solid as a bird under the soiled topcoat, no doubt. Something was filling out his clothes, but it wasn't him.

Maybe, like many a homeless derelict, he carried all his belongings with him, or maybe he scalped cheap, knock-off watches out from under the coat. Yes, he carried his house on his back alright, like a tortoise, making him no threat at all.

He'd flip him on his back.

"Time for you to go home, Joseph Xavier. And I mean *now*."

Father Mammock moved fast and grabbed Null's right arm, putting his stubby left leg behind his to hit the knee at the anterior cruciate ligament and crumple him down to the floor.

Instead, Father Mammock hit the floor hard when he landed flat on his back.

Null stood over him, motionless and dead seeming like a statue. His right arm suddenly jutted forward as if a mechanical blade on a hinge driven by a coiled spring. Father Mammock squinted. This poor creature was helping him up. Nothing more to it than that. Smiling and chuckling and shaking his head, he delivered a powerful right cross to Null's face, but missed and found himself dizzy, off balance and gushing blood from the jab that hit him square on the nose before he could see it.

He removed a handkerchief from the secret pocket one of the lonely, dowdy parishioners had sewn for him—Mary or Catherine or Hortense or something—what did it matter? They all led the same grim, gray, pious life that disgusted him.

"I'm afraid I'm going to have to call the police," he threatened, muffled by the yellowed handkerchief over his nose so that he sounded somewhat comical.

"I think I should laugh, but I don't know what's funny anymore. You won't call the police. We both know this."

"I know nothing about you, Joseph Xavier."

"Call me Null. Everybody calls me Null. When they can."

"I'll call you a rat bastard, now get the hell out of my fucking church!"

"It's not really your church, Father, though, is it? It belongs to the Archdiocese of Boston. It belongs to your Pope—isn't he a king now, by divine right? Or is he, in his greatly filigreed and regal appointment, humbly just a *prince* of the church?"

"You blaspheme!" Father Mammock shrieked.

"Let's just take that for granted."

"I've got nothin' for you to rob. You've struck out again, Mr. Null."

"What happened to Joseph Xavier? Where's the voice of the Lord now that we need him?"

"God is not mocked."

"Well, if he isn't he should be."

"You'll pay—"

"Oh, Father, we'll all pay. It's a law much older and much more potent than anything in your Bible. I have always paid, as far as I know—just as I'm sure that you will pay. Tonight, in fact."

"You'll pay with your balls to the devil in hell!" Father Mammock squawked.

"That's nice. They tell me such folktales are cute. I never know what to think, being that they're entirely irrelevant to the contemporary currency of human experience."

"It'll be your doom soon enough, Null."

"There's a better than even chance that it won't." Null paused and snapped his fingers, recited in a dull *sotto voce* like the speech feature on a laptop computer, "You know, it occurs to me now from my days at Boston Latin—that's right, the "mother of my soul," or alma mater, if you like. Both equally false. But I was there. Supposedly I had a full ride to Harvard coming to me even after my time in juvenile detention, but I chose a different path. I was forced to choose. And I took it without tears. Now, the pope isn't really a prince, is he? Far from it. But he is a bona fide King—The Holy See, which translates to the church having the seat of government, is itself actually a monarchy in which the pope is in fact the King, not so much by divine right, really, but by having been voted as such by the College of Cardinals.

"You—"

"I know. It's true. I blaspheme."

"Get! *Out!*"

"Eventually, but certainly not now. No, for now, you and I are going to take a trip down to the basement. And you'll need to be careful going down those dark steps. You could fall and easily hurt yourself. I think you'll agree it's best to keep you intact. For the time being."

"There is no basement," Father Mammock muttered with an utter lack of conviction.

"Let's go see, anyway. Just for fun."

"I'm not budgin'."

Null pulled his mostly all-plastic Glock 17 with suppressor from inside his topcoat. (Only the barrel, slide and one spring of the gun were metal.) His voice was a drone barely above a whisper:

"I don't think it should be necessary to keep putting you on the floor. And I think you'll agree it's a waste of time. You seem anxious. As with us all, time is always an issue. But that isn't what makes you anxious, though, is it?"

"You talk too much."

"Yes, I've been told that before. Think of it in the same way you might think of the squealing and squeaking of a bat—its sonar. The only difference is, rather than telling me where I am, it's telling me *that* I am."

"You're fucked in the head, boyo, well and truly."

"I couldn't agree more, Father. Have you a prayer for that?"

"The bat's in your belfry and the toys are in your attic."

"How fortuitous the opportunity for you to play with them then."

"Fucked in the head."

"I think that's already been well-established. Now, I'd like you to walk with me to the sacristy and open the door for us. You have the keys in the secret pocket you have in that cassock, right? I thought I detected a slight jingle."

"We take an oath of poverty—"

"But didn't Shakespeare tell us, "For oaths are straws, men's faiths are wafer-cakes, and Hold-fast is the only dog, my duck... Let us to France, like horse-leeches, my boys. To suck, to suck, the very blood to suck!" I have that right, Father?"

"You left something out."

"Yes, I did. But you got the gist, I think." He looked at Father Mammock with fisheyes. "Isn't that what you do, Father, suck and suck and suck until there's nothing left?"

"Shut your foul mouth!"

"Yes, you got the gist really well. Bring us to that door now or I'll have to put one in you to emphasize the need of your cooperation. You wouldn't like it if you were bloody and limping down those dark steps, with me hurrying you along. Frankly, neither would I. So please. Don't make me ask again."

Father Mammock lumbered forward through the shadows followed by Null, poking him with the suppressor of the Glock. He noticed with a small grunt of satisfaction, that Null already walked with a limp. Perhaps he could encourage him to tumble down those steep, dark steps into a quick, convenient death. He would give it his best effort. He was ready, even though he didn't fully under-stand what he was dealing with. He had never kept that close to the street, despite all charitable Catholic jeremiads that could have had him in the gutter with the sick, the wretched, the dying.

The sacristy was dusty despite decent, continuous use and was darker than the rest of the interior of Our Lady of the Sacred Heart. Null didn't direct Father Mammock to turn on the single bulb that hadn't yet burned out in the high and ancient fixture, but he clearly knew where the door was because he all but pushed Father Mammock directly toward it.

The priest shook with suppressed rage.

He'd make his move in the stairwell going down.

Father Mammock wouldn't fall; he knew every step by heart. He'd trip the damn gimp. Kick him hard enough to break his neck if the fall didn't accomplish that for him.

"Open it, Father, or I'll shoot the lock off and kick you down-stairs for causing a needless holdup. Do it, father. I'm infinitely patient, but that doesn't mean I'm not fast enough to keep from wasting time."

"It's dark and you'll be needin' a light."

"Neither of us need a light. No need to be hesitant. You've made this trip hundreds of times before. Just pretend I'm not here and open it. Now."

Father Mammock made a show of fumbling through his cassock for the keys, which jingled fiercely as he feigned trying to extract them.

Null pistol-whipped him across the face in an unexpectedly lightning motion without a thought. Father Mammock caught the blur right before catching the blow and sobbed and bellowed while recovering from it.

"You damned animal—you broke my jaw."

"Probably not. You're speaking unimpeded."

Father Mammock bellowed in grief as he opened the door leading down to the basement. He didn't have to be told to move again and when he began his descent, it seemed as if the darkness had swallowed him up, even though he moved slowly in hopes of Null coming close enough to him to be thrown down to the uneven rubble and dust piles of the basement floor.

Halfway down, Father Mammock cried out about his knee, and they both hesitated, He made grab for Null, who somehow feinted left at the right moment, turned his back to him and gave the priest a solid mule-kick that nearly caused him to bash his brains out amid the rubble and rocks at the end of the steps. This was thwarted by Father Mammock, who knew where some of the old railing that had been mostly removed was still intact and snatched it awkwardly.

"Keep going, Father."

"I'm in *pain!*" he whined, continuing down.

"Most pain, Father, doesn't last. I can vouch for the fact that yours won't."

"Why don't you just shoot me and get it over with?"

"It could come to that. But if it doesn't, then you and I will have some work to do. I'm guessing you want to live, so hold on to that thought better than you hold on to that broken railing."

Father Mammock grunted, threw the bloodied, yellowed handkerchief he had been clutching fiercely without knowing it so that it floated down to the debris and detritus of broken concrete of what was once a basement floor. Most of what was left of the flooring looked like a maniac had taken a pickaxe to it looking for treasure.

They both kicked away small chunks from under their feet and the grit of ruined concrete off their shoes when they finally reached the bottom. Father Mammock pulled a string hanging in mid-air and icy white light suffused the room.

"Brighter than I thought," observed Null.

"As you can see, Mr. Null, there's nuttin'. Nuttin' to be seen. I don't know what you expected to find, but dust and rubble and one of them new-fangled ten-year lightbulbs puttin' glare onto it all is what you've got. Now, if you're satisfied, please leave. Just go. And may God have mercy on your immortal soul."

"So, you'll pray for me, is that it?"

"Of course, of course. Just so."

"Your prayers mean nothing, do nothing, *are* as nothing. But you *will* be praying. That we both know to be true."

"I always do."

"That's part of a version of the immediate future that we can both agree with."

"To what point, Mr. Null?"

"Let's go down to the sub-basement and see."

That was the moment that Father Mammock thew himself back at the steps and would have been ready to crawl up them, but Null dragged him back and slapped him down into the gray rubble and dust. He kicked the priest hard in the solar plexus, who went over backwards with a yelp much like that of a wounded puppy.

Null offered his hand to the priest, which he took, and summarily yanked him to his feet with a fierce jerk that nearly dislocated his arm.

"I'd have done it myself if I knew you were going to cripple me."
He didn't bother to brush himself off.

"Let's not get ahead of ourselves, Father."

"Oh no, never let us do that. Joseph Xavier."

"It's Null. Call me Null. Some have called me DQ Null, for all my once-upon-a-time losses at the track, but only one person's left who'd call me that and he's a lifer in a mental institution. Some may still call me Joey X, but I never hear it. I suppose those who know me don't want to offend me for their own reasons. Most often, people don't call me anything at all. Those who called me Joseph Xavier are dead."

"And I suppose you're puttin' me in that category too?"

"I told you before, Father, it's a very bad idea for us to get ahead of ourselves." He gave Father Mammock a hard shove at the right shoulder he had wounded slightly when he yanked him up from the floor and the priest grunted and lurched forward without thinking, which brought them quickly to the entrance to the sub-basement.

"I don't know how you knew this was here when I didn't know it was here."

"But we both knew it was here. You'll have to find someone with a sense of humor to use those kinds of lines on. The sanctimonious Catholic priest whose every other sentence is likely a lie untouched by an omniscient creator who micromanages such things. Punishes venial sins. It might crack somebody up, I'm sure. But as you may have guessed, nothing cracks me up."

"So what now, boyo?"

"Down, Father. All the way. Down."

There was light at the seams of the door, which was a hard thing to miss. The meaning of it caused Father Mammock's hands to tremble, fumbling for the keys. Null betrayed nothing, but to look in his eyes you would see that he knew, that he always knew and if he didn't know he would know what had to be known with deadly quickness.

"No need for the keys, Father. Just open it."

The sub-basement was brightly lit in a soft, yellow glow. The light was bright enough to illuminate the stairwell whose steps were far less treacherous than the rickety near ladder of steps that had led to the basement. When they had both reached the end of the steps, it was a place that seemed to have been sandblasted clean. The floor was smooth and clear of dust, the walls had been recently plastered and a worktable was pushed up against one of them with a number of miscellaneous leather and wooden implements carefully arrayed.

In the center of the room was a naked little boy who couldn't have been more than ten, kneeling on an ergonomically designed bench where a lower platform supported his knees, the upper platform his chest, and his wrists were zip-tied behind his back, with a bright red ball gag (the shape and color of a clown's nose) strapped into his mouth. It could only be kindly described as a bondage bench, in circles where consenting adults frolic; it was a piece of sex furniture called, literally, a "fuck bench." The boy was making some kind of bird-like little cries, his voice too hoarse from having been screaming for hours without relent, the gag in his mouth too effective to have allowed for much else.

"This is outrageous!" Father Mammock cried. "It's bestial, beyond all humanity. If you have one of those smart phones, Joseph Xavier, I'll call for the police and an ambulance right now."

"No need, Father. I'll take care of the boy."

"What do you mean, you'll "take care of the boy." What are you suggesting in your warped atheism, your cruel and violent sickness? What do you think you're—"

"I said not to worry, Father."

"But this is abominable. What unholy criminal would ever do such a thing? We must release him."

"Do not touch him, Father." Null said sharply and nudged him with the suppressor of the Glock.

"I just—"

"Why would he have to be unholy, Father? Why couldn't he be the godliest of men?"

"Don't tell me you've fallen for all that propaganda of child abuse within the Catholic Church."

"Some very pious people deliberately mistake news for propaganda and propaganda for news. Catholic propaganda—dogma—is a beast all its own."

Father Mammock put his heart and soul into it. "I had nothing to do with this, I swear before God, Joseph Xavier! I *swear*! On the Father, the Son and the Holy Spirt. May God strike me—"

"Be careful what you wish for, Father, if you believe God is not mocked. I don't have to worry. I believe in nothing. So, you're trying to convince me that what we see here isn't your cherished little hobby? Right, Father?"

The boy's bird noises went up a few octaves to become a sustained high-pitched squeal.

"He doesn't seem to agree."

"The poor lamb is out of his mind with pain and terror so he can't tell you anything."

"I think he told me everything I need to know."

Null reached inside his topcoat and pulled out a blindfold. He dangled it before Father Mammock.

"What in God's name do you want me to do with that?"

"You invoke God a lot, Father."

"Of course, I do. This is his house."

"And he's in this room right now?"

"There is no place on earth so terrible that it would ever be forsaken by our Lord and Savior Jesus Christ."

"Okay. Let's see what Jesus Christ, Lord and Savior, does with our minor passion play here tonight."

"What do you mean? What is this blindfold for, exactly?" Father Mammock said as he grabbed it.

"It's for the boy, Father." Null waved the Glock at the priest to indicate that he had better get moving. "I'd like you to put it on him, please."

More squeals from the bound and naked boy, whose back and buttocks bore pink welts from what must have been a series of punishing blows. Some were brownish with dried, caked blood. He was sniffling and squealing. Both men seemed unmoved by this. Father Mammock did as he was told and the boy's noises were now a gargle of tears and snot.

"Why am I doing this, Joseph Xavier? Why are you making me do this?"

"A reasonable question, Father. I'll tell you."

"What despicable abuse do you have in mind, Joseph Xavier?"

"None, Father. It's just that no young boy should ever have to see what's about to happen here tonight. No child should ever have to look upon such horrible things. But I think it'll be very important for him—to hear you."

"*Hear* me?"

"That's right."

The boy's noises abruptly stopped altogether.

"What in the world would he need to hear from me—an *apology*? From *me*? Because you think *I* did this? That *I'm* culpable? Well, I won't be doing that."

"No, you won't, Father. I wouldn't expect that of you."

"What then?"

Null cast a long shadow across the floor as he moved toward Father Mammock, taking his time. He spoke very softly, but not so softly that the boy couldn't clearly make out the words:

"I just want him to hear you scream."

TWO

Five o'clock couldn't come fast enough. Detective Lieutenant Kay Boyd compulsively checked her cell phone for the time without any desire to do so and softly cursed herself for doing so. Still, being helpless before that petty habit was a lot better than being helpless before the almighty gallon bottle of Gilbey's cheap-ass gin. She switched over from the VICAP system to a refreshing game of solitaire on her PC, and that small act of defiance coaxed a smile out from behind her now perpetually dour expression.

Her dourness was predicated on the worsening conduct and ongoing problem of Joseph Xavier Null, deceased petty criminal, meth king of Boston. It was because of him that she wound up in exile, assigned to the headquarters of the Boston FBI on Maple Street in Chelsea, an eight-story building that looked like a massive Lego structure plopped down in the middle of a parking lot in the middle of a bunch of other more squat Lego edifices that looked even less well designed amid other contiguous parking lots and their respective but even lesser grim Lego structures.

The building was so new, the carpeting, even the walls, continually gave off a strong aroma of formaldehyde, which made the back of Boyd's throat itch for a shot or two of the miserable gin she still adored so much. Repulsed by the odor, her sinuses ached for the preferable scent of the damned gin.

"Do you really think that's the best use of the expertise you've been loaned out to us to provide?" asked Special Agent Joel Thrawn, peering at her computer screen over her shoulder.

"Jesus, Joel, you know how I hate that."

"I do. But I hate even more your theft of time during this period of budgetary constraints."

"I'm thinking, Joel. When I play online solitaire, it helps me think—"

"Let me just stop you right there, Lieutenant."

"Why not call me Kay, as usual?"

"I just want your attention, that's all."

"You're kind of a defensive neurotic sort, aren't you, Joel?"

"I thought that went without saying."

"We're at FBI Boston headquarters."

"Yes, true," Agent Thrawn said without the slightest lack of confidence. "And here at the FBI, we say everything—"

"And tell us nothing."

"How many months have you been with us now, Kay?"

"Not even one."

"Seems longer."

"So you were about to castigate me for playing online solitaire?"

"So you don't even have to download the game and run it, client-style? That's a nifty wrinkle."

"Fuck you, Joel. Everyone knows the networks here are blocked from any online entertainment sites."

"So, like everyone else, you found out that the Norfolk County Sheriff's Department website has a secret, special area where law enforcement may partake of some amusing games?"

"What else could I do? You impounded my phone."

"Along with everyone else's. My new rule. Unless—"

"Unless one of the dedicated phones sync'ed to specific cases."

"I try to promote focus."

"That's why you're the Special Agent in Charge, Joel."

"Yep. Discrete techniques developed over the hard, lean years of investigative forensic accountancy have finally proven fruitful."

"Think you'll be headed out into the field anytime soon, then?"

"Nope. You're as close as I'm ever going to get to that."

"So, you were about to tell me something that's worth waiting for, now that it's after five o'clock."

"So I was. I think playing computer solitaire can be quite helpful with some investigations."

"Really?" Kay Boyd swiveled her chair back and forth with her arms crossed defiantly across her chest, her high heels planted solidly in neutral colored acrylic carpeting. "Can you tell me how that works, exactly?"

"Easy peasy. Your mind goes empty as you play the game, concentrating on the cards, ignoring everything for moments at a time. When you've finished a hand, the thoughts come rushing back into you. Some old, some extremely old. And some new. Maybe very new. And with luck, one of them is like an Athenian head-birth—"

Boyd snapped her fingers. "Like from the brain of one god, out pops a goddess?"

"Or in this case, from a goddess to a goddess."

"You know the FBI has a no fraternization policy, right?"

"Of course, Kay, but you're not really with the FBI, are you?"

"No, thank God."

"I shall make a sacrifice to Zeus in your name tonight. As a show of gratitude."

"Oh, folderol, Joel."

"But still—"

"No drinks, Joel. But not because of you. Because of me."

"This isn't the, 'it's not you, it's me,' cliché, is it? No. I suspect that you happen to be a friend of Bill W's."

Boyd blushed a timeless blush and smirked. "Your suspicions are not unfounded. And you knew how? What was the tell, exactly?"

"Not really a single tell, as such. A hundred infinitesimal tells made it seem that you might actually be a *mutual* friend."

"Coffee wouldn't be out of the question, then, would it?"

"Emphatically not."

"But you're here for something other than ogling at me from a downward perspective. New thoughts perhaps?"

"On the nose."

"Fine. Go as deep into the paperwork as you like—*no*body knows who runs the Gangsta Boys drug cartel."

"Paperwork is my specialty. And I eyeballed that death certifi-cate for your old C-I—"

"*Decoy* C-I."

"Joseph Xavier Null—lowlife bagman and racehorse tout. Gambling and heroin addict. He dies after being tortured to death because—"

"Yes. Tortured to death by that mutt Cousin It. Because I gave him up. To the Family. Biggest mistake of my career. I tried to save him."

"You could never have saved him. You realize that."

"Not internally. No."

"It was never your fault. Amazing, you figured out what you did when you did. He was on a death track before you recruited him. Everybody was lucky he was smart enough to tip you off on the bust that did them all in—and that you were smart enough to take the hint. I read the whole thing."

"I gave him up."

"You couldn't know your real snitch was already reduced to a hunk of wailing meat by that swine Ignazio 'Cousin It' Cavilli before you did that. And you rescued him. The real flesh and blood, Joey X."

"If you want to call it that."

"So he's wiped off the board. Then, within a year after that, the entire Family's wiped off the board too. Kaput. Looks like some heavy hitter or hitters from New York or Chicago took them all out of play. Not the Rhode Island New England La Cosa Nostra though."

"No? Not the cheese boys? *Ya think?*"

"Okay, okay. I get that. They've got too many headaches for this."

"Aren't they FBI snitches too?"

"I think they're the only ones that aren't. Besides, they don't play well with African Americans."

"The late Joey X isn't *our* Joey X. Simple."

"No, it's pretty safe to say that the long-deceased Mr. Joey X. Null isn't running anything anymore—certainly not the biggest meth cartel in the northeast. The 'zombie/boogeyman' Obeah Voodoo yack we keep getting off the street from customers and resellers is just another sad urban fairytale born of the street. So why have our mystery man called Joey X, anyway?"

"Well, we needed an X variable and his was as good as any."

"Sentimental, I see."

"More than I used to be." Boyd began mindlessly gnawing on a hangnail. Agent Thrawn noted it but was too polite to mention it.

"The Gangsta Boys are moving up in the world it seems. They're spoiling for gang and mob clashes in the very near future."

"Exactly, Joel. They're not New York yet, but they're a powder keg, a timebomb waiting to go off. They're the only actual fully-realized American drug cartel, and the biggest meth slingers in the tri-state area—"

"And bucking for New York while they're at it."

"With a vengeance."

"They got presence down south too."

"Dixie Mafia's getting nervous. They're stockpiling guns."

"Not nervous enough to start killing over it yet, though."

"Remains to be seen. You read my report."

"I did. All the way through. So, we're really going to go on calling this guy 'Joey X,' right? As a sort of place holder."

"It's better than 'unsub,' ain't it?"

"TV did kinda ruin the term of art."

Boyd's hands were slightly tremulous, a tiny detail that might have gone unnoticed had she chosen something other than the act of lighting a cigarette to disguise it. "You can arrest me for this, Joel." She tried to chuckle but coughed instead.

"Now how can I do that when I'm not really here, anyway?"

"I'm about to set off a smoke detector, aren't I?"

"You are, if you don't put that out now." This was said with calm amusement and not an iota of either irony or tension. Agent Thrawn was never snide – even when he wanted to be. He failed at nonchalantly kicking the plastic waste basket close to her calf. He wasn't smooth about it, which made both of them laugh softly. "I'm guessing there's something in there you can snuff that out against —just make sure it isn't plastic. Because that'll set the damn thing off for sure. In like seconds."

She chose an empty, dented can of Diet Pepsi and they both heard the sizzle resonate when she plopped it back into the waste basket.

"How long sober now, Kay?"

"I got a six-month chip. Care to see it?"

"I think I'd like to see something else, thank you."

"Joel, are you trying to make me blush?"

Agent Thrawn broke out in a light sweat almost immediately. No, Kay—oh, geeze—really, I wasn't implying anything like that. That wasn't what I meant at all."

"I know that, Joel. Maybe one day, sometime, you will mean it though."

"That's a distinct possibility." He absently wiped his brow of sweat with a crisp, white shirtsleeve.

"Whoever's at the top of the Gangsta Boyz food chain is a ruthless, stone psychopath. He's thorough."

"Couldn't it be a she? Or even a *them?*"

"Them singular? Why not? Whoever our X is, he, she or they project a lot of fear. Soldiers would rather do time, even hard time, than serve 'im up. This isn't what I recall from my days at the B.P.D. O.C. task force. It's different. More clean and efficient. That's not like the Gangsta Boyz social club of old either. Way more stream-lined than what the Family put out. And you know it's not NELCN, which has seen much better days even under the Cheese brothers—"

"Big and little DiNunzio."

"And the very late Sallie "Jumbo" Palumbo."

"The mook that did the Freaky Friday robberies shot that guy right outside his house in Apple Valley. Broad daylight—no shame, no discretion, just popped the bastard and lammed."

"Sucks to lose a CI, don't it, Joel?"

"Yeah, it does. And he was one of the good ones. He'd been around forever and looked like he'd *be* around forever. But one quick pop and he's gone."

"Wasn't he running out of guys to rat out?"

"True. That does take some of the sting out of it."

"Now, the report I read said that they found eight shell casings at the scene. From a Springfield XD9 semi-automatic yet. Who shoots with that? What mutt would do that? So eight pops, really."

"That's precisely the kind of Moxie play our evanescent friend spooky old Joey X would have had to have done to keep on doing what he's been doing."

"That'd be truly neat if it were actually him. We could just pick him up."

"If we could find him," Agent Thrawn added balefully.

"But no. That mook in particular may definitely be bad enough and smart enough to be our guy, but he isn't. Because he's alive and my old CI's down for the big dirt nap."

"You know what? Special Agent Lockheart emailed me once that she was fairly sure that Freaky Friday was actually the Arrant family annihilator down there in Delaware—"

"The late Agent *Sharianne* Lockheart? Slaughtered in her own apartment in the Fens?"

"Yeah. Robbery murder. Butchered."

"Different shell casings, though."

"None, actually. You don't really think…"

"To me it looks like this Arrant creepo made her, broke into her apartment, lay in wait for her, did his business then made it look like a robbery gone bad."

"You have a bitter read on things, Lieutenant Boyd, you know that?"

"And proud of it."

"There could be a future for you at the FBI."

"I'm just happy to have any kind of future at all at this point. You know, if there weren't a shutdown of the federal government going on at the time, when she must've made Arrant in Rhode Island, which I just bet she did, she wouldn't have had too tough a time cornering him with a local SWAT team, instead of high-tailing it back to Boston."

"I know, I know: Because the Providence resident agency for the FBI on Dorrance wouldn't have been closed at the time."

"Sure you don't want to swap sides from being a Republican—?"

"No one's made me a good enough offer for that yet."

"Stick around, Joel. One may be forthcoming."

Agent Thrawn cleared his throat to break the awkward silence.

"Did you ever actually *see* this little desperado? A pasty little pear-shaped schmoe with a fright wig dyed blond-to-orange. His face is as hapless as Droopy Dog from those old cartoons. Looks like a total putz."

"A real schlemiel—"

"Schlamazel—he's the one gets the soup spilled on him, not the one just spilling the soup.

"Protective coloration, Joel. That's how he gets away with his bullshit. Looks harmless."

"Everyone underestimates him."

"His whole life."

"As Freaky Friday, though, he racked up an impressive number of corpses. Not just for a schlamazel."

"He also blew his wife and kids away with a double-aught shotgun, so he had quality as well as quantity covered in his kills."

"I gag at that image," Agent Thrawn said with a shudder, checking his cheap Invictus wristwatch even though he routinely told time with his cell phone like just about everybody else.

"Sort of takes all the romance out of bank robberies though, don't it?"

"They never had any romance for me, Kay. I wanted all those sons of bitches put away or executed since I was in diapers."

"No doubt you were a weird toddler, Joel."

"Good thing you're only one caught onto that fact."

"Too bad it ain't that guy either, Joel. So listen: *Someone* with real finesse is running this shitshow. Bust one of the street dealers and all he – or she – has to show is rolls of cash. Never any goods to prove anything beyond suspicion. Mopery. A public disturbance. Resisting. Whatever. Gangsta Boyz street dealers would rather violate their paroles or suspended sentences and go back to the slam rather than rat this fucker out. So, they've been trained and trained hard by someone who knows his business, and please spare me the superfluous pronouns."

"You're thinking ex-military, maybe?"

"I wouldn't rule that out. It's a definite starting point. There's absolutely no fuck-ups with these sons of bitches. From the Merrimac Valley and Lowell up through Brockton and Attleboro—these little fuckers are *nolle prosequi* down the line."

"So I noticed. No heavy busts, no deals. No one ever flips. Fancy lawyers duke out the bonds and fines. Ready cash to spare."

"Hence the reason for my being in your house and not mine."

"You came highly recommended."

"Don't bullshit me, Joel."

"Well, you should have been."

"And these kids—and they are *all* mostly kids. When they start making noises about flipping, no one can even locate the body."

"This is getting seriously out of hand, Kay. You know that. But do you want to know the worst thing about it?"

"I'm waiting with bated breath."

"Our boy's a bit of a fisherman."

"A fisherman? What the fuck does that mean, Joel? Is he a fundamental Christian? A fisher of men?"

"No, Kay. Not of men."

"Good god, then of *what* then?"

"Did you ever go fishing, Kay?"

"I did a couple of times at camp Beaver Day when I was a kid. It didn't sustain my interest."

"So you know what minnows are used for—how they're handled."

"Not really."

"You see, sometimes they're used to attract bigger fish to the hook, but that never works quite as well as chumming the water. So they just get in the way. Usually, when you catch a minnow, you just throw it back."

"And this has to do with the Gangsta Boyz drug operation how?"

"Thing is, our dude is using minnows."

"You're fucking with me. Fish."

"No. *Minnows.* That's what they're called, eight-to ten-year-old girls and boys who deliver the drugs. The minnows. They got that name because there's nothing we can do with them but throw them back and the Gangsta Boyz know it. The man upstairs did this. They have no legal parent or guardian, so we—I suppose I should say you—wind up having to interrogate them with a court-appointed *Guardian Ad Litem* in the room, which goes nowhere. By the time we get there, it's back into the foster care system they go and off they swim, never to be seen or heard from again."

"Jesus, you're saying the Gangsta Boyz shot caller has them blipped off?"

"No, they just disappear into the system."

"And how come no one just kidnaps a minnow or abuses one—him, her or they?"

"Fear. One of our late CI's laid it out that whoever touches one of the minnows will have a shelf life of exactly ten minutes on the street after the fact. All I can say is our dude is thorough and a man of his word. If he happens to be a man. Everyone's a bit hazy on basic facts there."

"I'm not with the OC Taskforce anymore. This change is a bit out of my depth."

"Well, if you can't handle it—"

"We can end this liaison anytime you like, Joel. You know *that*. My last hookup with a special agent makes this one look like a weekend at Disney World—Sandals, maybe, or something like that I never got to go on."

At that point, Boyd was willing to do or say just about anything to steer the joint Boston PD/FBI gang task force investigation as far away from Joseph Xavier Null as the space-time continuum would allow. Because that particular portal to real-time hell had been closed shut tight in the recent past and she was determined to keep it that way. The only problem was that what Null had done to make the Gangsta Boyz a crack unit of meth dealers was bringing down some heavy heat upon the whole thing that she just couldn't stop. So here she was at FBI LegoLand central, getting out in front of a plodding, dogged, bureaucratic investigation just to keep Null out of it. Volunteering to do it just to keep Null out of it.

She was hit by an off pang suddenly.

An urge.

It took much of the energy she had left for that given day not to laugh at the perverse phrase 'crack unit of meth dealers,' so she batted her eyes at Special Agent Thrawn, almost in satire, and hoped for the best.

And she told herself in the moment: "Yes, if hooking up with Joel Thrawn will help keep the FBI off Null's case, I'm down with it. I am right *there*."

She had made up her mind that Null was too virulent to deal with in any other way but by avoidance. He was like that flesh-eating virus—Streptococcus A. He was an opportunistic disease, finding his way in through any cut or crevice and then, well, you really didn't want to think of "and then" at all.

"Oh, *I* get it," Agent Thrawn drawled, pretending to just having realized Boyd's reference. "*That* guy. You're talking about Wilmer Quark, right?"

"The FBI's finest."

"Well, that guy's a straight-up hump; a walking hard on. Why do you think he got assigned to Boston PD in the first place and not vice versa?"

"No one's ever acknowledged that, you know."

"Well, I'm someone and I just did."

"So, Joel, are you willing to fulfill my dream and take me to Sandals, or what? Cancun maybe?"

"The thought had occurred to me, Kay."

Laughter followed that statement, which made Special Agent Thrawn visibly nervous.

"Okay, then. Hold that thought, Joel. *Just hold that thought.*"

THREE

"It's not him!" the old woman cried. She was about to get down on her knees, but Null stopped her with a clearly awkward, unemotional hug, lifting her back up. "It's just not him," she panted.

"Then I will find him."

"No one will find him. You don't know what the Sacred Knights are capable of. What they'll do," she whined. "It's hopeless."

"Hope doesn't matter. It never matters. Causation matters. Results matter. But you may hope as much and as hard as you please. Meanwhile, I'm making it part of my personal agenda to find your grandson." If Null would have been able to laugh at that, he'd have done just that, as he actually hadn't had any personal agendas since his simultaneous salvation and ruin at Mass General Hospital years ago. If he could be said to have had any personal agenda at all, it was to keep breathing—something he had to remind himself to do time and again as if he were a stupid cartoon.

The agenda was also to have an agenda.

He often lost the point of remaining alive and had to remind himself frequently that he had an established purpose, which had to be reestablished every few months or so. Forgetting what that purpose was would be tantamount to forgetting to be alive. And it was getting easier by the day to forget that he was, in fact, alive.

With no desire at all to be alive.

With no desire at all for anything when it came right down to it.

"Why, Mr. Null? Why should you care? Why would you want to listen to a pathetic old woman like me."

"Why wouldn't I?"

"Because you're a monster. A freak. You don't even look human, scarred up as you are. I don't know why I came. Why I was so crazy desperate, I had to drag myself to deal with a—a *thing* like you. Maybe it was like in that old movie "The Godfather"—where a very bad man can do good things for people in pain on his daughter's wedding. But you don't have a daughter, do you? There's not going to be any weddings, will there?"

"No, Mrs. Leporine. No weddings. Only funerals, and maybe too many of those for all concerned, yet never enough for me."

"Too many and not enough. I don't understand."

"Many of our dead lie forgotten. Not memorialized."

"In Christ's holy name, who would ever want to memorialize someone like you? You sell your poison to children. You murder anyone who gets in your way. Why would you want to bother saving anyone? Especially why would you even bother to save a poor little insignificant boy like Marion Slaughter? A boy with nothing, no prospects; barely a home and me. Just whatever's left of me and, as you can see, that's not very much. Nothing important for a bigtime gangster like you."

Null stared at her, calm and slack, unblinking and unmoved.

"Mrs. Leporine. All of us here know you're in pain, consumed with rage, surfeit with sorrow. Believe it or not, all of that's useful. It can be deployed, like a weapon. And I want to deploy it. Myself."

"These men—or boys—or whatever they are who surround you. They make me afraid. I don't even know if I'll be able to leave here alive. Why did I come? *Oh why?*" She made fists of withered hands and shook them at the ceiling, her face, with tears streaming down in rivulets like sweat, could have been considered itself to be a fist of another kind aimed with everything she had directly at Null's gut and, strangely enough, especially to the

Gangsta Boyz who were present to witness it, he seemed to actually feel it.

What she had said registered, and that realization was thick in the air of the room like mist or smoke. Just a minor shade away from being palpable.

He spoke with the calm assurance of an air conditioner, in exactly that tone and timber: a purposeful whisper carried by a low, vibrating bass note beneath. "No one here is going to hurt you, Mrs. Leporine. I think one of the men will see you safely home. You're not in any trouble with me or with my cadre of—friends."

Ronald, Desi and Dominic—three serious upper lieutenants of the Gangsta Boyz (now run by Shot Caller Null), wearing uniforms of jet-black skull caps, leather jackets and rap star tee shirts beneath (whose art looked like gang tags) grunted together a surly assent to Null's statement. It was plain that they wanted to act but had learned to be careful enough to do so sparingly when they couldn't anticipate the Shot Caller's word.

"Be chill," said Dominic, the largest and tallest. "You be cool up here in grandma's house."

"Real talk," added Ronald.

"Lady, you in this car, you *ride*," offered Desi, not meaning to be threatening even though his tone made it sound that way.

"I would hit you if I could make sure it would hurt you!" she sobbed.

"I would let you if you could."

"You are a loathsome scourge upon humanity. Oh, how I wish I had my husband's gun!"

"Use mine," Null whispered, reaching within his overcoat for his Heckler and Koch P7 and handed it to Mrs. Leporine butt first. She grabbed it with two quavering hands.

"Jesus wept! What in god's name do you want me to do with this...*thing?*"

"Don't drop it, Mrs. Leporine," Null said blandly. "It might go off."

"Just take it."

Null did that in a single, easy gesture even softer than his voice, with which he replied, "I'll take it as I said I'll take your rage, your pain, your sorrow. I will use them on your behalf. Tell me about these Sacred K nights—just who could such knights be in the modern era? The knights of Columbus perhaps?" he asked humorlessly.

"Christian knights of the Temple, the Father told me—you can't fight them. You can't even *see* them. They live in the shadows and darkness. Nobody can touch them."

"I'm not nobody."

"I don't know what you are."

"Temple, you said? But Christian? Catholic? You don't mean the *Knights Templar*, do you?"

"That's who they are, as I recall, now that you say it. I was told by the Father. Oriental Order of Knights of the Temple or somethin' like it, he said."

Null's breathing changed slightly, slowed and deepened even though the voice remained steady, calm and flat.

"I think I know what you mean. The Knights Templar. A secret order founded during the crusades in the twelfth century by the knight Hugues de Payens. They escorted Christian pilgrims through the Holy Land—Jerusalem, to be specific. In 1307, King Philip IV of France and Pope Clement V had decided that the knights had become a threat to their power and influence. So, together they charged Knights Templar grand master Jacques de Molay with heresy, sacrilege and Satanism. Routine stuff for undoing an opponent, so all the other leading Knights Templar were rounded up along with Molay and then were swiftly and summarily burned at the stake. The joys of feudalism, which America itself seems to be slipping into ever faster."

He seemed to stop breathing altogether, then blurted out sharply in a gasp: "That does seem to have failed to do the trick, doesn't it?"

All three Gangsta Boyz jumped at this.

"B-but Father Mammock. He said they were still of Holy

Mother Church. You cannot defy the church and if they are of the church, you cannot stop them. No, you cannot stop these knights, even if they've already skinned my poor Marion alive and ate him for breakfast."

Mrs. Leporine seemed to weaken at that statement and looked as if she might lose her balance and fall.

Ronald quickly put a chair behind her and gently encouraged her to sit down, then quietly moved off to the side, joining Dominic and Desi—Null's Praetorian guard.

"They were Poor Fellow-Soldiers of Christ and of the Temple of Solomon, Hugues the founding knight had claimed—but they turned out to be worse than that—or at least more extreme than that. Wouldn't you say?"

"So now what? They kidnap and murder children in the name of the Holy Mother Church? Why would they do such a thing?"

"It's well known that many a boy's youth and innocence had been sacrificed on the altar of lust presided over by lust-crazed Catholic priests still jealously protected by your Holy Mother Church. So, that could be a factor in the kidnapping and potential murder."

"I don't want to hear about that. We've all heard far too much about that."

"And yet I had to remove a small boy from a bondage bench in the sub-basement of the late Father Mammock's church where he was half-beaten to death, having undergone all the practices you don't want to hear about Mrs. Leporine, and bleeding from his ass."

"Help me, Jesus!"

"He's not here to help you. Maybe he was never here, But I am here, and I will help you."

"Late Father Mammock, that's what you said—what's happened to him? Surely, he's not part of these Sacred Knights."

"All I know about them I just told you, Mrs. Leporine."

"And the Father?"

"He's traveling a familiar road."

"I don't want to know about that."

"As well you shouldn't. Yet you want to know about the kidnap and murder of small boys, but not the priestly sexual abuse of any of them. Of all of them."

"Well, no I don't, but that's what they're doin', Mr. Null. And you may think you're some kind of big gangster, and maybe it's true you are, but that's not going to be enough to do anything. You're not big enough to take on the church, and how could Holy Mother Church be doing anything so foul and evil as to snuff out the life of a little boy like my little Marion?"

"History says that not only has the church done it, but they have sought to do it, and modern journalism reports that the archdiocese of Boston has, after agreeing to then pulling out of a $30 million settlement with eighty-six of just one priest's—one single little priest's—Father John Geoghan's—victims, the archdiocese re-settled with them for one-third the amount. $10 million, and is still negotiating with lawyers for other victims of other priests. Since the 90s the Catholic Church has sunk half a billion dollars in sexual abuse compensation for its victims. It seems even the pope accepts that these things have been done, and that the settlements carry an admission of sin. Of true guilt. And yet you ask how the church could be so foul and evil as to do ever do anything as extreme as mass child rape, use its power to hide it for hundreds of years, never mind the incidental murder of a single small boy? That may be carrying faith just a little too far."

"You make me sick, Mr. Null."

"No, Mrs. Leporine. It's your religion that's making you sick. Not me."

————

"Tea, Your Eminence?" Father Bricolage asked just above a whisper, fearful of interrupting the great man's studying of some old palimpsest, or was it just an old volume published on ageless vellum?

Cardinal Isidore Cromulent moved his lips gently, reciting to himself in Latin, his voice the faintest of whispers, softer than his steady breathing. He ignored Father Bricolage, though he was well aware of his presence even before he entered the room. Lilting tenor, contralto and soprano harmonies could be heard echoing just outside the door to his lush, baroque, lush—and continually under restoration—residence in the Basilica of Our Lady of Perpetual Sorrow on A Street in South Boston. Still reading, whispering, the venerable cardinal idly waved his left hand as if he were conducting the boy chorale from there, as if they were run on Wi-Fi from his listless, gestural command sent down by near field communication with the server.

The cardinal snapped the book shut and fixed his icy blue eyes on the dull and furtive gaze of Father Bricolage.

"Beautiful and unearthly, is it not, Sam?"

"Yes. Sure. Of course it is, Your Eminence."

"So beautiful it reminds one of the Elizabethan *castrati*."

"Yes, Eminence, and none of them have yet to
suffer—"

"Yes, yes, Sam. We're all too aware of their condition. If they didn't have it, where would we be with our grand initiative?"

"My apologies Your Eminence. I didn't mean to imply—"

"Imply? *Imply?* You stated it to a fare-thee-well, didn't you?"

"I didn't mean—"

The cardinal stood, stabilizing himself with both hands on the glass-covered top of his 18th century mahogany desk, fuming without pretense of pious restraint. "Father Bricolage, this is a most crucial matter attended to by the cream of American religious scholars, from the finest seminaries and divinity schools in this country. And you think we'd in any manner, in any way jeopardize this momentous, crucial and gracious mission by castrating little boys to freeze their vocal tones so that we may pleasure longer in the heavenly music God allows them to make. God offers them to us with his bounteous heart to enrich us with music, and so we should dictate terms to God himself for our own pleasure? For our delight? Such selfishness is deplored by church doctrine as you're aware, Father, are you not?"

Yes, Eminence, always, but didn't Saint Cecilia say, "Sing to God with songs of Joy.

The stifled snicker, caused him to make a little crackling sound in his throat. "That may be so, Sam, but I think our great Bishop and Great Western Father and Doctor of the church had this to say, "Rid yourself of what is old and worn out, for you know a new song... Let us sing a new song not with our lips but with our lives." Now, can these children be expected to do any less?

"But Eminence, those are but two lines of a longer speech that interprets Saint Cecilia's meaning."

"But those lines say what needs to be said. You don't disagree, do you, Sam?"

Father Bricolage immediately thought of this in silent rebuttal to the cardinal's rebuke, concluding words from Augustine of Hippo: "Your heart must rejoice beyond words, soaring into an immensity of gladness, unrestrained by syllabic bonds. Sing to Him with jubilation." How could any heart be jubilant, even with the song of the pure and innocent, harboring the knowledge of what these new "Altar Servers" were being set out to do. Granted, it was necessary, but it couldn't be that the cardinal and even the pope, whose approval had already been given to this special youth mission were in agreement as to the details. And yet the sheer importance of it was so staggering, he needed to concede Cardinal Cromulent's point and do it right away.

"Forgive me, Eminence. I yield to the wisdom of your insight into the works of St. Augustine."

"Come, come now, Sam. I chose you precisely because you could give me spirited argument on the holy word and sacred texts. Your work at the Harvard Divinity School, at The University of Chicago Divinity School and at Emory's Candler School of Theology has merited the attention of the pope himself and may perhaps one day occupy a valued place in the Vatican Library. You have a Masters and two PhDs. You don't have to take a dive in such a light-hearted exchange as this. Speak your mind, Sam. I can't imagine you saying anything that might be considered the least bit blasphemous or full of ugly free thought.

Father Bricolage knew right away that this was a direct order to shut up and be obedient. He had been in service to the cardinal long enough for the decoding of his subtexts to have become second nature.'

"No, Eminence. I would never, um, as you put it, 'take a dive.'"

"It's a boxing term, Sam. Probably not the most apropos metaphor. It's almost embarrassing to admit that in my youth I was a Golden Gloves fighter before Lord Jesus showed me the immense apostacy and hypocrisy of committing violence on men, even if only for sport."

"Oh, many of us have sport in our pasts, Eminence. I did a bit of track and field as a sophomore in college."

The grin of Father Bricolage masked a dilemma that gave him pause.

This was one of those moments when the cardinal was a difficult read.

He wasn't going to quote anything from *I Fioretti di San Francesco,* the anonymous translation of Fra Ugolino Boniscambi of Montegiorgio's *Actus Beati Francisci et Sociorum Ejus*, such as, "The weaknesses of the body are given to us in this world by God for the salvation of the soul. So they are of great merit when they are borne patiently." Was this what the pope and the cardinal might have had in mind in forming the *Defensores Fidei de Puero*? The patient bearing of the body's weakness, containing and hiding it until it at last dissipated, washing and healing the ill-repute of the priesthood, its swinish lust mixed with divine and sacred honorific adoration of the cherubim of boyish youth, in the precincts of Holy Mother Church. These boys, these especial fruits from the womb of life truly did belong in the church—for the church to protect and nurture them as they in turn would feed and secrete the festering moral sickness under the same vestments where, in the past, vulnerable sufferers were caught In *flagrante delicto ad pueros.*

Even to him at that moment, *Defensores Fidei de Puero* seemed like a lifeline of hope to curb the church's declining congregations and restore its moral authority without the poisonous hint of the blasphemous, the vulgar and low focus on the genitals, preempting and blocking the essential presence of the Holy Spirit.

"The hundred-yard dash, Sam? Was it?"

Never say no to the cardinal.

"I was a long-distance marathoner and a long jumper. I didn't make varsity, but I enjoyed doing it."

"But now your joy is contained in far greater and more eternal doings."

"All my actions from my first cry at birth to my last breath of seconds ago were all precisely and inexorably aimed toward faith in God."

"Faithful even as a baby, eh, Father?"

The priest said nothing.

The cardinal rose from his desk like some exalted specter and walked with silent silk slippers toward the walnut credenza, opened an upper-level cabinet door and retrieved a decanter of wine and two glasses. "Madeira, Father?"

"No, Eminence. I must keep my body pure and aloof from the physical temptations of this world as I strive to help clear the cluttered and compromised path to the next one."

With a mildness absent of rage, The cardinal replied, "Are you saying I lack bodily purity, Father?"

"Goodness no, Eminence. Your bodily presence and crucial involvement in the physical world safeguards and strengthens your protection and enabling of the most high, spiritual purpose of Holy Mother Church."

The cardinal sat back down on his high-backed, claw-footed Second Empire chairs at his baroque-finished mahogany Versailles desk, poured a half-full cut-glass goblet of wine for each of them. He held out a glass to the priest.

Hot on Father Bricolage's mind: *I must not say no to the cardinal.*

"I shouldn't, Eminence, as you well know. It would be wrong.

Cannot you hear the chorus of our *ángels exterminadores*? Their music hastens the call to chastity and purity."

The cardinal gave the priest a thin grin and downed all that was within his goblet, making no pretense at disinterest or detachment. It was obvious he enjoyed the wine. Then he leaned forward and whispered a whisper that was more threatening than any shout:

"Are you saying that it's my intention to fuck the church, Father?"

"Never at any moment, at any time, Your Eminence. Have you no trust in your chosen, faithful servant?

The cardinal shrugged a businesslike shrug and finished Father Bricolage's glass of wine in a single gulp followed by a long gasp of pleasure like the air escaping from a freshly slashed tire.

"But that's what you mean, Sam. You're bright—one of our very brightest—which is why you're managing the election of children into *Defensores Fidei de Puero* from the foster care system. You are their rescuer, their benefactor, their mentor, and an innovator in their program. So, it's just as well for you to know it. The pope himself knows it. The College knows it. You know it, but we'll all deny it. The pope will deny it in pastorals, bulls and edicts should there ever be a need to give even the slightest reference to this plan for the redemption and resurrection of Holy Mother Church? Yes, I *am* fucking Holy Mother Church, to be crude about it, but this is to use the petty lust of the flesh to cause her rebirth and renewal. And you know as well as I do that there can be no greater benefit to the Holy See than that. Now, some wine for you? Father?"

The priest pulled up one of the red-velvet upholstered chairs closer to the cardinal's desk, took one of the goblets and poured it full of the madeira and drank it all at once.

Their eyes locked, but the cardinal sustained a snide, thin-lipped grin. They both started to speak at once, but the priest demurred, and the cardinal spat out his message first.

"What are we going to do about this thug from the street—a *pezzonovante* inquiring after a failed member of our precious elect of *Defensores Fidei de Puero?*"

"Is he really a 95-caliber big shot, Eminence, like in some gangster book of trash?"

"He seems to be that, my son. Rumblings have reached my ears about the missing Slaughter boy."

"Rumblings?"

"Our cherubic defenders talk."

"Eminence, why on earth would they talk about such things in this near perfect, blissful setting?"

"They have a past that attunes them to such things. They know about the gruesome death of Father Mammock. Somehow."

"The Slaughter boy. Was he—"

"I don't know, Sam. You're hands on. *You're* the one who should specifically know."

"But I don't."

"And that grieves me bitterly, Sam. That you don't. *Know.*"

"I surrender myself abjectly before the wisdom and knowledge of the Holy Spirit who will alter, correct and enhance my understanding of *Defensores Fidei de Puero* even here as we speak. I will become better."

"Become. Well, let us hope then that the Holy Spirit gives you more good counsel and less needless comforting. Your comfort is inimical to this undertaking."

"Then I must ask this, and please understand, Eminence, that I ask solely as a means of sharpening my knowledge in order to help me more explicitly and effectively salve the wounds of Holy Mother Church, his Holiness, The pope, and, if I may make so bold, yourself as well, Eminence. If I may presume myself to hold such a lofty station."

The cardinal coughed ruefully.

"Did I ever tell you we were *wounded?* Are we some cornered, hunted beast? Are we some doomsday cult in hiding? Father, we have over a billion souls in our charge. It is to them we are looking and not just to our immortal church." The cardinal stopped at being just a single decibel shy of shouting.

"Forgive me, Eminence. I lack the verbal skills of the saints and can only aspire to them."

"You're forgiven, Sam."

"Your Eminence is beneficent as always."

"Well, go ahead then. By all means, ask your question. No need to shillyshally. Piety doesn't just belong to the meek, you know, but to the daring as well."

"Yes, Eminence," replied Father Bricolage, swallowing hard, forcing a thought and then sputtering: "Well, Eminence, what, then, if anything, does Holy Mother Church have to do with Karl Kellner, Théodore Reuss and that vicious scoundrel Aleister Crowley's group *Ordo Templi Orientis?*"

With a jerky motion, the cardinal knocked over his empty goblet and then shut his eyes.

FOUR

"Yeah. I said they sold me to *the Father.*"

"He's just a little boy with too much imagination. We simply lost him—thought he'd run away," the frowzy, dowdy, puffy-faced blonde mother said pulling her faux taffeta housedress more tightly around her.

The jowly, unshaven father slouched into the living room, cutting inches off his six-foot height with his posture, his gut spilling over his belted pants and came to her rescue in a laggardly way, offering gruffly, "This is one of our problem kids, y'know. Probably the worst. He tells all kinds of fibs, don't play well with the others out back. Does it look like we're swimming in dough taking care of six kids for the Commonwealth, including boy wonder here?"

"The house is bad, granted, falling apart in decay, but the furnishings are nice, maybe even a bit gawdy with all the gold-plated trim. The white of it all is almost blinding, yet neither of you are very clean. Why is everything else so spotless?"

"We put the kids to work in the house. Teaches 'em somethin' about life. Discipline and hard work, y'understand." The father, Mr. Kermit Banausic, plopped down with a great degree of difficulty on the coconut-cream colored sectional sofa that just about devoured the whole room. Doris Banausic, wrung her hands in distress, whimpering.

"Oh, my lord god Jesus, what do we do with a boy like this? What in heaven's name do we *do?*"

"We call this kinda décor "Mediterranean Flair" –it's classico, don't ya get it?"

"Yes. I get it."

"We'll take him back, Mr. Null, of course we will. But he'll have to be surrendered back into the system. We just can't handle such a rambunctious boy. He's what they used to call incorrigible."

"All boys are rambunctious, Mrs. Banausic. Even the ones you think aren't."

"But we've really got our hands full here with the other children. We can't handle little Clem Derecho no matter how we try."

"He ain't so little anymore, so you wanna take a good look at him and evaluate him for yourself. He's a porker, eats us out of house and home as it is. I was freaking relieved when he skedaddled out of our happy abode. We're living on a fixed income provided by these kids. Without them, I don't know what we do. As you can see, I'm too sick and injured to work doin' the pipe fittin' anymore. Doris would be okay out in the workforce, but she ain't got no skills."

"That's why we'd be so grateful, Mr. Null, for whatever you can do, in terms of emoluments."

"Do you understand where I found your Clement, Mrs. Banausic?"

"That's nothin' but a bunch of horseshit, Null. There ain't no better man in this whole parish better than the Father. He's one of those rare men of God who also happens to be the salt of the earth on top of everything else."

"We'd never have to sell a little boy to Father Mammock—"

"She's right about that one, pally. He wouldn't have to pay. I'd give the kid to him for free at the pointing of his little pinky finger."

"I don't believe the Father would do any of that to anyone, Mr. Null, let alone a small child."

"I keep tellin' ya, Doris: he ain't that *small*."

"I swear, Mr. Null! He was gonna stick his—"

Null gently put his hand across the boy's mouth and he made no further sound but that of shallow breathing.

"There'll be enough of that, Mr. Clement Derecho. Speak when you're spoken to or not at all," scolded Mrs. Banausic icily. "You can be punished, Clement. A bar of soap will fit very nicely into that mouth of yours."

"So, the Father gave you money?"

"Ya couldn't really call it that, y'know," drawled Mr. Banausic, flipping channels on his new Vizio P Series Quantum X 2020 flatscreen HDTV. "But, yeah, the Father was always helpin' out poor fellas like me who was down on their luck."

Clem made a muffled murmuring under Null's palm. He removed it from the kid's face, wiped it on his topcoat and the kid's eyes darted about, making a quick study of the room and all at once decided to say nothing.

There was a little click in his head that told him to stay quiet.

He didn't have to say anything. He could feel it. Null knew, and that was all there was to it or would be, he was sure. It felt wrong, this whole scene, and he knew enough about that, having been in enough rooms where it all felt wrong, and this was just like that, but with one key and special difference.

This time it wasn't going to go wrong against him.

"You have five other children, you said?"

"That's correct, Mr. Null. All girls. Wonderful little angels, I might add."

"You might. But angels are often dead, aren't they?"

"Not the ones in the Holy Bible. Well, they're beyond being alive."

"You mean never having lived at all?"

"Not life the way you understand it, Mr. Null."

"Life in which way, then?"

"Some kind of life we can only imagine in our dreams. The same everlasting kind of life we get—"

"After we die."

"Death is a beginning, Mr. Null. Surely, you've been taught that."

"I was, in fact, taught exactly that. But life has taught me a few facts—that those like you who extoll life after death are in no hurry to get there, doing whatever you can to drag out your presence in this foul plane of existence. Also, that death is a finisher, not a beginner. Death will end whatever evil one encounters—certainly any of the good—and it does seem true that the evil that men and women do lives on after them."

"You've reasoned it out for yourself, then. Vengeance is mine sayeth the Lord, and it certainly doesn't belong to us."

"Maybe not, Mrs. Banausic, but it does belong to the victim whether or not he or she can cash that in. And if they can, why then it belongs to the executioner."

"I'm not a philosopher, Mr. Null. I lack the schoolin' for that. But what has that to do with little Clement—"

"Jesus Christ, Doris!" growled Mr. Banausic. "I told ya that fuckin' hog of a kid ain't little."

"Let's not split hairs, Kermit."

"Just take his money and boot him the hell out of here. I'm sick of his droning on and on about nothin'."

"More rightly, Mrs. Banausic, you should be giving *me* the money, since I brought your child home safe and sound."

"But Mr. Null. We didn't really want him back. Safe or sound or in any other way. We thought he'd be a help to the Father. The church has programs for altar boys and servers that help the Fathers and groom them."

"*Groom* would seem the operative word here. By the way: I thought you said Clement ran away. Not that he entered into some kind of service with the late Father Mammock."

"Did—did you say, *late?*"

"I speak very carefully and well, Mrs. Banausic."

"Alright, fucko! Get your skinny, mutant-looking ass out the door, you creepy freak, before I kick it out the door myself."

"Oh, I'll be going soon enough. Relax about that, Mr. Banausic. Just one or two more questions, and then you can collect your reward."

"Hurry it up then, you disgusting freak."

"Where are all the other children—the girls?"

"Why, this is their playtime, Mr. Null. They're outside enjoying themselves."

Null stiffened and shouted in a sharp tone of voice like the cry of a carrion crow. "Shut up! All of you. Right now! None of you make a sound. None of you!"

The silence didn't hang, but instead pushed through the room like a force, a storm amid which everyone froze.

"What is it, Mr. Null?" asked Mrs. Banausic, trembling, her voice in vibrato form.

"When children play, they make noise. I don't hear anything but a few birds singing and some adult laughter far off. The occasional car passing by. Why might that be?"

"They're good girls, fucko. They ain't little hooligans like Clem."

"They're very good girls, Mr. Null. They never make a peep out of turn."

"When is their turn, Mrs. Banausic? When does that happen?"

"Whenever I say it does."

"You rule the roost. Yes?"

"Figure that out, did ya?"

"Clement. Go outside with your sisters for a few minutes, please."

"They're not his sisters. The little crumb ain't got no one."

"Go outside now, Clement. Tell the girls to relax. Make all the noise they want—*you* want. The more the better. So, yes. I'm telling you to be noisy. Go do that. Now." Null pushed the boy firmly forward, which caused him to scamper from the living room as if he were on fire. He had begun to understand Null—had a sense of him—and he didn't like it. He didn't like any of it but intuited that cooperating with the strange man who had rescued him from Father Mammock was his best bet.

"I'm not keepin' ya, am I, fucko?"

"Not at all."

"Then gimme the loot and scoot. We answered all your stupid questions."

"You did." Null reached into the left pocket of his topcoat, removed a bundle of bills kept together in a tight roll with a wide, elastic band. He tossed the bundle at Mr. Banausic, who caught it with ease, then gave a wide smirk.

"How much?"

"You can count it. It's the five hundred you asked for."

"Pisser. We're all set then. You can blow now."

"Yes," said Mrs. Banausic with a sigh of relief. "Go now, please."

Null cocked his ear. "Do you hear that? The both of you. Do you?"

"It's the children," Mrs. Banausic replied. "Such a racket."

"So what? We told ya to blow, so blow already."

"Certainly."

With a swift, easy, almost graceful movement of his right arm, Null drew the Heckler with the suppressor from his topcoat pocket and put two nine-millimeter slugs in Kermit Banausic's forehead, killing him instantly. Doris Banausic screamed.

"You can't do this, Mr. Null—you can't. You promised us money, promised not to judge us! You *promised*!"

"I'm a man of my word. I don't go back on my promises. I gave your husband the money and I'm leaving. I'm also not judging you. Rulers of the roost who abuse little girls must be dealt with, however. So too, mothers who sell little boys to priests must be held to account. Children need to be protected. I'm not here to judge you—"

Null grouped four shots into Mrs. Banausic's capacious chest before she could turn and run. She fell hard to the new mauve carpeting with a shuddering thud, lying on her side, blood trickling steadily from her open mouth. She looked surprised.

"I'm here to execute you."

Null pocketed the gun and then made his way to the backyard to gather up the little children.

FIVE

"Why am I here, Byron?"

"I wouldn't have ya miss this for the world, LT. I wouldn't have ya miss this one for all the Won Tons in Chinatown." Homicide Detective Byron Wurdalaka's lupine face was drawn and rum-blossomed more than Lieutenant Kay Boyd had realized or even remembered. She'd only been two weeks in FBI LegoLand—had in fact barely scratched the surface of gangland dope dealing in Boston before being dragged back here to One Schroeder Plaza and its antiseptic halls and rooms, its staid glass and metal flooded with migraine-making fluorescent light and sharp, flickering shadows. Just like back there in FBI LegoLand, there was no way to escape the damned light that was itself a hostile entity. She hungered for natural light, fresh air, blue skies with playful wisps of clouds, green, rolling hills and Gilbey's gin. A warm flow of Gilbey's gin. Oh, she needed that gin! Still! Even after the last detox. Jesus, Wurdalaka was looking awful, so much older than even two-weeks ago, even somehow frail. She wondered if he'd be taking early retirement. Fuck all. She wished he goddamn well would do it already.

She also found it hard to look at the silver-gray straw hat with the plaid band that threatened to fall over his baggy, crinkly eyes.

The persistent call for bad, cheap gin was rumbling annoyingly in the back of her throat. She lit a cigarette to get some relief and the somewhat stooped over, raffish looking homicide detective shook his head and chuckled, his ruddy whiskers gleaming in the hostile light.

"Just hit me with it already, will you, so I can get back to my joyous new liaison position helping out the Feebs on gang detail."

"You're just finagling yourself a government job. You ain't got a wisp of interest in Boston's subhuman element, do yez?"

"I'm here with *you*, Byron, ain't I?"

"Feebs succeeded where we failed, LT. They managed to give you a sense of humor at last. Oh, those sackless SACs over there in Chelsea are real goddamn wizards alright. They re-read Hawkins' "Brief History of Time" at lunch. They hand you out a copy to welcome you into the ranks of the clueless and smug? Or are you just a self-starter, checkin' one out of the lie-berry?"

"It's Hawking, not *Hawkins*, Byron. And everyone knows there's no one smugger than a Boston Police officer. They swagger around, honking their authority and act like they know everything."

"That include you, LT?"

"You bet your ass it does. So start the show already. I'm getting antsy."

Detective Wurdalaka was about to make a particularly un-PC joke about alcoholism but thought better of it. She had been known to punch a fellow cop in the face for doing just such a thing. No, it wouldn't be worth getting her written up over, it though. And no actual male cop would ever lodge an assault complaint against a woman for nailing him in the snoot. That would be a direct and open admission to having no balls at all.

A different kind of "suicide by cop."

"This kid is right out of the funnies. Strictly Twilight Zone."

"I don't get your meaning. Why isn't somebody interrogating him? Look at him—he's literally twiddling his thumbs there. Wait. You hear that?"

"Yeah, LT, I got ears."

"The little fucker's *whistling.*"

"You wanna take a crack at him? You're doin' the gang thing down in Chelsea, anyways."

"But I'm not doin' it here, Byron. Why do you even have him? You nursin' a homicide beef against the boy?"

"Oh, my shriveled little gonads stood right up at attention at the thought. But I don't got anything on him. Nothing. Except that maybe he's a lead into the Gangsta Boyz gang. Self-identified. He said it right at the desk. One o' your targets, I think it's safe to say."

"What's that tune he's whistling? Jesus, that ain't no rap tune, that's for sure."

"You can't whistle rap, LT."

"You know what I'm sayin'."

"I can name that tune, LT. It's 'I'm Forever Blowing Bubbles.'"

"Jesus Christ. If this particular mope ain't jammed up on anything, just pop him back out on the street and that's that. I'm steeped in enough bullshit as it is just dealing with the Feebs. I don't see the value for you, Byron. I honestly don't. I know you got cases to clear. No need to waste time with this kind of entertainment."

"Maybe yes, maybe no, LT. We take our investigative aids wherever we can find them.

"We do. But I don't go chasin' down bullshit leads when they come from homicide and there ain't no murder."

"These guys racked up more murders than I can count."

"But you can't pull down a one, can you, Byron?"

"No, I can't, and I'll level with yez. I'm losin' sleep over it."

"I got nothin' comin' here Byron."

"No, wait. I got an idea, LT. We don't wanna query the boy, let Nicky Andromeda do it. He's been an all-round man in Gangsta Boyz territory ever since he got the worse end of an exchange with that psycho CI of yours you claim don't exist."

"I never claimed nothin' about him."

"Well, he's here today prepping for court. Let's have him do a little tea dance with our sassy friend in there."

"He's not gonna smash the kid's face against the table or nothin', is he?"

"Not in the cold fluorescent light of day with you and me watchin' he won't."

"Okay. Go and fetch the dear boy."

Wurdalaka hustled from the room with his long stride and Boyd felt some relief in his leaving, but not nearly enough. She thought of smoking a cigarette, but the new smoke detectors installed this time were extra-hypersensitive and likely to cause a headache-making commotion that canceled out whatever relief she may have gotten. She felt alone, uncertain and weary beyond just the physical: it was like every thought in her head was labored and heavy, landing on her consciousness with a dull thud. She straightened up from leaning on the sparse metal desk with its two vinyl and aluminum chairs and peered at the whistling kid on the other end of the trick glass that didn't fool anyone anymore.

He knew he was being watched and just didn't care.

But he wasn't perp cool—no that was just an act.

No, this joker was frosty.

He leaned back in his chair with his fingers interlaced behind his head as if he might be surrendering, but his attitude proclaimed he had no intention whatever of doing that. No, he was assured of walking free from One Schroeder anytime he liked. He sat in that bleak blank room that carried the stench of fear, remorse and suffering and breathed it all in as if it were some kind of perfume that suited him. He was in no hurry. He had all the time in the world.

"Hey, LT. What're you doin' back? I heard the Feebs grabbed ya up."

"How are you feelin', Nicky? Any better?"

"I'm all good, 'cept I got a perma-limp courtesy of the zombie fuck that shot me."

"Cut the horror stories, Andromeda. They give me the shakes."

"Sure that ain't the DTs, Sarge?"

"Talk to the LT about that. She's the reigning expert."

"Shut the fuck up, Byron, already. You called us in here, so show us what you got. Shit or get off the pot, why doncha?"

"Okay. Okay, LT, I got you your man—somethin' you'd *never* be able to do on your own. Why don't ya go whip a little of that alpha bad-ass female energy on him? We *all* know you're one o' those."

"Y'know, the most badass feature I can display at the given moment, Byron, is not snapping my elbow directly into that slack ass yap of yours."

"Heaven forfend. You put me right in my place yet again, LT, yes you most certainly did. How *do* you do it?" If it were possible for him to have produced a hybrid of a chuckle and a sneer, Detective Sergeant Byron Wurdalaka not only would have mastered it, but would have delivered whatever it might have been right there and then, like a hard punch.

"You want me to sweat handsome Harry in there, LT, or what?"

"Why not, Nicky? I haven't really had a chance to evaluate those interrogation skills of yours lately. This seems the perfect opportunity to watch you strut your stuff."

"Show off for teacher, why doncha, kid."

Andromeda's face crinkled up into dimples with a grin.

"Why, Sergeant, I take remarks like that as your heartfelt gesture of professional respect and love." He air-kissed Wurdalaka to punctuate his sarcasm and entered the interrogation room with the kid, who was still whistling that eerie tune.

Boyd turned up the room volume to hear it better and sat down on the desk, kicking her legs a little bit as if she were sixteen-years old. Wurdalaka was leaning against the thickly painted, dun-colored plaster wall, his willowy height sinking into itself. Boyd focused on the scene in front of her, hoping there was something, *anything,* of value to be gleaned from this impromptu meeting. And it bothered her almost to the point of distraction that Wurdalaka was still softly chuckling to himself about the whole thing right in front of her.

They both watched Andromeda sit down in the one empty

chair at the table opposite the whistling kid, seeing him dig in without skipping a beat.

"Nice tune you're whistling kid. Which one is it? Some rap sample or what?"

"No sir. It's "I'm Forever Blowing Bubbles", an old jazz tune. I know it by the Original Dixieland Jass Band—not jazz, but jass, like ass—all white guys too, but they swung some. Gotta be a hundred years old."

"Where you gonna pick up a one-hundred-year-old jazz tune from? How could you even hear it?"

"You a cop, you should know things. Real talk. They pop that shit right onto CD. Been doin' that for decades. Where you been? Grandma's?"

"Very nice. Very tricky. I like it. Hundred-year-old jazz tune gone digital. I'll have to check that out. What did you say your name is?"

"Shit, cuz, you already hip to that."

"Okay, Mr. Manavelins. What is it that you came here to tell us?"

"You check me out, homes?"

"Yeah, we did. All I could say when I looked at your sheet was, 'Where's the beef?' because I couldn't find any. You're as clean as a vegan, Morris. You ain't got no beef. Not a one."

"Lacto-Ovo, my dude."

Andromeda jerked up from his seat and leaned into Morris Manavelins, shouting: "Alright, fuckstick, tell me who the fuck sent you and why or I'm gonna whip up a beef that'll jam you up so tight and final you won't never walk out of here. I'll lose your skinny ass in the tombs, misplace your jacket. By the time they find you, your little asshole be so wide I could drive a Subaru right through it. So spill it while you can, you little mope, or I'll start paintin' the walls with your insides. Do it now, while you can, shitbird!"

Manavelins looked worried, but not enough. His body tensed, lips pursed, but he showed no other signs of being as rattled as he should have been, much to the disappointment of the Third-Grade Detective. Maybe his timing was off. Maybe his heart wasn't in it.

Usually, the minnows collapsed into a pool of whining and pleading after yack like that. They didn't just sit there coolly mocking him like this little creeper kid did, even though he had an obvious, white-knuckled death grip on the edge of the table. And this kid didn't even have a sheet.

"You don't gotta pull no routine on me officer—"

"*Detective* Andromeda. Get it right punk."

"No need to try and put the whammy on me. I ain't your problem, Detective."

"No need? I got the whammy for yo' mammy right here, fuckstick."

"I ain't your problem, homes."

"You're not?" He forced a snide chuckle, bore down on the kid for real. "Tell me who my problem is then, shitbird. Gimme the message you put your skinny ass on the chopping block to deliver. 'Cause that's where it is and I'm holding the axe. C'mon shitbird, *give*. I don't got a lotta time. I got to deliver you to the tombs within the hour. Then we lose your jacket, keep you there till you smarten the fuck up. Maybe even let you out sometime."

That was good; he felt better about how this was going. He was on the muscle now, which is how you played it, if you actually wanted what you wanted.

And Third-Grade Detective Nick Andromeda had a big wants list.

Like this minnow's biggest fish, for one—the zombie fuck ghost who was the shot caller for the Gangsta Boyz. The guy that fucked up his leg. Also, the thing that really counted. He wanted a leapfrog promotion, and he wanted it yesterday.

"I ain't spooked, stupid ofay Dick. I can leave anytime I like. You do that to me, then in the hour, there come an attorney gon' track me down first, then you, motherfucker. Then we see what's what."

"Well, looky here, a fuckin' pipe cleaner wants to play. Okay, fuckstick: whistle me another tune. Make it one I can dance to. I got no patience for crud like you."

Andromeda kicked his chair hard just to make the kid jump a

little, which he did, then sat back down on it in an athletic motion to recover. The Detective bore down on the kid, leaning into him a little while watching his cool melt fast enough to provide a hopeful pang of relief. No, he really wasn't too shabby at all, when you looked at it fairly.

"Okay, Bojangles, get to it."

"You ain't gon' shut the Boyz down no way no-how."

"Now listen—"

"No, you listen, motherfucker. You just a ofay cowboy—everybody *know* that. Spelled backward, "cowboy" is a acronym for 'young, obnoxious, bastard we often con.'"

"I ain't that young, punk."

"Looks good on ya anyways, homes."

"Get to the point."

"You ain't big enough to bust us. We statewide now, not jus' Roxbury-Mattapan—Merrimac Valley up through Taunton, homes —and we motherfuckin' diverse as fuck."

"You're batshit, buddy. You ain't got the numbers—"

"Guess again you ofay piece of shit!"

"You got a mouth."

The kid spat.

Andromeda whiffed the stagnant air in the room with an open hand slap that purposely didn't connect with the kid's face, but that almost caused him to fall over backwards in his chair when he gave out with the big flinch. Sure, the kid was definitely rattled, just not *that* rattled. Andromeda stood up and glared at him.

Skinny little nothin', he thought. "You tellin' me you so big that BPD can't yank you out by the roots?"

"Yeah, motherfucker. You got nothin' but monkey mouth, Dick."

"You're gonna get taught some manners down at county, kiddo, after I book you, send you down there and misplace your jacket."

"Lawyer come find my black ass."

"You ain't been lost till I lose you, dipshit. I can hold you on nothin for two days straight and no amount of yapping from a brace of shyster lawyers can do anything about it. Chew on that,

Mr. Brock Manavelins. They can just pound sand and pile up enough pricey hourlies to make your boss deliriously happy."

"You don't get it, Dick. Ain't nothin' ever gon' make that mother-fucker happy. He never happy, or anything else. He say he know you, too. Ain't that somethin' of interest to you, though? Dick? He tol' me you was gonna be the one to try and slap me 'round. Fuck if he ain't on the money yet again. I don't get how he knew that."

"It does give one pause, kid."

Manavelins pushed back his chair with his heels making a screeching noise against the linoleum, smiling when he saw Andromeda scrunch up his face at the sound. That went down wrong, somehow. Very wrong.

"I got no record, no jacket like what *you* say. I ain't been in the system since I was a baby. I a damn honor student set to ma-*tric*-ulate at Northeastern in the fall. All paid, all set. You turn around sometime, maybe I gon' actually *be* one o' those pricey lawyers you talkin' shit about. So, you gon' hold me on nothin', assault me, put me in fear for my safety, all that, and then we all just go the complaint route—drop a file or two on you, tie up your brownshirt Nazi ass but good. Then we see whose jacket *really* gets lost."

Andromeda smirked at just how good a shot that was. Only a few feet from striking home, really. It was time to cool down, affect giving him a sympathetic ear—no, too far in the other direction. There was a more decisive middle ground to be had, so he took that.

"Okay, shitbird, just gimme the message and I'll let you scamper away out of my sight. Pukes like you gimme migraines."

"Botox fix you right up there, Dick. You don't gotta suffer on my account. No, you don't, Mr. Nicholas Andromeda, Third Grade De-tec-*tive.*"

Andromeda let it out, couldn't control it, couldn't hold it in— what could only be described as a bellowing horse laugh. This made Manavelins squint in discomfort.

"Cute, kid. That was fucking adorable. I get it. Here's my message back: next time send me a man. Not a boy."

"You axe-shully callin' me *boy*, Dick Nick?"

"Yeah, I am. Actually. But because you're a kid. Not because you're black. You're smart. I know I didn't confuse you."

"No, I don't think you confuse nobody, Dick Nick. Real talk."

"You memorize it? Or can you just give me the gist?"

"Why'n'cha go get me a soda, Dick Nick?"

Andromeda exploded into the table with nearly everything he had to deliberately knock Manavelins to the floor with enough of a shock effect to make the kid cross his forearms over his face to stop an oncoming blow and to make Wurdalaka and Boyd in the next room do a little inch-high hop from where they were watching.

Boyd nodded her approval.

Wurdalaka chuckled to himself and swore.

"You one 5150 motherfucker—*real talk.*"

"Take it easy, Manny. That's what the other kids call you, right? Manny?"

Andromeda extended his hand with a smile and Manavelins took it and found himself pulled up hard to his feet. "You go ahead 'n' call me sir, motherfucker."

"Let's take a good look at you, Manny. Turn yourself around for me. Don't question it, just do it."

"I don't do it, you do sumpm else I don't like, I guess."

"That's the spirit. Come on, kid. *Tempus fugit.*"

The kid spun around, aping grace and doing a not half-bad job of it.

"No worse for the wear at all. Everybody see that? Not a mark on the kid at all."

"I think they fell asleep on the other side o' that glass, but if they good then so am I."

"The message, Manny. Now. Hit, git and *split.*"

Manny cleared his throat and gave Andromeda a hard, practiced look.

"*No*body gon' be bustin' any Gangsta Boyz in this century, Dick Nick. We all trained. You find the cash, but no dope—never no dope. When one o' your ringers come round for a taste, buy a eight-ball, twelve-year-old bring it round later. You know this because those busts all die, little kid get out, he get recycled, probation. Costs and fees paid, hop on down to the next town. The slingin' don't never stop. Your buyers can't even get in on the bumper. No ride for them. Now, the guy with the keys, runnin' us all, he way too bad to be known—beyond 5150. No one sees him, no one *wants* to see him. He kill anyone make even a okay stupid move, tell some idiot lie. Harmless shit. Don't matter. It go up the chain, wham bam, good god damn. Insta-corpse. He don't kill for fun, he ain't reckless, he kill for—"

"Convenience? That's what you're tryin' to say?"

"Yeah, Dick Nick. That be 'bout right."

"So now I should be shakin' in my little custom-fitted booties?"

"What he say 'bout you? I bet you *know* this one."

"Surprise me."

"Next time he *take* that leg."

Andromeda froze, swallowed, recovered all in a heartbeat.

"Cute. Now he's gonna Peter Pan to my Captain Hook—lay off the funnies, kid."

"Ain't no funnies—we got iPads now and shit. I want a comic book I go stream a movie."

"What does that have to do with anything, Manny. Time's ticking."

"That motherfucker *know* you, Dick Nick."

"So he knows me, but I don't know the son-of-a-bitch."

"I ain't through, Dick Nick."

"I'm still awake, Manny, but not for long. I might just have to leave you for a while so you can collect your thoughts."

"You right 'bout the time tickin', Dick Nick. He kill your ass enough of it pass."

"Death comes to all men, Manny, even your shot caller."

"Yeah, but he still bring it fast enough. Get it to you 'fore you get the message. One way or 'nother, you gon' be communicated with, know I'm sayin'."

"Spit it out, Manny, then I can spit *you* out once and for all."

"Real talk: Monster man keep the little kids, the ones you call the minnows, dealin' gak so they never, ever get a chance to even *try* the shit. They all too scared o' this guy. Think he can see 'round corners. He the boogeyman. He also pay good, keep us *all* in the guap. Those minnow kids all get bank accounts—fuck, even the dumbest ones wind up with college funds."

"That'd be you, Manny, am I right?"

"You could be, Dick Nick. You could be."

"Anything else I should know?"

"Real talk, Dick Nick: The shot caller's a killer, a death dealer, no fuckin' around. No cap, motherfucker. This ain't a reputation thing. It's deep. He give you even a *chin check*, you motherfuckin' dead. Everyone in the Gangsta Boyz rather do time and live than give anything up about who's gon' kill you in a day no fuckin' sweat before he get breakfast. Before you think of a way out, yo' brains already be splattered across walls. He got total loyalty because—"

"Because he's a mass murdering psycho?"

"Yeah, that and he a ghost too. You never find him, he find you. And you never, ever want that to happen. He ain't for real. He like some dead thing, a—"

"A *zombie* fucker. You were about to say? Maybe zombie-fuck—"

"Don't even say it, Dick Nick. You don't know who he have on the payroll up in this bitch. We don't speak the name. That's 'cause he is what the name say: Nothin', nobody, Mr. Zero. A fuckin' ghost."

"Null. The defunct CI. You're talking about a dead man who no longer exists. He scare you with Santeria, some kind of chicken-gutting Obeah Voodoo shit?"

"Guess again, Dick Nick. He scare us because he just kills anyone in his way. He don't hesitate. He on you, kill you dead before you even *realize* you even wanna kill him first, plan a coup, defy a order. Blood and money. That's all it is to him. The money's hella good, which is why you can't arrest no one, anyone take him on or mess with even just *one* of his itty-bitty minnows, well that one already *be* dead before he pull shit. He stone dead—the body just don't know it yet. Pretty soon the man take on N-Y-C and he make that happen too. He don't miss a trick. We all got doubts he even human."

"And he knows you're talking about him behind his back this way? He knows you're running your mouth running him down like this?"

Manavelins shook his head with a sheepish grin, and suppressing a laugh, managed to say with a straight face: "My dude, he had me rehearse that whole speech with him right before I come see you."

SIX

"What the fuck do you think you're doing, Null?"

"You know what I'm doing, Kay. You always know—"

"Which is why I feel like having a goddamn drink all the time."

"You know that'll kill you. That it benefits no one and upsets what I intend to do. Your dying would be a monkey wrench in the works and a black hole to any sort of forward motion."

"You're shitting me. I thought you said you had trouble telling jokes."

"I never joke. Not anymore."

"That's not the way to prevent me from doing something—that it upsets your plans. Hell, that's a damn incentive to go ahead and do it."

"That's perverse."

"What's perverse is looking at you, knowing what you are, and hearing you say that."

"That cancels nothing out."

"Now you're making a joke?"

Null sighed like the air being let out of a tire—more like a hiss, really. "It tires me, sifting through the data, mining it in the voluminous cracked palace of my memory."

"That palace is more than just cracked, Null."

"'Palace is reaching, I'll give you that. It's a common metaphor for a phenomenology of mind."

"Whatever you want, I can't do it."

"I don't want you to do anything that you don't already have to do."

"That means locking you up."

"You'd have to join me if that were so."

"So if I kill you, I kill myself?"

"Are you talking to me or yourself?"

"I honestly don't know anymore."

"You're being morbid, Kay."

"Morbid. Me. While Mr. Meth-Dealing, Mass-Murdering, deranged fucknut is standing here in my condo telling me *I'm* morbid!"

Null looked about the barren space that lacked even the slightest pretense to style—even the minimalist style—sniffed the air and squinted his eyes a bit as he did. "Your place is a little sparse. The air's musty too. Maybe some fresh-cut flowers would help?"

"It's a little late in the game to tell me to stop and smell the roses."

"Even funerals have flowers, Kay."

"But you've never sent flowers to anybody, have you, Null? Even once?"

"I might have, but I too often have had more urgent demands on my time and attention, both of which are limited."

"And we *know* what those demands are—how they wind up necessitating a considerable subsidiary build-up of corpses."

"Hazard of the trade."

"And what trade is that? Meth dealer? *Death* dealer?"

"Have you ever thought about getting a cat, Kay? They don't require much care and it might help with the loneliness."

"I *had* a cat once. Remember?"

"H.H. Holmes?"

"Mudgett. The cat's name was *Mudgett*. As in Herman—of New Hampshire."

"That's right." Cool, empty.

"That's right. That is *exactly* right. And you know what happened to good old Mudgett, don't you?"

"Didn't I—"

"Yes, you did. You did. You killed him."

"I was on drugs."

"Aren't you *always* on drugs? Just to stay awake?"

"He was getting underfoot."

"That's your biggest problem, Null. To you *everyone's* underfoot. Everyone needs to be killed at some point if it suits a momentary need for expediency."

"I only do one thing, Kay. Just one thing."

"Yeah, yeah. And you're brilliant at it. So why bring it to my home and lay it at my feet? Are you trying to be a cat?"

"I lack the charm for that."

"You do."

"Well, your condo certainly needs something, Kay." Null waved an arm and the sleeve of his beige topcoat slid down revealing an arm that was all sinew and scars. "All this—your surroundings—make you seem even less alive than I am. Which isn't very alive at all."

"And you thought maybe a fresh kill or two might spark me back to life?"

"There are worse motives than that in the world, Kay."

Boyd sighed, shuffled her feet a bit, sat down on a rusted bridge chair, pulled out a Marlborough cigarette from its red and white box, lit it and blew a gout of smoke directly at Null. "You think?" she said without a trace of sarcasm. She put her knees together, crumpling her skirt and stockings, looking glassy-eyed.

"I thought that might have been true when you were interred at Lemuel Shattuck Hospital last year. I wasn't entirely wrong."

"What in hell are you getting at?"

"That's what I'm getting at. What brought you to liase with the

FBI and engage their interest in Boston gangs. Why I brought you to them."

"I can't steer their investigation away from the Gangsta Boyz. I wish I could, so I wouldn't have to deal with you at all. But there's a vendetta going on between the Feebs and the DEA, who'd like to wrap up all your band of kiddies in a bow and shut down what promises to be the biggest supplier and supply-chain infrastructure of methamphetamine in the northeast. My boss at the Feebs has a hardon for the streets, which means he has a hard-on for the Gangsta Boyz."

"Which means he has a hardon for me."

"You know the guy."

"The forensic accountant. Yes, I know him. He wants a big arrest with far-reaching impact and large numbers of busts, all solid, to make his reputation such that he can take retirement early and go out with a bang. That's why I put you there."

"To give *him* a bang."

"A broad phrasing."

"But that's you, isn't it? All the angles in broad phrasing."

"Enough that count."

"You think you missed something?"

"There's always something, yet my machinations—"

"Jesus Christ, yes! I got that. Like keloid scarring. Thanks for rescuing me from One Schroeder, at least. I was beginning to feel a little bit cramped in the hot box they were putting me in until you pulled whatever levers you pulled to get me a berth down in Lego-Land of Chelsea."

"I'll take out LegoLand entirely with a bang, if the accountant doesn't return to his spreadsheets and data analytics soon." His monotone went down to a coarse whisper, a sound like that of a straight razor slicing through paper. "If not, then, I'll wipe out the competition from them just as I have with others."

"But don't you get I'm trying to *sell* him the competition. You're not the only gang leader in Beantown you know."

Null paced the clean white dead space languidly, turning about in the light, uncaring as to the heat and glare that blasted his sensitive eyes, heedless of warmth, wearing a heavy topcoat under which was a machete hung from a lanyard around his neck swung to the back, a Heckler and Koch Tactical 45 with suppressor holstered in a specially reinforced inside right pocket, a Glock 9 with suppressor on the left within easy inside reach and an AR-15 Velcro-belted to his torso, yet he moved with an awkward grace as if merely hobbled by a damaged hamstring that had been sliced in two years ago and knitted funny. His limp gave him a false aspect of pathos. His flak jacket made him look slightly stocky.

His scars no longer shaded by his pork-pie hat that had looked sad and painful now were bold and shiny, glistening as though oily in the light.

"Give the Feebs at LegoLand The Mallet. He's got his drug operation and crew and I don't interfere with it unless he crosses over the line."

"But your line is Boston."

"Boston is mine. I own the town. I've taken it and I'm doing rather a better job with it than Honey Fitz did."

"You don't own the politics."

"If I have to, I will. You're with the FBI—get any trouble about it from anyone, even the captain who threw you in with that hump Quark? Your nightmare Feeb?"

"No. Parseeman, LaCuna even Byron Wurdalaka were happy to see me go."

"No trouble from Andromeda?"

"Always trouble from Andromeda. He's carrying a grudge about your shooting him in the leg."

"Tell him to learn to live with a limp. It's done wonders for me."

"He wants to frog march you down to holding."

"I'll send him down to City Mortuary."

"What else can I do for you—do that will make enough of a difference to get you to leave me the fuck alone? Do to get you out of my life? Really, Null, this anti-relationship just can't last."

"Nothing lasts. It's all a matter of when it breaks down."

"We're joined at the hip—worse than being married."

"Just do what you do. I've set you on the path. Work it out as it goes. There is one thing you might want to consider, though."

"And what would I ever want to consider on your behalf? Other than arresting you on *my* behalf?"

"Children are disappearing. My children—"

"You don't have any children."

"You heard Manny speak in interrogation. You heard all about my so-called minnows."

"Yeah. Sure. The ones too little— the ones that if we caught them, we'd have to throw them back."

"That's right. Except someone's been catching them and *not* throwing them back. They're keeping them. It's not a large number of them...right now. Just a few. But I did recapture one of them."

"Your minnow? So what's the problem?"

"No, he wasn't one of mine, or even the one a Dorchester lady prevailed upon me to find for her, with tears, the rosary and a votive candle. He was just another foster kid, hadn't hit puberty. Maybe he'll make a fine minnow sometime. We could send him off to Boston College, instead of the drunk tank or Titticut Follies where he was headed before I interfered."

"So you got him back. I cry tears of joy for that."

"I knew you'd be moved."

"What's the problem, then? It wasn't from a rival gang. You pretty much wiped them all out I thought."

"There are some stragglers afoot."

"Even so—doesn't really sound like a threat."

"I'm not sure."

"You? Not sure? You're always sure. Could it be you've found a criminal enterprise bigger than your own? One you can't fight? Or was it all just a misunderstanding?"

"It was no misunderstanding."

"Then who had him? I'm sure you meted out your usual brand of horror you call judgment."

"I never call it that. Not once. No, I exact no judgment. If I could feel sympathy, I'd give it to them right up to the end. But, unfortunately, I can't."

"I don't care what you call your murders. They sicken me."

"You didn't feel that way when you watched an angry group of teens and young men rip Gorgeous George Goodnature apart with Cutlery Corner knives."

"No." Boyd looked at her feet for just a moment then, when she looked up, Null offered her a lit cigarette, which she gratefully accepted. After a long drag and exhale of white smoke, she firmly replied. "I didn't feel that way when I watched that. I—"

"You were about to say you felt good."

"Maybe. But I did."

"I call it execution because that's what it is. Judgment, by the time I get to them, has already been handed down long before."

"And you need to tell me who you executed?"

"You should know."

"Should I? I'll play then. So who was it? And don't tell me it was the Ork. Malek's got it in for you since you took his right arm and left leg – feels a bit gypped, I'd say, but he doesn't have the numbers, the infrastructure or the will to do anything about it since you keep making his key players disappear every time they get a little fresh with your Gangsta Boyz. BPD *still* thinks they're the problem like we're back in the olden days of the Bloody Bean. Was it the ODDs? That clumsy criminal crew, O'Leary, Davidovich and Dionne? Sounds like a damn law firm."

"They don't do the law, but they *do* do order. They come in handy in a pinch. They're customers and contractors for us now, from Lynn, Everett, Fall River, Attleboro, even the Merrimac Valley. We outnumber them, solving the racial divide."

"They'd have the muscle, though."

"Maybe. A threat, perhaps. Yet peace prevails."

"Jesus, Null! Who then? Who grabbed up the damn minnow and didn't throw him back?"

"He wasn't one of the minnows."

"You know what I mean."

"I do."

"So tell me then why I should be worried. Why I should be looking into this. Who snatched the little tyke?"

Null looked hard at Boyd and recited the answer in such a nonchalant, matter-of-fact way it took her at least thirty seconds before the chill ran down her spine.

"A priest," he said. "I found him in the bondage dungeon of a Catholic priest."

———

"What is it going to take to kill this motherfucker? A goddamn army?"

"From the dirt I heard about the Family, that was already tried by the illustrious "Thing" LeCoeur. The *late* Thing LeCoeur, and he was better at this than I am. And I am superb."

"Then I guess you are just going to have to level up, isn't that right?"

"That's why I'm a professional. *Mr. Turbot.* That is your real name, isn't it? Turbot? Like the fish?"

"It's not American. It was shortened, no, bastardized by immigration thirty years before you were born."

"I shouldn't make fun when you stop to consider my own blessed moniker."

"Ah, your name," said Malek 'The Mallet' Turbot. "Innokenty *Gorets*—almost Russian, wouldn't you say? But no, not exactly that, is it? Not exactly Russian."

"Not exactly."

"A place near Chechnya, I think maybe."

"Not maybe."

"Ingushetia?"

Innokenty's boyish face brightened with surprise. He gave a low whistle that meant he was impressed. "Not bad. No, not bad at all." His eyes crinkled up at the corners when he smiled. "You've been there?"

"No, but I come from not far off from that region, a long time ago when I was only a boy who dreamed and hungered for more black bread and never got any. *Gortsy*, that's the plural. Is that right? You're of the Gortsy?"

"As a matter of fact."

"So what are you, then? An innocent mountain come down here to Boston to exact his price?"

"That's very close. A bit literal. And not really the point, now, is it?"

"We have no need to discuss that.

"It's your dime, Mr. Turbot."

"If it were only that, Innokenty. Just a dime."

"I charge Theron LeCoeur's same rate. And I should be charging you more, judging from what the objective did to the Family and then to your own operation."

The fat man spat. "A temporary setback, that's all. I just need to move certain impedimenta out of the equation and Boston will be mine like it was—"

"You mean like it was for a full five minutes before the Gangsta Boyz ate your lunch? Before the objective—"

"You're raising my blood pressure, Innokenty."

"I'm just trying to establish a baseline, Mr. Turbot, that's all."

"You are giving me palpitations, you little shit."

"Easy, Mr. Turbot. No need to lose your temper."

Malek the Mallet's face became flushed with red, and he shook where he sat as if he were struggling to rise but just couldn't, stuck in a moment of wearying exasperation.

Innokenty was perplexed, unsure as to what to do or say next, which was a rarity that irked him. Normally, he was at least two steps ahead of any situation he chose to put himself in. The only thing to do was to stand his ground and be determined enough to appear unflappable.

Then there came a steady beeping.

An alarm went off sounding like a truck backing up that instantly cued a tall man in a charcoal-gray Armani suit to lope into the room. He bore a wan, lined and weathered face, a receding hairline whose remnants were both tousled and sandy all set off by an icy, thin-lipped sneer. He slapped and snapped switches on the monitors, which stopped the initial beeping but produced another more keening sound that had just started up as he shut the other down. More frantic fingering made short work of that.

"You upset the Padrone!" he bellowed and took saltigrade steps around the organized crime chieftain, eying Innokenty as he fiddled with IV lines.

"*Padrone?* But Mr. Turbot isn't Italian, is he?" Innokenty asked with mock innocence.

"The title's hereditary," grumbled The Mallet. "I took it off a guy when I staved in his skull—"

"Yes," Innokenty said shrilly, clearing his throat. "With a wooden mallet. The legend still lives on in the street."

"Jesus Christ! Don't jiggle with those IVs, Toplofty. They're very painful!"

"I know, Padrone, but that's how we deliver the morphine into your system, to kill all the pain you're suffering."

"Well, it's not gonna kill *that,* is it?"

"I'll give you something that will," said the tall man in the Armani suit, obviously a medical professional, perhaps a doctor, perhaps something else.

"What? Shots? More shots to kill the pain, of the *other* shots?"

"Bee stings Padrone, mere bee stings."

Malek The Mallet, grunted, blew out his cheeks and screamed, "I'll pay you double if you whack out the son of a bitch so that he can *feel* it! Every single little bit of it, *inching his way toward death!*" Then he swallowed hard, exhaled all the harder with a scrunched-up face and added, "Make him beg to die. Then let him live. Just until he thinks he has hope. Then drive the point home slow."

No one spoke after that outburst for a good few minutes.

Innokenty nodded, not necessarily in the affirmative, but to show interest, not wanting to contradict The Mallet or insert himself into the action. He watched quietly, patiently, from where he stood in the center of the room, taking in the improbability of the whole scene, its very oddness: the spectacularly ancient, brilliantly hued oriental rugs, the notable impressionist and expressionist paintings displayed somewhat modestly against the Chinoiserie wallpaper, a Paul Klee, a Pissarro, an Oskar Kokoschka. With Second Empire furnishings that clashed in their disconnected opulence, mock Chippendale and Louis Quinze embroidered chairs and a monstrous, hepatitis-yellow divan that still failed to fill the sense of lingering emptiness. It was a setting that gave Innokenty an urgent sense of inner disquiet he hadn't yet completely defeated. In this chamber of squandered wealth that made a tragic yet at the same time impressive gesture toward taste, half the room was like that of a hospital CCU, ICU, or perhaps even just a Step-Down unit. Just as the artful aspect of the chamber was all business, the business of vulgar braggadocio, so too was the hospital half all business – the business of keeping Malek 'The Mallet' Turbot alive.

Innokenty counted five IV lines pumping fluids, nutrients and drugs—morphine and antibiotics, lactate of Ringer's and who knows what other sorts of private cocktails were being set on a controlled timed drip in the bargain—directly into The Mallet. Sensor pads were glued to his skin, their wires looking like tendrils of withered ivy giving vital sign readouts to various monitors.

Breathing hard, yet evenly, he said, "This helpful yet annoying *bozi vordi*—"

"Son of a bitch, you mean," Innokenty boldly offered.

"Yes." Mild, albeit genuine interest. "Why, that's right," The Mallet replied. "You speak?"

"Only a word or two, Mr. Turbot. The dirty words are always the easiest to remember."

"Yes, in every language, the true beginning of scholarship. Well, Innokenty, this tall son of a bitch here in the cheap suit is my physician, Toplofty."

The Doctor took a single stride to where Innokenty was standing and extended a brown hand that looked like it was wearing a glove of wrinkled parchment rather than skin. He looked hard at the hand and took a step backward, as though he had detected something unclean about it; possibly infectious.

"I'm sorry, Doctor, but I don't shake hands with anyone. It's a little superstition I have."

"No trouble at all Mr. Gore. We all believe in absurdities that bring us to commit atrocities."

"It's *Gorets*, Doctor. And that's why I'm here. Atrocities: those committed and those I must commit."

Malek made a gurgling sound from the back of his throat, almost like a geyser getting ready to blow, squirmed in his mechanical chair and spat in a half-whine, "*Atrocities*, you're talking about? You wanna talk *atrocities*? Just *look* at the atrocities that fucking *srika* did to me. Look at what that freak did to me!"

And even though Innokenty had gotten used to it after the first full ten minutes of meeting with Malek 'The Mallet' Turbot, it was a repellent display that could still provoke the gag reflex: the bloated, piscine figure of a stubby, swarthy man in what looked like a cloth diaper, although a Foley catheter led to a collection bag hooked to the side of wheelchair/scooter affair he was ensconced in, and another tube led out from the cloth diaper into a colostomy bag that was hooked to the opposite side.

The diaper's sole function was one of modesty.

More importantly, without even a blunted stub to indicate that they had ever been there at all, the right arm and the left leg were gone. And patches of pinkish coloration could be detected on the gauze bandages in both locations—a hint of blood mixed with Hibiclens, perhaps. Certainly not Mercurochrome.

Innokenty's nostrils flared with distaste.

No, the room didn't smell of decay or of crawling gangrenous rot, but it stank of a muddle of male colognes and aftershave products that Innokenty had no chance of separating out and identifying. He shrugged his shoulders, which meant nothing to anyone but him. *Why not?* he thought to himself. *The old man probably used all of them, maybe on my behalf to keep me from throwing up from the stench. Ah, such a host.*

"What was that you said, Innokenty?"

"I don't know, Mr. Turbot. I wasn't aware I was speaking."

"You looked like you were talking without words." The crisis averted under the approving eye of Toplofty, The Mallet seemed to have collected himself and relaxed somewhat.

"That's how I think, Mr. Turbot. That's all. A slight humming aloud. So what you detected must have been an echo of my thoughts."

Toplofty stepped between them.

"Well, echo *this*, champ. We don't call him *Mr. Turbot* around here. When you're in this room, on his premises and in his confines —his very *compound*—you use the term of respect, recognizing just who he is and what his position is over you." Toplofty delivered his mellifluous tones of practiced geniality with nary a drop of vitriol or acid. "Call him Padrone, Innokenty, and apologize when you do it."

"My deepest apologies, *mi Padrone*. I didn't get much of a briefing on this offer. I lack a substantial data set. If you'd like to send me a more ample packet—"

His shout was gruff, more like a growl, but loud enough to have been called a shout. "You don't need no more fucking information, *ubiytsa*. You need to move your dead ass out of here and bring me the corpse of that dead man!"

"Respectfully, a dead man can't be killed, Padrone."

"More respect in your voice when you use the proper title. Don't be snide or I may have to chastise you."

"He don't know what I mean. Go explain, please, Toplofty. Earn your keep, you suave bitch."

"Mr. Gore, the grim figure behind the biggest wholesale crystal meth operation in the northeast, has a certain mystique about him. They say he can't be killed because he's already dead."

"Another myth echoed in the street."

"There are no myths about the Padrone on the street."

"So this kingpin they call that Zombie fuck Null really did take the Padrone's right arm and left leg, just to show who ran Boston crime; whose drug operation would reign supreme."

"That soulless fuck gutted my operation from within with the damn niggers of the Gangsta Boyz. Now how does a skinny little white trash Irish punk with a limp suddenly run the biggest ghetto gang in town? They shoulda smoked his punk ass soon as he opened his whispering yap."

"He's got a scary kind of street cred, Mr. Gore—"

"*Gorets*, please, Doctor."

The Mallet laughed. "I love how everyone who meets the great Toplofty thinks he's a doctor, but you ain't nothin' anymore, are you, Eddie?"

"No Padrone. Nothing anymore is right."

"But you introduced him as your physician. Padrone."

The Mallet wheezed something like a giggle. "I do it to make him feel good. But when that good feeling gets in the way of business – and of the reality of position and place – well then, the truth must be told."

Toplofty's brow knitted, and his bottom lip curled. "But not right at the moment, Padrone."

"No, my good Doctor. Not right at *this* moment. But whenever I choose."

"As to Innokenty Gorets, Padrone?"

"You gonna take the gig, or what, my *Ingush* assassin?"

"What I don't comprehend, Padrone, is why a single, small man with a face like overdone hamburger has been so very hard to kill. Like anyone else, and I say fuck all to the myths, rumors and legends of the street, a double tap to the back of the head, a grouping of rounds center chest or a single, well-placed undetectable device will kill him much more dead than he's supposed to be."

"Are you serious, my little mountain man? If it's so easy, my only request is that you make him die slowly, so he feels every bit of it. If this phony baloney *urvakan* won't be any trouble, all I ask is for a nice up close and personal job. No bombs. Take your time. Make him squeal."

"Knives, I suppose, would be indicated."

"Yes, Innokenty, knives would delight me.

Innokenty scrunched up his face with displeasure. "I'll take the gig. But I just don't understand how LeCoeur lured this Franken-stein to George's Island with an army of Family soldiers, and not only did this Null live to tell the tale but whacked him out and the rest of the Family in the bargain, except the one with the lifetime pass to the laughing academy. How does such a little douchebag manage such a feat? You had a huge organization, rivaling the Family, and yet he's managed to whittle that down to a nub and reduce you to riding that mechanical hot rod you're perched on."

"What are you trying to do, mountain man—make *fun*?"

"No, Padrone. I only wish to make him *dead*."

SEVEN

Father Bricolage was pacing in the cold and spare main Holy Ghost Chapel of the Paulist Center at 5 Park Street, half a block away from the golden dome of the Thomas Bulfinch designed State House. The lighting was low, and the thermostat set even lower to save pennies on an energy bill that swelled every time mass was held owing to the high ceiling and generous modern waste space containing only pews for the faithful, balcony seating on both sides, crowned by the resplendent, artful Jesus Christ crucified.

There were three main pieces to this art of the Christ, installed in the chapel since 2004: a cross, an image of the Crucified Christ held aloft from the rood of his execution, and aloft from him a suspended magenta flame—the Holy Ghost incarnate. Father Bricolage barely gave this art a glance. Without the proper lighting, the power of its imagery was greatly diminished. He also had always privately detested this brute, modernist hagiography of a most solemn and sacred event, memorialized crudely for the billions but never so crass as this which bordered on a detached atheism daring to capture the Holy Spirit.

"Articulated flame indeed," he sneered under his breath to the answering echo of his contempt.

He was cold, he was uncomfortable, underdressed in a bilious yellow windbreaker worn over his flat black street clothes designed for minimum comfort and delivered on it. He could see the mist of his breathing in front of his eyes, which made him wince. The other priests had all adjourned for the evening and Father Bricolage personally relieved the senior priest of his light maintenance of the place and nightly lockup duties, for the sake of privacy.

He kept scratching like a small dog at the edges of his mind to find at least some reason, some aspect of a thought, a fragment—even just a crackpot idea to somehow make this *sub rosa* event more palatable to him—even to the slightest degree.

The motto "*Maior autem his est caritas*," was blazing in his mind. He felt dizzy and a little fatigued, largely because he had neglected to eat since his midmorning snack of walnuts and raisins. But he refused to attribute his weakness and discomfort to such a commonplace as incidental fasting and instead blamed it on the duplicitous, tainted, odious task that the cardinal had delegated to him even as the pope had personally and only *verbally*—another suspect contamination and mortification he knew that did nothing to purify the spirit—delegated it to the cardinal.

So now the cardinal had become a secret Papal Legate due to the Deputy of Christ himself, whose mission had become so low, so earthbound into a widespread rotted humus of paganism and shame so repulsive that several times in his service to the church, the worst of all demons had tempted him to leave the church altogether and find some other spiritual pursuit whose base elements didn't make his skin crawl.

And other than the cardinal himself, he was the only one who knew that he had been selected by the pope to be *nuncio apostolico* to Ireland and a few other Catholic-friendly governments to address the church's other scandal involving children: those of the clerics who had taken the vow of celibacy only to produce secret broods of children. "The Children of the Ordained." The pope also —*sub rosa*—had appointed him *nuncio apostolico* to the Eastern Rite Catholic Churches that allow clerics to marry and have children with the blessing of the Vatican to whitewash the effort. And—as always, to distract from the child abuse scandal that refused to fade from public fascination despite the vast wealth and power of the Vatican.

Yet the cardinal in his undisclosed position as Papal Legate had tasked him and him alone and had placed something profane yet at the same time sanctified in his care with the trust of his high office. Something too complex, rarified and full of contrary understanding to ever be allowed even to be referred to in the hushed whispers heard in the very worst alleys and gutters of the street.

His thoughts betrayed him.

Maior autem his est caritas cannot now be translated by Holy Mother Church as *practical utilitatem*—no matter how it may sustain and shore up the glorious body of priests, friars, bishops and even (he tried hard not to think of it, but naturally failed) *cardinals*. And was his cardinal doing more than merely casting his casual approval on the now sacrosanct children, the *Defensores Fidei de Puero*, sanctified by word of mouth from as high an office as that of the pope himself, or was he (unthinkable though it might have been) *window shopping* for a novel means of obtaining his own comfort?

Seeing to his *need?*

Father Bricolage nearly doubled over from a sudden pain he felt stab him in the stomach. He cried loudly to the stolid echo, "*Oh, holy, holy, holy!*" And in his mind, clarified by the beginnings of malnutrition, he spoke to what he believed was his own soul. *'This is God, the Christ himself, reminding me that the needs of the body are almost as important to attend to as the needs of the soul. Thank you, Lord Jesus Christ, thank you for this much-needed instruction. Perhaps you mean this for me to be a holy epiphany if it wouldn't be unseemly to think so and to have you know it?'*

"I am an idiot and of *course* he knows it."

"And if he doesn't know it, then we certainly do."

Father Bricolage was sweating, feeling ill, oppressed by the nature of his duties, but being entrusted with the will of a cardinal whose dictates were sanctified by the pope himself whose dictates contained the living will of the true Christ Jesus above all other authority, law, even meaning itself, were probably in hindsight more than he could bear. Yet he fought for this position, starved, studied, strove, prayed and suffered for this position. He wasn't a mere priest—damn the temptation of pride—but a courier, supplicant and factotum for what amounted to a crucial representation and advocacy for no less than what amounted to a rage in heaven, a spiritual force so powerful, frightening and worthy of abject servitude yet that could never even be implied, never mind symbolized, by an arch acrylic magenta flame suspended by thin fiber cable above a floating bastardized figurine that barely implied the Christ he knew of the fourteen stations of the cross, of the passion and of all the glorious visions that had soon followed after up to and including this needless fractious moment in woeful time.

His feelings were beside the point.

The Holy Spirit had taken him, had his way with him and anointed him into this perfidy, pushed him into it whether he had the strength or not.

"Heaven give me strength, Frater Phlegethon!"

"I think both heaven and I have come up empty on that one, Father Bricolage. You'll need a mickle of miracles before we're through to get what you want."

"It's not what I want. It's what the church needs, insists upon and has the entire Holy See upon which to materialize it anytime it likes."

"Really. Okay then, of what use am I, Father? Compared to the power of your church, I'm but a brother in arms of the Knights Templar. And we know what your body thinks of them. And why have this meeting with little old lowly me?"

"Your order wouldn't exist without Holy Mother Church. And we don't acknowledge your unholy existence."

"Yet my order exists in spite of your Mother Church, a great sow long past having one udder too many."

"You blaspheme!" growled the priest.

"Constantly and with great vigor, as one defunct Massachusetts politician used to say."

Father Bricolage used a silent votive prayer—there were no candles for him to light, so he offered all his subsequent efforts—and his own not inconsiderable will—to prevent his rebellious body from showing how it trembled due to both privation and outrage.

"The Order of Oriental Templars is a foul skidmark residuum of the Knights Templar we excommunicated and executed 700 years ago. You're fortunate to be of service at all in the church's and the pope's—"

"And the bishops' and the cardinals'—"

"Yes, yes to all of that, certainly. But you at last can maybe earn a fragment of the church's trust back as you help secretly mend its complex, morally deep, dispensatory plight. Its lasting wound."

"The world would never call it that."

"The world will never know beyond what it already thinks it knows."

"I keep forgetting to give your church its due, being the world's oldest and most successful criminal enterprise. Let them fixate on what the left hand has already done while the right ever so stealthily takes its place. I have to say, although it's definitely not elegant, it is in its very morbid way, kind of cute."

"Holy Mother Church allows you to think what you like—has no caring at all about what you think, in fact, only that you serve her appropriately and well in this matter and cause us no disgrace."

"The church has never been in a state of grace to begin with—has never been able to confer that state on anyone through bull, pastoral, dispensation or even by indulgence. It never mattered. You can't wash anything clean in the blood of the lamb when your principal means of operation is lamb butchery."

"It's pointless to discuss theology with you since you're so much lower than even the most neophyte deacon."

"To you, I'm lower than the laity, great scholar Dr. Bricolage. Do you know of Bartolomé de las Casas?"

"The Black Legend of Spain. What of him? *We* never abused Indians—that was a problem of Protestant Spain and the Americas..."

"In your Mother Church's approximated two-thousand-year-old-history, you've left a billion corpses in your wake. About as many murdered as you have devout followers in your current, much ballyhooed decline—exaggerated decline. De las Casas had this to say—"

"It doesn't *matter* what he had to say. He's no Catholic theologian and if he *had* been he'd have been excommunicated—"

"Would he now?"

Frater Phlegethon stepped out of the shadows into the light. He was baby-faced, freckle-faced; a fair-skinned, slight, red-headed man, anywhere from age eighteen to thirty-five. He wore a gray car coat with wooden buttons shaped like small missiles, khakis and Sketcher sneakers. His voice didn't crack, though, so he had left puberty far behind, something Father Bricolage hadn't been quite sure of until that moment. His hair wasn't just red, but fiery red, his eyes agate with pronounced flashes of red. The name his order had given him obviously must have seemed almost sarcastic every time he revealed himself to someone—a trumped up ginger messenger boy; a glorified intern—but he was strident when he spoke, snide with a continuous undertone of unironic anger. And he aped authority well enough to project it, touching servile nerves throughout Father Bricolage's psyche. This pronouncement was no exception:

"The reason the Christians have murdered on such a vast scale and killed anyone and everyone in their way is purely and simply greed.' And like Hans Kung on papal infallibility or Tissa Bala-suriya on original sin, The Virgin Mary and woman priests, he'd have been right."

"Apostates like you have no wisdom on the subject—never anything enough to affect the church."

"If I'm an apostate, then so are you, Dr. Samuel Bricolage."

"The church is the only arbiter of true apostasy, which cannot by definition take place within it – only without it. Tissa Balasuriya was excommunicated, and Kung was guilty of heresy, stripped of the right to teach within the church and is no longer officially considered a Catholic theologian."

"I thought you abolished limbo."

"He's in a new limbo—one the church designed especially for him."

"So much for apostasy not existing within the church."

"You're hairsplitting, Frater. I can do that too. I said *apostasy*, not heresy. Dr. Kung was a heretic who had not been shown to be an apostate. He differed on certain fundamental truths of the church. Oblate Father Balasuriya proved himself an apostate beyond all question on the matters of original sin and the immaculate conception, that cannot be allowed to grow as a cancer in the perfect body of Holy Mother Church."

"You mean because he wasn't a white western European, but instead a swarthy nigger from primeval, fratricidal third-world Sri Lanka."

"You can't besmirch Holy Mother Church no matter your blasphemous tack – and your cult cannot be compared to the church in any facet, especially with your long history of satanism, ritual sex magic and grave-robbing efforts at necromancy..."

"A short history compared to yours. And yet we celebrate Mass and the Eucharist just as you do, and we do it in a ceremony much older than the schism that birthed your criminal church. Our *Ecclesia Gnostica Catholica*, the Gnostic Catholic Church, is the ecclesiastical part of my order and we have every right to confer the sacrament of the eucharist of the Gnostic Mass as well as baptism, confirmation and even ordination of our priests."

"And you are so ordained?"

"I am, Dr. Bricolage. Puts me on equal footing with you, I think."

"Holy Mother Church gives you no such rights."

"I know, Father. We *take* them."

"Enough of your cant, Frater."

"And we spread them. So now we are thick as thieves."

Father Bricolage paused and looked up at the ceiling as if he might find a lofty thought there, then looked down sharply at the Frater. "Maybe one day a forgiving eye could perhaps be cast on your outlaw cadre perhaps by one of our good offices to somehow bring you into the fold, but not until this horrible flaw that has grown permanently within the church can be salved over and allowed to fade from the toxic consciousness of even those with sapient wit like yours."

"That wound will never heal."

"Yours is no place to say."

"I'll say what I like until I get your money."

"The love of money is the root of all evil."

"But not of your evil, now, is it?"

"If you submit to the Holy See—"

"Your offer's nowhere near as good as your money."

"I have your tainted emolument with me. You may befoul it further once I know your commitment."

"You don't need to know a thing—you know it all," the Frater dismissed.

Then he began to move on the priest.

In the bit of light that shown upon Frater Phlegethon, whatever truth there was in his taken name was there to be seen: fire shooting out from him in his gestures, his face red with a fatal blush of anger and his flaming pate of red hair sparkling in places when the light hit it. His gaze, though, was dark.

"Give it here," he commanded, stepping closer to the priest.

Father Bricolage swung his worn leather book bag around to the front of his cheap yellow windbreaker with the even cheaper black jacket and shirt that may have kept him from freezing to death, but not much more. Comfort was not his remit. His concentration faltered and Frater Phlegethon could see Father Bricolage trembling even as he held tight both sides of the bookbag. The boyish redhead lunged at him, again, crying loud enough to echo and cause the priest to jerk backward awkwardly.

"I can just take it off you!"

Shakily, the priest reached into the bookbag while the Frater stopped himself and stood stock still.

Wobbling in his left hand was a stainless-steel Ruger Mark 2 twenty-two caliber pistol. No need to ask if it was loaded. The Frater recognized it. Weapons were a specialty with him. It was no Bulldog .44, but it featured an easy one-button takedown. Good for a woman or a priest. And the damn priest didn't need to be any kind of shot to kill him at this range, or at the very least, seriously wound him. Then he'd abandon him there, leaving in a frenzied panic of guilt while the Frater waited for the EMTs to get there, his life on the line and all that money blown, which his order sorely needed.

And punishment within the order for this kind of mess was likely to be worse than this entire experience had been up to that moment.

"Well," the priest huffed with fake bravery, sniffling like a child. "Say something wise with that big, smart mouth of yours. Go ahead – spout off. I'd *love* to tell his Eminence that you weren't up to the job. Make me do it, hellion. Go ahead."

Frater Phlegethon was frozen in mid-lunge, stiff and tensed. While the priest waved the gun, however uncertainly, it was certain that his finger was on the trigger and that with no less than two doctoral degrees, the Frater could presume he was no dope. For all intents and purposes, the safety was off, and he had better move himself ever so slowly back into a less threatening posture. He slid his front leg back next to the left and let his arm drop, doing both extra slow and by gradual degrees a jerky bit at a time.

"Now, hellion, tell me your commitment to our cause!"

"Of course, Father. You don't really need the gun for us to finish this."

"Well, I say we do. Tell me what you'll deliver to us by discretion, stealth and secrecy without a leak to anyone who could ever talk about it, write about it, report it to anyone in any way. Off the books! Unburden yourself of what's due us from your rank, decayed and feculent soul."

The gun was still wobbling, but the Frater allowed himself to breathe more easily. This was a priest with very little experience in the world of the street. He was obviously too terrified to pull the trigger. Yet, it was best to play it safe, secure the payment and leave unscathed with no rounds to be removed by some clumsy veterinarian in the dead of night on the quiet.

"Boys, Father Bricolage. Boys as agreed."

"What kind of boys, hellion?"

"Young boys, Father. Boys just entering puberty."

"Lay it out for my ignorant Catholic ears to hear, so I may reward your perfidy with the sweet milk of Holy Mother Church."

"Singing."

"What about singing? What's important about the singing?"

"They have to carry a tune."

"No. Like the *Seraphim!* Like St. Cecilia would have them sing their joy to God!"

"Yes. That's right. Just like joyous little angels adoring God."

"Finally, you see the point. At last. So finally, even a Helot like you can come to concordance with our blessed church and our means of serving her."

"I don't know how I can guarantee the joyous part of the agreement. How could any child be joyous, having even the slightest inkling of what you and your church have in store for him?"

"Shut up, hellion! Each boy will learn his part of joy and solemnity from us. You merely need to supply the boy in good repair and spirits, and we'll take charge of him from there and do the rest. Many times over."

"I can take payment at any time now, Father. Now would be good."

"Of course, Frater. Now would be fine."

"And you can put the gun back in the book bag."

"Yes, I can do that. Still, I don't see it doing much harm where it is now."

"Not as yet, no."

"And how many of these children can you deliver within the discussed timeframe?"

"You shouldn't play with the gun like that unless the safety's on, y'know."

"I shouldn't? Well, thank you. I had no idea. Of course it's off. I couldn't very well shoot you if I left it on, now, could I?"

"Alright. I know you're not going to shoot me. We both know it. Not if you want this done. Back to business: I counted over thirty boys we could buy and/or spirit away from foster care families, all to your specifications. *None* of them tone deaf."

"Is that all? That's it? *That's* what we're buying?"

"The criminal enterprise I spoke to you about—they have quite a store of them too, all boys. All out earning in the street. I call them the Meth Kids. We could scoop those up too in the bargain."

"The count?"

"Over twenty, but I think that might be a little low."

"A little low. Are they, um, *tainted?*"

"All well-scouted in good condition. We've taken down the names of all those who did well in our little music test. How many do you want?"

The priest reached into his book bag, extracted an iPad tablet and tossed it to the Frater, who caught it easily with both hands. "Everything you need to collect your payment is on there. The VPN, passcodes, accounts, routing and SWIFT numbers. Just plug it in and rejoice."

"That seems easy," said Frater Phlegethon, calm now with the payment securely pocketed beneath his gray car coat with the sculpted wooden missile-like buttons. "How many do you want total?" he asked, the sharpness and hauteur having returned to his voice.

"All of them!" the priest shouted, then fired a single round directly at Frater Phlegethon's chest which, owing to nerves, inexperience and unabated wobbliness, hit him in the shoulder process, shattering his collarbone.

"Wh-why?" Frater Phlegethon asked absently, stubbornly refusing to fall as he staggered.

"You mocked the church."

"*What*?" Breathless, addled.

"You blaspheme too easily, Frater," the priest said, yawning, feeling strangely tired, and quietly let himself out of the building.

EIGHT

"Grandma's House" for this week was the long-shuttered Church of the Advent on Warren Avenue in Roxbury. It was a wood frame building with two awkward spires that seemed to be at war with one another. There was a half-attic sort of story above the second story that had been sealed off as unsafe back in the 90s, just as the second story itself had fallen into disuse as anything but a storage area for extra bridge chairs, broken pews and oddments of wood, also back in the 90s. Sometime around then, someone decided to squander the collection-plate cash of the faithful on an ultra-thin, faux stone masonry façade that had been slapped onto the building like cheap vinyl siding—the whole thing being intended to appear as one of those richly ornate and preposterous gothic churches dotting Europe wherever you went, but instead only managed to look like a skewed and lopsided Americanized parody of such houses of worship.

The church was a comic travesty that suited The Gangsta Boyz to a tee.

They sat on disordered pews, the cream of the leadership of the gang, looking somewhat small and lost without their boss, which gave all of them an edge of anger, frustration—and fear. This wasn't the image conjured by the profiteering news media and popular entertainments of every kind. No, the top shot callers of a ruthless, drug-dealing black street gang never were imagined being quiet, attentive, pensive and, beneath it all, nervous.

"It's all good," announced Brother Ray Carstairs, Gangsta Boyz IT specialist and purser. "We heavy in the black."

"You trippin' or what?" Ronald Brogan Jr. challenged. Ronald, like Cassius in Shakespeare's "Julius Caesar," could be best described as having 'a lean and hungry look.' His temper was barely held in check by pure self-interest.

"I ain't trippin'. We ain't losin' the mooga. Y'all got shares, now am I right?"

Dismissive mutterings and grunts were unanimous.

"We gots a J-Cat motherfucker as shot caller what gots to *go*," Ronald asserted.

Do-Rag, a short, skinny kid with a permanent case of the fidgets, trademark bandana in place around his head, got up from his pew and started pacing. "He may be a J-Cat 5150 chatted-out motherfucker, dawg, but I don't see the need. The brother put it best, yo. Shares and payments all on time and rounded off to the dollar. *Our* favor."

"It ain't broke," volunteered Desi, more a soldier than a leader with a loaded Mac II held across his torso to imply ready use—one with an adjustable metal stock, suppressor already screwed on tight and a swivel for sling/front strap mounting. Desi felt he could intervene. The Roscoe was his ticket to be taken seriously and he was plainly on the muscle. "So don't fix it."

"Fuck you, Desi, and don't level that gat at me, you know what's best for y'all."

"You go talk to the man upstairs, Ronald, you don't like me here doin' security," Desi drawled slowly. "If you remember how Legere of the KP society blew-up our damn club on Tremont Street, you unnerstan' why this ain't gon' be Grandma's House permanent no way no how. Like you thought it *should* be."

"Ronald, you best be way careful here what you sayin'," Dominic warned in a low, thick voice. "My brother got waxed for not doin' what the man tol' him to do. *Ordered* him to do, but him and Howard jus' had to hang and play X-box instead. Then blooey. Eve'ybody, eve'ything history. Then what the man do? He take the whole damn gang what did it apart one by one—"

Jo-jo, underfed-looking, gaunt with sunken cheeks with longish natural hair and wide, clear bright eyes, spoke up from the pew where he had been lolling, seemingly lost in thought. "Ronald got a better system or plan, I wanna know that right now. I was with the man rescuin' a busload o' kids from a KP super-factory. He also killed my friend Alphonse like he was swattin' a moss-*keet*-o. Nothin' to it at all fo' him. They ain't no bullshit 'bout him, that's true, but if Ronald wanna take over, I'll back his skinny black ass. The man never shoulda never let him live when he last throwd down at Desi's crib. He so hip, such a mean badass motherfucker, why he let his enemy live? Yet you so much whisper his real name to the wrong person and you get your motherfuckin' throat slit fo' you can say fuck all 'bout it."

"He did it to cement loyalty, numbnuts. Don't you see that?"

"Real talk, his spot be right on the line's I see it," Riley volunteered.

"Why we sittin' here yackin' 'bout the damn motherfucker— why we doin' it? Go on—gimme some kinda answer ain't gold-plated bullshit. We here to take back what ours from some outside ofay cocksucker."

"You best ease up, homey, he be spooky as fuck. You never know what he hears or sees or knows when you sure he ain't even around. He's got ways o' tellin' who done what when and how. And I don't like jus' how comf'able he is with a personal death tally higher than any dude I ever seed even back in the slam," Do-Rag explained.

Riley piped up: "*Plus* the fact, he so scarred up and dingy, I don't know zackly *what* race the man is anyway. Ever look direct into that motherfucker's fugly fuckin' face? How you possibly able to tell jack shit from that? He be like the same race as Freddy fuckin' Kruger from the Nightmare movies."

"Yeah. He be of a race aight: the burnt up, turnt up, *mutilated* race, you know I'm sayin'," Ronald rejoined.

Brother Ray laid it down solidly: "You know what? You got some kinda radicalized case of motorized monkey mouth, Brother Ronald. You better cool that shit down, and I mean as of yesterday. What you ever done for any of us anyway? I remember doin' some deeply piddly-shit rinky-dink scores witch y'all before the man set us up on the sling so fine and proper. Now we all flush—all our damn black asses are in the black and I don't care what race the shot caller is when he made us the goddamn cheese factory. I got more guap than I knows what to do with, but now you know I *do* know what to do with it and I know even better that I got no desire to give up any o' dat. Not for you or even the man hisself. I run serious IT for once; I do all the shit I *knew* how to do since I was 'bout ten years old, but no one would hire me to do—would even *let* me do. They just make me use my goddamn superior code and toss me aside like I was nothin' cause I ain't got no fancy diploma. Now I run a real IT department wit' a staff that answers to me and *maybe* the man. Sometimes not *even* the man. I make algorithms and set up A-I to make probability analyses and statistical modeling to yield better more effective predictive value slingin' drugs and makin' payoffs. Who gave me dat? You say my ability? Fuck yeah, but who the one let me loose to use it? Gave me the actual paying gig? Who back me and use me for the benefit of all of us just to sling drugs and make that work. You listen here, Brother Ronald. You can go fuck right off right straight to hell now, this very minute. Fact o' the matter is dat *I'll* be the one who sticks a shank in your heart and sends you there before he even get a *chance* to punch your ticket like he shoulda done months ago back at Desi's crib."

"You a bunch o' ass kissers—"

"You better watch that monkey mouth right now, yo, or I take Desi's Mac whatever-it-is and shove it right up your punk ass!" Dominic's anger showed in his face, and he snorted a little bit, which made you imagine steam exuding from his nostrils as if he were a bull in an old Max Fleischer celluloid cartoon. He wasn't in any frame of mind to be challenged, and not even Ronald was willing to test the limits of that possibility, though Brother Ray was already fashioning a probability model for that in his head.

"You wanna know why we here, stupid fuck? I'll tell you—not like everyone here don't already know. Not that even you don't know."

"I think the pussy done run off."

"Just shut the fuck up, Ronald!" Desi bellowed to less distinct noises of approval.

"Fack o' the matter is this: We ain't heard from the man in three days. Nothin'. Not a word. Now, whatever you wanna say, he some kinda O-C-D control freak about the day-to-day. I hear from him every single day least once," explained Brother Ray. "This just ain't normal."

"I hear that," agreed Riley, chief Gangsta Boyz chemist and meth cook. "He on the DM, the text or even voice maybe twice a day and I better answer even if I be at the crucial point in the middle of a cook. If I don't, I'd be the one missin' today. And that's real fuckin' talk!"

"Nobody know what the plan is or what the way forward gon' be. He's the only one that ever know. We got moves to make and we need to make 'em soon. This is the real problem," Do-Rag explained.

Jo-jo stood up and stretched, yawning for theatrical effect and then laid it down as heavily as he could: "Yeah, well the man don't show in a couple days, then Ronald oughtta get his shot to run things. Give him the keys to the motherfuckin' car and see jus' how he do. Cause if that murderin' psychopath ain't back in a day a two, we can ack like he already *be* dead and if he suddenly *do* come back, then we can make that state o' things permanent."

———

"Please don't make me, Mister. I'm scared and I wanna go *home.*"

"You have no home but where you stand, my son. Just stand here next to me and know that God is in his heaven and all's right with the world."

"Please, Mister. Can't I go back to where I was before?"

There wasn't a hint of darkness in the high, wide room. The lighting was so bright that shadows cast were faint and washed out because of it. The walls were painted a bright institutional white and the drop ceiling was a dated stucco pattern that gave a blue cheese effect should one look up at it for too long. (Although it was evident that no one had done that for years.) The purpose of the room was as blank and undefined as the room itself and its shining whiteness delivered no comfort at all, but was more a vapid yet deliberate sign of threat—a demand for those who entered it to be ill at ease, to be on their guard, to suspect everything which is exactly what the eight-year-old Asian boy standing next to the balding dapper, pock-marked man in the charcoal Armani suit with the red Hermes necktie holding the semi-automatic Walther PPK with custom-made suppressor against his left temple had made him:

He suspected everything.

More than that, he was terrified.

He was too young to know what to do and how to do it. Only old enough to be right about something bad, but not right enough to comprehend how much worse it was than his little mind had somewhat accurately read his situation to be. He knew not to plead anymore, and his silence brought some relief from the pressure of the hard aluminum rim of the silencer against his skin.

The gun was new-looking, burnished to near gleaming.

"I'll do stuff for ya, mister. I'm real good at cleanin'—"

"What you can do for me, son, is just be quiet and still for a little while. Not for too long, though. I know little ones like you have no patience which is why we adults must forever be developing and increasing our limited patience, to cope with your having none. All to serve you. Just for you. We *have* to do it. You are our burden and our charge. So you can shut up now and think godly thoughts, because soon our performance will begin and I want you to be ready."

"But I'm not ready," the boy whined.

"Oh, but I say you are ready. You know it's wrong to contradict an adult, especially one who's a delegate of holy orders such as myself. Yes, you just be silent now. As you can see, the star of our show is beginning to stir."

"He—he's alive. I thought—"

"I said silence, boy!" the pockmarked man snapped. "The last thing this material plane needs from you is any thinking at all. Be a statue; pretend you're a statue." And his leering anger wasn't concealed at all by the reflexive and practiced grin that bloomed into a smile that bisected his face, beset by stained, yellowed teeth that looked even more dingy and corrupted in contrast to the brilliance and clarity of the wide and oppressive room."

"He still looks dead to me..."

The pockmarked man smacked the boy on the cheek with the suppressor of the Walther PPK and hissed, the practiced, blinding smile still bisecting his wan, scarred, sharp-featured face.

But his scars were nothing compared to those of the other man in the room, crumpled on the floor, looking small, skeletal, almost fragile, pressed up against the baseboard heating vent like a pile of dirty laundry. His head had been shaved clean, with no evident stubble. He wore a long-sleeved olive drab military thermal shirt, gray fatigues, all its pockets suspiciously flat, all held together by a Sam Browne duty belt with two shoulder pieces for pistols not in evidence. The man's face was swollen with scars like boils, carbuncles and dark streaks shaped like leeches. His complexion was a swirl of uneven pigment, some pink, some red, some brown, some as black as an ancient scab. But for all that, the disfigured face was placid, peaceful, even as this roughed up, slight discard of a man returned to consciousness as if waking from a pleasant dream.

The pockmarked man and the small boy watched in wonder as he rose from the floor like a cheap special effect from a jerry-rigged Halloween haunted mansion. There was this difference though: his motion was smooth, easy—unhurried.

He didn't squint or blink, just looked straight ahead with a fixed blank stare.

"Welcome, Mr. Null. We're so happy to have you."

"You and the boy." A statement, not a question.

"Not the boy. No, the boy has no say in anything, as is true for most boys of his age. No, I meant we as in the holy order."

"Which one. I admit I've lost track."

"Mr. Null, no need for games. Your reputation precedes you as being a most knowing, most cunning individual. Hard to kill, so the stories of the street are told. Yet here you are, and I obviously have gotten the better of you, haven't I? 'Gotten the drop on you,' as they say in old gangster movies."

"I'll take your word for it."

"You have to appreciate the difficulty of what we accomplished."

"Anyone can get lucky."

"Anyone can, but skill triumphs over random chance and repeats itself enough to seem like good luck when it isn't. As in your being here. They were right. You were a most difficult specimen to catch."

"People exaggerate all the time. No one knows what's true or isn't true most of the time."

"They think you're some kind of monster—a zombie, a vampire, a ghoul. The fear associated with the mere mention of your name is immense. It took effort and resources to surmount that fear and find you. They all believe you're a dead man, Mr. Null, did you know that? Can you believe that?"

Nulls speech was clear, unhesitating and unwavering in its cool detachment:

"Well, technically, at least by bureaucratic standards, they're right. I happen to be officially dead on the record. You know how difficult it is to correct such deep administrative wrongs of official records keeping. So much easier to let a misleading ruling stand than to undo it—convene an inquest, go before a judge, make formal written requests in triplicate. Not really a worthy expense of my time. I have obligations to fulfil."

"Yes, I can see that. I know you do."

"Why do you have the gun on the kid when you could have it on me instead? I'm the problem in the room you need to solve, not the little boy."

"Well, he happens to be a problem in his own right, Mr. Null. Don't sell him short."

"I'm not selling him. Maybe you are. I don't know, but I have my suspicions."

"All in good time, Mr. Null."

"Null. Just call me Null."

"Children like him are little noisemakers and I like quiet. The order encourages much silent introspection and contemplation as essential elements of the will to power. You should know that, with all you've accomplished in the criminal realm. They used to call you the Meth King of Boston, but you've grown so much bigger than that now, haven't you?"

"In my own modest way."

"Yes. Modest. You're the top criminal in the tri-state area, not only Massachusetts. I hear even Rhode Island is about to cave and partner up with you rather than lose altogether."

"You don't need to explain anything to me."

"Oh, but I don't mind. We both have plenty of time. You're not going anywhere, and since I hold all the power in this room, I can set the agenda."

The pockmarked man shifted the position of the Walther PPK so that it was aimed dead center at Null's chest. Null didn't acknowledge this. He spoke a little above a whisper, dreamlike. "Release the boy. He has nothing to do with whatever your business is with me. He's been shaking like the storm door of a breezeway in a high gale, and he's peed his pants while you were crowing."

"It doesn't bother me, Null. Does it bother you?"

"Nothing bothers me."

"Then why mention it at all if it doesn't bother you?"

"Children are innocent. They need to be protected."

"You sound like you care so much." The pockmarked man's glee was obvious; his mirth was only shy of laughter.

"I don't. I'm stating a fact."

"My children are far from innocent. They are worldly wise teasers, sluts of a kind, grasping whores—no purity there, nothing at all to salvage—just like little Louie here."

"They remain children and you can't own their innocence no matter how many times you take it from them."

"I'm surprised at you, Null. What an absurd statement. Your reputation has you as a brutal logician of the street. Yet here you are, simpering over a child."

"Which of us is the one doing the simpering? Me, with a gun held on me or you with an upset little boy that you're minding to no ostensible purpose?"

"Good question. I think a single round from the Walther would put you out and validate that death certificate that's on file about you. I don't think you could get past one step before I put one in your heart."

"I won't argue that."

"Because you can't."

"This is the time when you get to the point. I mean, if you have an agenda—never mind whether or not you set it."

"You're baiting me, Null. You can't really do that. A flick of the trigger and you're Boston's deadest criminal."

"I already am. You can't improve on that. Anything you do will simply be a redundancy."

"And they say you're humorless."

"And what do you say? So far, I've heard nothing of substance or value from you. You're a clattering of empty buckets just to make noise. You seem to me now a ridiculous figure waving a gun that's too big for you and a child who's too small for you, like wet rags in a storm, with no understanding about how it all got away from you. And whether or not you know it—it has."

The pockmarked man's ravaged face went blank with confusion and its brow slowly furrowed.

"Please, mister, lemme *go!*" The boy whined to the point of squealing for a mercy that wasn't forthcoming. "Take me to a shelter or some *otter* place. Any otter. Gimme to da otter guy. I don't wanna be wit' you—"

Smoothly and without lowering his weapon, the pockmarked man knelt down to the boy and clapped his hand over his mouth to silence his whining. The barrel of the suppressor was aimed unwaveringly at Null's chest.

"Not a move, Null, not a step, or I'll blow a hole in your heart just to prove you have one."

"I don't have to say it, but I'll say it to make it clear even to you. I'm still. I'm standing still. Not moving."

The boy went limp against the pockmarked man as he stood. The man gave Null a practiced, lascivious wink.

"We're all adults here, Null. And even this boy is an adult in his own way. And he's going to help me explain to you the facts of life."

"Being dead, I've never felt I had any use for them."

"Do you have any idea just how much trouble you're in, Null?"

"Apparently, I never do."

"I'm recruiting you, Null. We're going to use you. You don't have enough power to resist."

"When that gun goes down, so will you."

"It isn't just my gun that's on you. It's all the guns that'll be on you soon enough. Work with us, profit and thrive—fight us and you'll lose and die. Slowly and in great misery."

"I've done that already. It wasn't all that bad, the more I think about it."

"You're not thinking it through."

"That's because I lack data. I need a baseline. Some hard answers to easy questions. Such as where am I? Who are you? And why are you using a child for a prop in this exchange?"

"I've stripped you naked, Null. As you can see, behind me in a pile are all your guns—the Glock 17 and the Heckler and Koch VP9 Tactical OR—the Bushmaster semi-auto rifle. The machete you wear under that topcoat hung from a lanyard around your neck. Oh, and your flak jacket? Thing's a bit worn down. You know, with all that drug money you're raking in, you really should spring for a new one. Getting you here, under my thumb so to speak? That was easy. They told me you were impossible to get—whispers of terror about you in the street. Yet here you are. Imagine that."

"I don't imagine anything."

"I believe you. Your spook bit is just a scosh hokey. Maybe more than a scosh."

"I don't do any bits."

"You're tiresome, Null. Maybe I'll put one in you just for the fun of it."

"You're nervous. You're likely to miss."

"So what? I'll take another shot, then put you down."

"You'll be dead before then."

"For a little guy, you talk pretty big."

"And you say nothing with too many words and waste time."

"Null, I am Frater Nostrum. And I am of that oldest of religions, Ordo Templi Orientis—"

"The Order of Oriental Templars. Not such an old religion, maybe not even as old as the Occult Circle founded by Karl Kellner and Theodore Reuss. Maybe it was the same thing. Who can tell with the Hermetic Temple of the Golden Dawn, the Rosicrucians, etc. It was a Masonic group chartered in 1902 by English Mason John Yarker, not Harker, by the way. You make the claim that you possess the key of all hermetic and Masonic secrets, which is nothing more than ritual sex magick—tantric yoga practiced within a circle to sustain and suspend an orgasm while you rant and chant and cast your drug-induced spells. McGregor Mathers and self-proclaimed great beast Aleister Crowley furthered it, hijacked it, and proclaimed in his great wisdom of random impulse that he named Thelema, 'Do what thou wilt shall be the whole of the law.' But there really was no law to follow at all, was there? Not that that ever mattered in the first place."

Frater Nostrum's smile returned, and it was more frightening and repellent than his determined frown with its curled and upturned lower lip.

"An over-simplification. A complete misunderstanding, but you seem to know something about us, which is unusual enough in this realm."

"They say child-rape Director Roman Polanski and John Phillips of the 60s pop group The Mamas and the Papas were part of it. As was L. Ron Hubbard of Scientology and Roger DeGrimston of the Church of the Process of the Final Judgment. All were involved in your perverse ritual sex magick practiced as a sacrament on little children. Is this why you have a terrified little boy half-passed out leaning on your leg and peeing in his pants?"

"Close, Null, but no, that's not the boy's purpose."

"Knights Templar, you aren't, executed and excommunicated by the Catholic Church. You'd only go back to the 14th century if you were original, and you're not, so, either way, you're far from the oldest. And whatever mistake I made that brought me here, I promise you I'll correct. After I kill you. But no rush on this. I see you have plenty of time to bloviate pointlessly at me. So. Continue."

"We are backed by the oldest, largest, richest, most powerful criminal enterprise the world has ever known. With a sacred mission sanctified by the highest authority."

"The Catholic Church. Crying poverty negotiating down civil judgements in their corrupt aiding and abetting of the child abuse and rape of small boys, like the one you have half-conscious against your leg. He your good luck charm? A rabbit's foot. Perhaps?"

"Oh, you'll know why he's here in a minute."

"You're the timekeeper, not I. So how did you get me anyway?"

Frater Nostrum shook his head and clucked his tongue to feign disappointment.

"Now, Null," he said in the tone of a scold. "You know you can pretty much get anything you want if you're willing to spend a million dollars to get it."

"Ronald," Null said softly, pensively.

"Oh, he was just one. You can hardly blame him. Clever little chappie. Just wants to get ahead."

"You're misleading me."

"What else would you expect? So, Null, it's decision time. We know you like children. We know you've shrewdly used them. Some call you the Pied Piper of Beantown."

"It's a gross exaggeration. I haven't taken rats or children, no instances of St. Vitus Dance and there's been no Goethe poem, *Der Rattenfänger*."

"You can't teach me a lesson, Null."

"What do you want, then?"

"We want you to recruit children for us, on a regular, rotating basis. Be *our* Pied Piper."

"Why would I do that?"

"My backers and I will make you rich."

"I'm already what's considered 'rich,' though it means nothing to me but utility."

"Do it to stay alive, then. We're powerful—two millennia powerful. You can't stop us. You can't even survive us, should we move against you."

"I'd like to put that to the test."

"Think again, Null. No single government can stand against my backers. Not even the schismatic United States of America."

"You know, the Catholic Church prelates were the ones thought to have murdered all the children of Hamelin to prevent their leaving the faith, just like they facilitated the rape of countless little boys across the world. That accounts for your prop, I think."

Now, Null was fast—faster than most men. Always a surprise when attackers, relieved by his awkward limp, his slight stature, his scarred face, dropped their guard and approached him unafraid. They learned to fear him too late. But this time, he wasn't fast enough; because even though he had barely blinked an eye, something he often had to remind himself to do, the thing happened within that space, that tiny pinprick of time. A shrug of the shoulder, a nod of the head, a nervous tick—

Not the breaking of a small boy's neck.

An almost inaudible crack.

With a sound like a sigh, the boy sagged down dead to the floor.

Null jerked forward and stopped.

"Uh-uh-uh, Null. *Condition zero.* You know what that means."

"You killed a small boy. A little child. Like it was nothing. They say I feel nothing, and I know I don't. It's not my choice, but it happens to be yours. We're alike then and then again not."

"This is our power, Null. This is what we can do. That little piece of chicken lies there on the floor to show you that we can do anything we want. Take what most matters to you, like the fragile life of a little, superfluous child. Sure. I feel nothing."

"I think you'll feel it very much when I rip out your tongue."

"By magic, Pied Piper? Remember, I have the gun. You're naked and alone."

"Oh, I'll get it done. However I need to do it. Whenever I can."

"You know that threats are beneath you, yes? You can't really take a bullet to the heart when your flak jacket is lying on the floor there behind me, can you?"

"I don't deal in threats. I provide executions."

"Well, here's mine: So, you either join us, or we kill you and dismantle your organization. A child at a time."

"They're not all children."

"To us, *all* your so-called Gangsta Boyz are children. Nigger children. And just like the Pied Piper, they'll follow you right to the grave."

"You're upset. I can tell."

"Not at all. Cool as a cucumber."

In the hesitation of the moment, the quiet was so intense the only sound to be heard was their asynchronous breathing.

"You're breathing hard, trying to hide it. You can't. Furthermore, your hand is sweaty, especially the trigger finger. You're sensitive, nervous. You're going to fire and miss."

Frater Nostrum bit his lip and the nostrils of his aquiline nose flared. "I can't miss at this distance."

"I see."

"Now you're getting it."

"I actually think you're right."

His relieved grin was knife sharp. "At last, you live up to your reputation."

Spoken with the passion of someone giving you the time of day: "Yes. I'm going to take your bet."

"*Wha—*"

Null covered the distance in a heartbeat. He leapt—

actually leapt—from where he stood, knocking Frater Nostrum down as the first gunshot went wild. The one that followed went wilder still and Null, with calm precision and careful focus, tore the Frater's esophagus and Adam's apple straight from his throat.

He left the tongue for last.

He took his time doing it.

The Frater made a sound like fresh popcorn popping as he gave up and died.

Stepping around the two corpses, darkened with new blood, Null found that the wall behind the dead Frater was nothing more than a light-reflective white canvas. He ripped it back and found himself staring into almost total darkness. He realized the room he was in was actually fashioned out of a causeway that was several stories above the ground. His eyes adjusted slowly to the extreme chiaroscuro of the scene. Null turned about, bent down and grabbed up the broken corpse of little Louie, walked over to the now-exposed railing and threw him off into the darkness.

Louie hit the floor below with the wet-punch-sound of a watermelon exploding.

"There you are!" Null announced, more than shouted into an echo. "Take him. Take your prize, because he's the last one you'll ever get. The very. Last. One."

As he gathered up his coat, his possessions (mostly weapons), dressed and arrayed himself as he had been before this unaccountable kidnapping, he realized precisely where he was.

"City Hall."

He spoke again into the vacant darkness over the railing. "I'm at City Hall."

NINE

"Just what exactly is your interest in this, Mr. Dzhugashvili?"

"The same as yours, Agent Thrawn. The course of justice."

"How does that compute?" asked Boyd, fluttering her eyelids for sarcastic effect.

"I'm just a licensed private detective looking to aid you in your investigation."

"We got enough dicks at One Schroeder as it stands, Dzhugashvili—"

"Please. Call me Josef."

"Alright, Josef whatever your name is—gimme the client and pony up whatever evidence you've scrounged up so far and let me get you served with an injunction to cease this, um, 'investigation' of yours—" Agent Thrawn made quotes around the word 'investigation' with his fingers in the air without a shred of irony, "–by tomorrow. That's right. Tomorrow. And if you raise a fuss, I'll have Detective Boyd here toss you in the clink, get INS to slingshot you right back to whatever shit-hole Eastern European country you hail from before you can say 'Beef Stroganoff.'"

"Maybe chicken Kiev is more to your taste."

"Look at that, Kay, a witty private dick."

"Don't be a public dick, Joel. Hear him out. You don't like what he's here to tell you, I can press the red button on the walkie I've got hangin' from my hip and sic a few blue goons on him to teach him some manners."

They were neither discreet nor soft-spoken. Not that they were yelling or hollering, but the friction wasn't quiet. It was still too cold in the false spring that had taken Boston in its usual teasing grip to be seated outside. You could have called the weather mild, but even transplants knew it was going to get colder before summer might at last finally break through the murk with some warm, golden days. And sometimes summer failed abjectly at that and wound up presenting a peculiar gray moistness all its own where a confused sun like a bored child spent little to no time on it.

The inside of the Café Paradiso was bathed in chilly silver light from its glass façade. Two other small glass-topped tables had customers, four obvious college girls feeling superior about not having to resort to Starbucks' for their lattes, overdressed for the weather, which is normal in Boston, where everyone is either wearing too much or too little at the wrong time for either, or the temperature decided to plummet to a flash-freezing thirty degrees before the afternoon was over. No one who knows anything trusts the weather in Boston. Of the three seated at the table least shielded from the unforgiving light, only the foreign national looked put together. The couple opposite him looked frowzy and frazzled. Dress to them, it was clear, was a last-minute consideration; and their hair bordered on the ridiculous, sloppy fright wigs one short, one grown out. And the balding agent's coiffure boasted wings spread out that were ready for take-off.

Innokenty wasn't as patient as he would have liked to have been. Even this minor meeting was testing his somewhat fragile limits. He had learned to be patient, but Putin's brutal moves in Ukraine where he served as a mercenary undid most of that. "You come on pretty strong for a guy looks like what you call a 'bean counter.' What do they do at the Feebs, Special Agent, Thrawn, rotate desk jockeys like you onto the street so they can remember why they were desk jockeys in the first place?"

"Zip it, Russian jagoff—"

"Ingushetia, Special Agent Thrawn. Not quite the same country."

"It's all one under Putin, pencil dick."

"Like it is under your former dictator Trump—the Putin asset the world knows as such, but not your great country with its pluralism of opinion. He plans and executes an insurrection and when luckily for you it fails, you enjoy it all like a reality TV show. Meanwhile his numbers, as they say, are just huge." Innokenty delivered this last parry waving his finger at Agent Thrawn as if he were pointing a gun he knew he didn't have to use.

"Okay, man of steel—"

"I love your wit, Lieutenant Boyd. *Horoschow.*"

"You're looking to do what to aid our investigation into the Gangsta Boyz drug cartel you shouldn't know a damn thing about? Exactly?"

"He's looking to get himself jammed up for obstruction and a few other charges."

"C'mon Joel, ease up. Maybe Mr. Dzhugashvili here can actually provide us with some help. Not listening to the street can fuck up any investigation. If what he says is garbage, we can kick him or you can arrest him for the added fun of more paperwork."

"Kay, if I arrest this jagoff, I'll refer him down to BPD and you can have both the collar *and* the attendant paperwork."

"Then let's kibosh that idea for the moment and hear the man out."

"Your kindness and discernment are noted and very well appreciated, Lieutenant."

"Just get to the point, mutt, or I'll find the appropriate drone down at division to handle the paperwork."

Innokenty smirked and gave out with a muffled, throaty chuckle. "Such a strong, modern American woman. "Badass" is the term you Americans use, is it not? They should award you a comic book or a documentary on the Netflix. The lessons of the 'Me Too' culture of abuse are not lost on you Lieutenant, not in the least."

"Heard of 'Cancel Culture,' Josef?"

"Of course, Lieutenant. Who hasn't?"

"Well, I'm going to introduce you to that firsthand you don't spill and spill fast."

Innokenty held up both palms in a stop gesture, nodding his head in agreement. "I'm here in the spirit of cooperation between law enforcement and professional investigators."

"Kay, get this son of a bitch's ID and run it. Then we can see what his cooperation with an active investigation actually means."

"Lay back, my friends. I'm here to help you. It serves us both if this supposed ghoul who runs the Gangsta Boyz is apprehended by you for his many terrible crimes. Shut down their operation for good, win glorious citations and profitable raises in pay. I can assure you that my client and I will be applauding zealously from the sidelines."

Boyd responded by splashing him with her cup of coffee, getting up from her seat, making her way behind the momentarily disoriented Innokenty and thrusting her forearm under his chin, squeezing hard. Agent Thrawn nearly fell over backward in his wrought-iron, valentine-shaped chair. (All the chairs were that way at the Café Paradiso—spidery and painted white.) She lifted Innokenty up by his chin and yanked his Craig Claiborne wallet out of the back-pocket of his immaculately distressed Diesel Safado skinny jeans and shoved him back down, leaving him coughing and choking. She laid the wallet down flat in front of Agent Thrawn, who picked at it hungrily, like a badger tearing through prey, then sat back down, looking satiated.

"Stalin you ain't."

Innokenty coughed, dabbed at himself with a fistful of napkins, took a breath to allow the smirk to return to his face and said with a chuckle of good humor, "There's something to be said for carrying a good thing too far with this 'Me-Too' approach."

"That wasn't a 'Me-Too approach.' That was a 'roust a dipshit' approach."

"Good to know."

The staff behind the counter, a middle-aged male manager with a harried look and a young woman barista with jet-black lacquered hair and dreamy eyes who doubled as a waitress, quickly disappeared into the back room and the college girls at the other tables had already scampered off, leaving cash and what amounted to forty percent tips. Agent Thrawn ran one hand through what remained of his hair while the other hand worked the wallet.

"So what are you really, Innokenty Gorets, international mutt of mystery?"

"He smells bad, Joel. I don't like it."

"You know we're going to run you, right, mutt?"

"Of course, Agent. I would expect no less."

"Let's have the pitch, Loverboy."

"Just as well, but no more coffee for you, Lieutenant."

"I swear we need to send this one down for a quick refresher in gladiator school. Brush him the fuck up."

"I assure you, Agent, I could teach a class."

"But Lieutenant Boyd already schooled you."

Innokenty laughed a melodic laugh like a tenor in a chorale. "Neither of you, you must realize, constitutes a threat to me of any kind."

Boyd slapped her Sig Sauer P365 semiautomatic down on the glass tabletop, so it rang. "Care to play steal the bacon with me, sweetheart?"

Innokenty chuckled with his best good-natured, dimpled expression.

"I know that game very well, Lieutenant. Though where I come from, we call it "Steal the *yokh*, but we do it with a Kalashnikov, not a popgun."

"Try to leave just yet, and I'll pistol whip you across the face with this popgun," Boyd snarled, picking the Sig up from the table and holding it in a position to do exactly that.

"I'm not here to be critical and judge you, but you have a much more difficult problem than you think you do. You're hunting a dead man—a man who's believed by criminals to *be* dead, maybe a ghost. No one's sure who and what he is. I don't think either of you can tell me that."

I can, Boyd thought and said nothing.

"Do tell, Mr. Gorets."

"With respect—"

"Well, that makes one of us, now, doesn't it?" Boyd batted her eyes.

"You were pretty once, Lieutenant Boyd. But that's not how it is today, now is it?"

"You might not be so pretty when you leave this meeting, Gorets. Adjustments can be made for an impudent fuck like you," offered Agent Thrawn with a gap-toothed grin and added, "on your face."

"Okay. Okay. Now that the niceties are finished, let me sit you both down on the brass tacks."

Neither Agent Thrawn nor Boyd cracked a smile at Innokenty's awkward usage. Boyd made the come on gesture with her index finger, stone-faced otherwise.

"*Horoschow.* You think you're hunting this jumped-up drug king-pin, but you are not. At all times this nimble little man is doing things that you don't conceive of. But uppermost of all of them is that *he's* the hunter. An experienced hunter. And as good as you may be, you're not really hunters. But that's all this man is at the bottom of it all. And the thing no one seems to realize about him except maybe his crew is that he kills as a default, as his principal reaction. He does it with ease. He seems a bit of a weakling, walks with a limp, not a big guy. But if you ever get close to him, he's already worked out why he should kill you, when he's going to kill you, how he's going to do it and how to slip away quietly, unseen."

"That all you got, Gorets? Some fairy story about the shot caller of the Gangsta Boyz crime crew?" Boyd asked already knowing the answer

"And one other thing you should know: he's already hunting us while we are only prepared to be hunting him. You should be worried," added Innokenty

"Stories of the street don't give me the shakes, bub," Agent Thrawn sputtered, trying to sound tough.

Innokenty made a church steeple of all ten fingers. "The stories of the street are myth. We all know that. But all myths are based in some kind of fact if you track them down far enough. What I told you is not myth. It's brutal fact. Now, you want this mug off the street, close down his drug factory of human despair? Pick the crew up piecemeal at your leisure and get ready for whoever the nature of things decides will fill the vacuum you left? Of course you do. And I want to help you do that and my client also agrees to help you."

"You're going to play the confidentiality game with us?"

"You know that game well enough to know, Lieutenant Boyd."

"We ain't getting in bed with any diseased whores, Gorets—you or whomever hired you."

Innokenty pursed his lips and made a dismissive pop with his lips.

"Plus, loverboy, for being so helpful, you ain't given us *bupkes*."

"I give you that he's hunting you—hunting *us*, my dear lady."

"Why should the head of a cartel need to hunt us down when he has a crew to do that for him? He wants to come after law enforcement, we're ready for him, FBI and BPD. But why would this kingpin ghost lift a finger himself when all he has to do is press a button? And why bring all law enforcement down on him while his cartel is expanding?"

"Lieutenant Boyd, you need to send this guy back to the office. He don't seem to know how things operate out here in the wild east."

"Wild west you mean, Innokenty. There is no 'wild east.'"

"No? Then who's killing meth heads from Methuen to Attleboro with gang muscle to back that? Who terrifies snitches and CIs in your greater Boston area enough so they'd rather tough out decade bids than serve up your mystery mug for a free pass? If that isn't wild, then I need to get a remedial on your language."

'I can tell you all about him, you Slavic scumbag,' thought Boyd,

'more than you could ever fucking imagine,' but instead countered with, "You got pictures on that, chief? Back up this mean little fiction you cooked up? Your apex predator shot caller hunting us down when he can find us anywhere? "

Agent Thrawn clumsily unsnapped the holster of his Glock 19 sidearm, leaned forward across the table, telegraphing his next move. Innokenty nodded and reached smoothly into the inside pocket of his jacket and flipped an envelope out onto the table, which slid toward Agent Thrawn and spilled photos out along the way.

"I think I did a pretty good job on these, Agent Thrawn. Note where he is—how close to you. Right outside that building that looks like a Lego structure. Also outside of One Schroeder Plaza, sticking out like a sore thumb, face full of scars. I hope you'll find them helpful in some small way." He stood, made a shallow bow and smiled when he added, "I'm at the Westin Hotel in Copley Square by your amazing library. Just ask for me, the desk will be sure to connect you. I want to assure you that I'm not hiding from law enforcement. In fact, it's my mission to be helpful to you. So, later gators."

Innokenty rose quickly and strolled out onto Hanover Street, whistling a tune neither Agent Thrawn nor Boyd recognized. No wonder. He was tone deaf in the strict sense. It was just an off-key version of "Dark Eyes." The door chimes jingled loudly as he left.

Boyd expected it just as intensely as Agent Thrawn shouted it:

"Run that fucking *son-of-a-bitch!*"

———

Father Bricolage hated the memory as much as he hated the rebuke.

It was like a kind of acid reflux burping up bile along his spine.

The cardinal was enraged, his face blushing with emotion and his hands unsteady as he poured himself a glass of madeira at his desk. He didn't pour one for Father Bricolage. There he was, splendid and expansive as Cardinal Wolsey behind his opulent, hand-carved and tooled Lord Raffles Lion Executive Desk, his robe billowing but his face soured, and it seemed somehow to have been withdrawn and retracted into itself like the toothy spiraling mouth of a lamprey eel.

He did not come across as fierce as the hand-carved visage of the lion facing Father Bricolage, who winced.

The hands of the cardinal that were almost turned blue by the nacreous veins crisscrossing them weren't shaking out of enfeeblement or palsy, but of a furious anger.

"Sam, I don't know what to say to you. How you've disappointed and betrayed us all in our holy mission to place and secure more candidates for our sanctified *Defensores Fidei de Puero!* You nearly killed Frater Phlegethon, and you did it without any authority to do anything, even to preserve your own safety. After providing him payment for qualified novitiates to sing in our new order, the—"

"*Defensores Fidei de Puero,* Eminence. Yes, I comprehend the ramifications of my misdeed. Surely there are other means of recruitment than consorting with pagan Satanists. We don't need to roll in the muck to secure these little worms. Surely—"

"Surely there are, Sam, but for heaven's sake! To call the inclusion of wanton, rejected little boys consigned to economic, moral and spiritual doom *recruitment* contains its own special blasphemy. It is itself reflexively blasphemous. This imperils your very soul, Sam. We're involved in a mission of sublime salvation, *not* recruitment."

"But eminence, these excommunicated Satanists blaspheme. Phlegethon himself embodied blasphemy and—"

"And you nearly killed him for it! Tell me, how did that profit us? How did this advance the kingdom of God in ways that bring strength and glory to Holy Mother Church?"

"His mouth will never again assault, defame, besmirch and tarnish Holy Mother Church again. He was what his selection of his putrid nomenclature proclaims him one of the five rivers in the infernal regions of the underworld, along with the rivers Styx, Lethe, Cocytus, and Acheron."

"Jesus Christ in heaven, Sam!" Cardinal Cromulent spat and slammed his cut glass goblet down on his leonine desk so hard that all the wine emptied out of it in a wave and the stem shattered, making him retract his hand in a jerk as if from intense flame, which didn't at all prevent him from getting cut.

"Your Eminence! Shall I administer first aid?"

"No, Sam," the cardinal replied in a soft, introspective voice, sucking his wound. "I'd like you to administer your ass to the address I've written down here and coordinate our efforts at Bethlehem Adoption and Youth Placement Services in Newton." He flung a miniature envelope at Father Bricolage, who caught it neatly, embossed with his own special ecclesiastical heraldry: a falcon-laden coat of arms mixed with that of the pope. "The soon-to-be-no-longer secular federal government of the United States is about to back us in our cause to counter your screw up. Great misdeeds at the southern border are about to benefit us all greatly."

Father Bricolage's face lit with excitement.

"But Eminence, don't you see? Isn't this God's way of rewarding us for defending his honor from willful sinners who were at best attempting to pervert the purity of our new cause? To at last stanch the taint of public corruption stemming from our most holy body's simple needs of the flesh so as to no longer impede his glory. And the continued sanctification of *Defensores Fidei de Puero?*"

The cardinal stood up from his impressive desk, his arms waving wildly, and screamed, "Get out now, Father. Go work out your penance at Bethlehem. Seek the confessional thereafter and you will abase yourself in front of the Grand Pater of Ordo Templi Orientis at their next Sabbath, beg his forgiveness for your attempted murder of one of his best legates, a dedicated confederate to our cause, and you will do so without that illegal pistol of yours which you will leave with me right now. Drag that thing out of your leather book bag right now and put it on my desk, *you sanctimonious, pedantic, suppurating asshole!*"

The cardinal's birdcage chest rose and fell with the exertion, the remembrance a fixed, still image in the priest's mind.

The recollection still stung his ears and now his eyes, which burned with the last withering image of the cardinal's venerable face, how his lips were like wet rags in the wind and his hair flew up like the feathers of a freshly shot bird falling from the sky. No falcon there, not like on his heraldic envelope, just bitter, flagrant moribundity.

"Father, are you alright?" came a voice.

And then he realized he had his index finger still urgently pressing the button to the chimes that announced his presence all through that bitter recollection. And the allure of the woman who met him at the door—in such outrageous array; her decolletage, her wanton perfume—made him want to vomit.

"Father Bricolage?"

"I'm sorry. You're N-Nonie?"

"Yes, Father. I'm Auntie Nonie Fomites. I'm the one you're scheduled to see. Please excuse the get-up, I'm usually quite down-dressed, even frumpy, but I'm speaking at a charity event tonight and I have to make sure I mingle sharply with all the big wallets. We need to keep donors loose, confused and happy, but always mindful of their Christian duty. Won't you come in, Father? Let me give you the lay of the land? So to speak."

The wink she gave was lurid; slyly corrupt.

She pronounced her surname Foh-mit- *tease*, which the Father found unnerving.

"Gladly, Ms. Fomites."

"Please, Father, call me Auntie. They all do. I prefer it."

"Yes. Auntie. You'll have to excuse me."

Father Bricolage stepped awkwardly into the foyer of what was a blinding white four-story mansion dating from the 19th century of Federalist design. He was immediately awed by its high-ceilinged grandeur, with its immense chandelier and its opulent oriental rugs, an enormous marble fireplace and mantlepiece in the front room, the subtle curve of it spiral staircase and the modern, burnished steel addition of two elevator banks.

"This is quite an historic property, is it not, Auntie?"

"Why, yes Father, it is."

The alabaster mansion was up the hill off Herrick Road near where the old Andover Newton Seminary School was located until it packed up and merged with Yale. The seminary itself was the product of a merger of the Andover Theological Seminary (founded in Cambridge, Massachusetts in 1807) and the Newton Theological Institution (founded in Newton, Massachusetts, the "Garden City," in 1825) to become the Andover Newton Theological School in 1965. Even before its removal to Yale in 2018, the school on its Herrick Road campus not only had created but stood by the educational model used by almost all Protestant seminaries today and pioneered a raft of training programs for prospective clerics as well as for field education and was in fact staunchly self-identified as an "open and affirming seminary," meaning that its doors were open to students of same-sex or transgender orientation and generally advocated tolerance of such sexual diversity in both the Protestant Church and in society as well – immediately marking itself as the sworn enemy of the burgeoning sect of Evangelical Christians and putting itself squarely at odds with the Catholic Church.

But money, the great religious lubricant itself that salved many of the wounds of sin and reconciled doctrinal squabbles that seemed quaint in comparison to the magic it provided, made strange bedfellows as wholesome and acceptable as homespun or, even better, a raiment of finest silk.

Bethlehem Adoption and Youth Placement Services may have acquired a select piece of the seminary's campus in the particular alabaster white mansion that was its east coast base and proclaimed a similar interest in the holy pursuit of the Christian godhead as the entwined seminaries had, but it was there that the similarity ended. Tolerance of any belief other than its martial interpretation of Christianity was at best a means to an end only if it facilitated a Dominionist and Opus Dei conquest of anything secular – and all the machinations of secularism were welcomed and exploited with the aim of ending secularism altogether.

Her distracting bosom rose and fell as she spoke. "You see, Father, we're interested in the future, not the past. We have no use for pomp and liturgy. The advancing of God's kingdom and governance in this world in the here and now is our mission. We're not interested in old-fashioned ecumenical progressivism. No, we are going to deliver Jesus Christ to the world with a sword, just as John the Baptist himself had envisioned."

"But Christ himself announced the sword"

"Yes, and in Nikos Kazantzakis' The Last Temptation of Christ."

"Auntie, the Vatican doesn't acknowledge that book as true Christian literature and certainly not as a valid telling of the Passion or the Stations of the Cross."

"But to have Christ live as a man participating in the struggle of this world! That's what we at Bethlehem are trying to bring to modern civilization. And to fortify Christian institutions, of course."

"You can hardly call the Vatican a Christian institution."

"Why, Father? You're saying it's not?"

"No, but it's a terrible example of damning with faint praise."

She stopped in her tracks, turned about gracefully on the heels of her fuck-me pumps, grabbed the priest by his shoulders, looking into his watery blue eyes, the nipples of her hard, too-spherical breasts stabbing him just under his collarbone. Father Bricolage was perplexed, uncertain if this was Auntie being humorous or deadly serious. He silently wished he had kept the pistol in his book bag against the cardinal's orders, then at once begged God for forgiveness for that thought, heartened by the slight punishment of nausea.

"Now, Father," she reprimanded, "let's not get ahead of ourselves, Father Bricolage. We all understand what a scholar you are. The cardinal himself recognizes you as a force to be reckoned with within the Catholic Church, not just in the Archdiocese of Boston."

"It seems we share some doctrinal differences."

"Follow me, if you will, and watch your step. There are lots of little half-step ledges in this place. I don't really think it was ever meant to house children, do you?"

"You mean the children are housed here?"

"Sure they are, Father. It's a big place. Three floors of dormitories, and one floor dedicated to your church's special initiative that we're all quite proud of. Just come with me. The office is right across from the nurse's station and administration to the right. Just keep your eyes on me and I won't lose you."

Father Bricolage did exactly that and found his eyes tearing with exasperated resistance watching her behind.

Auntie Nonie strode ahead of the Father as he shuffled behind, smiling brightly, past the young women behind the counter seated at their laptops and a twenty-something security guard in a steel-blue uniform that was too big for him and so seemed to be swallowing him up. At an old-fashioned door small enough to have been that of a closet, painted that same blinding white that defined the mansion, she swiped a key card through a black plastic reader bolted into it and popped up with a crisp snap.

"There's another half-step here with a sharp lip on it, Father, so watch it."

The Father wanted to say, *'Okay, I was too busy to see it, watching instead the sharp lip on you,'* but restrained himself. It was like there was a small apparatus in the dark back area of his mind—a sort of Maxwell's Demon separating sin from sanctity—praying autonomically to Jesus for forgiveness while the rest of his mind freely expressed the inexpressible that he had willed his body, especially his mouth, to suppress. And thinking this made him trip anyway over the steel-tipped lip, as he followed her into the room, which was as warm and inviting as a walk-in shoe closet.

Following that, he clumsily sat down in one of the two chairs upholstered with green leather that had been tacked down opposite the sparse, tempered glass desk that had nothing on it. Auntie Nonie moved in little steps on her fuck-me pumps and sat down daintily behind it despite the constraint of the tight black cocktail dress, the extreme stiletto-heeled fuck me pumps and the awkward ballast of her heavy spherical breasts. After she had sat down facing the Father, the door to the office gave out with a loud snap that jarred him.

"The door's on a self-locking delay. Helps to secure privacy."

"I understand you have much to hide."

"We're not so far apart there, Father. Our business is nothing if not confidential."

"The church has need of its secrets, Auntie."

"Some of God's most important work is done in the shadows."

"When necessary." Father Bricolage was grabbing the arms of his chair with two sets of white knuckles and was fiercely biting his lower lip.

"Does how I look distress you, Father?"

"I'm not used to seeing a woman entrusted with the care of children look like you—dressed like you."

She leaned toward him like a predator summing up her prey.

"Do my tits make you horny, Father? Give you the hots?"

"N-n-no—Auntie."

"Then do you like men, Father? We all have our predilections and temptations, don't we? Come, come. Don't *you?*"

"Never." Father Bricolage gave a dry cough to cover for the fact that his throat was closing up.

"Little girls then?"

The Father held up his palms at Auntie Nonie and waved them in denial.

"So it must be boys then. The crux of today's visit."

All at once Father Bricolage stood up and belted it out like a song:

"Heavens no! None of that at all—none of it in the very *least!*"

And unlike so many of the clergy, the Father was telling the absolute truth. All calls to lust, to the merest concept of sexual concupiscence, coition, fetishistic sexual objectification of any kind made him deeply queasy. If the physical fact of it ever came dangerously close to his person, he would find himself on the verge of passing out. Celibacy actually suited him, keeping him at arm's length from all manner of erotic connection, which in any of its forms disgusted him, made him physically ill. Yes, even the thoughts of his desperate errand to provide novitiates for the *Defensores Fidei de Puero* made him feel weak and sick.

"Nothing? No? Not what you see here in front of you? Not all *this?*"

She glided long-fingered, tiger-stripe-nailed hands along herself from her chest to her thighs with bright, polished smile, teeth distracting from moist, fire-engine red lips.

"Please don't try to make me unkind, Auntie. Just stop. Please."

Auntie Nonie barked a one-syllable laugh.

"So, you're trying to convince me that you're pure, Father Bricolage? As pure as your cause?"

"Auntie Nonie, the only entity more pure than Holy Mother Church herself is our savior Jesus Christ."

"And the procurement of little boys for your, um, Defense—of whatever?"

"*Defensores Fidei de Puero.* Truly a blessed cause to heal the wounds unfair secular judgment have visited upon our beleaguered and perfect church."

"You brought the money with you?"

"I have a dedicated tablet with me in my book bag. You have only to approve the transaction on the interface that will come up when you turn it on, and the funds will be transferred to your Swiss account. Your credentials have been programmed in as have ours. It'll be complete within minutes."

"How contemporary of you, Father."

"The Vatican understands we must function in a world whose changes and processes are liquid and mercurial even as ours are as stable and solid as granite.

Again, she demonstrated herself with supple hands and Father Bricolage felt a painful chill in his stomach.

"We don't have the massive wealth of the Vatican, Father. I have to do what I can to charm donors into supporting the holiness of our cause. Even though the government has eased some of our financial needs, funds must be finessed from the lust and venality of money men."

"But not from the church."

Auntie Nonie sat back and said in a low purr: "The purity of your intention doesn't have to be argued. It's obvious, and the government agrees."

"I don't understand."

"It's the legacy of our last president. God has delivered wayward children to us at the southern border by promoting crime, drug cartels, failed governments, desperate families flee all these plague conditions inflicted upon them by God to aid us both in our respective missions."

"Why would God inflict violence, privation and torment on Latin American countries? How could such a lingering disaster help anyone?"

"Oh, Father Bricolage, it's so elegant in its heavenly design."

"How could such a thing be considered elegant?"

"Oh, ye of little faith, Auntie Nonie countered. "Thanks to President Trump and his zero-tolerance deportation and separation policy at the southern border—"

"Wait. Are you telling me that such a despicable policy is not just another manifestation of that administration's incompetence? An unforced error, as I've heard them say on the news sometimes when I can bear to watch it?"

Auntie Nonie sighed, shook her head and grinned, saying unctuously, "No, it was a calculated strategy. You see, while claiming the illegal children were lost, the INS was directed to route as many of the little pests to Christian adoption centers like Bethlehem—centers dedicated to the defeat of secularism and the establishment of a dominion of true Christianity over all secularism. They are our soon-to-be beloved Christian soldiers marching as to war. And though we can't match the enormous wealth of the

Vatican, Bethlehem is owned by Betty DeVille, the SpamWay heiress."

Father Bricolage arched an eyebrow.

"You mean like Cruella De Vil, the cartoon villainess who wanted to make a coat of 101 Dalmatian skins?"

"Yes, except she wants an entire wardrobe made from the skins of undocumented Latin American children."

Father Bricolage pouted and his eyes narrowed.

"Not funny."

"Tough room."

"But how tough can I, a poor priest, truly be? If anything, what you really have to face is the toughness of Christ."

"Lighten up, Father. Our founder isn't doing anything more than the usual double dip of sacred Capitalism. American-style."

Father Bricolage went silent and contemplated it for a minute that was long enough to make Auntie Nonie sweat.

"The Trump Administration paid you money for each border-separated child that you'd house and feed until good Christian parents came along and adopted them."

"The Biden Administration too. They're still playing catch-up, trying to undo all of President Trump's good works."

"So, you're actually triple dipping, then."

"Come again?" Auntie Nonie looked perplexed by this at first, then a smile slowly played across her vermillion lips. "You're a hundred percent right, Father. For each child, we get paid by the federal government, by each set of placement parents and now by the Vatican."

"Let me correct myself, Auntie Nonie. Quadruple dipping."

"Now, wait a minute. That's going a bit far, even for you—oh, again. I get it now."

"I knew you would, Auntie."

"The Commonwealth of Massachusetts also pays us for each successful adoption and for each new admission we rescue from the nefarious abuses of the street."

Father Bricolage shook his head almost imperceptibly, wishing he had his 22 in the book bag instead of a dedicated single-use tablet loaded up with money. "So, it appears that Ms. DeVille and Bethlehem have made the kidnapping of children a highly profitable business."

"Indeed, we have, Father, and the fact that we have both state and federal tax-exempt status is the cherry on top."

"The blessings of Holy Mother Church, Auntie, are indeed manifold," replied Father Bricolage. "Even Caesar must yield to them."

TEN

"You're not really a doctor, are you Toplofty?" Innokenty oozed, popping a spearmint Tic-Tac in his mouth, not giving a moment to loll it on his tongue but crunching down on it hard, making a crisp snap.

Toplofty was pacing about his spacious office, which looked like the sort of space an advertising agency executive, vice-president of something or other might occupy, not an oncologist at Mass General Hospital. "It's an honorific, Yuri. You can refer to me that way out of deference and respect."

"It's Innokenty, Toplofty, not Yuri. You're thinking of the guy who succeeded a dog being launched into space. I don't have to respect you, Toplofty. I just have to pay attention to what you say, which I am hopeful will be a distillate of the drugged-out ravings of the former crime boss Malek the Mallet, who I doubt could make it across a room without your help."

"You can call me doctor as an honorific."

"I can but I won't, Toplofty. I work for you and the mutilated Mallet, which is not a situation I will in any fashion be continuing after I deliver one rather minor assassination to you along with itemized expenses and an invoice for the balance due."

"You disrespectful Russky faggot—"

"Careful, Toplofty. We Russky faggots have a nasty habit of repaying debts of honor with blood that's very seldom our own."

"I'd like to perform a procedure on your cranium that would give you flip-top face. Then I could open it up and take a shit down your neck, you little Russian fuck."

"Ingush, Toplofty, not Russian. We are a different people." Innokenty with a resigned sigh reached into the inside pocket of his jacket and smoothly withdrew a Glock G19 pistol and placed it gently on the office desk which was a steel and glass affair that showed no signs of ever having had any serious work done on its immaculate glass top.

"So what does that move prove?"

"It proves I know you don't carry a gun, Toplofty. Would you like to take your best opportunity? I give you what Bostonians call 'a free shot.'"

"If I massacre you, the boss loses out on your initial deposit and a supposedly top-of-the line assassin."

"Into each life a little rain must fall."

With a grunt to telegraph the move, Toplofty charged the much smaller, lighter Ingush national, which he sidestepped with ease. Toplofty was both burly and tall, and surprisingly adroit and light on his feet for a man close to sixty. He was in the starting lineup in both high school and college football. He had always been a successful, bullying jock, even when a co-department chair at Mass General Hospital. Lantern-jawed, aquiline featured, graying smartly only at the sideburns, he cut a striking figure, imposing, authoritarian, but not when he was lying on his back on the thickly piled rug. Innokenty put him down in two precise moves without breathing hard, without breaking a sweat.

Before Toplofty could say anything, Innokenty kicked him suavely in the side of the head. It didn't put him out, but it addled him enough to prove docile as he rose from the floor and dusted off his somewhat tight Armani suit.

"Toplofty, I prefer a more English cut to my garments—much

more forgiving of movement. Not that it would have helped you anyway, old timer."

"Maybe in a different venue—"

"You don't want to call me faggot again, old man. Just be aware of that before you speak again."

"How do you plan to stop this zombie that's running drugs up and down the Eastern Corridor?"

"I wasn't aware he had reached New York yet, never mind Washington D.C."

"Well. That's because he hasn't. Yet."

Toplofty did a little dip at the knees signaling that he might be ready to go down again. Innokenty went around the gleaming impressive show desk and pulled out the chair, slapping the seat cushion with his hand.

"You might want to take a seat, Mr. *Dr*. Toplofty so we might more effectively continue this discussion."

"I might. Want to. Sure."

Looking tired and slightly hunched over, Toplofty made his way to the chair and sank down into it.

"You're sitting in for Mr. Mallet today, so what does he want to know? Methods? Whether our original arrangement is in place? Timetable? All of it, none of it—what? You want his head in a basket as in some heroic movie. Maybe on a silver platter with mushrooms, truffles and parsley? Just what is it that you need to know about this not very complicated contract job I agreed to do for your has-been boss."

"He's not a has-been. He's temporarily—"

"I don't need to know what he is or what he isn't or even what he aspires to be, Toplofty. You paid me an inflated price to dispense with a crippled, damaged little man you somehow blame for the dismantling of a criminal empire neither I nor anyone else has really heard of. I'll do the job, but don't think for a moment I have any intention of participating in your little fantasy. This little half-dead creature you want planted in the ground or burnt up to ash is the biggest threat you have to reestablishing your criminal supremacy, I'll rub him out, collect the rest of my money and not bother with this again anytime soon."

"You don't get that *that's* what he does."

"Does what?"

"Makes you underestimate him. Think he's easy prey. Blink for a second and your flank of men are all eviscerated and he's already coming for you before you have time to squeeze off a single shot."

"You have faced this little manling in battle before, Toplofty?"

"No, but you saw what he did to the *Padrone.*"

"Yes. You mentioned that. He really did that? You're sure?"

"I am. I know he did that. The Padrone does not lie to me. Ever."

"What are you, his right leg?"

Toplofty winced at the remark, but decided to let it go, and not even correct him for having the wrong leg.

"No, but I'm important." At that, his nose began to bleed. He stanched it awkwardly with a handkerchief. Innokenty chuckled a low chuckle.

"Important? I see. So what is this important role you perform now that you're no longer such an important orthopedic doctor?"

"I'm *consigliere* to the Padrone." It sounded as if he were speaking into a rubber boot.

Innokenty clicked his tongue against the roof of his mouth. "Too bad for you, Toplofty. You should have remained a doctor. Because I intend to get rough. Very *rough* indeed."

"I don't get what you mean."

"Not a great *consigliere* are you, Toplofty. You see, once I take out this pathetic little zombie-man, what's going to stop me from taking over and running the biggest and only drug cartel in New England? I don't really think you could stop me, Toplofty. Do you?"

Toplofty reached feebly for the gun taped under his chair and Innokenty shot it out of his hand in the blink of an eye.

———

"Can't you just burrow into one of your hidey holes like a cicada and leave me alone for seventeen years, for Christ's sake already?" Boyd complained wearily in the dark as she entered her condo on Jersey Street in the Fens. She didn't have to see Null to know he was there.

"I'm much quieter than a cicada."

"So I noticed."

"Notice anything else?

"I can't get Agent Thrawn off your trail if that's what you're here for. He wants street cred and his way to do it is to nuke your Gangsta Boyz cartel before it spreads to New York and gets wrested from his palsied grip by that branch office."

"He should have stuck to forensic accounting."

"He is. He claims he'll get you on tax evasion in the bargain."

"He'll have to prove I exist first."

Dramatizing her exhaustion, Boyd set her handbag with the nickel-plated Sig Sauer semi-automatic in it and sagged down on her well-worn divan that sagged down even deeper as she did. She balanced a small pack of American Spirit cigarettes in her hand, withdrew one and lit it with the lighter that was waiting for her on the arm of the divan along with the seashell ashtray surfeit with ashes and crumpled butts, took a drag, closed her eyes and kicked both her feet, which relieved her of her high-heeled mules.

"That death certificate gag you have won't last forever."

"They can't call for an inquest without a body."

"Jesus, Null, hard to believe you could ever be this naïve."

"Kind of a joke, right? That I'm naïve? You're making fun of me."

"Nothing gets by you, does it?"

"Not much. But fun does escape me."

"I wish I could escape."

"Not much chance of that, is there?"

"Rub it in, why don't you?"

"I made my point."

"This is Boston. You want someone pegged for murder, no

corpse need apply. Bring someone back from the dead to sign an agreement? Go see Clarence Mahaney in Records down cellar."

"I have a better angle for Agent Thrawn."

"Don't tell me, let me guess. It's about the kiddies. Always about the kiddies with you. Now why is that? If I didn't already know how creepy you are, I'd be even more creeped out by that."

"But you know it's the opposite of that, Kay, so why fuck around?"

"Because the entire life I'm living now is nothing but fucking around. That's why."

"Steer him my way. I'll set him straight."

"Sure you will. You'll peel off his skin and make him eat it."

"It doesn't have to come to that. Not like the other Feeb."

"Wilmer Quark? No, not at all." She bit her lip, experiencing a quick, unsubtle thought. "And don't kill him, please. I *like* this one."

"Isn't Joel Thrawn a bit squishy for you?"

"Null, compared to you a bowling ball is squishy."

"We couldn't have been anything though, you realize. Those events were drug driven—"

"Everything you *do* is drug-driven. Still sampling your wares, Mr. Meth Magnate?"

"More meth mogul, when it comes down to that. And the answer is yes. I find sleeping an obnoxious waste of time."

"That stuff'll kill ya, you know." She tossed him the pack of American Spirit cigarettes. He held it up in front of his deep-set eyes and examined it as if he'd never seen one before. "Nicotine might help with the jitters, and it can also hasten your exit from this fucked-up world, so maybe I don't have to have your help ruining mine."

Null crumpled up the pack and made a neat arc with it as it landed in the wastebasket by the divan.

"And yet you must admit I help ruin your world at a pretty steady clip. And from time-to-time I also manage to save it. Then there's also George Goodnature. You remember him, don't you?"

"Here we go. Back to the kiddies yet again."

"No cheaper commodity in this world that brings in such a high price."

"How about sand?"

"Okay. Both lead to the same conclusion; use them up and there's no world left. There won't always be more."

"So you're all about saving the world, by becoming the first North American drug cartel of the great northeast. First in the world to look after the kiddies."

"Those Columbian drug lords like El Chapo did it first."

"True, but when the parents owed money to the cartel, the kiddies died with the parents just as fast and just as bad."

"No system is perfect."

"Says the Mogul of Meth."

"Running criminals makes it less likely you'll be their victim."

"Until they kill you."

"Yes, everyone wants to be the boss except the boss. Let's add Ronald Brogan Jr. to the list of those who'd like to send me down for early retirement."

"Why don't you just take all your meth money and run, for God's sake? Fuck off to Tahiti."

"Joy is dead for me, Kay."

"What in Christ's name does that mean?"

"I wouldn't experience the joy there that other men might so easily have. No, here is it for me. Dull as a raw March afternoon. There's an agenda here that needs my constant attention. So in my being bad, I'm good."

"You're as fucked up as they come, Null. You know that?"

"Someone reminds me of this at least every other day. But it's a very simple logical proposition: I need a purpose to keep moving. And as long as that purpose grows, so does my interest in continuing to live. And I happen to be in a growth industry."

"You know, Null, Joel's a pretty good agent. Getting onto you before anyone else does. Seriously, if he nabs you the way he plans too, he'll have carved out a neat little career for himself down at Legoland."

"Your remark about peeling him alive might have been prescient then. That would be regrettable, though I'm guessing here since I don't experience regret. I'm sure he's a fine Feeb, so perhaps it's best if we never met. But about the kiddies: my rationale isn't really the point. I can only say that in this declining world of horror, monstrosity and the ultimate depravity of humans enslaving other humans for money, well, children need to be protected. They must be saved, nurtured, if that can even be done anymore. Then, like a good Republican businessman, all bets are off. When they grow up and choose to buy my product, I'll even give them a discount. But until then, I'll do what must be done to keep them from being turned into sex slaves or live meat for predators whose time in this world has been a great overstay. These ophidian men, Medusan women for whom children are solely the loam from which profits grow—I shall make of them mulch for roses, if I have my way. And I'm usually very good at getting my way, modest as that is."

"You keep a low profile. Whether that counts as modesty, I don't know."

"You remember that picture I gave you on George's Island just before you nailed Detective Andromeda in the deltoid with a Kalashnikov?"

"Sure, sure—you old sentimental slob."

"Now who's being naïve?"

"I don't know, Null. I don't know anymore. Can't we dissolve this unwilling partnership of ours? Can't you just let me go?"

"I don't think you really want me to do that. And I won't let it happen until I'm finished. And that should take years…"

"Guess again, Meth Mogul. Joel and I had a sit-down with some Eastern Bloc jamoke named Innokenty."

"Yes, I know. Mr. Gorets. But I don't think Ingushetia qualifies as one of those Eastern Bloc countries. They're more in line with Chechnya, yet are defiantly non-Chechen."

"He's running you down, Null."

"Not yet, but I think that's his mission, unless he can snipe a few in my brain rather than having to get down in the dirt with me at street-level. Where I'll have the advantage."

"You think he's a hitter."

"You have a better take?"

"He's lazy. I think he wanted Joel and I to do his dirty work for him."

"How did we get back to the territory of telling jokes so fast?"

"You should have had that cigarette, Null. You seem a little jumpy, which isn't like you. *(Which it probably is, but I'd never let you know that. Oh, no.)*"

"I'm very possibly close to having a psychotic break, being that I haven't slept in a couple of weeks."

"You're not exaggerating."

"You know I'm not."

"How do you even know this?"

"Small indications, little show-and-tells. I sweat a lot and I'm losing weight. It's the same with the celebrated Ingush hitman. I have a man trolling the dark web twenty-four-seven for new likely challengers to the vaunted top spot as shot caller of the Gangsta Boyz."

"So what do you want *me* to do about it? He hasn't broken any laws yet."

"You think that's ever stopped the Feebs before?"

"Probably not."

"We have bigger fish to fry than a gypsy hitter working for a defunct crime boss, pricey though he may be. Greedy though he is."

"Sounds pretty big to me."

"This is much bigger."

"Trying to build suspense? School me the fuck already."

"No need to school you. All that's necessary is to supply you with one crib note for a pop quiz."

"I'm dying already."

"The kids say that when another kid makes a good joke— they're dying. They're dead."

"Null, for Christ's sake!"

"I was kidnapped by a cult member who staged City Hall for the murder of a child to convince me his cult meant business in hiring me to help them kidnap children. They're collecting boys. They only want boys. Boys who can *sing* yet."

"But why that? Who in their right mind—"

"You're not remembering your catechism, Kay. Think altar boys. Choir practice maybe?"

She shook her head as if to remove the cobwebs and enunciated dully. "The Catholic Church. Someone's kidnapping children and..."

"That's right, Kay. And selling them to the Catholic Church."

"What's the going rate for a child?"

"A child's life on the street isn't worth a penny, but the Catholic Church could easily pay thousands a head. Tens of thousands, if need be. They have the deepest pockets in world history."

"Holy shit. And with the vast tangle of all the civil cases, no one wants to do a criminal investigation."

"Not of the church, no. Those criminals must walk. They commit atrocities under cloak of holy orders. They can just buy their victims off for pennies on the dollar. But there's a loophole. Maybe the Feebs would want to look into it *if t*hey knew who the kidnappers actually were. If they weren't so holy. Maybe Agent Thrawn might like to make his bones with that. Forget about the insignificant, incipient local Beantown drug cartel calling themselves the Gangsta Boyz. Really just a bunch of glorified street-corner hoods. Agent Thrawn is way out of their league."

"Out of *your* league, you're sayin'."

"Let's not carry a good thing too far."

"Well, he could certainly go after the kidnappers without breaking any government taboos. No dicey, uphill arguments to fight against anyway. The president's Catholic, as you know."

"Yes, I know. But it gets even better for our Agent Thrawn."

"I can't wait to hear."

"The ones doing the kidnapping? They're an actual pagan cult."

"We have pagan cults. Right here in Beantown. They used to occupy Cambridge, but being priced out of there, they migrated to Somerville, but were priced out of there, so now they hang on tenuously there, so they definitely need the money."

"Yes. They do. And this one is an old one, known as Ordo Templi Orientis."

"That's nuts. You're talking Aleister Crowley? The guy whose castle Jimmy Page of Zeppelin bought to flex demonic? Is that even for real?"

"Boleskine House. He sold it in the 90s. All for show—never really lived there."

"That's the one."

"It's real enough. The Order of Oriental Templars has been involved with the Catholic Church since the fourteenth century. I mean until the church, for political reasons and the usual canon of pre-greed, excommunicated and burned them all at the stake."

Boyd dropped her smoldering cigarette to the oriental area rug and stamped it out with her stocking feet without acknowledging the slightest discomfort. "You're saying... You're actually telling me that...the Knights Templar...are trying to make a *comeback*?"

"That's a good way of putting it."

"I thought it was politics that made strange bedfellows."

"They do, but none more strange and profane than those made by religion."

ELEVEN

"I've never trucked it up to this level of Moakley before."

"Be glad we didn't have to truck it down to Big Mama's office in Worcester."

Like all Federal Courthouses, the I.M. Pei-styled John Jacob Moakley affair was just as bleak and grim as any other, despite its sweeping, modernist crescent shapes, its verdant, pleasant (albeit barren of people) courtyard overlooked by four stories of glass, its brilliant view of Boston Harbor hard by its famed North End, its Romanesque portico entryway and its human-scab-red bricks offsetting yet another four stories of glass. The bricks almost matched those of America's oldest streets in Boston but didn't quite. Its inner sterility screamed doom down its arteries of hallways; its rushing air from motion detector heating and cooling ducts both contained and gave out an unsavory odor of formaldehyde not just from the bristly carpeting found about the place in patches, (adding a sad stab of color to the place) but from too many sources to name.

"Why not Beantown?"

"Washington doesn't always err on the side of centralization."

"Fuck, who's the A-USA again?"

"You'll love the dude, Kay—a real old-timey Republican. He'll be all gung-ho about prosecuting an Afro-American drug cartel. The first in New England. He'll drool and probably make a pass at you – or he would if I weren't there to protect you."

"I can handle myself, Joel."

"One of the reasons you're here."

"I told you I got a better story than the usual racial ballyhoo."

"Yeah. Right. The Catholic Church. You know this guy's a full-out Christer."

"I'm going with the Knights Templar and their pagan activities. It can be a damn coincidence that their criminal pursuits have the inciting factor and happen to be done on behalf of the Catholic Church. People in Boston are used to evil having been done by Catholic priests in the archdiocese. It's the new catechism of shame."

"*Ordo Templi Orientis* – not quite the Knights."

"You know what I'm sayin'."

"Don't bang that drum until you have to. It's a bitter communion the politicos choke on swallowing. And you know—"

"Yeah. I heard. The President's Catholic. Who's this guy again?"

"Rocco Telluric. Likes to be called Muck, his old college football nickname. For having rolled around in enough of it."

"Jesus, not another BC jock processed out of Harvard Law."

"Columbia—Muck's one renegade move."

"Straight arrow?"

"Bent like all of 'em."

"Joel, you sound bitter."

"I want off accounting. Numbers make me feel divorced from humanity."

"Wake up, Joel. You're a forensic accountant working for the FBI. You *are* divorced from humanity."

"I know, believe me. But I need another chance."

"You can always date me, Joel."

"I can? You're serious. I think you're serious."

Boyd squeezed his shoulder a little. "You've got a chance."

Agent Thrawn badged them into a suite of offices occupied by the large part of the 100-plus Assistant First Circuit US Attorneys in various roles of criminal and civil. They passed the young prim, plain para-legal receptionist in a neat strawberry blonde bob, zero makeup and conservative rust-colored blazer who nodded at Agent Thrawn, recognizing who he was before he had a chance to wave for her attention. Her expression was practiced, vacuous, masking intimacies Agent Thrawn was actually afraid to think about. Every time he passed her, he realized she knew this, and wondered further if there was a secret contest between them as to whom would crack the first smile.

Rocco "Muck" Teluric's office door was open as he diligently tapped on the keys of his government-issue Lenovo laptop, citing chapter and verse case law that related to a questionable search and seizure, both Agent Thrawn and Lieutenant Boyd allowed the sound to glissade over their hearing as they missed the sense altogether. The fake wood-grained plastic slide-in placard beneath his name read simply "Interdiction." Young and athletic, wearing a too-starched blue shirt with a blazing paisley tie, Muck waved them in, and they sat down in two black leatherette chairs angled to face Muck as he sat at his black Ikea desk at the vertex of their angle. He was stocky, blocky, short, but with fine features that fought for notice with a buzz-cut military-style helmet of shocked hair. He chortled a parting remark to the party at the other end of the line and was all smiles as he stood up and reached out for Agent Thrawn's hand to pump it enthusiastically.

"Joel, how's it hangin' brother?"

"I forgot to check."

"You're being wry. I've always liked that about you, Joel. Who takes the time to be wry anymore?"

"You only think that because you're a short-timer, Muck."

"And don't I know it, but I don't see why a unicorn such as yourself wants to saw off his horn just to run not quite as fast along with all the other horses. You realize you're not really street, right?"

"You do this every time I come here."

"Yeah, sure Joel, but fuck me. This time you want a John Doe No-Knock Warrant for an address that's as-yet to be determined?"

"I know, Muck."

"Yeah, Muck, he may not be street, but I sure as fuck am."

"Oh, lady, I sure as hell see that, now that you pointed it out." He snapped his fingers. "Geeze, you're Boston Police Lieutenant Kay Boyd. I bet they even heard about you up at Main Justice. You is a legend, sister."

"Thanks for the compliment, Telluric, but that's more than just stretching it a little bit, I think."

"Don't play games with *me*, Kay. You can call me Muck. Everyone does. And maybe you're not too well-known at Main Justice, but we know *all* about you down here at Moaks. Believe it."

"Do you now?"

"You walked point on BPD's Organized Crime Task Force. Beautiful prosecutions, tasty cases. It was only a matter of time before the politics ate you alive. Truth be told, it's brutal down there at One Schroeder. And then you had that fucking hump on your back."

"I'm not exactly hump-backed, Muck."

"He's talking about Wilmer Quark."

"Judas priest, what do you *do* with humps like Quark down at Legoland? Guy's put in his twenty, begs for mandatory retirement, which policy ain't gonna give him, busies himself with bullshit and winds up an infected absolute pain in the ass for anyone comes near enough to him to catch a whiff of obnoxious failure. He's a pustule just won't pop, that one."

"Muck, you do know how to woo a gal."

Agent Thrawn nodded and grinned a grin broad enough to seriously challenge his hairbrush mustache. "Yup. That nails it. Wilmer's so damn bad at it, Muck, he can't even fail laterally, never *mind* upwards."

"So he just stays a grunt and grind human hemorrhoid down at Legoland, backbone of the Feebs, pride of the agency and all that happy horseshit."

"Your office don't got one of those, Muck?"

"Can't say that we do. Everyone's processed along so fast here that even the really good ones disappear before a regime change can give them a strong hint to hit the cobbles."

"You're hittin' 'em pretty soon too, right?"

"Depends on who wins the general."

"I'll say right now the warrant's valid. We'll get more than enough probable cause for at least one of two possible cases."

"Listen, Kay, this ain't no game license—it ain't a permit to go fishin'. We need PC before, not after the fact."

Boyd leaned forward halfway across the faux stone top of the Ikea desk and glared at Muck. "Fuck probable cause, Muck. We're goin' hunting, plain and simple. Joel's gonna get his first kill and I'm gonna be his guide to make sure he don't miss."

"I dig the Hemingway comin' out the mouth of a babe and all, but I need to know you got some kind of solid collateral before I set you guys up with a fourth-amendment blank check."

"I got the Catholic church," Boyd deadpanned.

Agent Thrawn's face went red, and he gritted spotless teeth. "Jesus, Kay, I told you not—"

"Too late, my man, the pope's out of the bag."

"I thought you said he was Catholic."

"Oh, he is. Don't let his appearance of apostasy fool you."

"I'm intrigued."

"Don't worry about your church, Muck. It's an end user we don't need to bother with. But the cult that's working for them? They'll make a nice target."

"Cult? As in Satanic? Judas priest. You wanna take a bygone trip back to the nineties?"

"Well, Muck, the church likes them. How Satanic could they possibly be?"

"Now, I'm worried. Whenever somebody tells me not to worry, little alarm bells start ringing. Joel, can you crunch some numbers on me, please."

"Sure, Muck. Let me tell you a little tale about the Order of the Knights Templar."

Muck held up his hands as a stop sign.

"Dude, save that one and sell me on your drug cartel, instead. Let's leave religion and the dark arts for dessert after you guys grab lunch."

"Lunch?" asked Boyd, confused.

"Sure, Lieutenant. You're not just going to wait around here while I get your warrant, are you? This isn't exactly a place anyone wants to hang out in."

Boyd slid back into her chair, showing Muck her palms, smiling. "I get it. So you know."

"Of course he knows. I told you he was one of the good ones, Kay."

"So, okay, Muck. We've got the Gangsta Boyz latest Grandma's House location, which is tough enough to do and a lead on their boogie man shot caller's latest illegal squat—"

Muck swiveled a bit from side to side, twiddling his fingers. "But again, no PC. A big, fat goose egg."

"Those eggs sometimes hatch, Muck. You know this."

"We'll sew it up PC, Muck."

"How? With a plant?"

"A squat has no expectation of privacy," asserted Agent Thrawn.

"Winner gets a kewpie! That's for this unknown space zombie masterminding New England's first and biggest drug cartel, right? Sure it is. So, fine and dandy then. I'll have a warrant in your hands for that before you leave the building. Then whatever that legal search yields will justify a no-knock on Grandma's House, if I can spin it just right."

"A floating location for the purposes of conspiring to commit a full-spectrum of drug-related felonies."

"Now *that's* a tasty opening. I'll use it. How come you never bothered to use that JD you got, Joel? You might have been good at it, y'know."

"I'm a Suffolk University alum, Muck."

"Ha!" Muck guffawed, licking his somewhat froggy lips and shaking his head. "Say no more, my man. Still, I'll use that precious one-liner as the capper in the carte blanche warrant I'll get when I put Judge Bob Droke on the case. His daughter OD'd last year, so he's got a rock-steady hard-on for drug runners. Serve him up a cartel and I'll have to bring an umbrella because he'll spooge all over the place."

"This may be an awkward time to bring it up, Muck, but what about that dessert?"

Muck's eyes narrowed and his fine face bore down on her with a puckish grin. "Kay, bring Joel back with you after lunch and we'll see whether that particular soufflé rises or falls."

"Warrant number two coming up," replied Agent Thrawn.

"Serve up good ingredients, Joel, or no soufflé for you."

"I'll make it rise if I have to infuse it with helium."

"The North End's right around the corner, Kay. Take Joel out for a pizza. His accountant's brain seems starved for carbs. Thinks I can whip up a souffle off nary a fart."

"Pizza's good enough for me, Agent Thrawn."

"By your leave, Lieutenant Boyd."

They left AUSA Teluric's office arm in arm, mocking romance, and as the inter-office DMs on his screen emitted low bleats, he said to himself, "Ain't thay cute. They probably really mean it, and everybody knows it but them." He sat back shaking his head in amusement.

———

"So, you're saying this place is like the "Soup Nazi" on that show?"

"But with pizza. I don't even like pizza."

"You will when I'm through with you."

"What are you intending, Lieutenant Boyd?"

"Why to woo you with tomato sauce, dough and cheese, Agent Thrawn."

"They'd better have some pretty great combos on that pizza to win my troth, Lieutenant."

"Cool your jets, Agent. They only serve tomato and cheese—"

"Only one kind of pizza?"

"That's it, Joel."

"That's positively unAmerican, Kay."

It was one of Boston's usual schizophrenic late-Spring days when the sun was shining at a blistering hot seventy-eight degrees and the wind was an icy remnant of the Montreal Express winds that each year blew Indian Summer in October to the dead of winter in November. No one knew how to dress for this weather. Everyone in the city was either over or underdressed and at the end of a long day could wind up shivering with a penetrating chill reverberating within them and topped off by sunburned face and hands. Not unlike most couples, on the walk from Moakley to the North End, down Atlantic Avenue toward Hanover Street, the huddled close into one another and with free hands wiped the sweat off their faces.

Hanover Street was uncharacteristically broad for the oldest area of town that went back to the early 17th century and whose other streets were hilly, narrow, twisted and conflicted with contrary one-way directions and parking that was so cramped and deficient that a more than a few lifelong residents made a profit off scarce resident parking spaces. It was chock-a-block with restaurants, coffee bars and pastry shops. Across from Mike's Pastry a block and a half down from Parmenter Street was a brick-framed, olive drab rolling steel door diner with a Coca-Cola sign that read Galleria Umberto. It would have been plain and unimpressive, as it certainly was in its late afternoon closure, but for the fact of a line that went out the door and around the block.

The clientele was assorted and entirely Democratic: students, rockers, lawyers, cops, bankers, road and construction workers, secretaries and goons all waited patiently, quietly, as the line slowly contracted into the store front. There were no arguments, no loud shouts of impatience, no boisterous insults.

"That's a long line, Kay. You think it's worth it for plain pizza?"

"It'll move, don't worry."

"It's weird. No one's complaining or making a scene. Are we still in Boston?"

"They don't want to be denied their pizza. The Pizza Nazi has no patience for impolite behavior."

"You're joking."

"Joel, these people, me included, are deadly serious about their pizza."

"Perhaps you and I could jump the line and present our credentials."

"Sorry, buddy," intruded a honk from two couples up. "I got FBI credentials and they cut no ice at all with these guys."

"Jesus H. Christ!" announced a tall black woman dressed as if an officer of some bank branch who stood in front of Thrawn and Boyd. "If that damn Feebie don't quiet down, he gon' get us all kicked out of line! And I got boxes comin'!"

"Cockblocked," Boyd observed drily.

"We've stepped into another dimension in the multiverse and I'm the last one to know it."

"I'm gon' get my damn boxes," the black woman in front of them muttered unself-consciously.

"Boxes. What the hell does she mean by *boxes?*" asked Agent Thrawn.

"Obviously, she phoned ahead," sighed Boyd. "Maybe we should have too. I'm famished."

"People do that?"

"They do, because sometimes—maybe too many times—they just run out."

"They run out of pizza, so you have to *reserve* it?"

"Yes, but there's a price."

"Other than money. Sometimes even in Boston, money just don't count."

"So what's the real price, then?"

"You have to have it take it with. They won't let you eat it here."

"We could take it with us back to Moaks."

"If we did that, we might not get any at all," Boyd said ruefully. "So to go is a no go."

There's nothing quite like the sound of a mass shushing in a long line waiting for pizza amid raucous traffic sounds of mid-day in Boston's North End—all varieties of honking failed to quash the desperate hush of the unrequited love of pizza. After interminable minutes of shifting weight from one foot to the other, idly checking phones and trading occasional muted flirtations, they at last crossed the threshold into the pizza Valhalla itself. Agent Thrawn's slackened mouth made it look as if he were about to succumb to heatstroke.

"There's nothing here," Agent Thrawn half-whined. "Nothing but brick and tile, a counter with a cash register and picnic tables. This is a restaurant?"

"Consider it a food hall."

"Why is this line getting longer again even as we get near enough to order?"

"I think they added stuff to their menu. It used to be just bread, pizza and dough."

"So you're saying they're coming for the arancini and calzone? One kind only? Are we in a pizza depression and this is a run on the pizza bank?"

"Probably for today. They shut down in fifteen minutes."

"I have to tell people I spent my lunch hour in a line for plain old cheese and tomato pizza with a pizza-obsessed police lieu-tenant and didn't get a single bite?"

"I'll give you a bite of mine, Joel, if you behave. Because, I don't know about you, but if I have to shoot somebody, I'm going to at least get myself a slice."

"Be still my heart. The line is moving."

Boyd grabbed his arm and allowed her head to rest upon his shoulder as they moved forward four baby steps, then were stopped by the loud clattering of trays onto the concrete tiled floor. There was the incomprehensible shouting of a male voice, possibly in Italian, possibly in distorted, accented English, and then two young men escorted three middle-aged women brusquely past the line and out the door. And then the voice became louder, enunciating each syllable clearly:

"No! Pizza! For! *You!*"

"Is this why no one is eating at the picnic tables and taking their slices outside?"

"I think so, Joel. Everyone's afraid of offending—well, you know."

"The Pizza Nazi. You're telling me everyone's afraid of offending the Pizza Nazi. You're a police lieutenant who's seen action in the field and, so I've heard, has fired her department-issue sidearm as well as a criminal property AK-47 and you're afraid of offending a little man behind a counter in a low-rent pizzeria who might refuse to sell you his piddling wares. Am I being pranked? Isn't all this staged for my benefit? C'mon, Kay, come clean. This whole thing is just a gag to haze the forensic accountant from the Feebs."

"Joel, you're going to be next in a few minutes. Please don't fuck up the order and get us tossed out. I really do have my heart set on scarfing up that pizza. So be polite, use good posture, stand directly on the X marked off on the floor before the counter, speak clearly and simply. Don't try to make small talk. The Pizza Nazi deplores and abhors small talk. That alone could conceivably deprive us of our pizza. Okay, Joel. It seems you're up."

She pushed him forward gently and he almost fell over, but he managed to recover himself, moving and speaking robotically and clipped, which proved a great success with the Pizza Nazi, who smiled and nodded after bestowing upon him eight hot slices in paper plates on a plastic tray along with a folded up paper box to put it all in—the meaning of that being unsubtly clear.

"My hero!" Boyd exclaimed.

"I gather we have to leave now."

"No wonder you're a Feeb, Joel. You deduce things so sharply and ably."

After demolishing their slices from the box on a bench in the smallish Rose Kennedy Park on Atlantic Avenue, they hurried back to the Galleria Umberto food hall only to find the olive drab rolling steel door dragged all the way down and locked up tight. The place was as formidable and unassailable as the local Federal Reserve Bank (just half a mile down Atlantic Avenue across from South Station) after business hours.

"Think if we both fired our sidearms at the same time we could lift that rolling steel motherfucker? Agent Thrawn proposed "Check for intruders, maybe grab us ten or twenty slices from the fridge. I bet it's even better heated up on the second day."

"Even unheated. I'd eat it cold with a beer a six in the morning without complaint," Boyd admitted.

"That's a good idea."

"Fuck the friends of Bill W."

"Fuck 'em—we need pizza."

"Do you think twenty'll be enough?"

"No. Maybe forty?"

"Think they have a handy carry bag in the kitchen? You know, for deliveries?"

"They don't deliver."

"Damn them."

"I told you, Joel. I warned you. And here you are, Jonesing for plain tomato and cheese pizza cut in squares off a rectangular bakery oven tray. No frills."

"Fuck anchovies. I'm going to live on this pizza until I die."

"Let's walk back to Moaks. You can undergo your cold turkey on the way."

"I revere you, oh Pizza Nazi. Yet I despise you!"

"I'm quoting you about this later, after you recover, Joel. You realize that, don't you?"

"I'm sorta counting on it."

"I knew you would."

TWELVE

"You're not worried."

"Think what you're asking."

"I know. You never worry."

"I don't feel a thing."

"Oh, but you did though, Joseph Xavier. Yes, Mr. Null, you *did* feel some things, especially with me. You don't lie, so don't say you didn't."

"I lie frequently now, but I had to learn how to do it all over again to do it so that it counted."

"Lie to me, then. I don't give a fuck."

"You give a fuck. That's why you're here."

"I'm just here to tell you you're burned. This nice little squat has been burned. Better bug out."

And if a squat could ever have been considered nice, the roomy first-floor studio apartment in Mattapan where Null chose to reside was exactly that. Pirated electricity alone made the room fairly bright, but the spotless white walls and ceiling reflecting that light made it nearly blinding. The floor was painted thickly with a glossy black that added a misty glare to the space. There was a Bose sound system that had fallen off the back of a truck. There was a Tempur-

Pedic mattress atop an iron frame. There was a refrigerator empty of food containing a kilo of Riley's newest and best batch of gak yet.

"Was it you? Did you burn it, Kay?" Null asked, unblinking.

"I didn't have to. The Feebs got resources. A little trip down to Moaks, a chat with an AUSA and forensic-accountant street-and-field naif Special Agent Joel Thrawn got us a bunch of warrants. They got a John Doe just for you. Joel wants to bust up the Gangsta Boyz and put you away. You been far too successful, Null. Your cartel-in-the making's finally on the federal radar, so any juice you got down at One Schroeder ain't gonna make a whit of difference. Congrats for that, by the way."

"Really? I knew it would be a case of you get what you pay for. They bribe, pretty cheap anyway, the BPD. That's a given."

"Cheap enough. After all, I do it for free."

"You have a stake in what I'm doing, and you know it."

"I don't know anything of the kind. So we fucked, then you went back to being a crazed, homicidal maniac—boo hoo. I don't got a stake in your business, whatever that happens to be, and I don't want a stake in your business. Ever."

"I'm a finder of lost children."

"Really. You. Gangster number one in Boston. A zombie. A dead man – the *bogeyman* playing into more criminal superstitions than Batman or the Shadow ever did."

"I don't have the power to cloud men's minds, Kay. I can only make them think more clearly."

"Right, while you're torturing them to the point where death is the only release. Oh, don't look shocked."

"I'm not shocked, Kay. You know I can't be shocked. I'm only listening."

"That's the story out about you on the street, Null. And I know it has to be true. The only thing that puzzles me though, is, since they *know* they're going to die and you don't hide that information from them, how do they wind up telling you anything?"

"Death is odorless, colorless. It has no character and no flavor. We add that. And in some way, if you had to attribute any real quality to death at all—still void of character in its indifference—it's a relief. Death can and will free everyone from the worst of all conditions life provides, relieve every painful kind of agony and in depriving you of that and everything else that comes along with it, you could argue that death was your friend, kind enough in the end to save you from all the terrible things I will do to you if you don't tell me what I need to know. And I'm like death in a way because I feel nothing, experience nothing but the dull domino logic of physics exerting its routinized yet random chaos upon the world where I'm only a complicit pawn, if anything a servant of death. Sometimes willing, sometimes not. I'm just a minor instrument, a blended voice in one of the many choruses that make up the symphony of absurdity that plays the only music of man's brief existence in the universe that will wink out before the acceptance of the fact that humanity is reflexive, fascinated with itself, relating itself to matter and energy that had allowed it to exist as only a fluke, a tick, yet still stubbornly assured of its supremacy, its primacy and the greatness of its value until it quietly ceases to exist. A casualty of a cataclysm."

"You're the cataclysm, Null, nothing else."

"And that doesn't even matter, as death in the end will make us all free."

"You don't even notice how you bore us all with these justifications for your being a stone vicious criminal, calling yourself things you're not..."

"I never do that, Kay. I may not be the alpha, but I am the omega."

"You're a psycho, Null, who needs to be put down like the sickly cur you are."

"I thought you loved me, Kay. Yet you want to murder me. So here you are: a voice in the chorus because that's completely absurd."

"Sometimes absurdity has a kernel of interior logic that makes sense when its conclusion is reached, Null."

"You ready to reach that conclusion today, Kay?"

"I should be, but I'm not."

"I don't think I could reach the Glock in my pocket in time if you were. This is your moment, Kay. This is the time."

"What do you want from me?!" Boyd shrieked, half in despair, half in the conviction that this was only a small part in her life—a life that was only going more wrong with every effort she made to make it go right. *"What do you want!"*

"I want to know where the local chapter of Ordo Templi Orientis is keeping the kids it's been kidnapping."

"I find it funny that you, the Pied Piper of Codman Square for Christ's sake, wants to find out where the kidnapped children are even as you exploit the most wretched little tykes to make drug deliveries for you."

"It's a good system, Kay. The cops either catch and release or put them in the foster system and I wind up getting them, anyway. With me, they have safety, some care and maybe a future. I even have a Social Services expert on my side to run things complete with schooling, nutrition—even some fun in the world normal kids are supposed to have."

"I can't tell you just how absurd that is. How ridiculous, your drug-dealer daddy daycare. I knew Mrs. Coelacanth, a professional. Knew how to bilk the system on the side of the righteous. She was one of the good ones." Her eyes narrowed and her jaw set. "Until you got your mitts on her."

"It was either me, or life on Social Security with a nearly empty joke of a state worker pension plan. Naturally she chose me."

"You make it sound like we all had a choice to be involved with you. But we didn't. You know we didn't. I know I didn't. Is that how it works with you? You plan these things in that pitifully corrupted, chemically masticated brain of yours?"

"You'd be surprised to learn just how many things simply fall into my lap. If you live in the span of the dark negative, a surprising number of good things come your way."

"Like me. I'm a thing that fell into your lap. A thing to be used and discarded."

"You're an important person, Kay. Don't fish for compliments or you may wind up catching the brutal fact that we're all to be used and discarded. Life is only for the living, only for as long as you're living. It's entirely indifferent to us when our moment has passed." Null cocked his head. "Or has been taken away from us."

"The Feebs—their nasty boys in their stupid get up—they're comin' down on this squat hard sometime today. Soon, too soon. We might both get caught here if we don't get movin'."

"I don't suppose Agent Thrawn bribes cheap."

"He doesn't bribe at all."

"I should burn it down."

"Why bother when they have your prints and your DNA already?"

"Call it urban renewal."

"Mattapan can take a fire on another ruined squat. But the crack crowd on the upper two floors will probably die."

"I have no compassion. Like me, they're dead, anyway. They won't notice it."

"Let's put this in a context you can relate to: It'd be an impractical effort that'd possibly cost you unwanted attention if you were to burn it down. Slipping out costs you nothing, gets you out fast and reasonably clean, which would be the point."

"I'm always ready to travel."

"Yeah, you surely are. Let's see if I can get this a right: A Glock 17 in one pocket, Heckler and Koch P30 with suppressor in the other; a loaded bump-stocked AR-15 Velcro-belted to your torso in front and a short, truncated machete hanging down from another lanyard in the back. Oh, I didn't want to omit the flak jacket you wear underneath it all. How do you even move with all that on you, let alone walk your funny little walk?"

"I walk a funny little walk because The Family sliced through my right hamstring. It knitted funnily enough to give me that funny walk when it finally healed."

"I bet those Gangsta Boyz of yours think you do it to look cool. And why not? You're the shot caller."

"There's no reason for them to think otherwise, is there?"

"Only when it's time for them to put a bullet in your head."

"They'll be as dead as I am then when the play is made."

"They could get lucky."

"No. Even in putting me down they'd never get lucky. Luck abandoned them long before I took them up."

"You're not really dead though."

"The certificate's on file. No one's bothered to correct it. They know it down at One Schroeder, but no one makes any bother about it. I'm the known unknown. And whether you accept it or don't, all of this that I've taken you through is a post-mortem."

"That's a fallacy. I knew you when you were alive."

"I was technically alive then, but was that really any kind of a life? The ponies, the dope, the petty servility to crime, the cheap beneficiary of evil. I'm much more alive now in my post-mortem state than I was before."

"You know I'm talking about me. Why can't you admit it? Why are you such an unfeeling prick?"

"You know why. You made me this way."

Boyd grabbed him by his seemingly scrawny shoulders, which felt like hot iron in her grasp. She released him, shook her head, turned away.

"I didn't! I never chose you for that. It just happened!"

"No, it happened because you chose me for death. You pulled the switch, and I can't help the raw fact that chaos switched it right straight back around to you. You earned what happened just as I did."

"Well, you and I are going to earn some quick lockup in the slam if you don't close up shop and get the hell out of here, and me with you."

"You still object to a burn out?"

"You still think killing some crack addict rando's is a model of efficiency?"

"You're right. It isn't. And the model of efficiency that the BPD is assures me that this intact squat with my prints and DNA all over it won't be a threat—"

"Yeah, except unlike the BPD, with all their bullshit, may not have an actual serious crime lab, but the Feebs sure as hell do."

"You're telling me I should be worried about Special Agent Forensic Accountant Joel Thrawn?"

"I am. I worry about the guy. He found you without my help."

"This is Boston, so Thrawn got some emails off the servers, an AUSA at Moaks invoking the rule change from Rule 41(b), limiting where the Feebs could seek warrants, to 41(b)(6), where a judge can issue warrants allowing the Feebs to virtually hack in wherever they like to secure incriminating communications. You know, there *is* something admirable in the forensic accountant's approach that applies these exploits to the present moment."

Boyd paced the short space and threw up her hands.

"Do you really want to go out in a blaze of glory when the nasty boys batter down the door and start pumping their burp guns?"

"Holding court has its appeal, but since nothing could ever actually appeal to me, we should just leave." Null took a clear plastic blue cigarette lighter from his topcoat pocket and flicked the flame, held it in front of him and stared at it, fish-eyed. Boyd slapped it out of his hand.

"We have to move, Null. I keep hearing them in my head."

"We can go when you tell me the other thing you have to tell me."

"About the guy."

"The hitter."

"I know this. He manipulated a meeting with me and Joel, tried to recruit us in some plan to get to you – presumably to put you down. We ran the mutt. Came up as Innokenty Gorets, an Ingush contractor, who doesn't exist. No other records anywhere. He's a ghost staying at the Copley Westin wanting to hunt a zombie who's hunting me and Agent Thrawn."

"I don't have to hunt you, Kay. And Agent Thrawn only *thinks* he wants to find me, but you know he doesn't. Yet you have to help him find me, even though you know already where I am, who I am and what I will do. Count on knowing that I *will* do it. The thing you don't want to think about it."

"I'm thinking about it now."

"No one knows this man who thinks himself a perfect shadow of death."

"Two men who don't exist canceling each other out. I can live with that."

"*Innocent Mountain Man*—the hitter's clever name."

"You don't speak Ingush."

"But I read everything."

"Where do you find the time?"

"It's easy when you never sleep."

"Time for that when you're dead."

"Not even then."

"I don't want to be here when they catch up with you, Null."

He grabbed her by the wrist with a quick jerk and twisted it.

"We'll leave together at a brisk pace. I hope my limp won't throw you off balance."

"No problem. Drop in the bucket."

"The Feebs are disappointing."

"They may be, but how would you even know?"

"Well, they're taking their time, now, aren't they?"

———

The neo-classical Greek portico of Bethlehem Adoption and Youth Placement Services was strategically illuminated to look placid and staid, unquestionably pretty enough to demand a quiet, momentary gaze before entering. The dark of night was the best time of all to see the majestic building, and like many such buildings across the world, what went on inside belied its appearance. A white Tempo Traveler Mini Bus pulled up in front of the entrance and that part of Herrick Road on the cool green historic grounds of the old seminary campus was so quiet that the sounds the vehicle made, rolling on smooth tarmac, braking to a full stop and cutting the engine so that the absence of that noise was a noise unto itself would have seemed deafening to any onlooker. The sound of the bus doors slamming was jarring at that late hour, but as yet provoked no lit windows in other buildings and houses and no cries for silence.

Two youngish men, one over six feet and the other at only five and a half, one bearded, one cleanshaven, both sporting tribal tattoos on their necks and on visible portions of their arms—both in similar costume of Old Navy tee shirts and blue jeans—but otherwise nondescript—hopped out of the front of the bus together, unconcerned about obstructing the driveway, and slid open the side door and out squirmed and wriggled a dozen young boys and girls of different shapes, sizes and hair color—Asian, African American, LatinX and Caucasian. They spoke among themselves in whispers and didn't have to be told to be quiet twice. Herded along gently by the two men, they assembled in furtive whisperings, in questioning awe and fear, telling one another to shut up or they'd be in even more trouble than they were in already.

The two men made motions to push the boys and girls aside but didn't have to touch them for them to immediately anticipate their need and perform to it. The shorter of the two pushed a tiny, recessed back button placed discreetly into the doorframe and a muted series of chimes sounded. The taller of the two men hiked his shoulders, turned the other and said. *"Ein feste Burg ist unser Gott."*

"What?" asked the short man. "What are you trying to tell me?"

"That's the name of that tune."

"Jesus. Don't get the kids started now that we got them all sleepy and shit."

"They're doing fine."

"They'll conk out right here on the doorstep if she doesn't answer the door already."

"I hear her coming."

Boyish voices piped up questions and complaints.

"Hush yourselves now," said the taller of the two. "You'll have snacks and TV inside if you guys can suck it up for a bit longer." His voice cut with an acid edge and the voices of the children cut with it.

"She takes her time."

"She likes us to know that she doesn't really need the money like we need the money."

"Everybody needs the money."

"Yeah, well, she has the one true God."

"You don't say. You mean the one divided up into thirds."

"That's the one."

The door opened without a sound and Auntie Nonie Fomites stood before them in a black peignoir and incongruous valentine pajama bottoms, her steely exaggerated breasts standing at attention as they always did no matter what she wore. She was a handsome woman with a tortured figure that seemed more plastic than flesh and that had been surgically altered to the point where it did more to repel than attract. Her hair was an obstreperous glistening red that hung straight down.

"You're late boys."

"Dipshit over here got lost and missed an exit on Route Nine."

"You were the navigator, Fuck-wit. Remember?"

"I remember that you didn't know how to use the GPS to get here, kept screwing it up until I had to take over and direct you."

"Talk about screw ups, that's the biggest one right there. You couldn't direct traffic."

"Stop bickering, you two. I don't care how long you been married, take the damn kids and sit 'em down in the cafeteria. One of you can keep an eye on 'em, give 'em some hot chocolate with more sedatives in it. I don't care which one of you does it, just don't overdose 'em like last time. It took weeks for us to scrub off the massive amount of shit *that* escapade dragged us all into. So pay attention this time. If you fuck up the bribe money comes out of O.T.O—*not* Bethlehem."

"Those are some pretty hot knockers you got there, Auntie. Up in an all-night salute, if you know what I mean," the short one oozed.

"Thanks, Dickweed. I had 'em put in just to torment schmoes like you. Don't they teach you tact down at your Hermetic Temple of the Golden Dawn?"

"You know Thelema, Auntie. Do what thou wilt shall be the whole of the law?"

"How could I forget."

"Don't get snide with me, Auntie. Giving us warehousing privileges allows you to triple dip."

"Quadruple dipping, you mean. You forget that with the kiddies we get routed to us from INS officers separating illegal kiddiewinks from their mommies and daddies at the southern border, the government pays us twice, state and federal. Income tax in reverse."

"Who says kidnapping doesn't pay?"

"Some TV show. SUV."

"That's SVU. Sexual violence unit, not sports utility vehicle, numbnuts."

"Special victims' unit, buttmunch."

"Okay, ladies, let's break it up. Buttmunch, have Numbnuts go and watch over the kiddiewinks in the commissary then and you and I can have a chat in my office."

"Hey, I'm more senior than he is. Why don't I rate?"

"Because numbnuts, he hasn't been steadily ogling my tits like you."

"That's only because he's afraid one of 'em might poke him in the eye."

Auntie Nonie shook her head, let out an exaggerated sigh and dragged the shorter of the two with her to the small office that was just off the foyer to left as you entered Bethlehem. Eighty years in the past, it might have been an oversized cloakroom, but now it was the drab, cramped office of a highly profitable and discreet criminal enterprise.

There were no windows in Auntie Nonie's office, and this was one of the reasons why she selected it when Bethlehem ousted the Greater Boston Crisis Center with a fat check, they weren't in any position to refuse. Capitalizing on interviewees' claustrophobia and provoking anxiety always knocked them back on their heels, giving Auntie an edge. Auntie always calculated any interaction with anyone and an exchange to be met by a sharp edge, an immediate, poorly disguised bid for control.

Such a style of communication dovetailed nicely with her past experience as a professional dominatrix. (Her favorite persona still was the "Rubber Nun"—requiring sexually perverted supplicants to polish up her latex habit with beGLOSS PERFECT SHINE Latex Polish, a bottle of which stood out prominently on her desk right then.) She was still considering whether or not to conscript one of the female rug rats to polish her up later on, should she choose to entertain clients again. And the only times in recent memory that she was able to achieve an orgasm was when she was being polished up by some little worm—age and gender just didn't enter into it.

They took their positions in the room and Auntie Nonie in aggressive fashion leaned over the desk just for the sheer joy of watching her little captive imaginary knight from Ordo Templi Orientis flinch and crab into himself as a feeble means of escape. She had him and he was sweating. It was always a wondrous kind of magic just how well her carefully sculpted fake boobs worked. It gave her unbelievable power over the mass of men—even homosexual and bisexual men—who were fascinated by her surgically reinvented mammary glands.

"Which of the Fraters are you anyway?" Auntie Nonie asked offhandedly, putting on a pair of glasses and shuffling papers as if unconcerned.

"It's really close in here," the tall young man replied, turning his head as if looking for a convenient escape route. "Maybe we could open a door?"

The horn-rimmed glasses slid down her nose a bit and she licked her lips. "I think we're going to need a little privacy. You have nothing against that, do you, my little Frater? I don't want your associate to hear."

"Why the privacy?"

"What is it you knights say? Do what thou wilt shall be the whole of the law?"

"It sounds chill enough, but when you get down to it, it's pretty impractical."

"Ah, I see we have a thinking man's O-T-O knight before us."

"Who's we?"

"Good point. There's just us here."

"We have Frater Manticore waiting outside—"

"The little one? It doesn't look like he's reached puberty yet."

"He's got pubes on his junk."

"Are you playing for the other team?"

"I don't suck dick. We got a communal shower down at the temple. That's how I know."

"So we've got him, all the babies in my charge and the squirming worms you brought with you tonight in the commissary, napping by now or getting ready to, I suppose. And you stuck us with little girls again."

"Yeah, so you only give us two-thirds payment on them. You don't do too bad on the deal."

"You *know* the church doesn't want girls. So we maybe get to double dip on them from Commonwealth and federal. Sometimes it's only a single dip, which isn't sustainable."

"Like I said. You clean up no matter what."

"Not when the boys we get are tone-deaf, can't sing a note, and we're back to getting only Commonwealth again."

"And you get to charge us back a twenty-five percent penalty for our trouble."

"Yeah, it's a handling fee, buddy. You're free of the little shits, but *we* have to warehouse them until we can get them adopted or lose them entirely, which is no mean feat, let me tell you."

"You still make out and we barely do."

"That's what you get for being a pagan satanist."

"Magic carries a steep price, I guess."

"What did you drug them with, anyway?"

"Thiopental."

"No doubt a little extra in the hot chocolate."

"That's right."

"Let's hope numbnuts doesn't use too much and kill them."

"Who cares? No one'll miss 'em."

"Well, Frater, frankly *I* would miss the revenue. Beyond that, maybe Thiopental might be a future option. Help us deal with the —umm—less-than manageable overspill."

"They're really no trouble, except one little wiseass kid from Southie. Marion Slaughter. He fights the drug and struggles to run off—he's not getting with the program. A noisemaker. A troublemaker."

"What did the Pater have to say about it?"

"He said if he causes any further trouble to break his little chicken neck and have done with him."

"You can do that here after our meeting if you need to. We have a good many nooks and crannies and vacant rooms where that could be done very discreetly, if you feel so inclined."

"What are you getting at?" snapped the Frater. "We're already losing money providing the church with kiddies they're tossing back either as too female or too tone deaf."

"Don't get excited, Mr. Beanpole. This is about business and only that."

"I didn't mean—"

"Oh, of course you *did* mean," Auntie Nonie said, waving away some of the rogue, copper-hued, cellophaned and tortured tresses that had flipped down comically in front of her left eye. "You boys, you men, I mean. Well, all of you, at least those of you who count anyway, you *always* mean that. There's never a time you don't. Which is good. As it should be. O-T-O is an earth-based calling, right? You follow the pagan laws of nature. So mote it be and all
that—"

"You're thinking of Wicca. That's not us, though we do reap the benefits of power derived from ritual sex
magick—"

"That's right—your Tantric Yoga trick. A couple fucking in the center of your magic circle. Works best with a couple of sexualized young children, hence your expertise in that kind of procurement. Let's see: the male's orgasm is suspended while incantations are made, beckoning the power of the spirits."

"Yes, and of the great demons, the princes of Hell we serve that provide power to the great Liber AL, the book of the law that binds our temple together: Pythius, Merihem, Dis, Mephistopheles, Dagan, Azazel—"

"Ah, Frater, it's Azazel interests me most."

"You think I'm surprised."

"No, Frater. What kind of Frater are you again?"

"I never said. Frater Frazil."

"A cold customer, then?"

"That's what great Pater Hadit gave to me, once I was recognized as being of his divine offspring Ra-Hoor-Khuit—hey, how did you know about that? About Frazil? You're of the decrepit Catholic Church, the embodiment of Babylon in cassocks and habits and clerical collars, beating people to death with mitre and crozier."

"Oh, I know a great many things, my little frazzled Frazil."

"Gee. I haven't heard that one before."

"My church agrees with Catholicism on some points, but we're much more aggressive and dedicated to infiltrating power and turning it toward the end of expanding and inserting the holy kingdom of God into the corridors of power and into all areas of so-called secular living. We are of the Dominionist group called The Family, secretly famous even though we've been on Netflix and in the Rolling Stone. No one wants to think we're that real, and so we gain more power by the day. Bethlehem Adoption and Youth Placement Services is just one of many Fellowship organizations profiting from the legitimate kidnapping of children at the Southern Border for their own good and putting them not only on God's true path but allowing them the sacred duty of financially empowering our franchise more than they could ever know."

"But all that's legal, umm—"

"Just call me Auntie," she said with an undertone of humming. "You'd be a natural member of the Fellowship, if you wanted to be, Frazil. I can see you have a good deal of talent."

"I'm just a holy apostle of Liber Al, Auntie, that's all. I don't see why you need us to provide you with bodies when the federal government does great doing that for you without us."

"Only because our Fellowship is in Congress and the Oval as well."

"I don't get any of it."

"It's part of our being altruistic even to those cults like yours in the spirit of comity. You know Father Bricolage is only collecting young boys who can carry a tune. But your group of disoriented knights managed to fuck that up without half-trying."

"No worse than that whacked out priest who nearly killed Frater Phlegethon with a pea shooter, one of the most favored of the Ra-Hoor-Khuit."

"You wouldn't be making much money at all if we weren't paying you half of what the church does per head, no questions asked, and no vetting done before cutting you a check."

"Why might that be do you think, Auntie?"

"What do *you* think, Frater Frazil?"

"You'd like to swallow us up."

"Yes, we would." She then abruptly stood and in a grand gesture —the spreading of her arms as if she were a stage magician executing a particularly complex and difficult feat of legerdemain —shucked her clothing off entirely. It was as if it had all been fastened together by Velcro and purposely designed to be torn away as if it were just another stage prop, which it was.

Frater Frazil bit his lip and squinted at Auntie, more wary and unsettled than surprised and titillated in some kind of boyish, tumescent awe.

"So, you'd like to swallow me up too while you're at it."

"It does seem that way, doesn't it. I *do* swallow."

"I'm really impressed about how they manage to point up like that."

"It's the surgical answer to the brassiere that Howard Hughes designed for Jane Russell in the movie "The Outlaw.""

"That definitely was a major feat of engineering."

Frater Frazil didn't notice Auntie Nonie eyeing the bottle of beGLOSS PERFECT SHINE Latex Polish on her desk. He thought she was looking at his crotch to see if he had had a response to her magic act. He did, despite making a considerable effort to will it away and seem so much cooler than he actually was.

"Dear little Frazil. How'd you like to make Auntie come?"

THIRTEEN

Knowing the history of Boston's many splendid religious properties, you might find its only cathedral, that of the Holy Cross, the seat of its diocese and the largest in New England, to be a little offputting. This wouldn't be because of its Gothic Revival splendor seeming so out of place in the South End, but rather its lack of the architectural ingenuity and presence of the Thomas Bullfinch original, which was razed in 1862. *That* Holy Cross Cathedral of Boston was an Italian-Renaissance structure dropped in the heart of downtown Boston on its Tontine Crescent (named for the Lorenzo Tontine investment scheme of a shared will) at what is now 214 Devonshire Street, where the old Underwood Typewriter Company used to be for many years, replaced at last by the anonymous business or state agency or tacky real estate placard that now occupies that address in the gray city zone of the present moment.

Still impressive in its stentorian way, the Holy Cross Cathedral at 1400 Washington Street in the South End serves as both cathedral and parish. The Cathedral Parish is made up of Boston's large, local English- and Spanish-speaking congregations, and has swallowed three Archdiocese-wide congregations: the Ge'ez Rite practiced by Ethiopian, Eritrean, and Egyptian Catholics; the German Apostolate; and the Tridentine Mass Catholic community. It also happens to be where the stripped-down, less than splendid, entirely modest (but entirely modern) office of Cardinal Isidore Cromulent was situated, the official seat of the cardinal's function.

There was a reception area that was easily three-times the size of the inner office operated by a rotating contingent of reverent mature ladies who had been in their various pasts secretaries or office managers. They were all zealous volunteers, often with chaste and secret crushes on the cardinal. It was enough for them merely to see to the needs of the exalted personage. No other recompense was necessary.

If you had managed to get an appointment to see His Eminence in this location, you'd find a very different Cardinal Isidore Cromulent than the one bedizened in his resplendent vermillion and white silk-lined cassock with deep scarlet fascia at his residence in the Basilica of Our Lady of Perpetual Sorrow on A Street in South Boston. No, here was a man dressed in a monk's simple robe of brown wool (but with a golden sash), again silk-lined to protect the cardinal's skin from abrasion as this raiment was for the appearance of discomfited penitence, not the fact of it.

The cardinal's inner, private office was soundproofed, void of mess and disorder and freshly dusted. A casual look would betray the fact that little to no work was done there at all – though there was an open "Space Gray" MacBook Pro laptop with sixteen-inch screen sitting on the glass top of the wide, squat mahogany ball-and-claw-foot desk and His Eminence's cellphone left next to it had a screen that pulsated as the thing made a tooth-rattling staccato sound as it vibrated urgently against the glass.

"Shall I get that for you, Eminence?" Father Bricolage asked ingenuously.

"Let it go, Sam. We all know who's calling. How she ever got my number, I'll never know."

"The pagan satanists aren't the most judicious of coconspirators, Eminence. A restrained and disciplined silence seems quite beyond them."

"No, and I'm beginning to doubt their competence in delivering to us the anointed boys who'll join with us in the most worthy pursuit of *Defensores Fidei de Puero*. That woman promises to deliver many more charges to us that the jumped up pagan satanists ever could."

"Then we should of course drop them like a hot potato, Your Eminence."

The cardinal shook his head, let out a self-dramatizing sigh, and sat behind his desk, twiddling his thumbs for a moment. "And yet, Sam, you know why we can't just drop them, don't you?"

"No, Your Eminence, I don't think I do."

Cardinal Cromulent smashed both his fists down on the glass top of the desk, which hardly raised a sound as the impact was somewhat feeble, but the abruptness of the gesture alone caused Father Bricolage to do a little hop backward. His face fell into a pout as the cardinal's face was flushed with rage. "You had to go put a bullet in their comptroller, Frater Phlegethon, you benighted idiot."

"But he deserved it, Eminence, I swear to you, blaspheming in a sacred chapel left and right."

"Do you realize what you've done—who Frater Phlegethon actually is?"

"No, Eminence. Clearly, I do not."

"He's the goddamn Head of Custodial Services here at Holy Cross. You mean to tell me you didn't recognize him?"

"I'm afraid he was invisible to me, Eminence. Perhaps he used one of their ritual-magick spells to make himself so."

"You're close to blasphemy there, Father. Tread carefully."

"I don't know what you want me to say here, Eminence. I am abject before your authority, as you know."

"Still wearing some kind of torturous hair-shirt under the cassock, Father? Mortifying your flesh to emphasize your piety and supplication before our lord?"

"I humbly do as God asks in all events and I'm eternally abject to his authority. And as long as I'm on this earth, Your Eminence, I submit myself with an open mind and heart both to his and to your authority and will.

"You do, do you Father? Good of you to say, and I certainly believe you, but perhaps you can tell me something?"

"Of course, Eminence. All my learning and knowledge is completely at your disposal."

"And both Holy Mother Church and I accept this great and bounteous gift with a fair amount of alacrity to be sure. Yet, aside from all that, would you kindly explain to me now where your twenty-two-caliber peashooter is at present? You know the one, don't you?" And here the cardinal snorted flecks of moisture from his nose in rage. "The one that nearly put Barry Weiss in his grave?"

"The—the—*janitor?*"

"Yes, Father, the janitor. And the only Jewish employee working in this Parish. That's right, Father. In your Byzantine genius, you managed to not only put one of the chief procurers of candidates for our exalted *Defensores Fidei de Puero* out of business, but nearly murdered the only goddamn Jew working in this entire holy cathedral!"

"Eminence, I—"

"I don't want to hear it, Sam. Just give me the gun."

"I misplaced it, Eminence."

"Misplaced?" the cardinal snorted.

"I don't have it anymore, Eminence. I surely must have misplaced it somewhere."

"You *misplaced* a deadly weapon involved in a serious crime that can tie both of us to that very serious crime? Have you lost your mind, Sam? That finely-tuned, scholar's mind you've cultivated at great universities for years? You've lost that *and* the gun? You had better be kidding, Sam. That vaunted mind of yours had better not have taken leave of its senses and you of that gun or you'll be taking leave of this parish lickety-split, and I mean as of yesterday. You didn't really misplace it, now did you? Tell the truth." The cardinal smirked at the priest in an almost lascivious way. It was as though he had regained his composure and had come upon a way to use this gaff of the scholarly priest to his advantage.

"It's a very small gun, Your Eminence."

"Tell that to Barry Weiss. He's at Mass General, no doubt being questioned by police detectives as we speak. You'd better hope Holy Mother Church's imprimatur and promised emoluments will be of enough significance to the Jew to keep his big fat mouth shut."

"A satanic pagan Jew of all things," the priest intoned with piety and crossed himself. "But he may yet be saved. 'Christ redeemed us from the curse of the law by becoming a curse for us, for it is written: "Cursed is everyone who is hung on a pole."' And so must it be for Barry Weiss."

With a scowl that scrunched up his face like an apple-sculpture witch, Cardinal Cromulent threw his cellphone at Father Brico-lage's head, which he neatly bobbed out of the way to avoid. The priest crossed his wrists in front of his face and quickly knelt down.

"Oh, I beseech both the benevolence of God and of Your Eminence Cardinal Cromulent to give me pardon and penance for my clumsiness and recalcitrance and accept my poor service and the entirety of my body in all humiliation for the favor of your grace."

"Stand up, Sam. There's no need for such a display. And hand me my phone, why don't you?"

The priest complied with head bowed. "Forgive me, Eminence. I thought there was."

"'When you were dead in your sins and in the uncircumcision of your flesh, God made you alive with Christ.'"

"Yes, oh yes, Eminence. 'He forgave us all our sins, having canceled the charge of our legal indebtedness, which stood against us and condemned us; he has taken it away, nailing it to the cross.'"

"Get the gun, Sam, or we'll both be nailed to that cross."

"Yes, Eminence. I'll find it and squirrel it away safely somewhere." The priest's face had gone pale, and his expression became an exaggerated mask of contrition. *He doesn't remember my having given him the gun, and therefore he doesn't know that I stole it from the ostentatious eighteenth-century desk in his residence in the Basilica of Our Lady of Perpetual Sorrow just after I had given it to him. God celebrates all blindness in the cause of helping us all see with a greater, more discerning light, just as weakness at the end of this life provides for the enormous strength at the beginning of the next.'*

"She wants bodies, Sam, the woman from Bethlehem."

"You mean more of the candidates?"

"No, Sam, I think she means priests, not children. Actually, too many children and the difficulty of handling them is the reason."

"Auntie Nonie."

"The buxom one."

"I never noticed."

"She is by design a honey trap for those who notice. But once again, God has protected you."

"Yet another Magdalene Laundress as far as I'm concerned, Eminence, in service to God. Her wanton displays have meaning only insofar as she facilitates our sanctified *Defensores Fidei de Puero.*"

"She supplies the boys."

"And I'm to supply the priests?"

"This will be your actual recruitment effort, Sam. This might help expiate your sins and chasten you from your recent lapse. Barry Weiss could destroy us all this very afternoon and his unbelief in anything other than that ridiculous Thelema puts us all at risk. He fears no divine reprisal and you have a blemish to expunge from your record of pious obeisance."

"But surely the confessional—"

"There's no need for you to confess anything, Sam. The Lord and I know your sins all too well and our forgiveness is boundless."

"You're not meaning to equate—"

"And why wouldn't I necessarily make that equation? I'm one of the most blessed and anointed of the College of Cardinals and on track perhaps in time to be the first American elected pope. No, I'm not indulging in the sin of pride, and doesn't God look favorably upon us when we celebrate our accomplishments?"

"God is never in the position of denying dreams, Eminence." Father Bricolage was breaking into a light sweat that the pain of his undergarment couldn't distract him from. His hands were shaking, so he hid them in the folds of his cassock. He was steeped in sin and his assistance to the cardinal was only worsening things. He desperately needed to give confession before God and adopt as many acts of contrition and penance as any good priest should heap upon him, but to what church would he go and what priest would take his confession without it getting back to His Eminence? Nowhere in this buttoned-up, crypto-pious city with its network of petty gossip, calumny and unwanted revelations that always worked their way to the top, thwarting the genuine efforts of pious men such as himself in the necessary execution of their labors. The unsavoriness of *Defensores Fidei de Puero* was making his stomach churn. He understood both its benefits and the totality of its righteousness, but even with that powerful understanding, it made his entire body quail in disgust whenever it crossed his mind, or heard its echoes as he was hearing them now.

"You hear the caterwauling, don't you, Sam?"

"Yes, it's awful. I thought your office was soundproofed."

"Oh, it is, but you forgot to close the door behind you as you came in."

The priest smacked his forehead with his right hand, closed his eyes, and looked heavenward. He sighed as he spoke, "Oh, my most profound and abject genuflections—"

"Relax, Sam. No one could hear us other than the sisters of Our Lady outside. They know not to speak of anything they might overhear while diligently serving the interests of this seat of the parish and of the cardinal."

"It's almost easy to forget that you're a man of true faith, Your Eminence."

The cardinal leaned back in his chair, upholstered in thick, dark green leather and gave out with an easy chuckle signaling that the storm of his angry impatience had finally passed. "That's true,

Sam. It comes with the true humility that only Holy Mother Church herself can confer upon you."

"That screeching—it's them, Your Eminence?"

"Sadly yes, Sam. Those who have fallen short of the fine points of the decree."

"The choir master—"

"Has had his fill of them."

"Cannot they be taught?"

"No, and I believe the sweetness and virtue of our liturgical music may, like discipline, have to be imposed on even the boys who show talent and a reverence for pitch as well as god. We have a most capable, pious doctor selected to ease our burden of further caterwauling. A sixty-year moratorium on the practice hardly trumps the thousand or so years before."

"And this doctor, Eminence? His skills cannot improve the situation with the others?"

"Sam—what works for the blessed cannot work for the cursed. The snipping off of gonads cannot imbue a boy with perfect pitch."

"But salvation is promised to all, Eminence."

"Of course, Sam. But in the next life. Not in this one."

"Surely, ear training—"

"No!" the cardinal shouted nervously. "They squall and cry and when one tries to entice them into the easiest of hymns, all he gets is backlash and unruly behavior."

"Do we release them into the wild, then?"

"To put it crudely, yes. I'm beginning to repine our affiliation with the Sacred Knights. They're not doing nearly as effective a job as the wanton aunt is doing, with her charges from the southern border. They, at least, I have it on good authority can – that *most* of them can carry a tune and are absolutely devout, abject before God, as opposed to the tone-deaf barbaric urchins the Knights manage to come up with. Caterwauling downstairs."

"But you're saying we're tied to the Knights because of Barry Weiss."

"*You're* saying it, Sam. And you're right. We'll have to buy them off to keep them quiet and make a token effort at accepting their offerings while the passage of time quiets them down."

"But what of their offerings, then?"

"Sam, you know we can't afford to have children making wild accusations to any adult, much less police and petty politicians, and the even *more* petty functionaries of social services. You know this. These wayward godless boys will have to be dealt with discreetly."

"You—you want me to recruit priests to do—to do—what I know you're asking me to do?"

"Their little souls will find more perfect comfort in heaven rather than in this veil of tears. Just to make sure fairness and trust is persevered, we'll match the Knights man-for-man in the cleanup effort. And they'll be needed to help Auntie Nonie deal with her willful and unruly boy problem. It's all been worked out with Grand Pater Hadit of Ordo Templi Orientis, down to the penny. And Nonie is badly understaffed. As formidable as she is, I don't think she can undertake this effort by herself. So, I'd like you to round up six priests to see this Holy Action of Holy Mother Church through. Matched by six members of the Sacred Knights too, of course."

"Will any priest at all do?" asked Father Bricolage, feeling faint of heart and as if he were ready to undergo some demonically influenced out-of-body experience.

The cardinal's eyebrows were raised in mild surprise. "Father Bricolage, come, come. You're surely brighter than that. I think you know to what kind of priests I am referring."

"I'm not really sure, Eminence."

The cardinal made a barking sound of disbelief and scolded, "Priests dedicated to the honor of God equipped with a pair good, strong hands."

"I see, Eminence. But why the emphasis on strong hands?"

Cardinal Cromulent replied in a husky, vicious whisper:

"To wring little atheist necks!"

———

Toplofty was keeping his cool with greater difficulty than he thought it should take. Who was this little Ingush prick anyway? This natty, trim little Eurotrash nonentity with the Gucci prep-wear and insouciant beard styling himself enough of an assassin to blip off the zombie fuck Null who had singlehandedly wiped out the Family and pared down the muscle of the Ork to the equivalent of the night crew at a KFC. So far, the target, this half-dead mutt Null, still managed to roam free, even after his mutilation of the Padrone. Even after crushing the Ork's citywide lock on Meth to turn his Gangsta Boyz into a cartel spreading gak up and down through the length and breadth of New England. The ghoul's sights were now set on New Jersey and then New York and the resistance to that bold infringement has been disturbingly, to date, unnervingly quiet.

Meanwhile, the Ork was still eating dust on its half-hearted crawl out of the hole that zombie fuck Null had buried them in and Toplofty himself had narrowly escaped being shredded to mulch by that stupid nigger crew the Gangsta Boyz. How could they ever have accepted such an ofay klutz as that half-dead zombie fuck Null to call the shots?

But the flagging crew of the Ork was all the former orthopedic surgeon had left after he bombed out his medical career with drugs and playing God as unofficial chop doc and medical fixer for any crime crew able to come up with the cash. Mostly robbery crews. The Padrone, though, had taken him in just in time, rescued him from that sad fate, bankrolled him, curried and groomed him as *consiglieri* which was the only thing that could have brought him back from that tragic second bid at Concord Correctional, where he barely survived the raging ass parties, routine beatings and forced feminization of the sicker psychopaths on the block that made him instantly and consistently and perhaps for all time as the privileged little punk he had fought tooth and nail against being for most of his life.

He fought it at school, in hospitals among civilians and fought it at last down in the bathrooms, showers, block and yard in prison only to have it brought home to him again and again that that's what he was; that that's what he always was and was always going to be: A privileged punk.

A punk at this point pushing sixty.

And what did he have to show for it? What was the great result? Living off crumbs from the Padrone's dwindling fortunes; bankrupt with a credit score that was an integer; a parole so tight it threatened to send him back to the slam if the monthly bribe was a day late. Oh, yes, let's not forget the plate in his head, the fused sections of his lumbar spine and the one glass eye that served as a constant reminder as to just how deep a punk he was.

Deceptive appearances, though, were Toplofty's saving grace. His body was lean and taut and whatever crepe-paper skin he had was hidden beneath Brunello Cucinelli suits and shirts that flattered his skinny frame. He strode falsely across the world with an easy-seeming grace developed through incremental years of solitary confinement. His full head of hair was the white that showed his age, thought to be "distinguished," but also bringing to mind the mane of the disgraced auto engineer, mogul and failed cocaine impresario John DeLorean. His jaw was square, eyes ice blue, cupid's bow lips pert – every inch of him tanned from tropical banking vacations to the Caymans and Macau. He cut a figure patterned after hated and revered original dandy Beau Brummel and much of these visual effects that benefited him now were what plagued him in the slam: he was an exceptionally pretty fish.

A walking rape-ass-party invitation and revelation.

Even now he still walked a little funny from all the unwanted action he racked up doing hard time back in the slam.

He was at this point in his life, and as it eventually was for Beau Brummel who died penniless and insane in Caen, a dandy in aspic.

Innokenty Gorets, considered the best contract hitter you could buy straight off the dark web, didn't miss a trick with his keen sniper's eye and made fun of him at their second, and last, meeting. He was an insolent little Puck, dark and wiry. Toplofty towered over him. The guy was, what, five-seven maybe? And that was being generous. A buck-fifty soaking wet, if that. And he should have been soaking wet with sweat. He should have been intimidated by Toplofty's greater height and weight, but he wasn't. No, he was calm as usual and ready to go at a moment's notice with a smart remark.

Yet his one-upmanship was calm, not desperate. He gave the impression that he had nothing to prove and was ready to prove that overwhelmingly at the least provocation. He did it within the course of casual conversation without missing a beat.

"So, Toplofty," he had said smugly in that awful Eastern Bloc labial drawl, "you still sleeping on your belly after all that savagery or what? It's easy to see you would have never lasted in a Russian or Chechen prison."

"Doesn't Ingushetia have a prison of its own?"

"No, it's far too small and poor and civilized for that. We had to borrow one from Russia and Chechnya."

"That's two, Innocent," Toplofty countered.

"Too true, my friend. That would be right."

"And with two prisons, I don't understand how you could be so free of tats."

"Tats, Toplofty? You mean Tattoos."

"I forgot. You don't make it out this way very often."

"More often than you might think, Toplofty."

"The Padrone's not in a good way, health-wise. He doesn't notice too many small details, being so much concerned with larger, big-picture issues, so I sort of take over where things tend to be a bit more granular. Now, what about those tats, Innocent? Or are you, perhaps, as we all know anyway, *not* so innocent?"

"You're on your game, Toplofty. Someone indeed has, as they say, lit a fire under your asshole."

"You mean ass, you fuckin' mook."

"Sorry, my friend. My English, as they say, has a few kinks in it. I mean ass, not asshole." Then he smiled and made a lecherous wink at Toplofty. "But in the final analysis, asshole isn't entirely off base either, Toplofty, now is it?"

Toplofty feinted a lunge at him, but the little assassin did nothing but smile. "Well, Toplofty. Let me know when you like to make a serious go at that, and I'll oblige you."

"You're a fake," Toplofty fumed.

"No. I told you my country was too civilized for prisons. So, though we might have borrowed two, we only borrowed none."

"No, prison time?"

"None. But if it helps, I'm sorry for your experiences there, if that's any help to you."

"Why is this Null fuck not dead yet?"

"All of the street is sure that he is dead. They say he's not a real flesh and blood man—some kind of zombie. Maybe a vampire. No one's clear about it. And no one wants to say anything beyond that. They claim he watches all of them all the time like some evil demon."

"And you don't know that's horseshit?"

"Now, how could I not know this, Toplofty?"

"Because you're not as smart as you think you are."

"What might I learn from you?"

"Humility, for one."

"Must we return to your ass in all things, Toplofty?"

The former orthopedic surgeon, disgraced and habitual, irrational, driven criminal stood silent as his face darkened with rising blood.

"This Null is not Papa Legba, Baron Samedi or Solomon Grundy, but a man who bleeds."

"Then, if you don't want to forfeit your contract, you'll get onto making him bleed then – to *death*."

The diminutive assassin smiled and delivered a throaty chuckle after only a moment's thought.

"No, Toplofty. Not at all. But you *will*."

And in that way, Toplofty was left standing with the task and the package and now in this miserable tenement stairwell in a decrepit apartment house in Mattapan, shivering under his tweed overcoat. The Ingush assassin was nowhere to be seen, and why not? He had opted out with the approval of the Padrone. The pack of gak in the pocket of his tweed overcoat was for the inside man in the Gangsta Boyz—the idea the Ingush *strunz* had to further humiliate him unnerved him, which for some reason, maybe its perversity, pleased the Padrone. Toplofty bit his lip realizing why it did.

There always had to be some humiliation game played on him to show him his place and confirm his loyalty. Toplofty shook his head in deference to the fact that he had to play it out and accept it. Even in his most brutish imaginings, his unsatisfying fantasies, he knew he didn't have much further to go. This was his last best chance at anything and, bad as it was, it was better by far than poverty or a rough ride back to the slam if he fucked up and crossed the Padrone. Weak as he was, Malek The Mallet still had enough juice to make grim things happen to such a weak player as happened to be his own consigliere.

So he'd better make any moves in the mission to nullify the zombie fuck Null not only count, but stand out in obvious excellence, if such a quality could be imputed to a drug gang assassination and takeover.

Toplofty whistled hard between his teeth a half-forgotten melody, softly marching in place to help warm himself against the lingering New England perma-chill that had completely claimed the squalid lobby of the dilapidated lobby that reeked of alcoholic piss, rotted food, the dank human stink of hopeless fear. It wasn't a direct, wet, frigid cold but an indirect, subtle, lingering cold—a ghostly cold. It was the kind of cold you could never get free of no matter how many years you stayed away from Boston. The stench, the chill, the weight of being played all dismayed him.

What he needed was heat and lights, color and pleasant sounds.

What he got was cold and dimness and the echo of his own footfalls and the coughing of a pile of loamy garbage in the far corner away from the boarded-up elevator bank that turned out to be human. He had stopped whistling. Therefore, while he waited, something else was needed. He tried humming the tune rather than whistling it.

That didn't work either.

So he sang, flattered by the echo:

> *"Solomon Grundy,*
> *Born on a Monday,*
> *Christened on Tuesday,*
> *Married on Wednesday,*
> *Took ill on Thursday,*
> *Grew worse on Friday,*
> *Died on Saturday,*
> *Buried on Sunday,*
> *That was the end,*
> *Of Solomon Grundy.*
> *Solomon Grundy,*
> *Born on—"*

There was a beat spat like a raspberry to imitate a drum machine.

Ronald Brogan stepped into the lobby—really more rolled into it than stepped—dressed in the usual low-hanging prison jeans topped with a black fish-mouth hooded sweatshirt that covered the lower portion of his face. He clapped his hands to provide a beat for a song that was no longer there. Even Toplofty could tell that he was trying to look more threatening than he actually was – give the effect of mystery to his mood and mien when it was easy to see he was covering for being nervous as hell.

"You gots to *rap* dat shit, nigga. This ain't da place to be singin' shit."

"You don't like music?"

Toplofty jerked himself backward a half step.

"Naw, I like rap. That was a dope lyric."

"Just an old nursery rhyme."

"Perfect up in this bitch. You born on Monday you betta know you gon' be dead by Sunday."

"That's dramatic."

Toplofty wondered if his own lack of cool was showing. He blew into the palms of his hands and rubbed them together, not so much a gesture against the lingering chill as it was to distract from the sweat beading on his upper lip. And that his hands had been trembling.

"Yo, I'm a hypin' motherfucker. Evvything in my life dramatic, Dr. Finger. You think this shit here ain't dramatic? You gots to *learn*." Then he began to beat spit raspberries, chanted and clapped along with the chanting, "Sol-o-mon *Grun*-dy, bon' onna *Mon*-dy, bucked on a *Tue-s*dy, squoze on *Wednes*-dy, netted up on *Thurs*-dy, got the Monstah *Fri*-dy—or the Monstah got him, *yo*—did a Dutch on Sadiddy, put'n his grave on Sun-*day,* then come back evvy *day*—he done come back evvy—mother—*fuckin'*—day!" He paused the chant but resumed the beat spit raspberry with the clapping, jumped up and screamed, *"Evvy motherfuckin' day, ofay cocksucker!"*

Ronald stopped there, half crouched glaring at Toplofty, who replied softly, "What was that about?"

"I told yez, homes. You *gots* to *learn.*"

"Learn what?" he spoke again softly. He was shuddering under his tweed overcoat, suppressing it as hard as he could, hoping it wouldn't show beneath the coat, both from the cold and erratic outbursts of one of the Gangsta Boyz that he didn't and possibly couldn't understand.

"Not to fuck with me."

Toplofty had blinked and there was the six-inch steel blade of a knife brandished in Ronald's hand.

"I'm not carryin', kid, so either put the knife away or use it. Do the latter and your little plan's blown."

"That ain't it, Dr. Finger. Try again."

"Sure, kill me and glom onto the package, do your thing and see just how fast you follow your boss into the next world."

"You a funny motherfucker, Dr. Finger. You is that."

"Sure. Funny, I was a doctor once, kid, but not anymore. Now, are you here to do some business or are you here to just fuck around?"

Ronald stood up straight, pulled up the fabric about the fish mouth of his hoodie and made the knife disappear into his prison jeans in one smooth movement.

"Now you can leggo yo' grip on the mini gat in your overcoat pocket. The twenty-two."

"How did—"

"Because I'm a smart nigga is why, Dr. Finger. Now you be chill and take that hand ouch yo pocket, we finish our business here and we can both kiss dat zombie fuck Null goodbye fuh-evah."

Toplofty removed his hands from his coat pockets and dropped them by his side, shuddering visibly, pouting, knowing this.

"Smart nigger, you say? You think it's really smart to bring a knife to a gunfight, kid?"

Ronald stomped his feet and bellowed laughter. "You so nervous, Dr. Finger, I slit yo' throat after your first two misses. Call me nigga again, I'll cut your heart out."

With a grunt, Toplofty reached into his right coat pocket and with a spastic, nervous move drew out a small package wrapped in green cellophane and tossed it at Ronald, who jumped back away from it as if it were a grenade. The Ruger LCP II twenty-two semi-auto pistol with Viridian E-series laser gripped comfortably, resolutely steady in his hand.

"How many you think I'll miss now, kid? I go."

"I s'posed be 'fraid o' that li'l ole popgun, yo?" Ronald asked, slowly picking up the little package of gak up from the filth-clotted tile of the stinking tile floor, which was once white but was now as sallow-hued as a wino with jaundice. He held up the package and waved it at Toplofty. "You been samplin' y'own gak, Dr. Finger?"

"I'm not a proctologist."

"No? Cause you way too far up my ass already."

"I'm going to crawl further up there still if you don't tell me you know what you're doing with that package."

Ronald had both his hands up, affecting surrender without meaning it. "Chill, now, Doctor Proctor. I know the game. Know what 'bout to get served to who's gonna *get* served. You can pocket dat toy gat now, real talk."

"So, you better be a smart nigger as you say."

Ronald took a step forward and Toplofty extended his arm that had the pistol at the end of it.

"Smart 'nough to of gone ta Boston Latin."

"Really, and you were never on the college track?"

"Money's out on the street, homes. I could be dead before I got my own self a corner office at the John Hancock."

"You had better be a smart nigger or we'll put your theory about the shots I can get off with this semi-auto before you put that blade in my stomach. And this toy holds six in the magazine and one in the chamber to start with. Want to take a guess how many shots I get off before you croak?"

"You ain't gonna shoot."

"Think in this part of Mattapan anyone will notice the little pops of my cute little popgun?"

"S'all good, Doctor Proctor – I feel ya." Ronald took his phone out of his prison jeans pocket, squinted at it and then stuffed it back in. He stuffed the small, green flat package of gak in his other pocket. "You want me to make my meetin' and be all prompt and shit, you *gots* to let me go do dat thing we *all* wanna see get done. I gots to know where Grandma's gon' be dis time. To do *da thing*."

Toplofty continued to hold up the Ruger twenty-two straight and steady.

"I had better, then, hadn't I?"

"Watchoo waitin' fo' homes? A apology? Better just fuckin' shoot my black ass then and be done wit' it."

Toplofty narrowed his eyes and leaned his upper body a couple of inches forward then lowered the gun and shook his head laughing to himself. He let the arm with the Ruger hang limp by his side.

"Kid, you better figure a way not to get any of that shit up your nose or the next time I see you, I *will* kill you. You got that?"

"Ya, I get it. I'm a—"

"Smart nigger. Yes, I know. Well, Ronnie, let's be clear here. This is your one chance to realize your full potential. This is your moment. So, I have only to remind you of what the Padrone had to say about it before I came here: *Don't fuck it up.* Because you know what happens when you fuck up out here on the street, don't you?"

Ronald shook his head resignedly in the affirmative and left the tenement lobby into the clammy Spring air, trading one kind of stench for another. Where the lobby stank of urine, feces and oily human sweat, the air outside of it stank of garbage, the heavy plastic smoke of something burning not too far away (but not in sight) and the repulsive cheesy scent of something dead rotting aggressively very close by. And as he made his way toward that night's Grandma's house, he distinctly heard Toplofty warn him again in an insane scream: *"Don't you?!*

FOURTEEN

The delivery of the drugged-out boys and unwanted girls was easier dealt with the next day when the staff of Bethlehem Adoption and Youth Placement Services in Newton showed up early that same morning. They were all nuns and unpaid volunteers, interns in various undergraduate programs on either the elementary education or social services track. It was understood that new residents about to undergo the standard intake procedure were to be quarantined to special dormitories reserved for that purpose on the third floor of the historic house, which boasted a blue plaque on its exterior identifying it as having been entered in the National Registry of Historic Places, but not really identifying why it merited that placement. The suspicion was that it had been a high-end bordello during the gilded age catering to Boston's elite and specializing, as legend had it, in cardinals, bishops and monsignors, and of course the usual politicians and captains of industry.

The incoming boys had been swiftly tested for their ability to carry a tune, hand-stamped yea or nay and kept in the same dormitory, drugged again with special ice cream for easy management and only the most trusted, elder nuns were allowed to see to their needs, toileting them, getting them to take in some form of easy nourishment, usually soup, and cleansed in the shower, doors opened and in sight of other nuns. The girls were being fast-tracked for the bi-monthly adoption showcases where prospective parents, in a near-classic Roman fashion, were allowed to pick and choose. The less presentable of the little female tykes were relegated to the foster care system after a few months of meager checks just from the Commonwealth, to yield some kind of reimbursement and profit on their upkeep and placement.

Failing that, comfortable berths in the generous bed of the muddy Charles River would be secured for them. That thought barely provided a twinge of discomfort, which she put out of her mind as soon as she felt it.

Auntie Nonie reviewed her situation, sipping a too-warm white Russian in her cramped office, trying to make the best of things.

The child kidnapping and resale scheme done under the rubric of Bethlehem Adoption and Youth Placement Services was proving far more profitable than the former bordello ever had. All that needed to be done was to route the bodies to their final destinations, collect the checks and wire them into the tax-free account of the DeVille slush-fund non-profit Tyndale Gospel Communications, take her cut then find some starving twenty-something MSW candidate—preferably a starry-eyed girl—to run the show while she fucked off to any destination that wasn't drenched in the permanent moisture of unremitting New England cold.

Even its heat was so damp and dank it somehow managed to chill you. You could never dry out and then the next cold wave froze you like no tomorrow. And it certainly seemed as if there were no tomorrow.

Tahiti at this point felt like a realistic choice.

The only interruptions that day had been the nuns doing their routines of service. The newest shipment of boys was still being served their three portions a day of drugged food, marched back and forth to the showers by the holy sisters and left in their locked dormitory until they could be physically separated—the good ones delivered to Cardinal Cromulent's residence in South Boston, the troublemakers and tone-deaf were to be disposed of neatly and discreetly by those bound by secrecy and holy edict who would never betray their faith and reveal the unfortunate mess of having to deal with unwanted children for whom there was no real place in the world. Foster programs were over-taxed with unwanted children and the Massachusetts Department of Children and Families had a long waiting list just for foster care placement. And Bethlehem was designed to be more of a processing center, a kind of waystation, than an orphanage in the classic sense, hence the twin true purposes of adoption and placement.

The business model of Bethlehem required a new meaning be given to the term of art "placement," that had nothing to do with actually finding families for tykes, merely places to send them to dispose of them. And if that place happened to be at the bottom of a quarry or of the muddy Charles itself, who was going to complain about it?

To be fair, Auntie Nonie had already seen to the niceties, such as which of the little dears could be kept around for a few months to keep the Commonwealth checks flowing, but only the least troublesome, and which of them couldn't. The difficult street urchins, the ones who lacked attractiveness, intelligence and charm (not to mention the ability to carry a tune) had to be cleared out to keep things moving. They had to be placed. *Expeditiously.*

Auntie Nonie was simply not cut out to be a house mother.

The irony of all this for her was the fact that in her deep desire not to become a brood mare for some schmoe working several jobs to keep some cracker box hovel in the boonies with a bunch of whelps screeching at her, she had somehow wound up absurdly responsible for so many children that she could hardly keep track of them. Yes, it was one of the lower DeVille acolytes who first felt an attraction to and a commiseration with her surgically perfect boobs and her greed. A few rolls in the hay and a lucrative gig rose from the ashes. The talents of the Rubber Nun were not to be underestimated.

How was she supposed to know that the gig required kiddie disposal as one of its chief requirements? She didn't know how she managed to swallow being a brood mare for a bunch of obnoxious pups by proxy but for the money.

Ah, the money was great. Nothing to sneeze at.

But this gig was getting old, and she had a bad feeling that some obscene iteration of daily chaos would carom into the damn operation and put one of her spectacular tits in the wringer.

Tahiti was looking like a better prospect as the day wore on.

The problem was all the busy work. Yet, who else could she have trusted to do it? Anyone intelligent might twig to what was going on that made Bethlehem such a wonderful, successful service of child placement to devout religious families, to Catholic schools that might board the children until they aged out and even to the rickety system of foster care. The nuns, luckily enough, were passive and obsequious and gave her little complaint and maybe just a few more meddlesome questions that might have been asked under normal circumstances. But Auntie Nonie had no trouble pushing these aside. She had a talent for distraction and dissembling. Sure, more than a few of the servile, volunteer nuns who came and went were lesbians, which was how religious torment processed those driven to carnal vices that were reserved only for the privileged male of the clerical species. Not surprisingly, boobs again came to the fore in satisfying all momentary qualms of the nuns, and those boobs were backed by a body worked on hard enough to carry them off well enough, driven by a mind adroit enough to be both overcautious and defensive that was also capable of having the mouth deflect and give all necessary false comfort to keep idle suspicions from becoming more active.

Keeping a lid on the problem meant that she had to do the books herself and submit to nerve-wracking periodic auditing by a CPA, adding her ability of distraction to lessen the impact of fudged numbers; she also had to do the ordering of supplies and the coordinating of outside services, such as technicians for cable TV and WIFI; she also had to deal with the gawky and disheveled IT guy who kept the Bethlehem intranet running, the website updated and maintained and cybersecurity updated, reinstalled and deployed. Worse, the guy puppy-dogged her just to get extra glances at her boobs, running around with an obvious erection under his soiled khakis. Still, the machinery of profitable kiddie kidnapping kept rolling on mostly due to her, and her cut of the revenues was all the larger because of it.

Auntie Nonie gave herself a small, satisfied smile in her somewhat dark, somewhat stuffy, somewhat overheated office, noting to herself that she worked hard for that ten percent of the gross revenues of Bethlehem. She was no parasite—she ran the show. She worked hard with a vengeful zest. Her swelling bank accounts reflected this. And, in the pragmatic sense, she was doing some perceptible social good, giving children who had no place to go places to go: the church, the religious school, foster homes and sometimes even permanent homes with religious families (or barren couples who praised Bethlehem as a Godsend).

And, sure, okay, sometimes to the bottom of the muddy Charles River; but those cases all had a predetermined trajectory not even her best efforts could alter. Certainly, it could have been worse. Like in the case of the difficult, unruly little girls—local girls—she encountered when she first had started at Bethlehem. There was simply no place for them. There were too many of them and they didn't at all suit the needs of the church. Having been virtually deserted, left alone by Betty DeVille's haphazard support staff at Tyndale and her at-best horizontally integrated organization, she was encouraged (if not ordered) to improvise and make do.

So she did.

The ten girls weren't adoption material, the money they brought in was only a piddly little single dip from the Commonwealth. There weren't enough finished rooms at the time to house them and so they had to be bunked with the boys, who themselves had triple-dip value for the most part, causing potential elopements, undue noise, fighting and general mess. So – again – she improvised.

And though she had found it too risky to convey those ten girls to the banks of the muddy Charles River even after she had drugged them to sleep, intending to place them to sleep peacefully in the river's generous bed without any help, yet another resting place occurred to her febrile mind before she set about accomplishing that task.

Amazing what miracles a little eavesdropping can provide, she mused.

There just happened to be a house in foreclosure in Newtonville off Highland Avenue with a bad foundation, a flooded, muddy basement and serious septic tank issues. It was an abandoned property that one of the agency's building contractors, a drunk, had made his personal house-flipping project. As with everything, he had given up on it, of course. Abandoned it in his usual feckless way. Even better. he had no deed or title to the property, just a set of keys, which Auntie Nonie, the Rubber Nun in all her glory, had eased out of him with very little trouble.

She had worked on the girls conscientiously and meticulously with an eye on the clock, yet avoided rushing, erring on the side of caution. And when she had finished, she was both relaxed and satisfied. A decision was made right then and there as she drove back to Herrick Road from the dump site that *that* would be the last time she would let necessary improvisation carry things so far.

Oh, well.

At least it was done humanely, prudently and with as little fuss as possible.

Besides, those children went where everyone's eventually headed anyway; they just arrived ahead of schedule. Got their secure place in heaven, no sweat. Yet, this knowledge didn't serve to comfort Auntie Nonie Fomites one bit.

She was getting nervous.

The experienced contractors that the DeVilles were supposed to provide her from DeVille scion Derrick's military subcontracting company, Yellow River, who were to give a quiet, invisible ending to the lives of problematic Bethlehem boys and girls, were no longer available. Already mustered. They had been swallowed up, dispatched and deployed to Kuwait, Iraq and Afghanistan as part of an immense (and hugely profitable) private security detail to protect the vestigial American presence in the region.

Yet another mammoth problem that was left to Auntie alone to solve.

Her nervousness was connected to her relying on religious forces to solve the problem—she should never have trusted the disposal effort to amateurs. Once again, her sense of economy had betrayed her.

Meanwhile, the tykes were about ready to be put down to full unconsciousness from their drugged out semi-stupor that was arrived at through wizened kitchen slaves who owed their continued existence to the DeVille family and who were now expert in dosing Thiopental, Dalmane and Thorazine at scrupulous intervals to keep the children docile, quiet and, more importantly, easily handled. It was getting late. Soon, she would have to do a bed check, take attendance, make sure there was no kiddie uprising in the works.

All it took sometimes was one mouthy kid to gum up the works, stir the rest of them up, mount some kind of futile demonstration that had to be swatted down with the kind of violence that wasn't good for anybody.

So many things could go wrong with an enterprise like this, and, like any seasoned performer, Auntie Nonie had a sixth sense about when to depart from the stage yet leave the audience clamoring for more. In her line, she was a seasoned pro. The best roper, the most expert hostess, the savviest front woman. She had never missed a performance in her life. But she wouldn't be giving any encores. No, by then she would be long gone.

They were late.

And she was sweating.

The clerics hadn't shown yet and her favorite Frater and his five buddies from Ordo Templi Orientis hadn't shown either. Now, to be fair, she expected that from the ersatz Knights Templar with all their ritual sex magick role-playing games and pretenses, but *not* from Holy Mother Church. Not from the piously officious Father

Bricolage, righthand man to Cardinal Cromulent himself. No, that was discomfiting. The man was punctilious to say the least. Deviating from protocols, timetables and scheduled meetings was anathema to that cassocked dude.

Their lateness made her nervous.

And their lateness lulled the agitated boys in the locked third floor dormitory to the false ease of darkness and sleep. Auntie Nonie prided herself on being right much of the time, which a lifetime of having been on the wrong end of a boot heel, a fist or a cocked and loaded twenty-two pistol, honed the skill of her constant suspicion to a fine edge. Could she have been right about how one little boy could ruin everything? Of course not.

Yet there was one lone boy shivering under the covers in that locked boys' dormitory even though it was only a cool fifty-four degrees outside, and the always cold Auntie Nonie had turned up the master thermostat to try and dry herself out from the persistent sweaty, perma-dank New England humidity. But the boy wasn't shivering with the cold, unless panic had a temperature.

He was shivering with fear.

His name was Marion Slaughter and he wanted out in a bad way.

"Larry," he whispered to a chubby dark-skinned boy in the cot next to him. "Larry, we gotta get outta heah. Pronto!"

Larry was unresponsive.

"Dude, get *up!*" A harsh, expressive whisper.

Larry didn't move.

Marion threw the covers to the floor, spun about sitting down, and kicked Larry with both heels of his feet. Larry woke up swinging, shouting, "What the fuck motherfucker? For fuck's sake!"

"You kiss ya mutha with that mouth?

"Don't gut no muthah—gut nobody, real talk."

"Anybody's gut anybody they don't wind up in this hellhole."

"But you gut a granny, bet."

"Ya. She ain't much, though."

"I'd take her off ya hands for ya. What you kickin' at me faw, fool?"

"We gotta skurt but fast, brotha."

"Why, homie? We got three hots and a cot in dis place. I don't see nothin' betta comin' f'us anytime soon."

"Yeah. True dat. We ain't got nothin' comin'."

"So why kick me in my black ass to wake me up?"

"'Cause I ain't ready to die yet and I don't think you ready for that bitch neither."

"Why you think dat?"

"'Cause we half-asleep alla time. Got no energy. The whole t'ing is feed us, move us, sleep us, repeat."

"Yeah, I guess I did see dat. Dey puttin' some kinda narco shit in the hot choc'lit. I can almost taste it still."

"They puttin' it in *evvything.*"

"Mus' be. I feel all sleepy 'n' shit."

Marion slapped his face hard. "Don't go back to sleep, mutha-fuckah!" Larry made a flurry of his fingers and hands to fend off the next blow, but none came.

"Shhh. You'll wake evvybody."

"Fat chance."

"I won't go back to sleep, already. I promise I won't."

"I figgered out why."

"How you know?"

"Some of us goin' somewhere but the rest of us, well…"

"I know. We ain't gut nuthin comin'. Shit. Dat ain't news."

"Shit, Lar', we ain't goin' nowhere at *all* if you hip to that."

"Now why they gon' do dat? Makes no sense."

"Ya, it does. Did ya check ya wrist?"

"Ya, they put a bullshit nightclub stamp on it. So what?"

"Didja see what it was of?"

"All smudged and shit, but it's some bitch cryin', I guess."

"That the Holy Virgin Mary, brotha."

"So what? We all got one. They all the same."

"Uh-uh. They *not* all the same."

"Look, you got one jus' like mine."

"Evvy kid in heah gut one like ours."

"Ya, who cayuz?"

"An' it don't mean nuttin' good, I'm tellin' you."

"I don' get it."

"Lookit, in the other room. Them guys all gut St. Augustine on theirs. I reckanize it off a book my gran has."

"If you got a gran, Mary, den why you wind up here?"

"Bitch sold me out. Call me Mary again an' I'll pop you one in da schnoz."

"Whut? You don't *like* Mary and Larry? Aww, you *know* we was meant to be together." Larry air-kissed his friend and was rewarded with a pillow in the face. "Cut it the fuck out. You'll wake evvybody up, you keep doin' shit like that."

"Fat chance again, assclown. I'd haveta kick all them guys awake like you and I ain't gonna do that."

"Why you so shooah, anyways?" Larry asked, still puzzled.

"Rememba when they had us try an' sing some stupid hymn when they got hold of us?"

"Ya. I blew it on purpose. You shoulda seen the look."

"I know, I did it too. I can sing pretty good, but not for these douchebags."

"*That's* why we been separated?"

"I think these fuckaz ah puttin a choir togethah. And they doin' somethin' else weird too. They want the dudes next door to sing *castrati*."

"Fuck no! You serious? Does that mean—"

"Yup, no balls at all. They scoop 'em right out and t'row 'em against a wall."

"If dat's what they doin' wit' *them*, what they gon' do wit' *us*?"

"I figger it like this: If that's what they gonna do with the guys they like—what ya think they gonna do with us? Sell our asses to Daddy fuckin' Warbucks?"

"I don' even know who dat is."

"The good news is, they ain't gonna scoop up our balls an' t'row 'em against the wall. No way."

"Okay, what da bad news den?"

"We ain't gon' live long enough to ever use 'em."

———

The light above the entrance to Auntie Nonie's cramped office flashed on and off, which meant at last there was someone at the door. She stood, smoothed her sweater dress down over her voluptuous curves with both hands and the hot pink nails glinted in the half-light like the wet talons of a predatory bird. She shook the cobwebs from her head, trying and failing to banish worries about the whole Bethlehem kiddie scam falling apart and going under before she made her nut—reaching the threshold amount that would allow her to fuck off permanently for good and all.

Yet the threshold kept moving further away.

There never seemed to be enough in the kitty.

"About friggin' time," she said under her breath, walking out into the high-ceilinged foyer that led to the front door. She threw the bolts, punched in an alarm code into the keypad recessed into the jamb behind a tiny door.

"Forgive me for the lateness, Ms. Fomites," said a weary-looking Father Bricolage, wearing his usual cassock, the clerical collar standing out brisk and white with a second-hand Burberry trench coat draped over him. "May I come in, please?"

Auntie Nonie frowned and stepped aside to let the priest in. The door stayed open.

"I told you before to call me Auntie, Father. Everybody else does."

"Yes, of course. Auntie. Forgive me."

"Sure, Father. You ain't expected to be as infallible as your pope."

Father Bricolage made a sour face at that statement.

"I don't mean to be rude, Father, but there's a time constraint here. Otherwise, I'd offer you a drink and a place to sit comfortably so we could discuss the matter at hand. But I think things are getting a bit *out* of hand here already."

"Yes, Auntie. I could certainly use a drop of something against the sultry chill of this place."

"I feel you, Father. It seems like a total bitch to keep warm in this old hovel. And I even turned up the heat."

"Something about being coastal—close to the sea—"

"Yeah, I swear at some point soon I'm going to have to have a talk with the folks at Tyndale to set me up somewhere inland, so I won't be cold all the time. And it's supposed to be Spring now, y'know?"

"Well, we're lucky it's not snowing. And if you do that, Auntie, make sure to avoid the Great Lakes region. It's much colder in Minnesota about now."

"Yeah, I know. Father. But something about this place—the Greater Boston Area—that's damp and sweaty no matter *what* the weather. Even in the summer, the wet air makes your skin crawl, and you feel, um, I can't think of the word. Moist, maybe?"

"Dank, Auntie. Dank. Is that the word?"

"Thanks, Father, that'll do."

Father Bricolage gave Auntie a dry, thin little chuckle. "You know, the kids use the adjective 'dank' now to mean something's excellent or of very high quality, not the usual damp, musty, and typically cold weather it applies to. I wonder how their etymology gets us to that meaning."

"Listen, Father, I'm surrounded by the kiddies all day long. I have neither the time nor the inclination to listen to them. I don't have the time to care about what they say and how they think. It's hard enough just moving them around and keeping them docile, feeding them and then getting them ready for the next and final move, which brings us back down to business, I'm afraid."

"I could use that drink Auntie, if—"

"I'll just bet you could, Father. But we're short on time here and we have some business to do before things get totally out of hand.

The census here at Bethlehem is too high—out of control as it is—and I've had to double up on beds. Security is becoming an issue. Worse, too many of the boys aren't really suitable for what you have in mind for them. Not really useable. So, we both know they have to be readied and prep'ed for another, more special journey—"

Father Bricolage held up his hand to stop her, and she made a little grunt when he did. "Yes, his Eminence has made me aware of this, which is why I'm here."

"Well, that's a big goddamn comfort, Father, or would be if you weren't standing here all by yourself, leaving me twisting in the wind. Where's your crew? Where's your van to transport the damn, umm, little cherubs to Southie? I didn't even see your car outside when I let you in."

"I took public transportation and walked from Newton Centre."

"The T? You took the fucking T?" Auntie Nonie blurted out, nearly choking on her words. "You *walked* here?" She began pacing the foyer, throwing up her hands. "This is a huge fuckup, Father. *Huge!* You want all those perfect young throats for your fucking hymns, but you're not only sticking me with the cherubs, but you're leaving me with the little devils too. The rejects. The ones no one wants or ever *will* want. If I can't get the census here down to something near normal, all the good work we're doing here could fall to shit under an audit done by the usual honest John CPA who thinks taking a kickback comes from the ass-end of a mule."

"Surely they're not that dull, Auntie. Self-dealing, however, is certainly a red flag to watch out for."

"Father, you have *no* idea."

"We've hit a bit of a snag there, I guess."

"You, *guess?*" Father? You *guess!* Fuck you, Father! You're supposed to be a goddamn professional."

"Auntie, it's just not that easy to find devout priests who would be willing even under the most extreme circumstances to take care of those boys the way we know they have to be *cared* for."

"What about monks? Haven't monks done the church's dirty work in the past?"

"Not since Thomas a Becket, Auntie."

"What about Frederico Cunha?" she seethed. "The deal was six burly priests willing to go to extremes on behalf of your cardinal and I wind up getting only half a one, which is you. I mean, maybe you're not even half a one." She grabbed both boobs with her hands and thrust them up as close to the Father's face as they could get. "If these don't race your engines, you *must* be queer!"

Father Bricolage reacted as if he had been hit in the stomach and nearly doubled over, his face contorted with disgust. "I'm celibate, Auntie. The only charms that work on me are the glorious exudations of our Lord and Savior Jesus Christ, so, please, Auntie, limit your behavior to the discussion at hand."

"Okay, Father, so you're queer. Big deal. Everybody already knows and no one cares anymore, but I bet they'd care a great deal if they got wind about our little charges up in Third-Floor Boys' Dormitory B. That might actually get you and His Eminence criminally charged."

"Now, Auntie, there's no need to jump to conclusions. I'm a priest and not expert in the ways of these things. I'm sure we have the manpower somewhere within the church who could commit such a necessary deed on behalf of Holy Mother Church. As for the bus, I'll bring it round tomorrow and take those selected for *Defensores Fidei de Puero* off your hands sometime in the afternoon."

"Jesus H. Christ. At least we managed to get *that* done. And what about the money?"

"This time I have but a paper check."

"No seamless, dedicated tablet?" she asked with false surprise.

"It's not enough to justify that."

"Too bad. I dug the tech."

"Old ways often prove to be best."

"The Fraters, I see, have pretty much proven to be a bust."

Father Bricolage thought with a shudder that she might shove her boobs in his face again at the word 'bust' and prayed silently that she wouldn't. He smiled broadly when she didn't, then quickly contained himself, settling his face back to a placid, humorless expression.

"We're both stuck with a bunch of faulty goods."

"The Knights have betrayed us since their last, best delivery—not enough of the right kind of candidates. We're warehousing too many of them and at the same time special procedures have yet to be done."

"You can send your surgeon here, if he's discreet, to do the snipping. Take a load off your and the cardinals back if you want." Auntie Nonie smirked knowingly, just shy of a wink, her index finger touching glossy, swollen lips. "Y'know, he *might* even help with that *other* thing."

Father Bricolage's eyebrows went aloft at that statement. "Indeed, he might," he said absently.

He then reached into his leather satchel, extracted an envelope, and handed it to Auntie Nonie. "It's a cashier's check for the full amount, the remaining balance, which I'm sure you'll know how to disburse so that Honest Kickback Jack won't be finding anything anomalous on the books."

She snatched the envelope from his hand, folded it and stuck it under her sweater dress between her breasts. "Thanks, Daddy-O. Y'know, you're only half the problem, really. None of the freaky Fraters have shown up either and they were supposed to be here the same time as you."

"I'll talk to Frater Phlegethon about it."

"You mean Barry Weiss? The guy you shot? Good luck with that,"

"I think it should be alright," said Father Bricolage, putting his hand on Auntie Nonie's shoulder in a comforting way, which she knocked off with a snort. "You'll find in the secular world that almost anything can be done with the right amount of emoluments applied to it and matched by faith of course."

"The check's helpful, Father. No shit. But it doesn't solve the problem. It's just so fucking messy. We *have* to get rid of those boys without much further delay."

"And the real reason for this is that you expect more lost children from the Southern Border, isn't it?"

"Of course I do. *That's* where the real money is. We should never have taken the church on as a client to begin with, but those damn DeVilles get all weak in the knees over the Catholic Church. I swear, it probably makes Betty DeVille wet to think you're involved with little old Bethlehem—damn papal groupie that she is."

"When *Defensores Fidei de Puero* is finished for the foreseeable future, we'll trouble you no more with the sacred needs of the Holy See."

"You mean of the *cardinal,* right?"

"That's right, Auntie. I misspoke."

"Like hell you did, Father, and—" Auntie Nonie's words were all at once caught in her throat. She swallowed hard with a strained and audible gulp and her face drained of color.

"What's the matter, Auntie? Are you alright?" There was no response for a few crucial seconds. "Auntie?" the priest asked tentatively again.

"H-holy mother of God, Father! Holy shit! We are majorly *fucked.*" She paused for a moment, then shrieked, her right arm extended parallel to the floor and her index finger pointing shakily out the door. *"We're fucked!"*

Father Bricolage turned around and looked out on the grounds from the open door to catch a glimpse of the jerky movement of little silhouettes that could only have been two small children running at top speed away from the lights of Bethlehem and toward Newton Centre down Herrick Road.

The priest took off after them, leaving Auntie paralyzed and shivering in the doorway from more than just the dank late Spring cold. His cassock spread like bat's wings in the darkness.

"Children, wait!" screamed the Father.

They didn't.

FIFTEEN

He was just another club-footed, crabbed little man of the shadows cast harshly in broad daylight, overdressed for the humid late Spring weather in bulky topcoat and porkpie hat, making his way down Washington Avenue toward decrepit Cary Square in Chelsea. He zeroed in on one of the larger, tumbledown structures of the square that still showed some activity in its comings and goings that weren't necessarily impeded by backhoes and bulldozers quite yet, but they were closing in. This was right along the edge of grim residential Addison-Orange neighborhood, named by developers for those central conduit streets trying to efface the poverty and despair that had queered attempts at reinvestment gentrification that had graced other such Boston neighborhoods for the past forty years.

The place was a dull, babyshit brown color.

A bent steel sign with broken enamel swung like a straight razor over the high plaster portico that defined the entrance, its door header having long ago crumbled away. Filling in the few missing letters of the swaying, creaking sign, you could make out the name 'Knights' and nothing else. Presumably the structure must have housed the Knights of Columbus, predating its Broadway Address. Those who came and went didn't seem like a

Knights bunch, all of them younger men, weedy or husky, bearded and intense with nothing in between the extremes. They all walked hunched over a little and didn't notice the equally hunched, crabbed and hobbled shape of Null approaching the entrance. Or, if they did, it meant nothing to them.

"They don't know me yet," Null mumbled to himself. "I would have thought they might, but they don't. They will soon."

The heavy institutional door with the tiniest horizontal rectangle of chicken-wire glass at six-foot level was propped open by a miniature boulder, and when Null walked through it, he immediately realized that it was several degrees colder inside than outside. The space also looked larger inside than outside, as if he had stepped from one world directly into another that was wider, larger, cavernous. One that was empty, gaping like a giant wound and the further up you looked the darker the high shadows became. The interior odor made Null's mouth taste of burning rubber and the scent itself was of cold, musty air and the emetic cheesy redolence of dead rats.

Despite the space being largely empty, there was a good bit of useless detritus cluttering the ground floor, as if the basement below it—and there was a basement—

had vomited up broken chairs, ancient broken wooden desks, the bottom halves of swiveling stools with their serrated threads and bent steel pivot rods pointing toward the door as if sending a message. Null could feel the dust collecting on his tongue as he walked to the center of it.

He ignored it all and even more coldly than the space itself or the unsettled late Spring air outside.

There was a man crouched over sitting atop one of the more stable halves of the busted-up, antique administrative furniture that looked solid enough even in its age to hold his weight. Many of the scattered dark and wooden bits and pieces furniture looked old enough to have been artifacts of the Great Depression of the 1930s. The whole place was a sad anachronism of useless decay and hopeless wreckage adumbrated by murky dust and filth.

None of that interested Null.

But the crouched-over man sitting on half a broken desk in the center of the space in the open black pea coat did.

He had mutton-chop sideburns, horn-rimmed glasses, and looked not much older than twenty-eight. He was idly kicking his heels against the broken desk like an impatient child. Mist came out of his nose and mouth, which made him seem unreal, but Null got the sense that that true irreality was somehow intrinsic to the man and was at the base of the man's character. The man's black pea coat was open, and the top of his shirt unbuttoned, but he didn't look uncomfortable, and he wasn't shivering. Null felt like shivering and hugged his topcoat closer into himself, not because he felt the discomfort of the cold, but because he didn't want his shivering to be mistaken for fear.

He was there to give fear, not the appearance of suffering from it.

"You're here to see a man, now, aintcha, boss?"

The man didn't so much as turn his head to look at Null. He was staring intently off into nothingness, into the middle distance, as if his gaze could somehow incidentally blast a hole in the far wall of the room.

"You're here to be seen I think."

"Is that right?"

"It shakes out that way."

"It's pretty cold in here, boss. You shakin' yet?"

"I can defeat the impulse."

"They say nothin' scares you, boss."

"Oh, so you know me."

"As much as one man can know another, boss, which is not at all. Really."

"That's deep. You're supposed to be a deep one—running this spectacular show I see." Null waved his arm about the room in sarcasm, but it was too wooden a movement to get the point across.

"People come to see me, boss, that's all. And I see to their needs when I can."

"Their spiritual needs?"

"This ain't no church, boss. I do the needs of the flesh and the fulfillment of the heart."

"And money, of course. Any means of raising cash that you can. I was told you're partnered up with an international criminal enterprise that puts you in with trafficking children. Kidnapping them, selling them and, in some cases, buying them to re-sell them to your partner. The great criminal enterprise."

"You mistake me for a priest, boss? It ain't like that."

The man didn't move, didn't alter his crouch, didn't alter his gaze from a broken wall whose bricks were showing and that had a few holes that let the waning daylight in. The daylight didn't catch his gaze, just the thick coat of dried-blood-red paint that covered that wall in places that had yet to crumble. He had no intention of looking at Null for petty reasons of power and control. Null was used to this and ignored it, completely at ease while talking to the back of the man's head.

"We all like money, boss. What's your point? You some kind of law, boss?"

"I'm not the law, but you embody a law, I think. Thelema, they call it, right? Do what thou wilt shall be the whole of the law?"

"Nothing wrong with freedom, boss. Ain't that what this great country's all about?"

"They say it is, you say it is. Everybody says it, but too few look beneath to realize how little freedom they actually have. And there's a big difference between freedom and a free-for-all."

Mirthless, deadened: "Good one, boss. I'll have to remember that."

"You think you're a member of the Catholic Church—your partner, isn't that right? I think the church might have a few things to say about that, and likely may take the opposing view."

"Where there's a will, there's a way, boss."

"You're admitting to me right now that you're involved with the church."

"Our lodge is very church-friendly, boss.

"Interesting that you say that, considering your order of the Oriental Knights Templar were excommunicated and executed 700 years ago. I don't see the rift between your religions ever mending so easily—what do they call you? Hadit?

"They call me Theo Teocalli. I ain't nobody's father."

"Oh? *Pater Hadit,* maybe? Are you sure you're not the living father to Ra-Hoor-Khuit, Lord of the Aeon and The Crowned and Conquering Child according to your Thelema? The babe in the lotus?"

"That's pretty dramatic stuff ya got there, Boss. I'm a pretty simple guy. It ain't like I'm involved with organized religion or nothin'."

"Maybe not, but it appears to me that you want to be."

"Well, there is a history there, boss. That's just a plain fact."

"You mean past your removal from the Catholic Church—your stillborn attempt to get back in, *Ecclesia Gnostica Catholica*? The new branch of your cult that considers itself ecclesiastical. I read somewhere that you claim to give sacraments through the eucharist of the Gnostic Mass. Why you even do baptisms, confirmations, and ordinations of your own priests."

"Maybe so, but we don't do no Bar Mitzvahs, boss. Ya can't have everything."

"You're group is a cult, founded in 1895 by members of a group called the Occult Circle. Germans, in fact. Carl Kellner, Heinrich Klein, Franz Hartmann and Theodor Reuss. Your great beast, Aleister Crowley, didn't get in on the act until 1904. They were fascinated with Tantric Yoga, the withholding of the coital orgasm for long periods. They intended to use it to allow for a magic circle drawn about the lovers to empower those gathered about it to do supernatural feats. Crowley came along and turned that into a religion, gave you his Thelema, all the while imposing the ritual sex in which he was already engaged in as a pretext for polyamory. Claiming that cocaine-infused fucking was the key to understanding Rosicrucian, Masonic, and magical symbolism in general."

"Heady stuff, boss. No lie there."

"Your exalted Thelema is supposed to mean divine will, inclination and, more importantly, desire and its fulfilment in pleasure. Essentially, it's all just an exercise in hedonism, because all it was, in reality, was high-minded justification for group sex, yet another swingers' sex cult along the lines of the defunct Esalen, David Berg's Children of God and this modern BDSM movement that's basically swinging in leather."

"You're harshing my mellow, boss."

"And it all goes downhill from there with Jack Parsons and his manifesto of the Antichrist, which was supposed to 'put an end to all authority that is not based on courage and manhood.' Not quite a match with Catholicism."

"You know more about it than I do, boss. Too bad we don't need no historian."

Dusk was beginning to settle, blotting out the sparse, bright daylight that had gleamed in from the damaged far wall and the stark light from the open entrance that Null had walked through. But it wasn't just the oncoming night that drove the light from the doorway, but a crush of human bodies. And it wasn't the darkness but the voices in heated conflict that growled and threatened one another that drew his attention away from the crouched man in the black pea coat seated with his back toward him back to the doorway. Then the violence followed.

What had started out as a group commotion among a tightly knotted group of men and women who had the sad, disheveled aspect, from what Null could see in the gathering darkness of the homeless, which shouldn't have been the case, as the nearest shelter was Crossroads in East Boston—a rough, tragic place where surviving a night's sleep was a dicey proposition. Null knew that fact all too well, having bunked there not so very long ago.

Null knew who they were.

Not the homeless.

Worshippers.

Their faces in the darkening light were contorted masks of

hatred and anger, contempt and disgust. They were fighting each other to get inside the decrepit structure, which, when you looked up, was as high and wide as an indoor stadium, but without real parquet floors (and with debauched, seedy linoleum in patches) and featuring a catwalk that bordered the entire space three flights up like a long balcony. The worshippers fought for something, but apparently it wasn't for entry, as not a single hand or worshipful foot crossed the threshold, not even by a fraction of an inch. They were stopped as if by an unseen barrier right at the line between the gray, filth-caked linoleum and the threshold itself. A forcefield, to use pop cultural terminology. And they weren't going to cross it without permission. Yet Theo Teocalli, or Great Pater Hadit, had no intention of moving from his perch or taking his gaze off the dilapidated wall, or even to shoot a single glance indirectly at Null. Perched as he was, he was beginning to appear in the shadows like a life-sized rendering of a medieval gargoyle.

Yellow lighting abruptly flickered on, causing Null to blink.

"Your flock seeks inclusion, Pater."

"Everyone searches for acceptance, boss. You know that."

"Why not let them in?"

"You can see that for yourself, boss."

"Because of me."

"There you go."

By this time, Null had to shout to be heard above the imbroglio at the door. Theo Teocalli matched his volume.

"You're a pretty evasive guy, Theo."

"Ya think it's some kind of virtue to be easy to pin down?"

Null sounded robotic in his counter to this: "Would I be pinning you down to say that your cover story – your assertion that there are great social and political implications for using blood, semen and vaginal fluids in sexual rituals within a so-called magic circle formed by your followers with a couple engaged in suspended-orgasm-tantric-sex in the center borders on repulsive satire?"

"Wit is the epitaph of reason, boss."

"I forgot to laugh."

"The truth can be strange, boss."

"Especially when your truth is the prime justification for orgies and generalized perversion cloaked in ritual robes. But no one's playing dress-up tonight from the looks of things."

"One man's meat, boss. One man's meat. Not everything is spiritual."

"You think your story's credible—that you're harnessing all the special power that flows through the physical universe, the human body and the social body alike achieved by your sex antics and flowery spells?"

"You're distracted by the sizzle and not the steak, boss."

"Your parishioners are getting out of hand, Pater. I can barely hear you."

"Hey, you guys!" Theo Teocalli shouted, high-pitched, again, without turning his head or looking at anything other than the dreary, dried-blood-red crumbling wall, not shifting his position a nanometer nor moving any other part of his body but mouth and tongue. "Pipe down!"

The silence that followed was like a thunderclap.

They had all stopped together as one.

"Cute trick," Null said flatly.

The flock at the door stood stock still, lined up like statues.

"What did you call it before, boss? Thelema?"

"You know, Pater Hadit or Theo or whatever you choose to be called. I came here to ask you about a recent incident."

"Don't you have some other place to be, boss?"

"No, but I believe that you do, Pater."

"For real?"

"Frater Nostrum called himself—"

"Oh yeah. Bill Dunning, I think, boss."

"He somehow—or you and your friends standing patiently by the door—kidnapped me, then made me a proposition. That I should help you gather up a bunch of kids for some kind of big financial reward. Claimed he could make me rich. Hard to believe that when you take in the surroundings here that seem suitable for the wrecking ball and not much else."

"You got a point, boss?"

"Maybe not. But your friend Nostrum did. He killed a child right in front of me. Just to make a point, show me how extreme and dedicated to the profit principal he was. How powerful you are. A flex. What could I, just one man, ever hope to do should I stand against you. Not worth a child's life to underscore the point."

"Dunno, boss. The world don't seem to think a child's all that. I mean, they tell you that, but alls they do is the opposite. Infant mortality, kiddie starvation and slave labor ain't never been higher. Kiddies come cheap unless you wanna rear 'em like pets—then it's like 300K-a-year. Better to whore 'em out and be done with it, the way I see it."

"Oh, I know exactly how you see it."

"Think so, do ya, boss?"

"Now, I don't mind one way or any other that you and your flock fleece marks and brainwash them into dedicated cult members. That's been a staple of power and control doubtless before recorded time. It doesn't matter much to me at all. People can surrender their will to any bad movement or two-bit demagogue they like. They're adults. They can do what they please. I sell gak and adults love it. I don't make them buy it and certainly, whether I do that or I don't, somebody is going to, so it might as well be done right. And I do it right, as you probably know."

"Don't know nothin' about that, boss. We don't do no drugs here. Not even no antihistamines."

"Which means nothing."

"Gettin' pretty dark, boss."

"It's going to get a lot darker."

"So you're the guy what tore poor Bill's tongue out of his mouth and killed him."

"I admit I was impressed by how you kidnapped me and set me up at City Hall no less. You have obvious skills and resources despite the sad story these surroundings tell. That and the stink."

"She cleans up nice, ya know? Like magic. Too bad you ain't gonna be on the list for our upcoming Grand Sabbath."

"You think I'll need an invitation to attend?"

"I think you're puttin' yourself in places where you're not wanted, y'ask me."

"We think alike in that, Pater. You are now in a place where you're definitely not wanted."

"You like westerns, right, boss? This town ain't big enough for the both of us and so on. I'd lay off the movies, boss, before you hurt yourself."

"You have it right, Pater. I'm giving you a chance right now."

"I ain't leavin', boss. I don't think you can make me leave. You ain't got the horses for that."

"I'm not going to make you and your cult members leave. You'll stay put if I have my way."

"How's that then? What do you think you're gonna do? Call the *authorities*? Your law don't got no place for us anywhere in it. You should probably take off, boss. I can't hold them kiddies back forever, y'know."

"Call them in. I'd love to meet them."

"I just bet you would."

"You're not getting the point."

"I didn't think you had one, boss. I thought you just liked to hear yourself *orate*."

"I don't like anything, really. Don't really love anything. But I'm decisive. And I only do one thing. Just one."

"Oh, now we come to the climax, don't we, boss? I got goosebumps already."

"We do."

"Lay it on me."

"I'm leaving."

"'Bout time, ain't it, boss?"

Null's throat was dry and caused his voice to rasp paper-thin as he spoke. But when he answered Theo Teocalli's question, he still sounded bland and unconcerned; almost bored.

"Yes, you're right. But I'm coming back. And when I come back, and you're here and your mischief of rats is here, I'm going to kill every last one of you. As slowly as the time and the situation permit."

Theo Teocalli clucked his tongue in numb wonder and said nothing.

Null then turned his back on Theo Teocalli whose own back had been turned toward him the entire time, and walked toward the doorway, the warped, patchy linoleum of the cluttered floor dampening his footfalls. The worshippers at the entrance moved out of his way and let him pass untouched into the night.

SIXTEEN

"We up in this bitch *for realz*, all ridin' the same cah and the man wit' da keys be takin' his time bein' late. We *all* disrespected," Ronald complained. "Shit."

"He got us up in H Block, maybe get us smoked by them Heath Street motherfuckers if da H-Blockers don't get our asses first, dawg." This from Riley, a tall lanky man who looked too old to be a gang member, yet he ran three separate labs in Methuen run almost on auto-pilot by three U Mass chemistry majors who couldn't afford to continue their degree programs due to the costs of an education that decades ago was virtually free.

Riley was lolling on a black beanbag chair in a green asbestos-tiled and white-painted, nondescript room in an abandoned three-bedroom apartment in the Jesse Jackson Towers on Humboldt Street deep in H Block where that particular gang owned the streets.

No self-respecting Gangsta Boyz member would ever be seen walking H Block. And if he *was* seen, he would have literally been caught dead. Just a little bit north of Franklin Park, that small corner of Roxbury—Boston's most virulent and persistent ghetto—was known as H Block due to the fact that most of its street names began with the letter H: Humboldt, Homestead, Harold, Harrishof and Holworthy. The Jesse Jackson Towers, yet more low-income housing in a neighborhood that was surfeit with the same, was set back off a tarmac parking lot that had been reduced to rubble over the years. Only the few abandoned cars jacked up on concrete cinderblocks (that were never going to be moved) implied that it had ever been a parking lot in the first place. The Towers was far less imposing than its name declared, being squat rather than tall. In that area, which was close to the Bromley-Heath housing project in Jamaica Plain, the Towers was both overshadowed and forgotten but by the rats and the worst denizens of the street, including the Gangsta Boyz.

Only squatters and crackheads lived there now that nobody kicked up rent to anybody.

Yet it had become a universal Grandma's House—a gang demilitarized zone.

The worst of the Boston gangs—the H-Block gang, the Heath Street gang and even the NOB Gang (an abbreviation for the Norton/Olney/Barry streets in Dorchester)—could meet there with an expectation of survival if a heavy tithe were paid to the non-participant gangs. So far, there had yet to be a double-dealing gang massacre and every gang expected it and it was that unfulfilled expectation that kept the universal Grandma's House viable.

And, as Do-Rag, said, "Chill, homes. Da shot caller paid some hefty cake get us this place. He come in his own time. You know he got a plan. He *always* got a plan."

Ronald was pacing nervously while everyone else in the large main room, den or living room as you please, while everyone else was seated in mismatched chairs or on the large, cream-colored sectional sofas with stuffing popping out at the seams like little clouds frozen in time. The room was a hot bright white where the asbestos tiles ended. But it was also darkened with smudges of black due to the dust and collected filth that had creeped in from all the users of the room, be they dealers, junkies, more half-dead crack heads or spindly meth tweakers (courtesy of Joseph Xavier Null, undisputed meth king of Boston). All of these made themselves scarce when word came trundling down the cold, vacant yet grubbily cloistered streets of Roxbury that Grandma's House that day belonged to the Gangsta Boys and that weird, menacing zombie fuck Null who was some kind of Obeah Voodoo deity on the same level with Baron Samedi—and *no*body was going to fuck with that.

Desi, one of Null's street sling vassals, was a gaunt, quick-eye lifer of the streets, pushing twenty going on fifty-five. He strove to look relaxed, silently reciting mantras about money and the good life he had already accepted as being something that he would never live, flexing his fingers hard, rocking back carefully in a bridge chair.

Do-Rag sat in a corner hugging his knees to his chin.

Meth master Riley, another gaunt, slope-shouldered youth, got up and paced with Ronald, whom he towered over.

Dominic, a tall, well-muscled youth just barely twenty, standing an imposing six-foot five with a saturnine expression didn't speak. He didn't have to. His known loyalty to Null for having arranged a full-out merk crack at the doer of the explosion that killed Howard and his brother Edgar told you where he stood. And since joining up with the Gangsta Boyz—which didn't even require a serious beatdown for initiation—mooga flowed, cake was served, mooga and guap came down from heaven and wallpaper just pasted itself up every goddamn where.

Ronald bit his lip, refusing to sit down, though there were in fact ample chairs, all mismatched and of several different kinds, glaring at everyone in the room as he shifted his weight back and forth from foot to foot, rocking his thousand-buck Balenciaga sneakers. Like Cassius, one of the assassins of Julius Caesar, he had a "lean and hungry look." Yet he was only just a little more impatient than the rest of the lead crew of the Gangsta Boyz: Do-Rag, Riley, Desi, Dominic, Brother Ray and Jo-jo. If they weren't all deadly sure about why zombie fuck Null called them to meet all at once instead of by his usual surprise impromptu visits that never failed to scare the bejesus out of every single one of them every time he pulled one, they would have considered running off from the demilitarized zone double quick, as zombie fuck Null might have decided, thanks to Ronald, to smoke them all as a house-cleaning move.

And all the Gangsta Boyz took it as a bad sign that there wasn't a case of cold beer waiting for them when they each converged upon the place at the appointed time. Not one of them, not even Ronald, was going to be late to this meeting. And it didn't matter to any of them that Null was late.

Null was spooky, hincty, a buggin' J-Cat motherfucker from the jump. But stupid and frivolous? Never. Had he ever made a false move at any time that any of the Gangsta Boyz could determine, or even mention? Never. Was there always a dead-ass cold-fact solid reason for every move he made, no matter how stone seven-thirty it looked? However whack?

Yes. Dead-ass *yes*.

And crucially: Did that motherfucker bring in the guap?

More than they had ever made since they changed their name from the Crispus Attucks Crips back in the day when the actual Crips made it clear no one would make it to twenty if they kept on using that name.

"Watchoo so nervous 'bout, Ronald. You look like yo haid 'bout to eck-*splode*," japed Brother Ray, breaking the tense silence, tilting back in a La-Z-Boy lounger that looked like it had been narrowly rescued from a dump back in the 1970s.

"I'm fuckin' frosty, motherfucker. I gut nothin' to worry about."

"Huh!" Desi snorted. "You sure enough got somethin' to worry about the man come in here blazin' gats after your skinny black ass, he findin' you actin' all squirrely and shit."

"Ya, Ronald, don't be grillin' us like you don' know for a fack jus why da man call us here. He still gots the keys and that should be enough for you. Yooz all know why we here anyways."

"C'mon, y'alls know that when da man give explicit instructions he mean every damn syllable." This from an only slightly agitated Do-Rag.

"I don't give a shit *what* the man say," Ronald complained. "I think the whole thing sus. I'm 'bout to book."

"You should always look before you book, Ronald. Not doing so might get you killed."

That flat, dead, precise voice.

Colder than the room itself.

Null.

They all (though they would to a man deny it later) suspended their breath in that moment as one. Even Ronald, who had to emit a loud, guttural grunt just to collect himself and gather the nerve to respond, had frozen stiff. He managed to grunt a second time to unfreeze himself while Null stood giving him the fish-eye, then blurted, "'Bout time you brought yo' skinny chatted-out ass down here. We alls been waitin' on you."

"It's my car, Ronald. I call the time; who's late and who ain't. Unless you want to take the keys off me. So, *do you*?"

Ronald rubbed his face as if suffering from an intense headache – perhaps a migraine.

"Are you coming for them, Ronald?"

Null braced himself, his legs spread apart like an arch, his torso bent slightly forward.

Ronald held up both hands, palms front.

"Don't gut no intention o' doin' that, dawg. You gots the keys. I knows it." Ronald was astute enough to read that no one in the room had any intention of backing him at that moment.

"Very good. We should all work together in solidarity then."

They all assented to Null's statement, even though they weren't altogether sure what he meant by it. Especially since they all had seen too many bodies fall that hadn't taken the full range of meanings from just one of Null's seemingly casual statements. He was a timebomb, a walking landmine. And if anyone who knew this got twitchy enough to pull on him, they hit the ground dead before firing. "Did everyone here follow my directions?" Null filled the gap of silence. "Everybody comply?"

And the assent that followed filled the room and made its echo bark.

Ronald cleared his throat at a higher pitch than his grunt had been. "We alls know why the sling gut slowed down not by some but by a lot—them minnows been disappearin'. I don't think they runnin' on home to momma's cause they all don't gut no mommas."

"That's the fact, boss," agreed Brother Ray. "Revenues been sorely impacted."

"I may be just the cook—"

"No, Riley. You're not just anything. You're running three labs out there in the wilds of Methuen that nobody's caught onto yet. No bad incidents, no cataclysmic explosions, no fires—nobody knows. You spread the cake around right. Production's the best it's been."

"You ain't lyin, boss."

"I endeavor not to. And do so only when pressed."

"Endeavor what, you chatted-out motherfucker—"

"Slow down Ronald. Try not to get ahead of yourself. You're holding iron, aren't you? Packing heat? Got yourself a gat?"

"We *all* gots dem," Desi interposed, chuckling ruefully.

"Who—who don't?" asked Do-rag cheerlessly.

"It's straight up kidnapping," a flustered Ronald sputtered out, fuming.

"That's an A plus for you, Ronald. You are hands down my best student. That's it exactly."

"It ain't just the minnows," Brother Ray sighed. "It's losses. We's hemorrhaging da gak. An' our delivery system is all fucked up."

"Is that on you, Ronald?" Null asked with a vacuous tone that betrayed zero emotion, sounded almost innocent. Everyone there knew the question was far from that. Very far. "Can we chalk that up to how you run the sling?"

"You go 'head an' do that, cracker motherfucker. You playin' up in this bitch on ass and eve'ybody here know it. You ain't got too long and that's a fact."

"Is that right, Ronald? You're my number two and want to climb up to be number one—replace me, is that too a fact?"

Ronald smiled broadly and shook his head as if in deference to the shot caller. When he raised his head and slit his eyes, it became apparent that deference wasn't his stance. "You'd like me to pull, wouldn't ya? Then you'd see who ackshully supports yo boney ass, wouldn't ya? You *know* I gots maybe anotha betta cah comin' up soon. Figgered out that much, didn't ya, you chatted-out monkey mouth zombie fuck?"

"I know you've been talking about me when I'm not in the room, Ronald. I accept that. Who doesn't really?"

"Ya might say dat. You might. Why not axe the fuckin' room? You frontin' I say. I bet eve'yone agree wit dat. Real talk, homes."

"Okay, Ronald. Since you're not going to pull—"

"Shee-it, cracka! You think I'm a damn idiot. I bust out a gat and start blastin', we all fucked. They find out I'm the one broke da law and I get exampled right quick. Find me hangin' off Zakim Bridge, or off a lamppost at Grove Hall."

"On the beam again, Ronald. H Blockers and everyone else are going to enforce the peace or nobody gets anything anymore—no neutral place to make deals and armistices and so forth—and N-O-B and pals don't want that. Wouldn't take long to know who fired that killshot either, now would it? And maybe they kill some of your friends before they finally get to you." Null clucked his tongue. "Not good, though, no, any way you slice it. Maybe you think they'd kill me if you missed. Then again, I'm outnumbered here. You think you got the keys, but I could bite the big one here and now without anyone firing a shot. Isn't that so? And you wonder *why* I haven't killed you yet?"

"You still a monkey mouth chatted-out J-cat cracker mother-fucker." Ronald was breathing hard, feeling cornered where before he had felt the tide turning in his favor. The room was not his chorus.

At that, Riley rose up from his seat on the black bean bag chair and spoke calmly but loudly so that it echoed with a bounce effect throughout the sparse room that was so much larger than its contents.

"Respeckfully, boss, Ronald wants you to get a ho check, know I'm sayin'?"

"I know. You *all* know. You ready for that?"

"You buggin' zombie fuck—eve'ybody know you packin. Shee-it. We *know* how you do."

"Do you, Ronald? Because I'm ready for all of you right fucking now. And even you can be replaced, Riley. You know it because Jo-jo's seen me do it."

"Shit, this scarred-up ofay freak bastid done Alphonse like he was nuttin' just cause he fuck up an' kill a kid on a run. Like he was scrapin' doggie doo off his shoe. And he right ready to lay down the molly-whop on us all!" Jo-jo crouched down like he was a coiled spring.

"Anyone here kills a child, I'll do for him as I did for Alphonse. You want to ho check me already, let's go here and now. I've been ready for that since before I got here. Jo-jo's right. I'll lay down the molly-whop on all of you before you can blink an eye. Like a challenge? Well, here it is, gents, come one, come all—"

"No, no, *no!*" cried Riley. "We not here to give dipshit Ronald the keys. He couldn't drive no car, not the way you do. We *alls* know this."

"Well, Gangsta Boyz, if you don't come and ho check me now, I'm going to ho check *you.*" Null's voice was unaffected, even soft as he knew the echo would carry it. He might have been asking someone to pass the salt at dinner.

Ronald began to quake, from anger or fear, no one could really be sure. Perhaps from both.

"Think 'bout why we here!" cried Do-Rag, popping up from his corner of the floor. "We don't find out who's kidnappin' the minnows—den we got no cake no matta how much gak Riley chefs up in da kitchen."

"True dat," Riley chimed. "No minnows, no cake, no matta *how* much gak I bake."

Ronald did a quick spin about on his heels and saw out of the corner of his eye Null reaching for any one of a number of guns in his coat, all semi-automatic.

"A'ight. A'ight!" Ronald squeaked. "I wylin. I be wylin *and* stylin'! You can all chill—you gots da damn keys, boss, an', no, I don't need no heart check, no ho check an' no check at all! We don't gotta take it there."

Everyone sat back down but Ronald and Null. Ronald was breathing too hard to conceal it and Null looked like he wasn't breathing at all; as if had never drawn a breath in his life.

"You have something for me, Ronald, isn't that right?"

"Yeah. You right. You want the thing?"

"Sure. Hand it over."

Ronald tossed him the sickly green colored plastic package of gak to Null, which he caught one-handed as if he weren't paying attention.

"This supposed to be more gak?" Null asked as if distracted, examining the package.

"Fresh outta da lab, done up by a itty-bitty startup com-pe-tit-*tor* of us. They chef be dumb, though. Real talk."

"Riley does just fine."

"Naw, I ain't sayin' Riley need to go, but he runnin' three labs down in Meth Town. Dis chef straight up MIT chemistry genius. Give dat gak a taste, you see what I'm talkin' about."

Null tossed the sickly green, postal-taped-up pack of gak back to Ronald, who caught it shakily in both hands. Then Null pulled a French serrated switchblade from his coat pocket, strode over to where Ronald stood in confusion, grabbed the pack from his hands, made a slit in it with the knife, scooped some powder onto the flat of the blade and held it up level to his face.

"Take it," Null whispered.

"I don't mess wit dat shit. Yo go haid, boss."

"I'm telling you to do it now."

He didn't have to say he'd use the knife on Ronald. His eyes said it. The room knew it. So, with all the bravery he could muster,

Ronald snorted it off the blade quickly without a rolled-up dollar bill to help him. Naked to the blade, no hesitation.

"Tell me, now, how righteous that gak is, Ronald. Let us all know."

"I guess it's 'bout's good as ours."

Ronald's eyes watered and his face went slack.

"I thought it was some kind of super gak. Leave old Riley and Meth Town in the dust, right."

"It just—"

"Just what, Ronald?"

"Okay, boss. Okay. Just *O*-kay!"

"You don't look so good, Ronald. Maybe you should take a seat?" Null waved his hand and indicated a debased faux Victorian parlor chair whose upholstery had been eaten away decades ago. It made a loud creak when Ronald sat down in it, rubbing his eyes, allowing his head to hang down.

"Righteous gak," Null remarked absently. "Totally righteous."

"We gotta take back the street. Fuck dose tykes—get men back on the sling, no one gets kiddie-napped, know I'm sayin'?" Jo-jo belted out, not bothering to stand as it might have been taken for a challenge he had no intention of making. "I'll run them streets wit' Ronald and we back doin' a cakewalk."

"You have ambition, Jo-jo, which is good. Useful, to be truthful, so I appreciate that. But ever wonder why since we've implemented cast-off children—minnows—as our delivery system why arrests and court appearances of Gangsta Boyz have gone down to nil?"

"Eve'ybody know dat," remarked an impatient Desi. "Don't matter we don't de-liv-ah. Don't mean shee-*it*."

"True, Desi, yet it's good to not have Gangsta Boyz mouthpiece Wat Tyler Schulman earning his retainer, isn't it? No warrants to dodge, no messy skip traces to outrun, no appearances before rueful elitist judges to make. Not the worst state of affairs."

Dominic didn't have to stand to command attention when he spoke, loud and low, the tone of it projecting a quality of looming presence from where he sat. "Security gots to be upped. We should all be watchin' them itty-bitty kiddies."

"We got men eve'y which way, no one sees nothin' and I hear-ed tell some spooky crew tryin' to be like you, Mr. Shot Caller snatchin' up dem kiddies." Brother Ray opined. "You knows what's gotta be done—put in the damn work on the streets."

"Put in da work," was repeated by all in the room, but Null just stood there, unblinking.

"Put in the work," Null at last repeated and the echo barely carried it.

"Gentlemen, I know who the doers are—at least half of them. But I don't know who the other half is, and I don't know what they're doing with our minnows. But one of them murdered a child right in front of me."

Riley jumped to his feet, seething, "Shot Caller—you betta fuckin' know or maybe dis room put the molly whop on *you!*"

Before Null could react, Ronald slid off his chair down to the dust-ridden floor, white lather oozing from his mouth.

Null had yet to move, yet to speak and all the Gangsta Boyz made a squawk round robin that was cut off by the door to Grandma's House blasting open and a gang of blue-jacketed FBI agents with drawn Glock 19 millimeter sidearms storming into the room, all of them male and all of them reflecting a practiced rage. Not even Null resisted being cuffed and put up against the soot-smeared wall, still speechless.

Special Agent in Charge, Joel Thrawn, followed behind the agents along with Detective Lieutenant Katherine Boyd close in, both flipping badges, the former grinning ear-to-ear and the latter looking harried, beleaguered and defeated.

"I think the kid on the floor might need some medical," Boyd sighed.

Agent Thrawn walked over to the impassive and cuffed Null, patted his scarred and swollen face and said, sounding almost giddy, smiling broadly: "Don't tell me—*you're* the zombie fuck Null?"

SEVENTEEN

The tumbledown, creaky-looking "no-tell" motel had been sandblasted clean, all signage and come-hither lighting removed. A soiled banner had been draped over the once brightly lit sign announcing The Muddy Charles Motel and vacancies aplenty, correcting your vision in rust red paint that there were no longer any vacancies there and that there may never be any again, sloppily proclaiming: "Closed for Renovations."

If you had stopped your car without having zipped by it on your way to Harvard Square or to Storrow Drive heading toward the Central Artery, the Ted Williams Tunnel, Logan Airport or home on either shore, you'd wonder why anyone would have ever wanted to have anything to do with the place anyway. And now it had seemingly been stripped of all color—the bilious green, jaundice yellow, nosebleed-red hues of signage were gone and left in their place was just a gray blocky mass and black cast that even in broad daylight looked to have been overcome by shadows and a heavy, grim resignation that was an absence of color all its own.

The defunct motel looked as if it had been plopped down as an afterthought by an angry god fed up with loose human depravity onto a large traffic island right on Soldier's Field Road between

Market Street in Brighton and the Eliot Bridge in Cambridge. You may think that maybe such a god as this was evacuating his bowels, didn't care at all where he did it and that that may have been the case if such gods existed, but even if they didn't, the Motel stuck out as something wrong, out of place and maybe more than a little foul. There it was between Harvard University and Hell—a former brothel of disaffected male teen prostitutes formerly run by the defunct world kiddie-porn player Hebe Group that was now no more and had no chance of ever again asserting its claim in the highly profitable world of child trafficking, murder and abuse.

Permanently broken and crippled as all such enterprises should be and too few are.

There are clichés we all know about fighting fire with fire and that two wrongs don't make a right, and yet the miserable, repulsive business of child sex trafficking called kiddie porn had been stopped cold by a brutal and remorseless criminal so horrible, so coldly terrible that it was a serious risk even to just carelessly mention his name on the street.

And it was that unfeeling monster who killed with abandon, quickly without blinking, slowly with dedicated care and attention to applying the maximum amount of pain until the subject longed for a death that was being withheld to make the extremity of torment that much worse, that much more unendurable, taking it that much further into the gray zone of excruciating human pity where there could be no pity, where there could be no mercy, where there could be nothing but agony in the space of a dream that seemed to be everlasting until the last light of hope whimpered into darkness.

The two small boys zigzagging on foot where there was no walkway, dodging cars and trucks, less terrified of dying that way than from where they had just escaped barely made it, sweaty and determined and not nearly as terrified as they should have been had they only known better. But they didn't know much of anything, and their knowledge of the world was a patchwork genome of human frailty that contained only small fragments of right answers.

And so those intermittent fragments of haphazard connectivity brought them to the absolutely wrong place for exactly the right reasons.

Maybe not so wrong a place as at first it may have appeared.

"You really think this fucked place gon help us? It ain't even opened up," whined Larry Grouse, shivering with the last of the winter chill. It wasn't just that he was in his pajamas—half his shivering was motivated by a knowing fear that his best friend was right about their impending murder of convenience.

"Naw, Lar, I see lights. Looka the office. There ain't no sign lit, but I think there's a guy in the office," replied Marion Slaughter.

"We gotta get inside somewhere quick. My balls is ice."

"Ya, I know. But I'd rather die out in the cold than be murdered by the lady with the big tits."

"They shoulda lifted her off the earth and into the strat-*to*-sphere already them balloons, that freaky biatch."

"We don't gotta die out in the cold if the guy at the desk let us in."

"Charge then, you crazy mo-fo!"

"Fuck yeah."

"You coulda been killed back there in the orphanage faw droppin' the F-bomb too!"

"Yeah. They like they kiddies obedient, nice 'n' dead. No F-bombs evah!"

"Fuck the F-bombs and charge that muthafucka!"

Holding hands in a fleeting gesture of innocent trust, the two small boys dreaming they were in a movie with everything heightened in meaning and aspect, exaggerated into a great adventure starring two equal heroes, just like that old cowboy movie *Butch Cassidy and the Sundance Kid* throwing everything they had at a precise goal with so much effort and hope, how in the name of the god that defecated out the former Muddy Charles Motel could they possibly fail?

The sound of two small bodies thudding against the thick glass door to the office woke Brother Ray's right-hand IT assistant, Noggin Wintle, from his reverie. Noggin (for the size of his head, which rivaled the corpulence of his body) had been playing with a pirated version of Quick Books, importing one XML file to replace another and testing out a free online XML validator to fix the kinks in his hurried coding and to perhaps lessen the tedium of the operation. The office was warm—well-heated as was the rest of the former Muddy Charles, still half-full of hangers-on from the days of Hebe Group, not having yet determined or committed to finding another place to land before their inevitably being turned out into the street to face whatever came. Noggin himself had been daydreaming, half-asleep after having completed the myriad of tasks texted to him from his boss' cellphone. He hadn't yet encountered it directly, and he hoped to God he never would have to, but the cold, airy disapproval of his boss for even a minor mistake could very well result in his being macheted to death, bludgeoned to death or his being the merciful recipient of a Teflon-filled nine-millimeter round lodged permanently in his agile brain.

And if his boss, the *big* boss, not the cool, affable Brother Ray Carstairs, but Joseph Xavier Null—a.k.a "that zombie fuck Null"—knew that he had had the slightest thing to do with Ronald Brogan's ill-fated plan to take over the Gangsta Boyz gang from an unstable, unpredictable criminal psychopath who murdered with unparalleled pain and efficiency as if he were brushing lint off his overcoat, well, his fat ass would never be found.

Even as he puzzled over the strange thudding at the door, he shook the cobwebs from his beleaguered brain and felt relieved for the job that, although it definitely put him in danger of an unwanted encounter with a homicidal maniac, it ironically kept him too busy working all the gang data with his IT skills to be rounded up with rest of the Gangsta Boyz in the latest mass arrest at Grandma's House in the Jesse Jackson Towers on Humboldt street in Roxbury.

Sometimes that kind of relief was enough.

Even better: no one knew what had become of Null, his own personal deity of plenty and death.

That was when Noggin felt a jolt of courage run through him like an electric charge, so, emboldened, he went to the door, wiped the condensation of his breath from the glass and peered out onto the empty parking lot. "Nothin'. I need to wake the fuck up."

He sighed and looked back on his workstation set up at what remained of the motel front desk with the three jumbo flat-screen monitors, three separate towers as many motherboards and processors (with multiple cores within them), more RAM than he could possibly use, triple hard disk capacity, and a huge ergonomic keyboard that sprawled in his lap when he sat in his ergonomically specific 400-pound capacity multi-function black mesh office chair with adjustable sliding seat depth. When it was all said and done, he smiled to himself knowing that there were far worse places to be —far less enjoyable places to be and tasks to do than what he was confronted with daily, managing the last vestiges of the Muddy Charles Motel.

He was jarred when the thud came back again.

This time it was the two small boys, Larry Grouse and Marion Slaughter, their faces ugly and distorted pressed up against the glass like snails sticking to the glass of an aquarium.

"Get the fuck out y'here, you kids. This place be off limits fo' childrens!" he warned.

The two boys shouted back a jumble that amounted, after several high-pitched repetitions, to this: "They wanna kill our asses and cut off our nuts!"

With a shrug and a sigh to the benefit of exactly no one, Noggin Wintle, went and snatched up his set of master keys from the crowded workstation, shambled to the door, unnerved by the knocking and shouting of the two small boys, who, after he let them in, ran right into his legs and hugged them for warmth. He gently pushed them off and knelt down to their level.

"Watchoo two childrens doin' outside half nekkid in this weather? You was already riskin' freezin' ta death already."

Marion and Larry tried to tell their story coherently to the Gangsta Boyz assistant IT manager while he made them both Swiss Miss hot chocolate in red Solo cups from the hot spigot option of the water cooler next to the employees-only restroom entrance. Of course, Marion and Larry couldn't express what happened to them in a cogent, orderly way. Fortunately, one of Noggin's specialties that made him useful and kept him alive in a blood-thirsty street gang was data mining.

They were slurping greedily from their Solo cups of instant hot chocolate—the kind with little marshmallows, the kind that came out dry from a paper packet. They didn't care if it burned their mouths.

He realized soon enough that he'd have to order out some pizza for these boys.

And before he did that, he never had to ask the one question preying on his mind.

"We came here 'cause of that zombie guy—the dead guy that runs this hoorhouse."

"It ain't that no more, Lar. The dead guy killed everyone but let the gay hoors stay here free. Maybe he got more killin' to do?"

"He *always* got more killin' to do, childrens. He never stop killin', which is why yo' little asses need to go—"

"They say the dead guy pays kids to deliver gak," Larry explained. "Take care of 'em good, too—better'n the folks that sold 'em."

"Ya—we dint finna crawl all the way from Snootin' Center to freeload. We wanna work. No cap!"

"We excaped!" Larry cried, half with joy, half with worry.

Noggin shook his head, suppressed a worried grin, collected the red Solo cups from the boys and went about making them round two of hot chocolate with little marshmallows, not quite sure of what else to do.

"So, you say they gon' smoke ya little asses at a Christian orph'-nage b'cause ya can't sing some shitty song ya don't know? That's whacked," Noggin told them to ensure that he had at last gotten the gist of their fragmented squeals and cries.

"Ya," said Marion with wry pride. "We got 'em fooled on that."

"True dat," said Larry, neatly high-fiving Marion without a thought, as that was the cue for it.

"You say the big-boob lady gon' kill youse f'a *fack?*"

"Nah," Larry blurted, cutting off Marion who was eager to answer that in drastic terms. "She got priests to come and break our necks. priests'll do dat—like with chickens."

"Priests..." Brother Ray repeated half-aloud to himself.

"They got *two* kinds o' priests," added Marion. "Two! The *catlick* ones and the ones wit' da hoodies."

"Hoodies?"

"Yeah. Bathrobes too."

"They stone seven-thirty suckas runnin' aroun' in them black bathrobes," Marion explained with what he thought was perfect understanding.

"Black. Bathrobes," repeated Noggin aloud, thoughtfully, as if an information dump were being performed by one part of his brain upon another.

"*Love dem hoodies!*" cried Larry happily.

"Hoodies be dope f' the *pope!*" cried Marion just after, as Larry's hand extended up to meet his for an on-cue high five.

"Hoodies," Noggin repeated emptily even as his brain filled with reason. "Pope," he whispered his thick lips making a small, round O. "Pope."

"Where you goin', Mister Noggin?"

"Ya, we dint finish tellin' ya 'bout dat crazy boob lady," added Larry.

"You guys kin sit down now in those two chairs by the exit to the stairs. The green ones. It okay if you spill sumpm' on 'em. They the kind wipes clean. I got to make a call."

"You maybe orderin' dat pizza?" Larry pleaded more than questioned.

"Dat, my little brotha, is the *nex'* call I gon' make."

———

"Ten dead girls," Special Agent Joel Thrawn said between gritted teeth.

"Don't know about that," Null spoke as if he were checking in a hand of Texas Hold 'Em.

The interrogation suite at FBI Boston Division in Chelsea, walking distance from the cold and roomy shambles that was the main Boston temple for Ordo Templi Orientis, could have doubled for a conference room. There was nothing of the offputting and crude appearance of security that was provided even in the most deluxe interrogation suite offered by BPD at One Schroeder. Granted, it was spartan, staid and stolid, but not entirely unpleasant.

There were no windows, of course, not even ones that would look out on the busy main corridor of the fourth floor, but the lighting was soft, and the room aerated by fans that moved the vitiated air about in an emulation of fresh air that nevertheless remained stale. It was all meant to relax the subject yet keep them addled with the staleness of their own exhalations.

"What the fuck, Joel?" Boyd snapped, nearly tipping her chair over backward as she sprang to her feet. "You get your main suspect runner of Boston's up-and-coming drug cartel to come up here and capitulate and *that's* what you have to ask him?"

"Settle down, Kay," Agent Thrawn replied in a harsh whisper. "It's unprofessional to side with subject. Even down at One Schroeder, they know that. *You* know that."

"I don't think she's siding with me, Agent Thrawn."

"I'll let you know when I want you to speak, shitbird!" Agent Thrawn hollered as if a Drill Instructor for the Marines at Parris Island.

"Joel, what in Christ's name do you think you're doing?"

"I'm closing a case, Kay. A big one. And shitbird here is going to help me do it."

"I—I don't really—get what you're doing."

"I get it, Kay."

Agent Thrawn swiveled around in his seat, leaned across the table and put his face as close to Null's as he could get and snarled, "If you call Lieutenant Detective Boyd here 'Kay,' one more time, fella, I'll knock your teeth down your throat!" Tiny flecks of saliva dotted the stale air and hit Null in the face.

Null looked bored, not bothering to move a muscle or even blink.

"Calm down, Joel. Null's my CI too. He's been calling me Kay for a long while now."

"Yes, Agent Thrawn. At some point soon I'll be calling you Joel. It's an inevitability whether you punch me in the face or don't."

"Don't do it, Joel. Null's taken more than just a punch or two and his pulse never gets above sixty."

"I'd like to put that to the test, Kay."

"Fine with me as long as it's tit for tat, Joel."

Agent Thrawn jumped up from his seat and took a swing at Null, which didn't connect. Null, as if no one existed in the room at all but him, sat impassive and unresponsive, patient as the Buddha Statue of Hyderabad.

"He doesn't rattle at all, does he, Kay?"

"Not that I've seen. And I only wish he would."

"Listen, fuckstick. I've got all your crew—pretty—

much the important players arraigned. I'll get more of them too, and you too in the bargain, I don't get me some good answers pretty fuckin' fast."

"I've got some answers for you, Joel. You're not going to have me arraigned because I'm going to be your informant, your CI, which is fine by me. I accept that deal."

"How do you know I want that, shitbird?"

"Well, gee, Joel—"

"Agent Thrawn!"

"Joel. None of the Gangsta Boyz are going to court once our counsel Wat Tyler Schulman has them post bail. You don't have them on possession for personal use, possession with intent and not even that extra-special eighteen months in jail, up to five years in state prison for possession of an unlicensed firearm, which begs review as it happens to be *prima facie* cruel and unusual punishment, as it denies the offender due process of law and violates the separation of powers doctrine of article thirty of the Declaration of Rights of the Massachusetts Constitution."

Agent Thrawn stopped pacing the room abruptly and asked, with a nonplussed expression, "Is this shitbird for fuckin' real, Kay?"

"Who do you want to be, Agent Thrawn—H. Paul Rico? Maybe Joseph Connolly? They both ran Whitey Bulger and Steve "The Rifleman Flemmi" and both did time. You planning on doing time, Joel? I got friends and contacts in Concord and Walpole that might help you out, if that's what you want to do. You can't have too many friends, now can you, agent?"

Boyd sighed as if she had heard this question one time too many, although she hadn't. "Too fuckin' real, if you ask me, Joel."

"I'll get you for conspiracy off what we found on your lieutenant, Ronald Brogan—"

"Joel, you can have Ronald. I gave him to you, served him right up, if you recall. You have no recorded evidence, not a single syllable. And what you have on Ronald extends only to Ronald, which is a definite on the eighteen-month bid for an unlicensed firearm and even the gak he had on his person. All my guys will testify he tried to give it to me, and I refused it. I even shoved it up his nose with my knife."

"Which was well over the allowable size for a pocket pen knife, so that's a misdemeanor concealed weapons charge right there."

"Do you really want an AUSA to prosecute me for that? While I'm working the street as your confidential informant, which is what the whole brouhaha was about to begin with? You had no interest in me as Boston's alleged meth king. You never had any intention of doing that at all, especially when we both know that I already have the Boston FBI's savvy and expert drug interdiction team on my case. But you and I know that even they can't make their case, now can they?"

Boyd gave Agent Thrawn a slit-eyed look.

"Joel, tell me right now what the actual fuck is going on here right now or I'm walking out the door, which will mean we're done. And I'll be done with all this bullshit too once and for all."

Agent Thrawn slumped forward a little, wiped the beads of sweat off his brow with his shirtsleeve and sat back down, not bothering to look up at Boyd or even at Null, his head bent, and his eyes focused on the mauve wall-to-wall carpeting of the floor.

The eyes abruptly rose up, looking at nothing but the olive-drab walls which looked as if they were carpeted as well.

"He's right, Kay. I wasn't going to break his little drug gang. Not even the Interdiction Unit could do it, and they've been on this little fucker's ass for about a solid year. I just wanted to develop your legally dead CI into *my* legally-dead CI."

"So that's why the original request that saved me from lousy paperwork details and that hump Wilbur Quark? Fuck, am I blind."

"Ain't we all, Kay."

"He's not really street, now is he, Kay? Not in the slightest, I say. So, what was he doing really, down here with the Feebs? No, don't tell me – forensic accountancy. Right? It's a stink all over him like flopsweat." Null sniffed the air loudly and made a face to punctuate his point.

"I hate that you have a knack for that, Null. I really, really do."

"I'd just love to take that free punch to the little fucker's face about now."

"But you won't, Joel, will you? Because you know you need me. I read the street better than any of your fellow agents or any rat you know of and—congratulations. You win. You got me. I'm *your* CI now."

"I'll let Kay borrow you now and then."

"You don't have to be so magnanimous, Joel. You can have him. Let him move in with you, for all I care, because that ain't going to happen to me and I don't want you to die of loneliness."

"Don't get romantic, Kay. This isn't the time."

Null looked distracted, spoke perfunctorily.

"I can tell you this, Agent Thrawn. I live, work and breathe the street. All of it all the time, to the exclusion of all else. A crime goes down in my city, I know all about it, and if I don't know about it, I'll *still* know quicker than Ronald Brogan hitting the floorboards face first after having snorted a bump of poisoned gak. How's he doing, by the way? Elude your clutches, after all?"

"He'll live, close call though. They should have let the fuckwad die, then I could get you on a righteous murder bust."

"If I could laugh at that, I would. He was trying to kill *me* with his bad gak, not the other way around. How was I supposed to know it was poisoned?"

"But you knew, didn't you?"

"An educated guess isn't knowing, Joel. For all I knew, it could have just been shittier product than the stuff I allegedly make."

"If I blood-tested you for gak, I could get you on a possession rap, sweetcheeks."

"Just because I'm your newly minted CI, Agent Thrawn, doesn't mean that you don't still need a warrant for that. Cut the tough talk. It'll make things quicker and more efficient if you do. Besides, everyone in Boston and his brother or sister who needs to know already knows you're not street and never will be. You were made before you ever set foot outside of Legoland."

"Just do what he says, Joel, for Christ's sake, and quit fuckin' around already. Let us all know right now: What. The. Fuck. Are We. *Doing here?!*"

Agent Thrawn sighed again. Then he repeated with an undertone of weary ferocity the same curt phrase: "Ten dead girls."

Null and Boyd returned the remark with blank stares.

"What does he mean, Null?"

"I honestly don't know."

"I meant what I said in the first place: *ten dead girls.*"

"A shame, if true," Boyd said for lack of anything else to say.

"It's not just a shame, Kay. It's *everybody's* shame."

"Holy shit," mouthed Boyd.

"Never heard of it," Null replied in a half whisper, realized he was lying but hesitated to add anything further. It wasn't necessarily what he was thinking of, was it? Because if it was, he had more than just one thing to add to that disclaimer.

"You're not makin' sense, Joel. That ever happened here in the bloody bean, it'd be bigger news than the indictment of Donald J. Trump."

Agent Thrawn pounded his fist on the table. "And that's the trouble, Kay, and even for you, there, fucknuts, it would be just that kind of news. Exactly. And yet even on hearing it you reject it because as even fucknuts knows, it's the kind of news nobody needs in this town at any level and on the side of any agenda. No one can use it and all it does is hurt everyone. It has to be cleared and cleared so quickly that by the time the whores of the Fourth Estate hear about it, it'll just be the ghost of a rumor. But maybe it ain't so bad for me, because I grabbed it, took the initiative. This is my ticket now. I clear this shit, I get that sucker punched.

"Bit of a rough way to go just to be a street field agent, Joel," Boyd said, perplexed.

"You think they'd let a forensic accountant like me loose on the street any other way? Think they think I'm suited for it, do you?"

Null sat there, silent, glassy eyed.

"Got something to add, fucknuts? I know you're pretty good at yacking anyone's ear off who'll listen. What does it mean when you go quiet. Pissin' your pants, are you?"

"I hate to say it, Agent Thrawn, but your plan isn't quite as terrible as it sounds on first hearing."

"Well, Katy, bar the fuckin' door. Praise from Caesar."

"Here's your problem, Joel, the way I see it. We now know something you're doin' that sounds pretty much off the books from where I sit ain't soundin' much better the less we know. A little knowledge can be a dangerous thing. In this case, for *you*."

"Look who's interrogating whom, Agent Thrawn."

Agent Thrawn rose up slowly from his chair.

"Shut up, Null. No one's supposed to know. Very few are in the loop on this. It's been hushed up hard and fast, because it's a huge scandal. A terrible scandal. Ten dead girls were unearthed in Newtonville—yes, I know, almost as hoity-toity as Wellesley. A septic tank went bad in one of the foreclosed-on houses—yes, that happens even in toney Newton, and when the foundation went and there was a bit of a collapse, a bulldozer came up with ten broken dolls wrapped up in burlap bags like potatoes. Ages eight-to-twelve. Fresh. Months old if that. We caught it immediately, the Newton PD being basically ceremonial and not much good otherwise. A lot of departmental pull and political muscle went into keeping it hushed up."

"How could that even be done in a roiling mire of gossip and rumor like Boston?"

"That would have been huge news, Kay—international news— if even the most rinky-dink of the weekly handouts caught hold of it. It'd explode into reverberating echoes of outrage that would last years online, constantly popping up in the news cycle, and occupy more of our time than any other case."

"This was Kennedy territory then," observed Null mirthlessly.

"To put it crudely, Null, that's exactly what it is. And must remain, even *if* we clear it."

"I don't get what he means, Joel."

"Sure you do, Kay. If the Kennedys could hush up all their violent miscreancy and criminal conduct, why can't the FBI take a page from their book?"

"If it got out, confidence in all local law enforcement would land right in the toilet," Boyd agreed.

"Not that there was much of that to begin with," Null rasped.

"Yeah. Smart mouth, fucknuts. And everyone would look to the FBI to solve the damn thing and even now we still haven't got bupkes on it. No ID on the girls, forensic evidence got fucked up by groundwater and sewage, all the teeth were smashed out of their mouths postmortem with a hammer. This was an organized body dump, not even likely to have been committed on site. The broken-up floor of a basement in an empty, foreclosed-on house at the bottom of a hill where flooding was almost guaranteed was a smart choice. Somebody knew what they were doing, which is why we don't got bupkes. As fucknuts pointed out, we're already in the shitter with PR as always, but *this* fucking monstrous outrage is deadly. Radioactive. It's going to shove us so far down the toilet, we might as well be broken-up, toothless corpses in burlap bags drowned in sewage ourselves. So, okay, Null. I played your game. Now riddle me this: who did it? And when you sell me on the who, don't forget to sell me on the *why* – so I don't have to shove it back into your fugly disfigured face and make you eat it."

Null and Boyd as one: "You're not street, Joel."

"But I will be."

"Maybe sooner than you think, Agent Thrawn."

"Sucking up won't put you on my team so quickly, fucknuts. It looks to me like you and Boyd have something going on that I'm not a part of."

"I'm not sure what your jealousy should evoke, laughter, tears, or my default, which is indifference. But I have a question that may contain an answer for you."

"Jesus fucking Christ, then lay it on me already!"

"Did you find a nightclub stamp on their wrists—the ten dead girls?"

"Why would any of the prepubescent girls be wearing a night-club stamp on their wrists? "Who would bother to do that?" Boyd asked dully.

Agent Thrawn's eyes went wide, and his mouth went slack.

"How did you know that?" he asked in a small voice.

"There's a follow-up question to that one, Agent Thrawn. If you were able to make it out, was it the image of *"La Pieta?"*

"From Saint Peter's Basilica in Rome?" Boyd asked, reaching a grim conclusion but stopping just shy of uttering it.

"Yes," Agent Thrawn answered absently. "They all had them, but the stamps were so faint and smudged we couldn't make out what club they were from. We could make out the image of one of them faintly."

"Christ," Boyd said reflexively.

"*La Pieta*," Null rasped.

"That's right, fucknuts. The virgin Mary contemplating the dead body of her son, Jesus Christ which she holds in her lap."

EIGHTEEN

The squat was new, immaculate, lit from a single bulb that hung down from a wire fixture connected to the ceiling, swaying gently with the cold draft from half-rotted window casements and sashes. Null and Boyd sat on ancient metal bridge chairs incompatible with the equally ancient bridge table that was set up in front of them. Peering over the tabletop were two scared little boys, Marion Slaughter and Larry Grouse, both wondering if they had blithely waltzed into what might be their last moments on earth. Their eyes were red with stress and tears.

"Okay, boys. Tell the lady exactly what you both told me. Do it slowly and include every detail you can recall. You boys have good memories, I think, so don't stint on any detail," ordered Null crisply.

"I don't think I can do that, sir," Larry pleaded. "I don't know what a stint is."

Marion just gave up an sank to his knees, "Please don't kill me like you did gramma. I won't say nothin'."

Boyd left her seat and got down on the floor next to the boy and was given pause by how clean the rough-hewn wood planks of the floor were.

"Jesus, Null. Whoever you had scour this dump might have caused these floors to collapse."

"No dust though. Granted they have a little bounce to them."

"Bounce. I like that. I damn near went through them to the basement getting down here with the kid."

"You might as well get comfortable, Kay. The kid has a tale to tell."

Marion without provocation let himself fall into Boyd's body and buried his face between her neck and shoulder and she reflexively stroked him, lying to him that everything would be all right several times until his sobbing at last died down.

"Well, speaking of tales, Null, why don't you tell me about your latest homicide?"

"Not much to tell."

"I don't know why he does shit like dat, missus. He ain't human, dis freak," offered Larry to take the heat off the exhausted Marion, quietly breathing, slumped in Boyd's arms.

"Nobody knows why he does what he does, kid. You know it so you're wise beyond your years."

"Is he gonna kill us too, missus?"

"Well, Null, is that the next part of your insane plan? Off the tykes?"

"Insane plan? A legitimate point, I'll grant you. Will I kill a child? Not if I can help it, and even if I can't, I won't."

"Relax kid. The freak never lies."

"I lie only when I have to, Kay. You know that. I used to think it was unnecessary to lie. I've revised my opinion since then. I lie as part of a strategy, but that's it. Sun Tzu is popular with all the villains these days from his "The Art of War," surpassing even Machiavelli's "The Prince" in its cynicism. "All warfare is based on deception," said he. True enough. So I lie, because I'm fighting a war."

"Against whom, Captain Nutbag?"

"Let little Marion tell you his story, Kay, and find out."

"I'll fill in the blanks too, missus."

"Thanks, Larry. You do that."

Boyd lifted Marion's head, wiped his tears away from his face with her hands, and spoke directly to him. "C'mon, kid. Tell the freak your story."

"You know," he sniffled, then blinked. "My name's Marion. And don't call me Mary, neither."

"Mary and Larry, Mary and Larry!" teased Larry to bolster his courage.

"Hey! Shut the fuck up, Larry!"

"Why would anyone name a kid Marion?"

"It's a boy's name and it ain't so bad. Some old cowboy actor was named Marion."

"Marion Morrison," Null interposed. "John Wayne. The right-wing cowboy. True to form, he didn't like Indians. Odd to name a boy that."

"Not so odd if you want to humiliate a boy for life."

"Like a Boy Named Sue?" Null asked humorlessly.

"Exactly like that. So, go ahead; tell us your story."

Unexpectedly, Marion blurted it all out at once, letting it all run together, not as if it were one sentence, but if it were just one word. For some reason, that didn't matter, the intensity of his delivery brought the message home. And at the end, he collapsed into Boyd yet again and she didn't stop him, stroking him as he sobbed.

"That's the craziest shit I ever heard."

"Think he made it up?"

"Kids do a lot of that, you know."

"No, missus. He tellin' it true."

"Marion, show Lieutenant Boyd your right wrist."

The boy didn't comply, so she gently took his hand, then dropped it. He barely noticed.

"Holy shit."

They said it together as one without meaning to: *"La Pieta."*

To which Larry replied, "You guys is whack."

"Well, Null. You're Special Agent Joel Thrawn's new CI. I guess you'd better set up a meet and break the news."

"I don't think he'll believe it, do you, Kay? Honestly?"

"The creeps in the black robes, okay."

"I watched one of them kill a boy in front of me. They had the muscle and know-how to find me, drug me, stage the whole thing at City Hall and clean it all up by morning without a trace. No news, no Internet."

"And the kid had the *La Pieta* stamp."

"Like the ten dead girls, we could presume."

"And we don't know how many boys."

"I know," whispered Marion Slaughter. "I stopped eatin' ice cream and drinkin' hawt chocklit. I paid attention. Bed check said twenty."

"Eighteen now, Mary."

"Shut the fuck up, Larry!"

"*D'oh!*" Larry japed, giggling.

"So they know."

"You think they *don't* know? And even if they don't, beneath that confusion is the clarity of the threat and the facts. So, they in fact know."

"Why don't you think he'll buy it?"

"Bethlehem Adoption and Youth Placement Services in Newton have a connection to the Archdiocese of Boston, which obviously is a strong appendage of the Catholic Church."

"Which is still settling out lawsuits on criminal acts of child abuse."

"You heard Marion's story. He and Larry pretended they couldn't sing."

"We fooled 'em good, ya freak," piped up Larry.

"Without question you did," replied Null without delay.

"You don't think the FBI wants to investigate the Catholic Church about the ten dead girls?"

"And eighteen dead boys," said Marion, coming to life after seeming to be asleep against Boyd's shoulder. "Eighteen of em f'sure gon' get the big bitch."

"They ain't dead yet, Mary,"

"Shut the fuck up, Larry. They gon' be."

"You don't think it crossed Agent Thrawn's mind when he got a gander of the *La Pieta* handstamp?"

"No, Kay. He associates that with the nightclub element. Ordo Templi Orientis—pagan satanists with rituals and robes bespeaking new age hedonists and old-age hippies. Those are ideal perp's for the Feebs. Easy pickin's. The Catholic Church? Let sleeping pedophiles lie."

"But they're not sleeping, Null."

"Agent Thrawn hopes they are and won't pursue it."

"You think Holy Mother Church is at the crux of the whole thing?"

"I think they set it in motion. And not just a rogue priest, but some higher ups."

"How do you get there? You killed Marion's grandma because she sold him to a priest."

"And not the first one, either."

"So, you whacked out two of those, then an S&M priest, a Frater from the local pagans—"

"Ordo Templi Orientis."

"Thelema. 'Do what thou wilt shall be the whole of the law.'"

"So you know."

"I used my cell phone like anybody. How do you get from there to the Catholic Church and its higher ups?"

"Why the emphasis on singing, Kay?"

"They're putting together a boys' choir?"

"Very good, Lieutenant. You're on the money,"

"I am?" Her expression went blank.

"A very special kind of boys' choir. A choir in service to priests, Maybe the first of many such choirs to keep their priestly antics in-house and under the safe rubric and sheltering basilica of Holy Mother Church and its Holy See."

"Oh my God. And *La Pieta?*"

"The ones who've been marked for death wear that wrist stamp.

I'm guessing there's a different stamp on the wrists of the anointed. It's how they tell them apart."

"Which means they're doing a volume business."

"No flies on you, Kay."

"Little girls aren't much use for randy priests – are they?"

"They're not. Their procurer made a mistake. Ten or more."

"You think their procurer is Bethlehem Adoption and Youth Placement Services in Newton?"

"I do. And Ordo Templi Orientis. They're procuring too. Bethlehem also procures boys from the Southern Border – the ones separated from their parents by ICE agents under Trump's zero-tolerance immigration policy. They get sent to Bethlehem."

"Where they get federal, Commonwealth *and* Catholic money for rounding up good Catholic boys who can carry a tune. A triple dip."

"Kidnapping children can be a very profitable business. And the Catholic Church has *illimitable* resources, the oldest, most successful and largest international criminal enterprise in world history."

"Joel won't go near that."

"Even if he knows the full story. Even if the Feebs know it, it's not the kind of bust that makes careers, but it could certainly break them. Without a perfect case, the Feebs could wind up taking more PR lumps than they've taken since Waco and Ruby Ridge. There are no perfect cases, and they want to steer clear of religion. Especially the Catholic Church."

"Joel thought he was onto some sort of serial-killing psychopath."

"Well, Kay, in a way he was. Except the psychopath wears the miter, crosier and resplendent robes of a cardinal."

"Or a pope."

"Can you guess why the boys are afraid someone was going to snip off their nuts?"

"You're kidding."

"I never kid. In 1599, Pope Clement VIII approved the castration of young boys to sing in the church choir."

Boyd screwed up her face, bared her teeth. "That's barbaric."

"There's a book about it, "Angels Against Their Will," by Hubert Ortkemper."

"Only you would know that." She sighed.

"Not only me. And it seems to be a golden oldie making a comeback. The Catholic Church allowed the practice as late as 1959. No price too high to pay for songs sung in boyish voices with all the power of grown men."

"That's gross," Marion chirped between hiccups.

"Ew," managed Larry.

"Just imagine how sweetly the young *castrati* will sing, each attached to the service of a priest, fulfilling a lifelong path in the church as a dedicated catamite until they age out and become little more than eunuch slaves. And the church has always loved slaves. Meanwhile, more boys are pressed into service. The priests are satiated and protected with no outside entanglements and messy accusations, all is quiet, harmonious and holy."

"No one's going to blow the whistle?"

"Do you think Sinead O'Connor has recovered from her moment of whistleblowing yet, when she was actually *right?*"

"There's a movie about that."

"Haven't seen it."

"They don't care if the boys they abuse are castrated?"

"They think it's better if sexual pleasure only goes one way. No confusion about sexual identity or gratification on the part of the choir boy, later left devastated as a man. Perhaps the men too will wear a telltale handstamp that determines their futures. But the music will be heavenly as slowly boys mature their way through hell."

"You're a truly warped, sick individual, Null. Some days I ask myself why I don't just bite the bullet and put one in you like the mad, rabid dog you are."

"Yet who's going to stop this, Kay? The Feebs? The BPD? *You?*"

"Holy Christ, not me. Never me! You've made a murderer of me already, twice over! I'm not going back there. Not ever."

"Then perhaps I'm just warped and sick enough to deal with something that much worse."

"Yes. I know. You do one thing. Just one thing."

"True enough, Kay. And when I do it this time, all of them will die. Every. Last. One of them."

"Oh, god."

———

"Kay, I do believe I've been shot."

"What? I didn't hear anything."

"That popping sound."

"That's what that was?"

"Left shoulder process, I think."

They had been walking down toward Ruggles Station on the Orange Line. Blood trickled down Null's coat, collected at the bottom seam and then made heavy dark droplets on the broken pavement in the streetlight.

"More shots!" cried Boyd, drew her Sig-Sauer P226 nickel-plated semi-automatic, knelt down and returned fire.

"No need, Kay. He's done. He did what he set out to do and now he's halfway home.

"Yeah, well, I bet I can tell you who he is and where you can find him."

She stood and holstered her weapon back under her coat in a single quick gesture.

"Kind of a heavy piece of iron to run around with strapped to you like that, isn't it?"

"Look who's talking

"True dat, as the Gangsta Boyz would say."

"They gettin' closer to killing you yet?"

"I think when Agent Thrawn and you arrested us, you saved my life."

"Not much of an arrest. No drugs, no guns, no money—shitty arraignments. Everybody kicked, including you. Except the guy who's got a hardon for you. We got him on possession with intent and possession of an illegal firearm. I don't know if we actually saved *your* life, but we definitely saved his. He didn't seem in much of a position to shoot you, lying there vomiting on the floor. The gak he snorted was no good. Laced heavy with aconite. Only you would figure to use something as recondite as that." She paused and clucked her tongue. "Recondite aconite. Poetry."

"No proof of that, though."

"None. I don't even think Ronald is sure you tried to kill him. Since he was trying to kill you in the first place."

"He's gonna get a bid for poison gak?"

"Gak is gak. The law enforcement position here is that it's all poison, and you are the gak master of Boston, aren't you?"

"I have heard tell."

"You don't even have an appetite for that, do you?"

"I use it, but I don't need it."

"Do you even eat?"

"When I remember to."

"How do you know the sniper's done?"

"No more shots, Kay."

"He could be waiting until you get into better position."

"Think it through, Kay. I'm not a big target. I'm wearing a heavy overcoat and a porkpie hat. He's hundreds of feet up and away, we know not where. He fires four rounds. Three were around our feet, hitting nothing. A headshot through the hat would be tough. He knows I wear a flak jacket. So, where does the fourth shot go? Right into my left shoulder, not even my right. Of course not. He assumed I was right-handed. He was wrong, of course. I'm fully ambidextrous. But he had no intention of disabling me. And if that's true, he didn't want to kill me. No. You know what he was doing, don't you?"

"Yeah. I get it. He was gaming you. Setting you up."

"That's right. He wants me hurt, scared and on the defensive."

"And you're not."

"What do you think?"

"I wasn't asking. But I bet he assumes *you'll* be asking."

"That's right. I'll ask you who he is and where I can find him."

"Yes. And I'll do that. And it'll be the trap where he kills you."

"It might be an opportunity for me to kill him as well."

"Probably not."

"I don't know, Kay. This assassin is pretty bold, pretty sure of himself."

"That he is. Made a very pretty show of introducing himself to Joel and me—even told us where he was staying—offering to serve you up on a platter, supposedly to save us the trouble while also saving himself the trouble. A real shitbird's pitch."

"He didn't mean a word of it."

"I see that now."

"This doesn't feel like a Gangsta Boyz hit."

"No, it doesn't. Any ideas?"

"None, detective. When you're the meth king of Boston, there's a long list of rivals desiring to take your throne. Murder is a small price to pay for that."

"You oughtta know, your majesty. You murdered your way up the chain to get to where you are."

"Again, no proof."

"Only anecdotal. Is Agent Thrawn going to hold multiple child endangerment charges against you? For your minnows—your prepubescent slingers?"

"Didn't you and Detective Andromeda look into that after I sent you my message?"

"We did. We unfortunately hit a brick wall."

"Yes. My expert HHS professional Ruth Coelacanth runs a program out of the Dapper O'Neil Shelter and Service Group in Brookline. A revolutionary work-study initiative for children in the primary grades. Very successful and well-funded."

"By your fucking drug money."

"Yes. A successful public good adventure in what Republicans call 'bootstrapping,' where the children are actually out there on the street earning the money that keeps the program that directly houses, feeds and benefits them in business."

"That's where you sent Marion and Larry when you put them in a cab. You're making them minnows."

"Yes. You say that like it's a bad thing. Yet, I can assure you that it's a vastly better deal than what the Catholic Church had planned for them."

NINETEEN

The sixth-floor explosion at the Westin Hotel at the Copley Square Mall—a crazy quilt of a building that looked like some Dymaxion atrocity designed by defunct pop-culture guru R. Buckminster Fuller—caused everything to freeze in Copley Square but the birds and the children and the leash-less dogs that zigzagged through the stupefied crowd on the sidewalks and crosswalks, too petrified to move. There was an instant traffic jam, which in Boston isn't at all unusual with its crazy-quilt network of streets, many of which were well-trodden cow-paths as late as the 1920s. What was unusual was the crush of police cruisers, ambulances and fire trucks to the point of overkill being that a strict city ordinance required a firetruck and a police cruiser accompany any EMS personnel dispatched to any scene, bringing welcome emoluments to all concerned, even if it happened to hinder rather than help emergency response time.

The lack of any forensic data, internal and external, didn't stop all the local cable news affiliates and all the remaining daily newspapers in the greater Boston area, sprawling out from Allston-Brighton to Eastie, from speculating and editorializing to fill the brazenly empty pocket of content. And stretching these few facts in a failed attempt to fill that pocket:

1. The room was registered under the name Josef Dzhugashvili, who claimed to be a priest, which was also Josef Stalin's real name, back when he was studying for the priesthood. The security cameras appeared not to be operational that day, or someone ensured that they wouldn't be operational. Or deleted their contents.

2. There were no fatalities, though a Domino's pizza delivery man received third-degree burns merely from having knocked on the door to deliver that week's combination special.

3. The room had been wired thoroughly with sensors, rigged to trigger the explosives even from a knock on the door, but the true focus of the rigging was the window. It was as if the elusive former occupant expected a break-in from there. The rigging of the door looked like an afterthought, fortunately enough for the Domino's delivery man.

4. The explosives used were only sufficient to kill anyone in the room, not outside of it and didn't significantly damage the physical plant of the hotel. Weight-bearing walls were left intact without a single wall having been breached. The explosives were sufficient to blow the door off its hinges, putting the Domino's Pizza delivery man in a coma.

5. All of this added up to there having been a shaped charge deployed by someone highly skilled in demolition, possibly out of the military or even presently serving.

The FBI hadn't yet gotten involved, and the BPD was taking its time investigating while its PR flack of the moment was busily making teasing denials and awkward spin to network cable and streaming media ground forces laying siege to the lectern, he was fending them off from behind. (The BPD had yet to figure out that having a woman PR flack as opposed to a pensioned off former hack inspector would have made their denials and spin far more effective and implied a progress from within that might someday actually happen. But no, it was always another craggy-faced silver-haired Joe who delivered all the bad news.)

Her name was Janis. Her last name was unimportant, because it was subject to a continual state of change, as was her occupation. You could call her a hitter (hitwoman would have been a bit too dramatic), torpedo (just a tad phallic, as she was nothing but feminine; "All girl," she might tell you), assassin (fraught with obvious intrigue), but no to all of that. If you had asked her, she would smile and disarm you with a joke and a shrug and evade the question altogether. And this would work. You'd go along with it because she was unquestionably cute. Likable and ingenuous, even if you struck sex-appeal from the equation. Janis wore no make-up, which lent an innocence to her face. Agate-eyed, strawberry blonde, dressed down to almost a unisex appearance in yoga pants and hooded sweatshirt, although her fully feminine shape was easily discernable beneath. Her gait was panther-like. She had a bright, clean, white smile, like that of a child.

And she could put a bullet in your brain with the offhanded ease of applying chapstick to her full lips – and do it in a heartbeat.

She was walking next to Null, keeping pace with his slight limp, neither racing ahead or falling back behind.

Behind them both was every available member of the Gangsta Boyz who didn't have a pending appearance scheduled down at Suffolk District Court.

They walked with deliberate purpose down Washington Avenue, heading toward Cary Square in Chelsea—really not far at all from regional FBI headquarters at Legoland on Maple Street. But the square wasn't their destination, no. Instead, it was a battered, beaten-up, broken-down mid-twentieth-century public building, cheaply built out of glazed brick and cinderblock concrete—one whose appearance inspired such remarks as *dysfunction hall* and *wrecked hall*. Its public purpose had long ago passed into oblivion and the structure faced no revival in sight.

Except for this night.

Saturday night oozing slowly into Sunday morning was the Ordo Templi Orientis hour of power and they were going to use it. This was the time to hold their Grand Sabbath in celebration of their potential re-entry into the bosom of the Catholic Church for their assistance in making collections for *Defensores Fidei de Puero* – plus the outstanding balance for boys delivered and miscellaneous services rendered. This was the most propitious moment to extract divine energy from the sacred circle and to accept Amrita into their bodies to achieve immortality.

And the suspended orgasm achieved in the center of the circle by two young virgins would complete the sacrament—everyone drinking from goblets that contained as much fresh sexual excreta as could be sampled and mixed with wine.

The Gangsta Boyz that marched behind Janis and Null made a hum of low-resonant sound, too apprehensive to be silent and too fearful of Null's all too quick hair-trigger response with one of the guns he carried or, worse, with a sawed-off machete he wore hung around his neck by a lanyard which he could access and swing before you could exhale a breath. Janis too spoke low, but entirely unafraid, a vein of steel running through her words like a razor.

"This time, I'm just a straight-up hire. Not like last time, Null."

"No, this isn't like last time. Last time you put your foot in a trap saving my ass."

"I draw the line at children, Null. I may be a murderer, but I draw the line at children."

"I thought you didn't use such direct terms."

"I don't normally, but I can with you."

"Because I'm a fellow traveler?"

"No, because you're just so much worse than me."

"I thought that might be it."

"That's why you're here."

"But you don't want me to go in with you."

"No, I'm saving you for later."

"Why didn't you have the Lieutenant come along too? For extra protection, too. She'd do it for free. Me? I get my standard rate."

"Yes, you do. I thought of asking her, but she seems to resent my having made her a murderer once already. She's not looking for a second bite at that apple."

The modest parade stopped in front of the dilapidated building, its ancient, busted up steel and porcelain sign swaying back and forth in the unremitting, sea-dank wind, like a pendulum. And if you listened for it, you could hear its abrasive creaking that sounded like a perturbed cat. There was no other pedestrian near them on the street, just the usual late-night number of cars all going way too fast to be concerned about a group of blacks with some shadowy figure standing at the head of them beside a single curvy white MILF.

"You just want me around back?"

"Follow me there – hurry up and wait."

Do-Rag, shuddering a bit in his thin windbreaker with the dirty chill of sea air off one of the many landfills of Chelsea, repeated what he knew to be his orders in a definitive tone, not allowing his voice to rise up an octave at the end, making the statement sound like a question. "You press da button, we take flight and lay the molly whop down on 'em good."

"Anyone who isn't carrying step out of line," Null said crisply, flat and matter-of-fact.

Not one of them did; not one of them breathed a word. The fate of super-slinger Ronald Brogan was still uppermost in their minds. They didn't know how he had done it, but Null had somehow poisoned his biggest rival amongst their ranks with his own gak. Put him in the ICU. Without lifting a finger. None of them wanted to engage with that.

The desire right now was to keep living to keep earning. And whatever you wanted to say about the zombie fuck Null, when you followed his orders, you earned. He had the keys to the car, and no one wanted to take them from him.

"What else we do, Do-Rag?"

"We, uh, well...bust a fucking nut on every last one o' dem CHOMOs. No one gets out alive."

"And the other thing?"

"Get whoever's in da basement da hell outta there."

"Letter perfect," replied Null in a half-whisper, disappearing with Janis into the deep blackness of pervasive shadows behind the building.

Inside, the building was without heat, and the lighting was spotty and haphazard and wasn't helped much at all by the mismatched pedestal candelabras situated close to the outline of robed worshippers who, with bowed heads, crowded around the sacred circle at whose center were two naked children, one boy, one girl – both looking confused, cold and scared. Positioned in front of them on a small platform raising whomever stood upon it only a few inches, was a single robed figure whose hood was thrown back, exposing a man's head. It was Theo Teocalli, better known in this circle as Pater Hadit, or, as he put it, raising his voice to dull echo: "Merry meet and merry be, for I am the living father to Ra-Hoor-Khuit, Lord of the Aeon and The Crowned and Conquering Child —*the babe in the lotus!* And I am also Heru-ra-ha—Ra-Hoor-Khuit and Hoor-paar-kraa—*Nuit and Hadit*, but Hadit especially as I am to all of you Pater Hadit!"

In a communal yet off-kilter grunt, the robed figures replied, "Hail Pater Hadit! Merry meet and merry be!"

"So mote it be!" the Pater replied.

"So mote it be," approved the communal grunt.

"We now call upon the watchtowers of the east, west, north and south. And the great grey wind!" Pater Hadit shouted in trumped up ecstasy.

"The great gray wind sends channels through our bodies."

"The wind that drives us!"

"The wind that blows!"

"And the song must be sung!"

"The song shall be sung!" responded the robed worshippers.

"We sing it now together!" exhorted Pater Hadit.

And so they did:

> "*Wind in the north, rush through branches like bees*
>> *Three times three, let it be, let it be*
>> *Bound to the circle beneath the southern tree.*
>> *Three times three, set them free, set them free.*
>> *Fires without, fires within, dining is west, know ye no sin.*
>> *Three times three, will you see, will you see?*
>> *The circle is cast, now flow east to the seas!*
>> *Three times three, bound to be free, bound to be free.*"

Pater Hadit withdrew a ceremonial dagger—an athame—from his robe and he waved it about with forced portent. One of the robed prayerful allowed her robe to drop to the floor and stood naked, arching her back, head and breasts upturned to the sky. Someone handed her a tacky-looking goblet "bedazzled" with plastic gems and sloppily covered with Testor's cheap gold modeling paint. She took the goblet and, affecting sultry moves clumsily, walked up to Pater Hadit, lifted his robe and descended to her knees, proceeding to give him oral sex. He climaxed quickly and easily with a flat note sung at the end and the woman spat his ejaculate into the goblet, rose silently and left the circle for a table of objects adjacent to it. A decanter of wine sat with glasses on top of the table. She poured some of its contents into the goblet, sidled up to Pater Hadit, who brought it to his lips as if about to sip from it, but instead held it high and intoned:

"Amrita alone is the goddess for one!"

"Amrita with one is the goddess of many!" answered the robe-bedizened rabble lustily.

"Two for immortality!"

"Two for the power within the circle!"

Pater Hadit made a sharp gesture with his left hand, and the robed proselytes quieted down and bowed their heads in reverence. He then stepped off his plinth and walked toward the trembling, frightened children at the circle's center and walked counterclockwise about them, assessing them, making wild facial expressions and a clawing motion with his left hand as if he were mimicking a lion, when he was only an awkwardly posturing man. He bellowed rather than spoke from homemade doggerel:

"When the Goddess walked
   The Gods all trembled
   Took back their power, and stealthily stalked
   By remaking themselves after whom they resembled
   The Pentagram as set beneath the feet we see
   They cut inside, consumed, entombed
   And created themselves after she, you see
   In becoming the goddess themselves, you see
   In becoming the goddess who blooms in me
   Amrita – medicine held 'twixt divine and profane
   Beyond our lips, we are she, we are she.
   As it was remade, as it was ordained
   Blessed be, blessed be, blessed be, blessed be!
   Amrita for immortality!"

Pater Hadit then got down on his knees near the children who were too scared to move. He thrust the goblet between them and opened his mouth to say something soothing to quiet their crying but never got the chance.

He was interrupted by a voice that was loud but mechanical that broke up into a squawk at the end that reverberated about the place. If there could be a sound described as a cold squawk, then that would have been it.

"Amrita may be for immortality, but I am for death!"

Pater Hadit stood again in the center of the circle, lifting his head toward where he believed where the shout had come from—somewhere above on the rickety catwalk maybe, but the impoverished lighting couldn't penetrate the shadows under which the speaker was doubtless hiding. Perhaps he had been here before.

"You blaspheme! Your impiety is what means death!"

"Correct on both counts, Theo Teocalli."

It was him, the nosy spook who tried to roust him a week before the Sabbath. The recognition made him sputter and lose control of the room for a crucial moment as the worshippers began to mutter. He made a guttural growl of rage and frustration and decided to go with a threat that it took another long minute for him to realize that it was one he could back.

"You've made the greatest mistake of your life, boss!"

"I've made so many, how could one truly ever tell?"

"They'll know because your miserable, unbelieving life will end here."

"With some modification, I was going to say the same about you."

In the small gap of silence made by Theo Teocalli deciding what to do, the cold and frightened children stood up and cried for help with jumbled words in rapid succession. The naked female member of the congregation ran over to them in order to shut them up.

"There's your indictment, Theo Teocalli, and your final judgment. All that's left is—"

"What, you intruding misshapen little fuck? What's left do ya think? What are you gonna do about anything? Nothin's left for you. Nothin'!" Teocalli shouted in return.

"Execution is what's left. That's what I was trying to tell you before you interrupted me."

"Execution, you dumb fuck abomination?"

"That's right. Execution. I'm going to kill every single one of you. And do it as slowly as I possibly can." Null shouted this with all the passion of a television test signal turned up loud.

Pater Hadit or Theo Teocalli made a circle in the air with his left arm and crowed, "I like the odds, you little freak. There's just one of you and many of us. It won't take long for us all to get up there and feed you to the little animals down in the cellar! Ladies and gentlemen of this Holy Hermetic Temple of the Golden Dawn!

Show this pipsqueak just how we can darken what he thinks is a light!"

Null had been pressing the redial button on his burner phone of the day and Do-Rag wasn't responding. He methodically yanked the AR-15 Bushmaster from under his coat, chambered a round, with his right hand while he released the bolt by pressing it with the thumb of the left hand, which he also used to insert and lock in a fresh sixty-round mag drum, the thumb being already there and ready to release the bolt.

He spun about with it as if he were himself a gun turret.

At the same time, the robed parishioners of Ordo Templi Orientis boiled up together as one, snarling a tangle of ear-splitting epithets, dividing in near equal parts to get to the tortured, corroded wrought-iron steps that led up to the catwalk on either side so that they might meet Null in the middle and put an end to him.

As loud as he could to give them pause, Null shouted with empty authority, "No need!"

In the one uncertain moment of hesitation that affected the robed parishioners of Ordo Templi Orientis—who, despite a forced malevolent mystique had no great experience in murder, even in such a simple situation of vastly outnumbering such a small, unprepossessing victim. They were stumped without specific instructions from Pater Hadit as to how to kill the victim even though at a glance it looked deceptively simple. Without the Pater's input, group-think filled the void and creakily ticked up to the easy determination to trample the poor clod where he stood.

But the poor clod in question was Joseph Xavier Null, Meth King of Boston, Shot Caller of the Gangsta Boyz street gang and FBI informant. And, since his ascension to the Throne of Meth, he had never experienced what anyone might call, even at first blush, "one uncertain moment."

And in that uncertain moment, with the first round chambered and the mag drum in place, and with icy efficiency, he began mowing down the robed parishioners of Ordo Templi Orientis even as they were clambering up rusted wrought-iron steps with the unanimous intention to trample him to death. Their only fallback position was to literally fall back—.223/5.56 millimeter rounds having ripped a good portion of them up to nothingness and dropped them down.

Rounds that could pierce just about any protective vest, especially the one Null wore almost at all times.

"You freaky faggot punk!" roared Theo Teocalli. "I got more proselytes on the way to ice your bony ass. Your gun don't mean nothin'!"

"Funny you should mention that," Null said, finding humor in exactly nothing—even in the fact that the Gangsta Boyz, led by a weirdly intrepid Do-Rag, had broken open the doors to the building just as he had said that and crashed in shooting from a variety of different sidearms—from Lugers to Raven Arms MP-25s and other Saturday Night Specials. Do-Rag himself was firing a weighty 357 Magnum, deadly serious at murdering as many of the faithful as he could. Null didn't need to bark out orders to them as they crashed through into the expanse, firing at anyone wearing a robe, avoiding the wild man waving his fists in stunted fury at Null and who stood right next to the two naked screaming children just as Null predicted he would be.

As Null had calculated beforehand, they were going to be hostages.

Even accidentally wounding one of them would be a death sentence decided in seconds. All the Gangsta Boyz knew that going in and sharpened their aim accordingly.

"I saw this in a movie once," Null shouted from his position on the catwalk. "I thought I'd try it out." And with that, he jumped off the catwalk.

He had grabbed just before the jump an oily rope hung from a ceiling girder, embraced it, still firing the Bushmaster in an awkward pan of the expanse and shinnied down a bit too fast to the ground floor, picking off a few more of the stray robed parishioners on his descent, emptying the remains of the 60-round mag drum clip into them.

"Gonna blip me off too, punk ass faggot?!" Theo Teocalli screamed and spat. "Better be a marksman. And as for the writhing little tots down cellar, I got more of a congregation coming to wring their pretty little necks too. So fuck you, you bullshit wannabe gangster. Just bet they'll take care of you too, even if you somehow manage to blip me off in the process."

When he hit the ground, Null tossed the spent AR-15 aside to the floor and stood up close to Pater Hadit, who was shaking with spittle dribbling down his chin.

"No, Theo Teocalli. I promised I'd do you slow. And I always keep my promises."

Blankets were thrown on the two children and they were spirited outside by two nervous Gangsta Boyz who knew that botching any move that Null might judge would put them in their respective graves. Desi and Jo-jo each had grabbed hold of Theo Teocalli and another of their ranks handed the goblet to Null, who peered into it, crinkled up his nose and cast it off to the side, where it clattered to the floor and splashed its contents against the nearest baseboard.

"So much for Amrita," Null sighed.

"I'm ready to die, motherfucker!"

"What's your hurry, Theo? Going somewhere?"

"Up your ass, motherfucker."

"Uh, Dawg, you gots timing issues," reminded the perpetually worried Do-Rag.

"You carry a lot of tension, Do-Rag. I'd say you were a candidate for a stomach or duodenal ulcer if I didn't know the cause of that was the bacteria helicobacter pylori. An anti-biotic wouldn't cure your ills, would it?"

"This a good time for jokes? You say you gots a appointment, homes."

"Correct. I suppose I should hustle a bit, shouldn't I?"

The only answer came from Theo Teocalli, who quipped, "Move that ass so I can kick it."

"Gentlemen, you can let him go." Desi and Jo-jo both did so unhesitatingly with a shrug. Theo Teocalli immediately put himself into a fighting posture, his legs splayed, his body half in a crouch, his right arm defending his face, his left fist ready to strike, quavering yet otherwise motionless.

Null shook his head.

"Theo Teocalli, you're ridiculous," he observed offhandedly. He paused, stiff for about a minute, waiting for Theo Teocalli to make his move, while at the same time Theo Teocalli was waiting for Null to make his move. "Somebody please give Mr. Teocalli a knife – so that he'll feel confident that this will be a fair fight?"

Do-Rag stepped up, produced an "out-the-front" sliding switch-blade from the pocket of his painter's pants nearest his thigh. He released the blade and slapped the knife into the moist palm of Theo Teocalli's outstretched hand, whose fingers then curled tightly around its black lacquer handle.

"Dawg," Do-Rag whispered into his ear. "I'd say run—make yo way to da door right quick, but that won't do ya no good. Maybe jus' drop da knife and take what comes—cuz he gon' take that blade off ya before you can use it anyways."

"Shut up. The freak'll be dead in a minute."

"A minute?" asked Null ingenuously. "I know I have somewhere to be, but I promised you more time than that."

"Don't sweat it, boss. You're never gettin' there anyway."

"Keep time for me there, Do-Rag."

"You cuttin' it close, homes."

"Not yet, but soon."

Theo Teocalli screamed something unintelligible as he stabbed at Null with the knife, which flew off to the side and skittered across the floor.

Do-Rag counted to himself, not quite silently, just how long it took.

It wasn't nearly as slow as Null had proposed.

Null did it in ten decisive moves with barely a pause in between, but at the same time seemed unhurried by the effort.

Silence weighed heavily upon the expanse of the hall as the living looked upon the dead and found that there was nothing to say. Pater Hadit had gone the way of the sacred golden goblet of Amrita, his life having spilled out as a noisome mess over the ersatz parquet floor. It had the color and consistency of red mud. Without a sound, as had been prearranged, the Gangsta Boyz filed out quickly and neatly through the front entrance. Do-Rag was the last to leave.

"You were exactly right, Do-Rag," Null remarked as Do-Rag turned to leave with the others.

"I was?"

"You were."

A chill ran up Do-Rag's spine, not knowing where this was leading and also not wanting to know. He stopped breathing. "How?" was all he could manage to get out.

"I did actually cut it close."

Neither of them said anything after that. Do-Rag went out the front entrance and Null went out the back. His pace was easy. He walked as if he were just marking time. And perhaps that was the only way he could see it – made any of it make sense to himself. All he did, every death, every showdown, every score, every criminal conquest. Just something he did when he wasn't asleep.

Marking time.

TWENTY

The back lot of the "Knights" hall hadn't much room for parking, which was worsened by the three rusted-out abandoned old makes of cars that had probably been there since the last century. Null stood there for ten minutes waiting for something to happen, and nothing did. As much to give himself something to do as well as a little more light, he lit a cigarette, puffed on it urgently, then spat it out, having gotten nothing from it and the light it gave was short lived.

The sound of slow clapping got his attention, and he froze where he stood.

The sound grew louder, accompanied by that of footsteps crunching in the busted up tar and concrete rubble that led in a path up a grassy hill that leveled off where Null stood in the back lot level with the second story of the hall. When the clapping and footsteps reached their diapason, the person who produced them became visible in the low ambient light of the flickering streetlamps.

"Truly impressive, Mr. Null. Efficient and on time, as always."

"You can drop the 'Mr.' Call me Null. Everyone calls me Null."

"Only those not too frightened of you to mention your name at all though, isn't that right?"

"I don't give that much thought, to be truthful. But you're not one of those, am I correct, Innocent Mountain Man?"

"How sly, Null, but very good. So my reputation precedes me."

"It does. So I did a little light reading. So what's the real moniker?"

"It's been lost to history, so let's leave it that."

"Which side were you on, Innokenty, in the Bosnian War of the 90s?"

"I'm Ingush, Null, let's leave it at that."

"Of course. Lots of shame to be had whether you were Serbian, Croatian, Yugoslavian, but you were a mercenary, that's for certain, and so your life path had been set. I didn't have to Google you further to know that. That dirty little war amounted to a good deal of fun and profit for soldiers like you."

"Do you really wish to antagonize the man who's come to kill you as if that would help your cause?

"No, but it would help your cause. As a paid assassin, I'm sure you were promised a fat bonus if you made me suffer as you took your time killing me. And we both know who has that particular axe to grind—Malek "The Mallet" Turbot."

"I don't see how you would know any of that, Null. That's not a subject for Googling."

"No, it's not. But it's pretty easy to deduce. You're a trained sniper. You could have had me when you shot at me when I left the squat and wounded me in the left shoulder. Since your capabilities are fairly obvious, the only answer is that the best money in this job is in how you kill – not just *whom* you kill."

Innokenty chuckled with relief tinged with wariness. "So, Null, you can't shoot me, now can you, because all those bodies on the floor in the hall took all the rounds you had. If I'm wrong, go ahead and shoot me with one of your pistols."

"Unfortunately, true."

"You're waiting for someone, Null, but I don't think you were waiting for me. You had no way of knowing I'd be here."

"Maybe," Null replied. "And maybe not. Either way, the cat's not dead."

"Yet, Null. Yet."

"Cats don't have nine lives, nor do you."

"It's the one life that matters."

"The knowledge you think you have can mislead you."

"Your guiding principle, Innokenty."

The assassin snapped his fingers in mock revelation. "You're waiting for the FBI. That's it, isn't it?"

"Maybe we both are."

"Now, why would you say that?"

"Because my knowledge hasn't misled me."

"That's because it came from me," a husky voice sounded, its speaker hidden in the shadows of the trees that kept the hill intact alongside of the Knights' Hall exterior.

"Lieutenant Boyd," replied Innokenty. "How charming of you to attend. Is your new boyfriend and the rest of his Feebs right behind you?"

Boyd stepped into the light, checked her cell phone for the time.

"They're about ten minutes out, Innokenty. Still processing the former address of O-T-O in Jamaica Plain, which should lead them here."

Innokenty cut her off with his loud, mirthless chuckle. "And what will they find but a bunch of dead wannabe knights or monks or whatever thing they thought they were and some squabbling brats in the basement. Everything tied up neat. So, obviously, Lieutenant, you found the tracker."

"No shit, Sherlock."

"And trackers can work both ways, which I should have remembered."

"Again, you get the prize, you Ingush piece of shit." She pulled her nickel-plated Sig Sauer from her shoulder holster and pointed it straight at Innokenty.

"You're not going to shoot me, Lieutenant. You don't want Null to make you a murderer. Word out on the street—as you say it here —is that you killed for him in the past. No?"

"You're right, Innokenty. I'm not out to kill you."

A loud shot blasted out. And yet another unseen voice followed it.

"But I'd be happy to push the button on you anytime, Innokenty."

Innokenty looked wan and ghoulish in the scant lighting. His right hand was pressed against his left shoulder. "I've been shot," he said with no small astonishment.

"Funny that," said Janis, stepping into the light next to Boyd. With an agreeable nod of her head, Boyd holstered the Sig Sauer while Janis kept her Smith & Wesson CSX nine-millimeter pistol trained on Innokenty's perplexed face. "I kill for sport, sonny, and when I shoot, I do not miss."

"Wh-who the fuck. Are. You?"

"My name's Janis. My last name's whatever you want it to be. Odds are I've already used it somewhere down the line."

"You can't tell me Null planned this. This insignificant, deformed piece of shit can't have thought all of this up."

"Seems pretty significant to me," Boyd countered.

"Me too," agreed Janis.

"Here's how it plays, Innokenty. Short and sweet. Either you let Lieutenant Boyd arrest you, tied to the all the dead of Ordo Templi Orientis and the kids in the cellar, and you get deported back to wherever your phonied-up passport says you came from or—"

"Or what?" Innokenty chortled. "You're going to kill me?"

"Bingo."

"You think just because I took what has to be a nine milly to the shoulder that we are equals now? That the fight you think we're going to have when I kill you will be somehow made fair? There will be no fight, but you're right, there will be death."

"There doesn't have to be. You're just a hireling of Malek's. A proxy. You've never hurt or killed a child that I know about. And I make it my business to know."

"No, I have not."

"You don't have to die, if you just walk away."

"But think about how my livelihood will suffer. A walk-away would seriously cut into my bottom line and my reputation on the dark web. This I cannot do."

Janis wagged her Smith and Wesson about as she spoke. "Oh, you bet there *will* be death, alright, Wile E. Coyote. I might just murder you myself. For practice."

"So much for fair."

"I never said anything about being fair, Innokenty. But why not? Janis, if he kills me, let him walk."

"Then the lieutenant will arrest me."

"I can be fair, Innokenty. The world and the police, on the other hand, play a game that's a bit different from mine."

"The world," coughed Innokenty, scornful.

"Maybe not the world then. Call it chaos. And maybe my game isn't so different at that."

"Well, Null, chaos has always favored *me*. So, I'll take your bet and then deal with the women as I usually do. When I'm done with you. I'm favored there too, don't you know?" He winked and tried to smile, breathing hard.

"Kay, favor this man, please, and take all his guns—

you know where they are. I should hope," Janis added wryly.

"No need for hope, Janis," she said, patting Innokenty down. She held up each gun to be seen in the scant light as she retrieved them: a Glock 19 from his shoulder holster; a 22 Magnum mini from his ankle holster and a cumbersome Smith and Wesson Model 637 Chief's Special Airweight from his jacket pocket. "He don't got no knife."

Null tossed her the late Pater Hadit's "out-the-front" switchblade, and she caught it one-handed. "Give him this one. For fairness."

"You're tired, spent—haven't eaten and slept for days, snorting the gak too, of course."

"Of course."

"And knowing you as I do from the excellent profile my client provided, your shoulder wound is very likely infected, since you don't like doctors so much. You're not what they say at all, Null, no. You're not. You are no preposterous monster, no dark voodoo god. You aren't of the walking dead, a zombie. No, you are just a much-less-than-ordinary man. Which makes you nothing—soon to be even *less* than nothing." He spat and then grinned.

Null stood there, impassive, not so much like a statue, more like a mime holding the pose of a statue, a little bit tremulous at the edges, the pose itself ready to crack. The only thing holding it all together was spit and flimsy will.

Null whispered as if reporting a fact: "Death is for you, Innokenty Gorets."

Before Null could take a single step forward, Innokenty was already on him, stabbing him repeatedly in rapid-fire prison-yard-style succession, like the piston of a powerful engine. Satisfied and affected by the effort, his shoulder wound still bleeding from Janis' gunshot, Innokenty staggered back to admire his handiwork.

Null, speechless, dropped to his knees, then fell over on his side.

Boyd and Janis stood stock still, their breath suspended. This wasn't how it was supposed to go. Did Null actually mean it when he told Janis to let the assassin walk if he killed him? It was clear that Janis wasn't about to stop aiming her gun at Innokenty no matter what a dead man wanted. Her arm trembled more from emotion than from fatigue.

Innokenty chuckled a throaty, high-pitched chuckle, then stopped himself, and took out his cell phone. "I hope he isn't dead yet. I have to get some real agony out of this *durak* so I can earn my bonus. So, I must shoot a little movie of his finale." He approached the fallen Null confidently, cell phone in one hand, switchblade in the other. He raised the blade up as he was about to get down and bring the half-dead Null around to face his expert use of it on his eyes, his face, his tongue – but he never made it.

An unexpectedly alert Null had his sawed-off machete already up and slicing into Innokenty between his legs. Then a substantial sideways hack into his belly, which produced a gout of blood. Innokenty staggered back, just barely keeping his footing. Null stood up, taking his time. The knife fell to the rubble from Innokenty's hand.

"Y-you're dead."

"I've been hearing that a lot lately."

"But, but, I *killed* you!" he cried.

"Lemme blow his little head off, already," pleaded Janis, her Smith and Wesson still aimed at Innokenty's face.

"No need, Janis. He's about done."

"You can't be alive after that. You. Can. *Not!*"

"It's okay Innokenty. You've just been trumped."

Innokenty's reply was lost in a gurgle of blood.

"Chaos may favor you, but death... Well, death has always favored me. And I only do one thing. Just one thing." Null, standing strong, significantly bloodied up in the front, his overcoat having fallen open, coolly delivered a sideways blow with the edge of the machete, which just about decapitated Innokenty, who sagged where he stood into a heap in the rubble.

"They're going to be here in a minute, Null. We'd better hustle."

At a glance, Innokenty now looked like any nebulous bunch of garbage you might find behind any dilapidated building in Chelsea that you would hardly notice or might never have noticed at all, but for the blanched and twisted face mask that stuck out of it from an awkward angle.

"I don't want no truck with the Feebs. The only radar I ever been on was with Hebe Group, which doesn't exist anymore. I'd kinda like to keep it that way," answered Janis.

"Can you even walk, Null?" Boyd asked in near panic. "I mean, I can't even. I just *can't.*"

Null swallowed hard and hissed, "I can make it to the car. Drive with a lead foot to Mount Auburn Hospital. Missy Crocus is working the night shift in the E-room tonight."

"Don't tell me you checked."

"You know he did," replied Janis.

"Don't worry about the Feebs, if we can all start moving. They're already here but haven't quite made it back here because they don't know that back here exists yet. But they will soon."

"Fucking Joel," Boyd sighed.

"Jesus, Null. I was sure that son-of a-bitch killed you."

"I'm not so sure he didn't."

———

They called it a compound, the misnomer kept alive on the street by the defrocked doc known as Toplofty, right-hand man and officially unofficial physician to what remained of the once powerful head of Boston's Ork gang, now reduced to the unseen behind-the-scenes comptroller of bookmaking and prostitution running from Eastie all the way up through the North Shore. The building was a by-the-numbers adaptive re-use of a 100-year-old clapboard tri-decker in the 40 block of Orient Avenue in Orient Heights. Ironically, it was a short walk from the 35-foot tall statue of the Mother of God at The Madonna Queen of the Universe Shrine, which remains the national headquarters of the Don Orione Fathers (also known as the Sons of Divine Providence), an order of Catholic priests founded by St. Luigi Orione, who was canonized a saint only recently back in 2004.

The irony is how closely situated Malek the Mallet was to the flash point of his nemesis Null's current enemy, which would, on the face of it, seemed to have been the archdiocese of Boston itself, if not the whole of the Catholic Church to boot, grinding all the way upwards to the pope and his secret *motu proprio*. Though it must be fair to say that the Sons of Divine Providence were ignorant of Cardinal Cromulent's *Defensores Fidei de Puero* as well as the Papal bent behind it. And they were likely to remain so. For the near term, at least, the Sons of Divine Providence were only a potential enemy just as long as the critical Papal *motu proprio* remained secret.

Might they have metamorphosed into something more malevolent if they had come into direct knowledge of the Papal *motu proprio*? Would they accept it and further dicta that might come down the line?

Who can say?

What course might the Sons of Divine Providence take to protect the priesthood, the Holy See and the pope himself against such barbaric criminals as the apostate Joseph Xavier Null and his Gangsta Boyz?

Frederico Cunha, Miroslav Filipović, András Kun, Konstantinas Olšauskas, Hans Schmidt and Christian von Wernich—all priests convicted of murder.

Haven't the holy righteously murdered to protect the divine?

Sixteenth-century Catholic theologian John Calvin (the founder of Calvinism) endorsed the murder of heretics with a citation from the Old Testament, Leviticus 24:16, "The one who blasphemes the name of the Lord should be put to death; all the congregation must stone him. Any foreigner or native who blasphemes the Name should be put to death."

Had there been no warrior popes?

Pope Julius II (Giuliano della Rovere, Pope 1503–1513) is still known as the "warrior pope," having taken his name not from a saint but from Julius Caesar, who used warfare to conquer the Papal States. Weren't the casualties of his battles righteous murders sanctified in the eyes of God?

And if so, what about priests serving only the divine?

Meanwhile, the more gnawing problem facing all who knew of it—perhaps even including the pope himself—was that hard evidence of *Defensores Fidei de Puero* had already been bubbling up to the surface, perhaps soon to be recognized for what it was. This was particularly true in the case of the ten dead girls found in Newtonville with a smudged club stamp of Michelangelo's *La Pieta* on their wrists that was now in the diligent care of Special Agent Joel Thrawn.

And Agent Thrawn was sure that he was running street-scum-meth-honcho Joseph Xavier Null to close out the crucial case of the ten dead girls and win his street cred, but just as had happened with former Boston gangster number-one, Whitey Bulger, who just happened to be a confidential informant of FBI Special Agent John Connolly, Null was deftly, even maliciously, running *him*.

The not-so-secret dictum of Malek The Mallet, however, was another story altogether. All over the street – in every cul-de-sac, alley and walkway – reports of Null's impending death had already been interpolated into the ongoing buzz of underground commerce. First as an urgent morning whisper, then a mildly inter-esting afternoon factoid that by evening, whether true or not, accomplished or not, no longer mattered.

No one cared and Null's name was still tough to say in any part of town.

They said he was already dead.

"Tell us," went the common thought steeped in realistic fear, "how do you kill death?"

Besides, Malek had gone from feared leader of the most violent and defiant crime crew in Boston, rivaled only by the creepy Fami-ly's Gomez Gomelsky for the top spot, to nothing more than a prison-yard, chatted-out J-cat monkey mouth motherfucker no one took seriously anymore.

Malek the Mallet had become a lost and mythic boogeyman of fun – a joke told on the street time and again to crowd out the mention of Null, the single syllable even the lowest mope was afraid to utter in public (and perhaps even when alone).

No question that it would have been easier to call the Madonna Queen of the Universe Shrine a compound than to call the lightly guarded gray-hued clapboard rehab that housed what was left of the top leadership of the Ork such a thing, but even those of the street who still openly mocked the infirm Malek 'the Mallet' Turbot allowed it to be called a compound as a passing gesture of respect, though not without a good deal of sarcasm in the bargain. The BPD did token drive-bys, to be sure, but the Feebs couldn't have cared less, both having written Malek off as an inconsequential light-weight, a living postscript to the rich history of the gangs of Boston whose most vicious crew was now headed up by some alleged zombie who knocked poor Malek off his perch and off his pins.

Even as a pathological homicidal maniac, Malek had to take a backseat to Null.

When Null showed up at Malek's compound on a drizzly Wednesday afternoon flanked by Gangsta Boyz Desi and Dominic, who between them carried an unwieldy-looking black nylon zippered bag that held some sort of bizarre shifting shape within it, the two soldiers at the door buzzed them in, then parted, opened the doors and let them pass. They knew who it was and probably why it was and that it wasn't worth putting up a fight when the Meth King of Boston himself had deigned to pay a visit to the ailing and broken Malek the Mallet's compound in broad daylight.

A murder at that level would more likely be a massacre carried out at night with multiple automatic weapons firing hundreds of rounds to finish everybody off all at once, with the compound burned to the ground and not with the Meth King himself in attendance.

The interior of the house was entirely new, neat and immaculate with an austere, hospital level of sterility and cleanliness. The three dragged the unwieldy bag in through the vestibule and then up a steep flight of robin's-egg-blue carpeted stairs that led to the second floor, which revealed a suite of offices attended by clerks, accountants and straight-citizen types both young and old, their laptop computers and a serious rack of cloud servers at the far end of the hall blocking an ancient window. The workers were unruffled and unmoved at the passage of the three gangsters and their oversized bundle who continued on to another flight of stairs up to the third floor, which, at the landing, entered directly into Malek's personal apartment and privatized ICU set up.

Malek was seated in a thick brown leather La-Z-Boy recliner attached to a kidney dialysis machine that thrummed ceaselessly underscoring all other sound in the room: the electric clock, the stertorous breathing and the oily voice of Toplofty barking into a phone in an adjoining room.

The odd hybrid of hospital room and connoisseur collector's showplace had no effect on the three but for the two who carried the burdensome bag to drop it down onto one of the ostentatious, ancient, uncannily hued oriental rugs, where it made a squishing sound. Famous impressionist and expressionist paintings, either startling originals that had once been museum catalogued and featured in pricey coffee table books or astonishing fakes whose brush strokes were so vivid they could have been applied just a few days ago as opposed to as much as three-hundred or so years ago – were displayed somewhat modestly against the off-white Chinoiserie wallpaper.

Null counted right away a Paul Klee, a Pissarro, a Modigliani and an Oskar Kokoschka.

The almost comfortable surroundings featured incongruous Second Empire furnishings that clashed with the mock Chippendale and Louis Quinze embroidered chairs and an ill-chosen hepatitis-yellow divan that boasted more a connotation of nausea rather than comfort. This was nothing less than a chamber of squandered wealth and failed criminality that made an even more failed attempt at gentility that fell flat as soon as you noticed that half the room was exactly like that of a hospital CCU, ICU or Step-Down unit.

Malek, wearing his amber wraparound sunglasses, chuckled throatily at his uninvited guests. The stumps of his amputated right arm and left leg were covered in gauze stained yellow and pink. His face was dappled with sweat and spittle oozed down his chin.

"Sweet set-up you have here, Malek," Null announced. "Let's see, you have five IV lines pumping fluids, nutrients and drugs into what's left of you, morphine, of course, antibiotics, lactate of Ringer's and I guess an antibiotic or two, maybe even a special concoction or two formulated by the de-frocked Toplofty?"

"Why ain't you dead? You should be dead by now," Malek asked softly, almost whispering.

"I've been hearing that a lot lately."

"Then why didn't it stick?"

"It might have stuck, but I wear a Kevlar flak jacket pretty much most of the time. Now, I know what you're thinking. You're thinking, 'That won't stop a blade.' And yes, that's true. It won't. But a good, thick vest can slow a blade up a bit and maybe keep it from going in too deep. Rapid-fire knife wounds delivered prison style can certainly still fuck you up when you're wearing a vest. But they won't necessarily kill you. That your assassin was aiming for the heart didn't help. More Kevlar there than at the belly."

Malek the Mallet began chuckling softly which increased in volume with every other chuckle.

And as the chuckling grew louder, wilder, wires that provided the data for the readouts of various monitors for the crime boss's vital signs connected up to an assortment of sensor pads glued to his skin began to move. They went from moving to violently trembling when his chuckling transitioned into a coughing jag that caused Toplofty, still barking commands into his cell phone, to stride into the room.

He made minuscule knob adjustments and checked the IV lines. Lastly, he placed his palm on Malek's forehead, ended the call he was on abruptly, and slipped the phone into the pocket of his navy-blue Amani jacket.

Taking in the tableau of Desi, Dominic and the scurrilous and execrable Meth King Joseph Xavier Null, Toplofty went to reach for his Ruger EC9s semi-automatic pistol in its shoulder holster, but Null's Glock 9 was already drawn before he could finish the move. He withdrew his hand from his jacket tremulously and raised it up with the other one, both palms facing front.

"Good decision, Toplofty," Null expelled like a heavy breath. "I have no reason to kill anybody here today. In fact, I come in peace."

"Listen to the guy who fucking mutilated me talk about coming in peace. If I could get up from this stinking machine, I'd take that same axe he used to do this to me and show him the real meaning of peace – in *pieces!*"

"Can't we just let bygones be bygones, Malek?"

"Don't tell me that you come bearing gifts," he spat, the spittle failing to leave his mouth entirely.

Null suddenly went stock still, his mouth open and slack eyes wide. No one in the room had to guess what was going on with him. He was like a machine gone wrong, its programming stuck on a fatal calculation, like the deadly Diophantine equation that's sometimes known as the "summing of three cubes" that not even Einstein could figure out. But no, it was just Null calculating irony.

Weighing, measuring.

Snapping back to the world at hand, Null spoke almost brightly. "You know, I wouldn't have thought of putting it that way, but yes, very true Malek. I come bearing a gift just for you."

"If it's a bomb, set it off already and be done with it. I don't mind being headed in advance to the next world as long as you and the niggers are coming along for the ride."

"None of us is going anywhere, Malek. And make just a twitch more movement, Toplofty, and I'll put a few rounds directly into your heart." The Glock 9 was still up and in Null's hand. He had made the original movement so fast, the gesture itself seemed a feat of legerdemain.

"Relax, Toplofty. He ain't here to kill me. No, not yet. He got more plans in that mutant freak mind of his, like maybe makin' giblet gravy outta my guts while making me watch. Like in that movie where the FBI agent was made to eat his own brain."

"I'm not Hannibal Lecter, Malek. I'm just a guy tryin' to get along."

Toplofty's face went red.

"Let me pull on the sonofabitch, Padrone. I think I can shoot his lights out before he can cock that Glock."

"We both know you can't, so don't."

"No one has to die today, Toplofty. In point of fact. It's amnesty day for your poor Ork."

Null nodded once in Desi and Dominic's direction.

At that cue, they unzipped the bag and dumped its contents out onto the brightly antique oriental rug on which they were standing.

Malek bucked up from his specially configured La-Z-Boy recliner as if he had been defibrillated though the paddles were nowhere near him, recessed as they were into a plastic wall unit.

"Look what you're doing to my 7th-century hand-knotted Kerman rug—you're defiling it, you stupid *apush!*"

"Would you look at that. I thought most of it would have dried by now."

Toplofty growled and said nothing, mindful of the Glock that was still aimed toward him, center chest.

There at the heart of the geometric center of the rug lay the bunched up and broken bundle of what had once been Innokenty Gorets, world-class assassin, oozing crimson goo onto beautifully knotted silver, gold and cerulean blue cords of the oriental rug. Innokenty's face stuck out at a weird angle, eyes wide open, looking like a carelessly crafted fright mask.

"You have ruined everything you have ever touched, *apush*, and you just don't give a damn do you?"

"No, I suppose that's true, Malek. In my favor is the fact I never hired an assassin to deal with you – what work was done on you was work I did myself. And I have never ruined the life of a child. Can you say the same, Malek?"

"I don't foster maggots. I eradicate them when I have to."

Null clicked his tongue and shook his head.

Malek the Mallet was seizing, wheezing as he gulped for air and wriggled in the La-Z-Boy, trying, seemingly in vain, to reposition himself. Amid the sighing, not even the thrum of the medical machinery could obscure his sharp grunt of surrender.

"Go help him, Toplofty. I won't shoot you. Just move *economically*. Try not to trigger the trigger."

"He doesn't need it, you wretched clod. He can take care of himself."

"I admire your ability to lie to save face, Toplofty. A very much protean skill in your case."

"You want to tell stories or show a respect for *economy* as you just said and let us know terms?" Toplofty pronounced and puffed out his pained chest.

"It's admirable, Toplofty. Here you are, pushing sixty, physically damaged, putting up a truly convincing façade, yet feeling every second of your age: sporting a prolapsed rectum from years of anal rape down at Walpole. Branded a criminal, you take up with the worst mob in Boston as maybe the worst *consigliere* ever only to have it all taken away from you by the simple, dedicated handiwork of yours truly. Now, you know I'm not bragging, so don't bother with that accusation. But I realize you're just itching to proffer a rejoinder. So let me suggest one to you. Say 'thank you.'"

"Go fuck yourself."

"Close enough. I don't beg for miracles."

"You shall never get them. God will find a place for you."

"You could be right, Malek. I doubt it, but if you are, then he found this place for me right here and the time to be right now and bade me to work my will from there as I see fit. Isn't that right? I know all you criminal Christers believe in free will. Well, who am I to argue? I'm not Paul Tillich, but if he were here, I'd argue with him about this. No, by your crude little belief system I'm exactly where I should be. But then, they're all crude little belief systems, now, aren't they?"

"Get on with it, *partvogh mard!*" belched Malek. "My beautiful carpet," he whined immediately after. "My God!"

"Yes, Malek. Your God. I'm going to deal with him right after I deal with you."

"With whom, *apush,* God?"

"Precisely that."

"You are stupid as well as crazy, then," Malek tried to spit, but he was out of saliva.

Dominic moved a single step forward, glaring hard in the direction of Toplofty, just standing there, his shadow looming.

"You don't dis da man, cuz," he said crisply. "He the plug, not you."

"Toplofty! He's *still* bleeding on my fucking rug already!"

"Padrone!"

"Move a fraction in any direction, Toplofty, and I'll put you down. I'm pretty good with the Glock at this range. And I've had a great deal of practice recently."

Toplofty threw up his arms in front of him and then compacted himself down into a seated position on the bloody rug, crossing his legs.

"Go ahead and shoot me, freak. Anything's better than listening to you natter on."

"Relax, Toplofty. I said today's amnesty day and I meant it. By the way, don't worry about the blood, Malek. He's been dead for a while, so lividity will keep your rug from getting too damaged by it. But the point I'm trying to make here is this: I'm not going to kill you."

"You said that already."

"Shoot me already, punk. Enough of your sad yack."

"He talks to hear himself talk, Toplofty."

Dominic and Desi broke character at that remark and burst into laughter. They abruptly stopped when they together realized at the same moment that Null could just as easily put them down with the Glock and there was little to nothing that they could do about it in the moment.

"Brave face, Toplofty. Failed consigliere to the end. Alright gentlemen, here's your terms. You can have your bookmaking, your whores, your little plots and plans. Just know that I'm the plug. Interfere with that, I'll shut you down and put you down. Stay away from the kiddies—no KP for you. Not ever. They belong to me exclusively. The assassin you hired on my behalf, well, as a token of good faith, I brought him back to you. Hire another one, better look into a restoration expert for your rug, because there's going to be a lot bloodier ooze on it before we're through."

"I don't understand what the fuck you want," Malek whined. "Why not just end it here while you can, you *partvogh mard?*"

"Just let him spew and screw. No one cares what he has to say.

Burn us now, burn us later—same goddamn fucking difference," Toplofty droned.

"You two just keep playing your little games. I might even help you from time to time, should I see a reason. What you and what's left of your little Ork are to me is simply this. *Placeholders.* You're the loyal opposition who will invest in a very public antagonism against me. Please do make bold with that. You'll prevent the power vacuum that might cause me and mine an unwanted level of harm by being just as irrelevant as you are right now. And with you two harmless comedians working against me, I can own Boston Street crime in its entirety as a monopoly while the citizens believe there's some healthy capitalist competition going on in a pointless struggle to obtain something as fleeting as a sneeze."

"*That's* your fucking plan?" shrieked Malek, wild with pain and shame.

"Yes. That's my fucking plan. To make use of you."

"As what, you sad little freak?"

"In the printing and software development worlds, I believe it's called—*a dummy.*"

The three of them turned their backs on Malek and Toplofty and made a quiet and unobtrusive exit that even the guards at the outside door in front hardly took notice of at all.

TWENTY-ONE

Mass General Hospital (MGH) is a city within a city.

It sits on its haunches like some enormous architectural toad at the end of a large cul-de-sac off Fruit Street which in turn is off Charles and Cambridge Streets, the main drag of the long ago famous but now nearly forgotten Boston Brahmins of Beacon Hill. (Charles Street now has fewer antique shops on it than MGH has buildings.) The main entrance at 55 Fruit Street is not unlike the entrance to a cathedral. All it lacks are the Gothic arches. But Charles Bullfinch's original design – still intact in the building that bears his name, also on Fruit Street—*does* boast a neoclassical portico with columns.

The old building also includes a structure known as the "Ether Dome," where in 1846, local-dentist William Thomas Green Morton gave a public demonstration of the administration of inhaled ether during surgery – not the first instance of the use of anesthesia, but the first to be documented. (A reenactment of the Ether Dome surgery was painted in 2000 by artists Warren and Lucia Prosperi. They used MGH staff to pose as their counterparts from 1846. The Ether Dome is still open to the public.)

Established in 1811, MGH is the third oldest general hospital in the United States and has a capacity of 1,011 beds. Together with

Brigham and Women's Hospital, it's one of the two founding members of Mass General Brigham (formerly known as Partners HealthCare), the largest healthcare provider in Massachusetts. MGH admits approximately 50,000 patients, the surgical staff performs over 34,000 operations and the obstetrics service handles over 3,800 births per annum.

And to consecrate it further, MGH was also the first teaching hospital of the Harvard Medical School.

If that fails to impress, bear in mind that MGH also takes in around 1.5 million outpatient visits each year at its main campus, and also at its seven satellite facilities in Boston at Back Bay, Charlestown and Chelsea and in the neighboring towns of Everett, Revere, Waltham and Danvers. With more than 25,000 employees, the hospital is the largest non-governmental employer in Boston.

None of this daunted Null as he walked in through the main entrance in broad daylight, alone and stripped of all weaponry but the nearly all-plastic Glock 9, which he need not have done, as there were no metal detectors. In fact, none of the foregoing impressed any Bostonian in the slightest. MGH was as all-encompassing and easily ignored a fact of life as was the miserable weather and the fact that most residents could never explain to outsiders – or even perhaps to themselves—how to get from this street to that avenue, despite having lived within blocks of both destinations for fifty years or more.

MGH was simply a prevailing condition of Boston life, like terrible driving and endless rotaries.

And Null was aware that out of the approximately 50,000 admitted MGH patients, a bullet-wound sufferer wouldn't be all that difficult to locate. He had surmised that his target was somewhere in the thoracic surgery department.

Null negotiated what might have been a mile and a half of heavily reticulated and twisted corridors, some separated by flights of stairs and some causing him to double back twice. At last, drenched in sweat due to the hyperactive heat brought on by the ever-persistent cold and his heavy clothes, he reached the Thoracic

Surgical Unit located on Ellison 19. The patient he was there to see had a private room. He had only been moved there from the Post Anesthesia Care Unit the morning before.

It was still visiting hours, so a busy nurse (they're always busy, now, aren't they?) showed him to the correct room. The nurse had to suppress a wince and a grimace, getting a glimpse at Null's face under strong fluorescent light, permanently swollen and distorted by bulging keloid scarification. She did nothing about it because she had seen worse, and Null reflected a mild, non-threatening manner.

She couldn't have understood that Null always reflected a mild, non-threatening manner.

He stepped into the room and there lying in bed covered by bright white sheets with even more IV lines in him than Malek had and a catheter that emptied into a graduated plastic container hooked onto the aluminum frame of the bed, was a red-haired, pale- and freckle-faced boy, the sight of whom was so jarring even to Null that he almost did a doubletake. But he didn't. He never disclosed even the most benign of responses. He retained the appearance of being lax and harmless, as the good nurse deduced earlier, albeit somewhat odd-looking with his heavy topcoat, his porkpie hat and his lumpy, disfigured face.

"Frater Phlegethon, I presume?"

———

"He shot you only once with a twenty-two."

"Yeah," wheezed Barry Weiss. "But it was a bad round. Broke apart inside me, fucked up a lung, nicked my spleen and my guts. This is the third surgery I've had."

"Must have been an old piece."

"Probably old rounds too, if you want to really think about it."

"Lead is lead. You don't like the irony of being shot in the chest by a priest?"

"He was so bad at it, it almost did the job of killing me. He wasn't there to kill me, though. He was supposed to *pay* me."

"He wanted to renege?"

"No. He paid me first. Then he shot me."

"Why do you think he shot you?"

"He lost his mind is my best guess."

Weiss had to pause for a deeper wheeze that resolved in a sharp and painful sounding mini-coughing-jag.

"Do you want the nurse?"

Weiss waved both hands above his head, which shook wildly. "No."

"You'd like to finish our talk – or we can discuss other options?"

When the coughing jag stopped at last and calm was restored, Barry Weiss spoke with hoarsened voice. "I know those options, so no thanks."

"Not too many survive such discussions, Barry. So far, your odds don't impress me. You want the nurse to come in and give you oxygen or something? I can always come back."

"No, don't do that. I'd like to get rid of you once and for all."

"It seems we share a common goal then."

"I got a nurse comes in every four hours now to help my breathing using this dingus over here." With the thumb of his right hand, Weiss indicated a clear plastic graduated cylinder a little over a foot tall with a little yellow plunger inside resting at its base and a green rubber tube coming out of it. "They call it an Incentive Spirometer, so I get to suck wind a little hoping for a nurse worth lookin' at who's lookin' back at me."

"The abyss is looking back at you right now, Barry. You know this yet?"

"How do I play this then?"

"And live? I thought you'd never ask."

"And they say you have no sense of humor."

"They also say I talk too much. I'm unaware of both conditions."

"Not much for me to say until you tell me what you want to hear."

"Option one is that you tell me everything about the connection Ordo Templi Orientis has with the Catholic Church—more precisely with the Archdiocese of Boston. Option two is that I feed you to the Feebs since I'm now a confidential informant."

"That isn't really a thing, is it?"

"Barry, it's been a thing since before Johnny Depp played Whitey Bulger in that dog of a movie."

"Why feed me to the Feebs?"

"You get to have the ten dead girls murder that Special Agent Joel Thrawn has been investigating to get his street cred pinned on you. Everyone else from your lodge is dead. Yet another item I haven't heard yet in the news. How many were there, I wonder?"

"Eighteen not including Pater Hadit."

"Regardless, you're the last man standing, as you lie there. So you get to take the fall. Slug it out in court and then in the press— who will at this late date finally get wind of at least some of it."

"Is there an option three?"

"As a matter of fact, there is. I call it quits right now, put two in you with the Glock 9 in my pocket and walk out of here clean as a whistle. That's if you keep asking the questions and not giving me answers."

"That thing didn't set off any metal detectors or nothin'?"

"Surprisingly, no. And that gun may be mostly plastic, but not all. Not the suppressor I fixed onto it though. So it was still a risk. Who knew I didn't need it? Oh, well, it's certain to do the job without too much noise, thanks to that suppressor. By the way, that was your last question, Barry. The next thing you say will determine my next move.

"Listen, the whole thing started as a goof."

"You're saying you weren't serious?"

"Not at first. I didn't know it would be a real thing that brought along real money with it. Suddenly it just took on a life of its own."

"Explain that."

Sure. I was working over there at the Holy Cross Cathedral in the South End. I'm just a janitor mind you, and a Jew to boot. Who woulda thunk it?"

"You tell me."

"You got me, boss."

"Don't start talking like the late Theo Teocalli."

"You did him too, huh?"

"Yes, but slowly. I'll do you a great deal faster." Null yanked the Glock 9 from his pocket and rotated it in the air to encourage him to continue.

"Okay, so I'm a snoopy kinda guy. You already know I'm hooked in with the local lodge of the O-T-O, which is always hurting for cash, none of its members having much more than a pot to piss in. And there I am, working for the largest and richest criminal enterprise in the world."

"I killed Frater Nostrum who described it in just such a way."

"You know I've done one short bid at Concord Correctional for kiting checks, right? And the archdiocese hired me for the great optics: a Jewish check-bouncer gets a break from no less than the Catholic Church."

"You overheard something—eavesdropped on someone somehow?"

"I did a little spyin' on the cardinal to break up the monotony."

"You were looking for money."

"Everybody's looking for money."

"You thought the cardinal had money."

"What do you mean by 'thought?' I knew. The Catholic Church has more money than God."

"I can get behind a man who wants to tell jokes with his life on the line."

"It's like nervous laughter."

"Get on with it."

"Glad you approve. I caught the cardinal bitching out a guy he called the choir master about the quality of the boys he had to work with, saying he needed more and better, then on a call with this former sexworker who runs some holier-than-thou Christian adoption center in Newton, I heard him bitch her out for bringing him little girls when only the boys would do. Wynona Fomites was the name. Auntie Nonie Fomites. I looked her up and ran her down for the lodge."

"You were hands on then," Null whispered gravely.

"Oh, no. Not me. It wasn't like that. I was more mind than muscle."

"Show me."

"Okay, so good old Auntie, with the big boobs out to here." And Weiss made a grand, outflowing gesture from his chest with his hands and coughed a little. "She used to be called the Rubber Nun back in her sexworker days – now she just helps the Trump people like her boss, Betty DeVille, the SpamWay heiress, kidnap kiddies straight off the Southern Border when ICE separates them from their parents. She gets paid for accepting them three ways: State, Federal and Placement fees. That bitch is plain raking it in. Kidnapping as a business model, no ransom necessary."

"And how did you know this?"

"I'm no mathematician, but even I can do basic arithmetic."

"You had a chat with his Eminence then."

"You think *I'm* terrible? Listen, he's an oily fuckin' creep. Stinks of roses, lavender and shit. His eyes lit up like the Terminator's when he heard what business Nonie's in, and *then* I pitched him how we of the Boston Lodge of O-T-O could figure into the mix. You know. Help out."

"So it was all your idea?" Null commented vaguely, checking his phone for the time.

"I look like Pater Hadit to you? He's the shot caller at the lodge, not me. I'm just a helper."

Null silently rotated his gun again.

"Okay. So, then the Rubber Nun fucked it all up by taking in too many little girls and had to replace them all with little boys. You know how that went, right?"

"I do. Child trafficking for idiots. Sounds like Boko Haram in Africa."

"More like Joseph Krony, don't you think? Boko Haram just kidnapped girls—Nigerian Chikbok girls, to be precise."

"I do. The self-appointed 'messiah' of the Lord's Resistance Army—boss of the gang still waging Africa's longest running war. Kidnapped over 30,000 children, forcing the boys to become soldiers and the girls to become sex slaves."

"Yeah, well, Cardinal High-and Mighty sure didn't want no girls. He made that clear. He wasn't going to pay us for no girls. Any of us."

"Why all boys?"

"I gotta spell it out for ya? Are we that low?"

"Yet another question, but I'll allow it since you're correct. No, we ain't that low. Who did the ten little girls then?"

"Not me. No one from the lodge, I'm pretty sure. My best guess is it was old Auntie's mess. I think Cardinal Grand Poo-Bah had her clean it up and we of the O-T-O weren't getting paid for any more tone-deaf boys we delivered. So they had to be taken care of too."

"I presume you helped with that."

"I didn't. The Rubber Nun's a formidable woman. She handled it."

"Really. This woman."

"You don't gotta believe me. The Rubber Nun ain't exactly frail, y'know. But that stuff's way too skeevy even for me. Like I said before, I'm not muscle. I'm all mind. I did money—bookkeeping, planning jobs around the lodge. Strategies. I didn't really want to think about hurting anybody, much less children. It wasn't my end. I handled IT stuff, wire transfers. And not for nothin', but the O-T-O delivered some real tone-deaf wonders to the church who wound up being held over at the Rubber Nun's place until who knows when. The church don't want 'em. The Rubber Nun don't want 'em. They got nowhere to go. They're stranded at Bethlehem Adoption and Youth Placement Services. I know this. *You* know this."

Null cocked his head to the left and the arm whose hand held the Glock 9 stiffened. He looked stuck.

Barry Weiss began panicking as he faced the gun and saw the

nurse who had directed Null to his room stopped cold in the doorway. She was doing a quick check-in, got a hard glimpse of the gun, froze for a moment, and then sped off.

Like some delicate apparatus that had been temporarily knocked out of whack, Null appeared to be resetting himself, rebalancing his processes, adjusting his perceptions. He abruptly snapped back from his reverie to the present moment.

"You're right, Barry. I do know this. You know I found two of the boys, escapees from Bethlehem. They had club stamps on their wrists of *La Pieta*. You wouldn't know anything about that, would you?"

"I wouldn't, but it don't take no genius to guess what that means."

"No, it don't, do it?"

"You might want to hurry things up. I think security will be here in a few minutes."

"The nurse?"

"She saw your gun."

"Oh, that. Fine," Null said absently, and relaxed his arm back down, slipping the Glock 9 back into the lining of his coat.

"Security's pretty slow, but they're still coming."

"Yes, you're right again, Barry. About hospital security. When they have any at all, hospital security is always woefully slow."

"Do you shoot me now, or what?"

"Lying in bed like that makes a person fairly anxious, doesn't it? Wouldn't you say, Barry?"

"I would."

"I think I'll take my leave before it's taken from me."

"Is that it?"

"What more do you want?"

"A thank you would be nice."

The only response that the former Frater Phlegethon of the Boston Lodge of Ordo Templi Orientis got when he blinked his eyes only once was that Null had quietly disappeared.

TWENTY-TWO

Boston was hit by yet another punishing rain. This wasn't unusual for the short season that followed winter that only the wildly optimistic recognized to be spring and which only led to an unpredictable summer that might be marred by a continuum of gray skies and cool temperatures or be graced by a hot spotlight of brilliant sunshine, scalding heat and days that went on far too long. (You could call those days dog days, when snakes go blind, the morning dew is poison to open wounds and all dogs go mad, but no one would hear you). An admixture of those two conditions made the general populace of Boston even more crazy and violent than they might have otherwise been.

And Boston has always been a crazy, violent town, filled with race hatred, class hatred, barbarous tribalism and goofily stupid crime that kept the Boston Police Department busier than it would have liked to have been. Anyone who knows the tortuous nature of Boston crime knows that the worst of it was kept far from the light of day, seldom if ever spoken about, was never reported and, as time passed, wound up being relegated to the half-whispered legends of the street.

Joseph X. Null was such a legend.

Everyone wanted him dead. There was a weird unanimity in

that. The BPD wanted him dead, the FBI wanted him dead, Malek the Mallet and what was left of the Ork wanted him dead and BPD Detective Lieutenant Katherine Boyd wanted him dead.

They all wanted him dead, both in legend and in fact.

Acknowledging his existence as a legend, Null had reconciled himself to his own death on all counts, fact, fiction, fancy and fate. If he could have been comforted, then it would have comforted him to become as unnoticed as a passing shadow, a cold, ghostly draft, a muffled cry in the night. To live as a mere suspicion, a suggestion of terror was his personal summum bonum. All the rest he would work out diligently with bullets and blades and, now and then, a garotte.

Meanwhile, Auntie Nonie Fomites didn't know anything about Null. His existence hadn't reached her yet and though it might have had relevancy for Betty DeVille's crew of upstanding criminals who always kept a careful ear to the street, they had no interest in Boston at all. To them it was an atheistic, cosmopolitan sinkhole, a paste-gem imitation of bigger cities with much bigger profit centers to attend to. Ah, but even with its dwindling religion, Boston meant Newton and Newton meant Bethlehem, which meant to them the upscale precincts of Newton and a test case for continued business with the Catholic Church, and Boston's lingering Catholic faith and its strong archdiocese marked a cash-positive avenue for the further kidnapping and relocation of children to advance God's kingdom. And Betty DeVille wanted a cardinal in her pocket and the cardinal wanted the ear of the pope, and now had achieved it, thanks to a serendipity of need and the endless administrative cover-ups of venal priests who were the sacerdotal life's blood of Holy Mother Church.

Auntie Nonie was pacing back and forth in the foyer of the mansion that housed Bethlehem Adoption and Youth Placement Services, rubbing her hands together anxiously, trying not to lose her cool, ticking off the logical problems in her mind. She even experienced a frisson of relief with a short giggle that the mansion which sported one of those hoity-toity blue plaques from the

National Registry of Historic Places was there for unspecified reasons that weren't at all too occult for Auntie Nonie to dope out. She knew all about it from some leisure time spent idling on her Toughbook laptop. She held the conviction that she was, on some spiritual level, the new conduit for all the vile and perhaps misunderstood shenanigans that went on within the pleasant walls and beautifully restored confines of the Herrick Road mansion over 150 years ago.

"So this is where all the town worthies used to get their ashes hauled and smoke up some opium, well, it couldn't be more fitting that a child trafficking and kidnapping scheme replaced the house's former function as a whorehouse. Meanwhile, nobody's really gettin' fucked. We just move the kiddies in and move the kiddies out and the profits just keep rollin' in."

She paused reflectively, for a moment then abruptly kicked the baseboard with the toe of her Jimmy Choo stiletto-heeled shoe and screamed, "Except for those goddamn worthless duds that I'm stuck with and have to get rid of! *Fucking hell!*"

Auntie Nonie looked at the clock and quietly, inwardly, panicked all over again at the lateness of the hour. After another fifteen minutes of pacing, she sat down on the stairs that led to the second floor and pleaded to the God she had never at all actually believed in, wailing, "Where are my busses? Where are my six burly devout priests who are supposed to be solving my surplus pest problem? I'm in a jam here and, no mistake, none of this feels right. I've got my ass hangin' out there in the endless downpour, for Christ's sake. Where oh where, you worthless, stupid deity is my goddamn *deliverance?*"

The pounding rain gave her its most calloused, indifferent reply.

The wind snarled at her just as if she were like anybody else, and she knew that anyone who had met her since she was a teenager would never walk away from her with that opinion. *Never just like anybody else,* was her ethos, her creed and calling. Those she let walk away from her knew what they had just managed to elude. And those that didn't? Well, they never forgot the ride she gave them, whether it was behind the wheel, in the sack, off the ledge of a building, at the deep end of a swimming pool or atop a wrought iron fence. And if their memories had to be truncated—cut short by whatever the given moment had dictated to her that she do in that one rare offering life and time had always given her again and again—the window of opportunity—she always understood autonomically how fast to act and exactly what to do.

She had never been caught short and exposed fumbling with necessity too late—a day late and a dollar short.

That was never her and she kept those dollars flowing so she would never be short. Not once. Not in anything. Not ever.

Even the worst thing she had ever done—those *girls!*

She understood clearly more than anyone else equally positioned to do so but refused, refused to take hold of the grim truth, squeeze it hard enough to extract gold from it and bury the remnants where even god could never find it. That was her knack. That was her triumph and that was why creepy God-a-holic and dedicated Christo-fascist Betty DeVille had picked her. Her aggression and naked greed sealed the deal from the scary dowager with the physique of a skeleton who was nothing if not an oozing, quivering wretch of naked need, festooned with jewels and silks and implants not half as nice as her own with a lacquered yellow fright wig that resembled a helmet (and that you could never comfortably call blonde).

And why not?

Didn't the billionairess style herself a soldier in God's precious army? Wasn't her billionaire brother, Derrick, some kind of big-time mercenary PMC—private military contractor—delivering bodies and ordnance to patch combat and security holes throughout the Middle East, despite being illegal for the US Government to hire under what Betty DeVille had called the Anti-Pinkerton Act of 1893? Not to worry. Derrick spun off and merged so many versions of his BlackPool PMC business that not even the Pentagon knew precisely who the protean entity was that was working with them at what given time for who knows what. Or even what they were doing and, as it turned out to be the case in Iraq, just whom they were slaughtering to advance the highly profitable glory of war. It was what Betty's brother often referred to with outright glee and laughter as "our beloved permanent war economy."

Derrick King would have understood Auntie Nonie's problem with the little girls at a glance. Any no-nonsense, pragmatic, tough-minded, mature person of business could and would have understood it without any explication at all. Still, it was better for the optics of the thing to keep quiet about it. Absolute secrecy was required, and she understood that in her meticulous and stealthy execution of the only viable solution at hand. And even if those girls were somehow discovered and dug up—how could they be traced back to the pious administrator of Bethlehem Adoption and Youth Placement Services?

A tireless, selfless advocate for the fragile little lives of children and a good Christian woman in the bargain.

No, the problem wasn't the ten girls in the basement of a condemned building in Newton Highlands, but the fifteen raucous, difficult boys upstairs on the third floor. No, those fifteen boys would sink her—would sink everybody, even little miss deniability, Betty DeVille herself. No, they had to be spirited away in a different condition than just the perpetually drugged state she was keeping them in.

And the cold icy creature made up of equal parts fear and despair crawled lovingly and passionately up her spine, taking its time.

It wasn't fifteen boys anymore. Two had escaped.

Two useless, stupid, untalented little boys had escaped.

The creature made its way into her brain, icing it up so fast it was like ice-cream brain freeze without the ice-cream. The headache rush was instant and severe.

She screamed long and loud, then stepped out into the whipping wind and pounding rain and sat under the ledge of the entryway that kept her somewhat dry and illuminated by warm, soft yellow light behind her from the open door.

A cross draft slammed the door shut and then, just as abruptly, threw it open again. This repeated three times. And Auntie screamed.

She screamed once more when she got the door closed sitting in the rain for what she felt was a long time and, predictably enough, nothing happened.

Auntie Nonie suddenly found herself jostled and shouted at, though she could hardly make out who was doing the jostling and shouting or what the words meant.

Father Bricolage knelt down, put his arm under both of Auntie's, helped her up and then in, where there was warmth and light and a dampening of the sound of the pounding rain when he closed the door behind him. Auntie fluttered her wet eyes open and smiled at the sight of the priest. Before she could think of doing it, she flung his arms off and apart and pushed him backward so hard that if the door hadn't been closed to stop him, he would have wound up on his back on the tar driveway in the torrential rain. It had become second nature to her to do it, recalling decades of unwanted manhandling, and she felt a modicum of remorse for having done it to a celibate priest who was only trying to help her.

"I'm sorry father. Old habits die hard."

"That's alright, Auntie. Sometimes those habits only die when we do and face the final judgement of God. But in the end, final absolution given by a sacerdotal member of the brethren of the priesthood will see your soul safely to heaven." He was about to suggest that he could perform that service for her at any time she liked, thought better of it and bit his lower lip instead.

"That's if you believe that death has a life of its own, Father, which I don't."

"But can you know that, Auntie? Know for certain whether or not your very soul is imperiled or safely aimed in a heavenly trajectory?"

"No one can know that Father, but I'm fairly sure."

"Now how could you ever be sure of such a thing that has warranted the attention of all the greatest theologians the world has known?"

"Of course I couldn't be, Father, which suits me pretty good at this time when we've had ten little angels sent to their reward in heaven and we have thirteen to send there tonight, and some other angels your church doesn't seem to know what to do with who need to get their little tickets punched as well."

"You know that our choir can't accept little girls. You're going to have to find a home for the little dears. Or perhaps arrange for foster care."

"All systems are stressed to the max. They'll age out by the time I get beds for 'em and they're hard enough to handle as it is. Ain't no place for 'em. State only pays so much and federal don't pay nothin' except for those got off the Southern Border. We got homes for those, no prob' – but the rest do no good for nobody. And you couldn't come up with a few burley priests to help lighten my burden, could you? They can't all be tall, scrawny faggots like you. Yet, you're all I get. A useless fag."

"Auntie, I'm celibate."

"We speak the same language, don't we?"

"I don't take your meaning."

"You know I know what your defense boys are all about."

"Defense boys? There's no such thing."

"It's Latin, Daddy-O. Parse it out."

"Oh!" Father Bricolage exclaimed, feigning befuddlement, knowing perfectly well what Auntie had in mind. "You mean *Defensores Fidei de Puero*?"

"You're going to fuck the little choir boys, aren't you? They're just fresh catamites for priests like you."

"Not like me, Auntie, no. I am a true celibate and a devout instrument of God, a servant of God whose vocation is the continuous state of life that God has asked me to live in which, by choice, I shall never depart from, even when I depart this life, only to further serve his glory in heaven then as I do here on earth now."

"I suppose it'd be pretty tough for you to serve God as a pimp in heaven like you're doing in the here and now, which is a good thing because you're really pretty terrible at it."

"You imperil your soul talking to me in such a way. You should take confession and recant what you just said to me. The foulness of it. The arrogance."

"Stick it in your ear, Padre. We're both stuck up a creek without those bodies."

"You mean *with* those bodies, don't you?"

"Same difference."

"But you had the doctor coming—the special doctor?"

"He's late and you've come without priests. Without help of any kind. Nothing to help me with these disgusting disposal issues."

"But I drove the mini-bus to get here."

"That's for the St. Augustine boys, I take it? You're washing your hands of the rejects, then."

"My hands are clean, Auntie. It's the filth of your own hands that needs the washing."

"Bullshit, Daddy-O. You're in just as deep as I am."

"I have the church, Auntie, what do you have?"

"I have a Christo-fascist billionaire and her mercenary war-loving brother advancing what they call 'The Kingdom of God.' Could be a standoff, ya think?"

"I think I'll take all my good boys and leave you and all your other charges in peace. But before I do, there's still a part of our contract that you have yet to deliver. And I cannot take my boys without it."

"Okay, Daddy-O, and what do you think that is?"

"You know what it is."

Auntie Nonie took a deep breath, made claws of her hands, which she used against the air of the room and screamed: "Don't play games with me, Daddy-O! I'm stressed half to death, and the bodies are everywhere! *Everywhere!* And he's coming. I keep hearing that he's coming. On top of everything and all the bodies are falling on me—"

"My child, you can't—"

"It's all over the street. It's whispered everywhere. The monster, the spook—the goddamn zombie people are afraid to say his fucking name. I don't even got his *name*."

"Calm down. Not everything you hear in the street is real. Oftentimes, my child, it's just a word and a concept with nothing behind it. No proof, no material reality or fact behind it. Only fear to bolster it, begging to make it matter and repetition of a sad story that has only an empty threat behind it."

"Fine. Sure. Whatever you say."

"You're stressing out over a myth, a non-fact."

"Oh, you mean like Jesus Christ, then? Well, that makes it all clearer, now, doesn't it?"

"I won't be baited by you, Auntie. We'll wait for the doctor to arrive. Do you think your doctor might apply those special abilities to the disposal issue?"

"I suppose if he's good for one thing he'll be good enough for the other."

"We paid you enough to cover that, obviously. We're not liable in any way."

"I don't know, Daddy-O. I think we have a kind of a *force majeure* issue here. I think there'll have to be an upcharge of some kind."

"I don't have all night, Auntie, and I'm not here to argue or dicker with you. I'm here to take receipt of my good boys and return to the Basilica of Our Lady of Perpetual Sorrow with all due haste. This isn't a night fit for man nor beast to be out in, let alone a group of perfect little boys."

"You mean imperfect. They won't be perfect until—"

"Yes, I didn't mean perfect. Nothing is perfect in the eyes of God who is the master of perfection and is himself so perfect that he could never duplicate that perfection in any living thing—as that would kill it. And the imperfect must be preserved and protected to give voice to the glory of God. And after the delicate procedure that will protect them from sin, cloak them from sin, and bring them closer to the Lord's embrace, its blessing will only multiply with time. The very nature of their sacred singing will deepen in power as they age, which, uncannily, will reach higher and higher grada- tions of voice, yet with more richness than any secular male voice ever could match, achieving the widest possible ranges of soprano, mezzo-soprano and contralto—"

"And will they sing just as heavenly when raped by your priests?"

Father Bricolage put his hands over his ears and squinted his eyes as if enduring a migraine or some equally painful incursion into his brain through the ear canals, though it didn't have to be the decibels and frequency of the sound itself, but just the quietly artic- ulated words spoken.

"I will not tolerate such cant, Auntie. There will be no rape. The boys of *Defensores Fidei de Puero* will give of themselves freely to their assigned priest, whom they will also assist in all his duties, whether prosaic or sacerdotal. If there is no carnal response of lust in the boys of *Defensores Fidei de Puero,* then they can be absolved of all sin. They themselves are a perfect solution and will prove to be a healing balm to the great wound done to Holy Mother Church—"

"By her reprehensible and fully corrupt priests?" interrupted Auntie Nonie, sashaying seductively toward the priest, who pushed her away violently. "My, Father, you *are* a little fag boy, aren't you?"

"I didn't come here to argue with you Auntie or to play your sordid little games. I am here in furtherance of a sacred mission. This very mission to 'increase the honor given to God by the church in union with Christ, its Head. Sacred music likewise helps to increase the fruits which the faithful, moved by the sacred harmonies, derived from the holy liturgy.' I'll await your doctor to come and do his enabling duty and then will trouble you no further."

"You quoted that pope, didn't you? I think I heard something like it from Betty DeVille herself. She said it was from that *good* pope back in the forties—the one who knew what to do about the Jews."

"That is a most manifest lie against Pope Pius XII, the infallible voice of God on this earth at the time."

"He gave Hitler the church's okay on extermination of the Jews—"

"I will not debate that alleged embarrassment with you, Auntie. The Holocaust has been used too many times as a weapon against the church, to injure and besmirch her. Never mind the petty six million Jews of alleged Catholic Hitler's annihilation. So what if the pope played the politics of the time and appeased Hitler which was the only sane course to follow at the time? Better to question the atheist monstrosity Josef Stalin and his deliberate murder of over 100 million people in excess of his disastrous clashes with the Nazi war machine, which our beloved pope managed to avert by making a tacit alliance with the dictator for the good of all. Just as he did with Mussolini. The survival of the Holy See depended upon it."

"Pope Pius XII wasn't going to war, was he?"

"Good question Auntie. Perhaps he was and it is in this that we can find agreement. Now it's cold, and pelting rain. Couldn't we adjourn and move to somewhere a bit warmer and perhaps have some hot tea, or perhaps something a little stronger if you have it?"

"Not the worst idea, Daddy-O. But I've had a little playmate of mine looking into matters of relief that I suppose will help us both. Even if the Doctor doesn't come."

"You're not thinking of having *him* do the procedure, are you, Auntie? Is he even qualified?"

"No, but he can be helpful. I tricked the place out for medical so the Doctor when he gets here—if he gets here—will have a sterile work area stocked with whatever he needs in the way of med-surge. For what has to be done. Hopefully quick and neat. And there are good sized trash bags, double reinforced too, for the large-scale medical waste that will have to be carefully disposed of after the fact. Pounds of it."

Father Bricolage made a face, turned his head away and held up his right hand in a 'stop' motion to emphasize his point. "Not my department, Auntie. But it seems for all your hysterics that you have matters well in hand regardless."

"Well in hand?" Auntie Nonie squeaked. "Well in *hand*—"

"Yes. You're resourceful, which is why you're in the position you're in and anointed by god to do business with us—"

"Jesus Christ, father faggot! Don't you see what's happening? This thing is unraveling faster than we can even track. I don't know if someone leaked what's going on, but between the zombie fucker that's supposed to be dogging us, the cops and the damn feebs, we could all wind up getting blanched in boiling water if we don't get things back on track. And soon."

"How long ago was your doctor supposed to have gotten here?"

"A couple of hours ago."

"Was he driving in this mess? I ask that because as you already know, the weather made me late driving the bus."

"I don't think he has a car. He was taking the T."

"Green Line to Newton Center? So that's just a walk from here. I've done it myself."

"Well, as far as I know, the T's still running. Not that the thing doesn't shut down at the first real sign of our usually shitty weather."

"No, Auntie, not that it doesn't."

"Could be he ain't comin'."

"Let's hope otherwise."

"Hope away, Daddy-O. Pray on it, why don't you?"

"You're sarcastic, I know, but I'm always prayerful about much in the back of my mind. I pray constantly. I never want to lose the instantaneity of prayer and homage to God—"

"So you do it all the time, then? There's spontaneity for you. What else do you do all the time, Daddy-O?"

"I won't debate the niceties of worship with you, Auntie, but I will add a continuous prayer in the back of my mind for the salvation of your immortal soul."

"Good of you."

"It'll be a very short prayer, but it should suffice."

"A short prayer from a faggot priest with a short dick."

"Short lifespan, Auntie, if you're not careful."

"Back at you, short-dick motherfucker."

"There was a crooked man, and he walked a crooked mile. He found a crooked sixpence against a crooked stile."

"What the fuck's *that* supposed to mean? Poetry at this very exactly shitty moment? Are you kidding me?"

"That old poem reminded me of something I saw in the rain as I was driving up here. A lone man walking a funny little walk that I passed on the way. Reminded me of that rhyme. He was precisely that, because he looked crooked."

"Oh, great. So now you think—"

It was like an alarm had suddenly sounded.

The electronic ringing of the doorbell, really an almost resonant artificial ringing with a bass undertone of a loudly humming buzz broke the tension. It's uncertain as to whether it was the frequency of the sound or the inchoate chill of the unwavering New England dampness exacerbated by the incessant rain that made Father Bricolage shudder so violently when Auntie Nonie opened the door, but she didn't notice it and neither did the man at the door who rang the bell. The priest made the sound of frigidity with his lips and that, combined with the shuddering of his body, seemed to warm him up.

"You're the guy, right? The one who was supposed to be here two hours ago?"

"Beg pardon. The weather slowed me down and I didn't have a car at my disposal."

"Glad to see you, Doctor. We were worried you weren't going to make it at all," Father Bricolage interceded with cheer.

"You drove the mini-bus, sir?"

"Yes, that's right."

"I saw you pass me as I trudged up the hill looking for this place."

"Yes, that's right. We saw each other. If I had known, I'd have given you a ride."

"You're a priest, aren't you?"

"That's correct. You can tell by the outfit, huh," Father Bricolage responded, aiming for humor and missing.

"Being that you're a priest, why didn't you stop and offer me a ride?"

Father Bricolage positioned himself to argue but stopped himself taking in the state of the drenched little man with the damaged face. He reasoned quickly that the hat wasn't just to keep the rain off of him somewhat, but to cast a shadow over the ruined face. His finger was raised up to make a point, his mouth open to make an argument and he had taken a single step forward with his right foot, but he froze and stepped back, nervously adjusting his collar.

"You're right, Doctor. I'm sorry. I should have. By the way, if I might have your name, so I may address you properly."

"Geeze, the guy needs a towel more than he needs an introduction. Your name's, what, cat nip or something like that, right?"

"No, that's not my name, but rather what I do. Khatna, khafz, khafd and khifaad32 which is female circumcision. FGM—female genital mutilation—is how more civilized quarters refer to the practice. By the way, I can also act as a moil if a boy is in need of circumcision. I'm skilled at both, although not quite so much on the ritual, though I do have some key prayers memorized."

"That's all great, Doctor, but let's get you inside and out of the foyer so we can get you all toweled off and set you up for the task at hand."

"Doctor, you're forgetting something."

"I'm sorry, Father. What might that be?"

"Your name, Doctor, if you don't mind."

"Call me Null. Everybody calls me Null. When they can."

Auntie Nonie sidled into Null where he stood, forcing the contours of her body into him, but not getting pliant flesh beneath the heavy topcoat. Instead, there was metallic rigidity in uneven places, which made her draw back. Father Bricolage clasped his hands together, nodded and bowed slightly, his face twisted by a broad smile that set his face into a painfully held spasm, to cover his uncertainty. Null squinted in the brightness of the light of the anteroom, splashed hot white by halogen bulbs set high in the ceiling. Yet for all that splash, the foyer was cold and Auntie Nonie shuddered.

"You have a lot of hardware under there, Doc, y'know?"

"Are you trying to make a joke, Ms. Whoever you are?"

"Auntie can be very charming, Dr. Null, as you can see, but I'm certain she meant nothing by it."

"Auntie?"

"Yes, Doctor. Nonie Fomites. Everyone calls me Auntie. You may as well call me that too."

"I'm Null. Everyone calls me Null—"

"When they can, right, Doc? Nice tagline, by the way."

"What you felt was merely my being prepared."

"No, I was just noticing, Doctor, that's all. Of course you need equipment for what you do."

"Yes, I do. And I like to travel light. Keep on the move as the procedures you require are a bit too rarified for the average American to accept, and so must necessarily be swift and sure and clean and kept underground in the shadows, out of the course of normal events."

"Well Dr. Null, just step inside with me. We'll get you dried off and set you up."

"You may need to towel off also, Auntie. You're right. I am rather drenched. But I don't have much time, so I'd like to get started right away. I understand that there's quite a bit of work you need to have done and not all of it in my principal areas of expertise. A disposal issue, if I'm right?"

"Oh, yes, Doctor Null. You hit the nail on the head."

"Once again, Doctor, let me apologize for not having picked you up along the way. I should have recognized at once that it would take a driven, purposeful man to be out on a night this, trudging up Herrick Road as you were in the torrential downpour."

"How could I not forgive a man whose profession is forgiveness? Don't give it a second thought, Father."

The foyer of the antique mansion led to a narrow front hallway and a flight of stairs facing the entryway with a door at the end of it, which led to the basement. The walls had been scrubbed, primed, painted and repainted an alabaster blistering white. The door that led to the basement was low and angled at the top to mimic the diagonal of the staircase. Even Null had to bend down to fit through the doorway that opened into a cramped stairwell whose ancient wooden steps sanded smooth that were as steep as a ladder. And he was shorter than both Auntie Nonie Fomites and Father Bricolage. The stairwell had been whitewashed just as the remainder of Bethlehem had been and was so brightly incisive it could be seen as that even under the niggardly illumination of a single energy-saving lightbulb.

The basement itself was an explosive nova of light with high-wattage surgical lamps that caused both Null and the priest to shield their eyes with hands. Before doing that, they caught a glimpse of a tall, robed figure throttling a small boy who was gulping and gasping for help, thrashing his body about to get out of the grip of the strangler. The boy freed himself, managing to bite his assailant and run toward the far west wall of the basement, crumpling in the corner near two other boys who both looked terrified sitting on the floor hugging their knees. Their whimpering was louder than the two imposing gray Vornado fans that kept the air circulating in the dank space and the dehumidifier that was vainly beating back mildew with its surly hum.

Auntie marched forward toward the robed figure and gave him a wide arc smack across his face that set him back on his heels.

"Frater Frazil, you disappoint me! I send you down here with just three wee little ones, and they're *still* running around and acting up. It was one simple little thing I asked you to do. Do I have to keep ordering you around in the nude to get you motivated or what? Let's see those balls of yours be good for something—"

"You thought they were good for something this morning."

She smacked Frater Frazil across the face again and after a couple of heartbeats they both smiled at each other.

"The Doctor's arrived now and he'll handle things from here. Still, go grab the one that got away in the back corner and show the Doc how we do things at Bethlehem."

A sound like a great popping of exhaust shook the room.

Auntie jumped back and held up her hands in front of her face. "Oh my God—he's squirting on me!" she squealed. "He squirted blood on me!"

Another pop went off and Frater Frazil collapsed to the floor.

In near shell-shocked confusion, Auntie fell back on her heels and narrowly avoided hitting the floor near the already fallen Frater.

Father Bricolage made a half-swallowed gasping sound that would have proved amusing coming from a puppet but disturbing coming from a middle-aged priest. Null appeared to be both slack and relaxed, calmly marking time. The priest took advantage of this gap in the action and pulled his twenty-two pistol and cocked it.

"It's unpardonable, Null. You just killed an innocent man outright. Even you must understand that judgment belongs exclusively to the lord—"

"That's convenient, then." Null sighed sounding bored, "I don't deal in judgment, and I don't recognize kings, lords, popes and priests."

"You just murdered a man for nothing, and what have you to say for yourself?"

"It looked to me like he was trying to strangle one of those boys over there against the wall. So, maybe not for nothing."

"In your judgment."

"I don't do judgment, Father."

"What would you call it, then?" The priest was so enraged his face took on the hue of freshly cut beef and the hand holding the twenty-two shook hard."

"Execution. Judgment would have been superfluous here."

"I could plug you right now, villain."

"No, you couldn't."

"I will now, if you don't comply."

"Comply with what, priest? I comply with Diderot, who said, "Man will never be free until the last king is strangled with the entrails of the last priest."

"Foul-mouthed encyclopedist."

"Sure. He founded the Encyclopédie to help advance the Enlightenment. All priests should rightly despise him, just as you do. Kudos, priest, because enlightenment kills off fanciful cults like Catholicism. And in this case you are the last priest, but since no king's entrails are handy and the Frater there beat us to the strangulation part, I'll just have to resort to other means—"

"He's dead, you horrible creature! You killed him!" Auntie bellowed in the midst of a tear-soaked tantrum.

"I'll plug you if you don't stop," Father Bricolage stammered.

"Oh, keep still, Padre. Your hand is shaking so badly you'll miss anyway, even at this close a proximity. And, if you'll notice, I have a gun that's right up against your belly." Null turned his attention to Auntie. "Is he really dead, do you think, Auntie? I shot him twice and this ain't the Sunday funnies. I guess the reason you got squirted on was because I luckily hit the carotid artery. The other was a headshot, dead center, also really difficult to make despite movies and TV. I think I've been getting the hang of handling sidearms like this one, though. This one's a Heckler and Koch P7, German. Especially good craftsmen, the Germans—no slapdash American-style handiwork labeled and billed as exceptional, which the world has come to know—thanks to Trump—as meaning exceptionally bad. This item's an easy point and shoot, which I did, and it worked out remarkably well. Don't you think, Auntie?"

"Shut him up, will you already, you Goddamned Jesus fucker!"

The priest looked down and his trembling hand was empty.

"You know, twenty-twos are thought not to be quite as deadly as the higher caliber pistols, but they really can't be beat for lightness and ease of use. An even easier point and shoot, if you ask me. This one's a pretty good example. Unfortunately, when the hand that holds the gun shakes as badly as yours, at this light a weight, the gun really can't steady it the way a heavier pistol might. The gun just goes wherever your wrist goes, so, you were out of luck well before I grabbed it off you. It's a nice piece. A Ruger Mark twenty-two. It's no wonder you nearly killed Barry Weiss with it. Frater Phlegethon—head of building services at Holy Cross Cathedral. Funny coincidence that—like right out of a John le Carré spy novel. But this is way funnier, because it's real, and a real threat to you and your church, don't you think?"

"I don't know—"

Null clucked his tongue. "You should have finished Barry off when you had the chance."

Auntie Nonie stamped her food and screamed: "Do something, you cocksucker! Don't you get it? This twerp is the guy the whole street warned us was coming for us. *'He's coming. You can't stop him. He's a killing machine. Blah, blah, blah.'* Well, he's here, you stupid priest. You're bigger than him, so take the goddamn sonofabitch down already, why don't you?" Auntie spat blood that had trickled down to her mouth between her lips to underscore her point.

Nobody noticed that the boys who had pressed themselves up against the west wall of the basement had gone entirely silent. And the Vornado fans hummed quietly beneath the voices and added a slight growl to them as powerful fans are wont to do.

"I suppose this is my reputation preceding me—it just gets worse and worse. No matter what I do, I just can't keep a lid on my existence. Life would go so much more smoothly if you two didn't know anything. Sadly, you know too much."

And with that last statement, Null pistol whipped the priest up from under his chin, which delivered a massive shock to his brain. Stunned, he collapsed backward against the door jamb and sank to the floor. Auntie ran at him, shrieking something incomprehensible, Null shot her once in the leg with the Ruger twenty-two and she went down.

The boys against the wall were still silent, but all of them were smiling.

TWENTY-THREE

When Auntie Nonie struggled up from the floor, she flopped right back down again. Blood was trickling steadily from her upper left thigh. Trickling, not gushing. The pain wasn't terrible, just dull and thick, thudding along in sync with the beating of her heart. She was sure that if she collected herself for a few minutes, and caught her breath, she could then make herself stand and then lope out of this perverse dungeon of despair and get herself to an emergency room in one desperately quick hurry.

The only problem was that the idiot priest and the scarred-up little freak who shot her were still blocking the exit to the stairwell. Forcing herself to her feet, feeling as unstable and goofily off-balance as a newborn foal, her blurred vision cleared hard and fast and nearly with an audible bang, and then she realized what she was seeing was the sick little freak on top of the stupid priest mashing his face to pulp with the Ruger Mark twenty-two. The sounds of chirping birds distracted her for a moment, and she had to concentrate to figure out what that sound meant.

It was terrifically difficult to interpret sensory input when the entire experience of life given in the moment was like being at the bottom of an aquarium. After several deep, cleansing breaths of the variety she had once experienced in yoga class, she realized what the chirping was.

The little boys, those sad, lost little fuckers whose destiny was to become mulch in some prosperous person's garden (maybe even her own, which brought a smile to her lips) were laughing. They were laughing and making fun of her and the stupid priest. How dare they? A hot flash of desire scorched her chest from the inside out, which made her only want to murder them more. It was followed just as quickly by a black depression made of fragile ash that she couldn't do that and survive this grotesque melee.

It was at that ashen moment that she realized she was in shock and huffed a little self-parodying laugh about it, because that didn't mean that she lacked presence of mind. No, she would always have that. She hadn't come this far and escaped successfully all the ragged traps and pitfalls others had lain in her way, which no doubt would have cooled out any lesser woman permanently. No, she was perpetually ready for the worst, and she huffed out another little laugh that this pipsqueak of a zombie making pâté of the late Father Bricolage's face was the only danger standing between her and a fast Uber ride to Newton Wellesley Hospital.

No, no, *no!*

Auntie wriggled a bit of her practiced wriggle that nearly caused her to keel over but allowed her at the same time to slip the knife from the inner sheath of her dress and grasp it in a way that gave her confidence, which she mistook for energy. So with a weirdly stiff and courageous awkwardness, she lunged at Null, who was too busy mashing the late Father's face to notice.

At the downstroke of the blade, Null caught Auntie's arm just before she caught his, took the knife from her and made a calculated slash across the top of her breasts with his right hand holding the knife, then straight punched her with a left jab to her face, breaking her nose. He was rewarded with an angry spout of blood, which he neatly dodged. Auntie hissed like a cat, which gurgled a bit, as it was overtaken by the blood running down her throat.

They both paused when an explosion of commotion intruded into the room that was so loud and multi-sourced that it sounded like a stampede of hydrophobic cattle crammed into a pit and being burned alive by flamethrowers. There were screams and hollering, loud shouts of urban threat, the pleas and cries of women and children and footfalls—seemingly hundreds of footfalls storming the floors just above the basement, stamping, stomping, tapping, scuffing, shuffling. It was a din that had sprung up as if from nowhere. Null, as was so often the case, remained placid and serene. There were loud screams matched by hollers as well and all of it gave him a moment of pause, and Auntie was grateful for it until she realized what all the noises signified.

Immediately in the moment, though, Auntie recognized secondarily what the noises *didn't* signify. Cops. No cop sounds whatever. Nothing at all that sounded like a cop. No loud bullying brag. Cop-victim sounds abounded, sure, that was true. But cops barking orders, threats and the brutal thudding of their routine beatdowns weren't in evidence. Not a peep from their squawking walkies either, whose crackling crosstalk infected every scene they arrived at, even before they managed to manufacture something routine into a self-serving crime scene.

The lack of crosstalk gave her a chill that it might be something much worse than just the dull-witted police intruding on a scene they hadn't yet fucked up which was getting more fucked up, with every passing second. Then a voice broke through the silence of the room that had been defined by the cacophony just outside of it.

"I *knew* it!" cried the boy that Frater Frazil had been throttling a little less than fifteen minutes ago. "They here! The damn cavalry's come to get us!"

"Maybe somethin' worse I bet," came a glum reply from a smaller boy who was hiding his face between his knees."

"Okay, boys!" announced Null in a monotone. "Turn around and face the wall. You're too young to see this. You shouldn't see this. Just turn. Look away."

"Okay, boys!" announced Null in a monotone. "Turn around

and face the wall. You're too young to see this. You shouldn't see this. Just turn. Look away."

"Mister," piped up Frater Frazil's former victim, "We ain't gon' do that. We wanna see all of it. We deserves it. So go 'head. We *down!*"

"Yes, you're right kid – the cavalry has arrived."

Auntie Nonie wavered forward a bit, spilling more blood as she took a step closer to Null, who swiped at her jutting breasts, deftly slicing into each, but not along the bottom suture lines that had healed years ago leaving nary a scar.

"Don't worry, Auntie. I'm quite handy with a knife. I'm no surgeon, mind you, but it takes much less skill to destroy what refined medical skill has accomplished. Snip, snip and there we are."

She lunged at Null, her torso moving much more forward than the rest of her, which seemed dug into the concrete floor, nearly toppling her over before Null caught her and steadied her. That was when Auntie gaped her full-lipped mouth open and screamed up from the diaphragm so loudly the word "help" could hardly be made out at all.

"No Auntie – you just don't understand. They're here to help *me*, not you. And we're not really in any hurry for that at all, as if you couldn't tell."

"I'll kill you!" she said, breathless.

"Time for you to take a nap, Auntie."

"Fuck!" Auntie replied just before Null flattened out his right hand and gave a hard push to her bleeding breasts which sent her falling backward while Null wiped the knife – a plain dagger with a six-inch double-edged blade – with the hem of his coat. He pinwheeled the knife in the air twice, caught it neatly then stuck it hilt-first in the outer pocket of his topcoat – a garment already over-burdened with ordnance.

When Auntie went down, the loudest boy laughed that much louder while the other two looked on, not in shock or astonishment, but in wonder at how such a drastic change in their grim reality could be worked with such violence and in so little time.

"Oh, yes he did!" cried the loud boy. "He *did!*"

When Auntie woke up lying bloody on the basement floor, the boys and the bodies of Frater Frazil and of Father Bricolage were gone and Null was talking in low tones to two young black men, one was tall and thick – a bruiser, Auntie would have said, if she could have spoken at that moment, but it was still taking all she had to keep her eyes open and remain conscious. Jo-Jo, was a name she heard Null say, followed by Dominic. She thought that was odd. But then, why couldn't a black man be Italian – or at least have an Italian name? Names were crazier these days than ever. Meanwhile, she had taken notice that blacks and Latinx's and Asians were filling the roles of Russian and British aristocracies on cable and streaming TV and even at the movies. She dredged up the word 'anachronism' from her brain and was proud that she could do it.

Yes, that what it was. Ridiculous. But the rubes always pay extra for the ridiculous and if it's one thing she knew Hollyweird could provide in a heartbeat, it was the ridiculous.

Funny the things you think of when you're dying.

No. She was far too tough and mean to die.

There was a way to survive this little encounter and she was going to find it.

What Auntie didn't know and couldn't know was that Null had the very same idea in mind.

Buses. They were discussing buses. But the father had come that night in just one bus and he wasn't going to be transporting a bunch of the good, useful choirboy geldings anywhere anytime soon. Or to the home of that Cardinal, the Basilica of something or other in Southie. Her body wanted her to laugh but even before she could smile the pain stopped her. It hit her like cold water. The freak had his gang bring up another bus to shuttle all the little kiddies – even the most useless of them – to somewhere else where no doubt he'll get a pretty price indeed for each little tow-headed soul-sucking vampire. So, another means of making child kidnapping profitable had made itself known to the little fucker. Well, she wanted in on that action. In fact, she'd rip it away from him at the first opportunity and get those black studs on her side for an improvement on the deal after she murdered the son-of-a-bitch.

He thought she was still unconscious and oblivious, so certainly the best course was to play along with that. She just needed to lie quiet, marshal her strength and strike at the little zombie fuck at the first open opportunity that presented itself.

Oh. Fuck.

Wait a minute. She realized as she was lying there on the cold concrete floor that she was bleeding to death. The longer she laid there, the harder it would be for her to get up and the more likely she would just die lying there. Auntie consoled herself that she had everything figured out now. All she had to do was to act.

The black men made sounds of subservient agreement to Null – obviously their boss or leader or whatever they called it now. Head honcho? That sounded creaky. She didn't know how many of them there were, but there must have been enough to muscle all the night-time support staff of nuns and graduate students before herding all the segregated kiddies into one sloppy bunch and get them off to the busses as if they were going to a carnival or the zoo – but God only knew where the little fiend was sending them. If they had known, why they'd overtake the gang and come down to the basement and rescue dear old Auntie. That was an impossibly fun thought.

She cracked a smile even though it hurt her to do it.

No, it wasn't the smile that was hurting her –

No, it was the zombie-fuck Null straddling her and slapping her face to bring her back to consciousness. And she was conscious now, wasn't she?

"I'll kill you!" she screamed, to which Null replied with all the enthusiasm of an undertaker:

"No, Auntie, not even you have to die tonight if you play things right." He fished the knife out of his coat pocket and held it up to the light.

Auntie had resolved to play for time.

"What happened to the Doctor. Habib, or Ibrahim or whatever his name was –

"Saladin, I think it was. Peace through faith."

"Yeah, him."

"I cut him apart – deconstructed him on the Green Line Riverside Branch of the T on my way to the Newton Center stop with the shortened machete I have hanging from a lanyard I wear around my neck that lies flat against my back at this very moment."

"You're barbaric."

"Aren't we all, Auntie."

"Murdered him outright, just like that."

"Yes. Premeditated murder, if you want to get technical. I like to think of it as an execution. You know, he castrates little boys and administers clitoridectomies to young girls, effectively castrating them too."

"They can still have kids."

"But they can never have joy."

"Joy is the casualty of the modern world – even they rich don't get to have it."

"Not even billionaires Betty and Derick DeVille?"

"Maybe the saddest of all."

"So your doctor, your man of faith, maimed children for life – happily. No remorse, all delivered in good faith. For a price, he'd even dispose of unwanted children entirely who have nothing, no place and nowhere to go. Easy money. Snaps their little necks like killing chickens for Sunday dinner."

"I have strength through the power of Christ!"

"That's good, because you're going to need it."

"Just do it."

"I'll take my time, Auntie. You can be sure of that. I'm going to work on you for a while with this knife you so generously provided me with. I'm going to carve you up into a splendid disasterpiece – which isn't just a song by Slipknot – and you're going to make it out of here on your own. Once the ketamine I gave you wears off. By that time, this place should be pretty well ablaze. But you have some advantages. For one, it's raining cats and dogs outside which ought to slow down the fire; and for two, I'm allowing you to keep your arms and legs."

"Help me! God *help* me!" she screamed unabated until her throat no longer worked.

And Null did take his time with her long after she had been rendered silent.

———

"Thermite," Null said quietly. "It should work with the primer charge. Burn this mansion down in a hurricane."

The busses idled wildly set against the angry roar of the rain and the shouts, titters and squeals of small children, some of whom hadn't yet woken up, even when dragged from their dormitories downstairs, shaken about and tossed by unruly Gangsta Boyz into the busses, some crammed in three to a seat, the busses vibrating close to bucking, stalling out and giving a jolt when started up again. Jo-Jo was already in the driver's seat of the big dingy MBTA bus stolen for the purpose and the neat little Mercedes-Benz bright white minibus which bore no markings whatever boasted Desi up front, wired and cranked to boot that bus all the way to University Place at Washington Square, Brookline to Ruth Coelacanth's place, the Dapper O'Neil Shelter and Service Group.

Known otherwise by the Gangsta Boyz as "kiddie central".

A tank overfilled with minnows.

Meanwhile, Riley, ace chemist with a crack Jones that had ejected him from every undergraduate program he scammed his way into. Brilliant at first, lackluster at last, Riley finally thrived in the challenging environment of the Gangsta Boyz meth operation, given a budget and a wide enough berth to improve product quality and delivery in an ever-improving complex of methods. He was the man of meth methods in Methuen with a lab of twenty apprentices under him – so for him to be reduced to concocting and laying thermite charges to blow up an orphanage in Newton Center hurt him much more than he could ever admit.

And calm logic was the only thing that cut any ice with Null. He may have been a psychopath, no question, but the most expedient and extreme logic applied to any problem yielded a happy result with the quirky Shot Caller. But you had better take aim and not miss, because if you were wrong or slow or confused, he might determine within his own bizarre ratiocination that shooting your lights out in the heartbeat of a decision would be best for everyone – including you.

Yes, he was so fucked up that his steely reasoning could decide offhandedly that killing you would be the best way of saving you.

"I knows how to set a thermite charge, boss man. Iron oxide, aluminum powder, and a strip of magnesium. I puts down a MG strip – a nice long one – light it up then hustle back to the bus."

"No primer needed."

"Nope. The MG strip do it all, as long's I got this li'l' Bern-zomatic torch with built-in ignition to heat up dat strip proper. I got alla the strips long enough fo' me to hop on da bus and we all peel out wit da big burst o' flames jus' behind us like in the damn movies."

Riley was smart enough to correct himself from saying that Null might be behind the times or perhaps not as versed in pyrotechnics as he should be. He understood that laying and igniting thermite charges throughout a building was a good deal safer than laying a single charge on Null and not even have a chance to second guess yourself before the resultant explosion had already taken your life.

"I am behind the times a bit I think."

"Don' matta. We got ya back, Boss. Ain't none of us goin' the Ronald route on ya, real talk."

"Haul ass, then, Riley - and watch out for Auntie. She's a bit of a mess now the ketamine's worn off, since I cut out her implants and scarred her up. I also shot her in the calf. People tend to get crazy when things like that happen to them – and she's in a race against time, seeing whether she bleeds out, burns up or gets hit by a car as she lunges, caroms and stumbles her way to a fast or a slow death. Personally, I'm advocating for the latter. But I digress. Haul ass, Riley – and I mean haul it *now*."

Riley leapt from the bus and loped into the mansion before Null could have a chance to add to his digressions – which could prove lengthy. He added to them anyway on impulse and gave no sign of caring how much it might cost him or anyone else for him to be heard or ignored.

"Light a fire under what remains of Auntie's ass, Riley!" Null shouted.

And Riley had no idea who "Auntie" was.

The children on both busses had all gotten a strong inkling of what Bethlehem had in store for them. The ones that were still drugged were awake and alert because the strength of terror and adrenaline countered the cold somnolence of now-obsolete Thiopental. The busses idled noisily, haltingly with a violent stutter. Some of the children cried and whined scattershot while others shouted and whined and there was incipient violence and desperate punches delivered by tiny hands. No one was doing a thing about it, because the Gangsta Boys knew by heart never to dare to anticipate the needs of their Shot Caller, who might just put you in a situation where killing yourself was the best option. Or maybe he'd just shoot your lights out. Either way, it paid in too many ways to list to hang your imagined actions on his every word until he permitted you to make them fact.

It was an acknowledgement beyond fear.

It was recognition that the Shot Caller stayed in place because of the money, and what he inflicted on the street, which was something you could only call meta-terror. If you were one of the Gangsta Boyz, wherever you went in the Northeast Corridor, no one gave you backtalk; no one challenged you on anything because the death toll that Gangsta Boyz exacted led by a whispering homicidal maniac was enough to earn even the least member a measure of deference and respect.

Every Gangsta Boyz member knew that deference and respect

was the true sought-after quality prized highest by every street gang.

And because of the scarred-up whack job that ran the show, they had more of that than any other street gang – even in New York City, where each separate member was eyed with skepticism and contempt, but the worst of the gangs from the Bronx – ABG, Sev Side and Third Side - knew to keep a respectful distance and to keep their mouths shut in even the briefest and most trivial confrontation with the Gangsta Boys from Boston – lest a shooting war break out. And if their boss was a stone 730, J-cat, chatted-out kill-crazy motherfucker – what kind of lieutenants and soldiers might he have amassed, running gak up and down the Northeast Corridor? Worse, there were already gun-running rumors about the Gangsta Boyz impinging on their New York territory. Spark that and you spark a war.

Did the disunified Bronx street gangs want to bring that kind of zero-sum action down upon themselves?

No, as it stood, the Gangsta Boys were a swaggering bunch rocking a chip on all their shoulders, held back only by Null, the Shot Caller, a leader they had never chosen but who nevertheless muscled himself right into all their action and successfully killed anyone who disagreed with that. Not that they wanted to be fair, but since the zombie took over, ridiculous amounts of mooga kept flowing into Gangsta Boyz pockets – not just from slinging meth, but from special jobs that mattered only to the Shot Caller and no one else. But the shrink wrapped packages of hard cash paid up front virtually guaranteed near 100% of Gangsta Boyz volunteers for every run that Null offered them, for whatever the fucked-up reason.

Null did his talking with cash and the barrel of a gun and that was a language the Gangsta Boyz understood and accepted easily – just as they accepted a Shot Caller who would rather kill than back down, once that fact was dramatized to them in smoke and blood.

And cheddar, mooga, wallpaper, guap.

Non-stop guap.

It was with his shrink-wrapped block of guap in mind that Riley laid the charges of Thermite, lit the magnesium strips and bounded from Bethlehem's entrance as if he had caught some of that fire with his requisite prison jeans that was burning up his own ass. He bounded up the steps of the big bus in two lopes and nearly crashed into Null who waited calmly standing by the coin box as the bus stuttered furiously, perilously close to stalling out.

"Did you see the woman?"

"Ya. Almos' knocked dat bitch on her ass. Damn, what you do to her?" As soon as he asked the question, he regretted it and scrutinized Null's face carefully for the remotest sign of his impending death and took a breath when none came.

"But you didn't. Knock the bitch on her ass. Did you?" he whispered.

"No, I dint touch her, I swear. I passed her jus' after the last charge. I don't know she make it out 'fo' dis bitch go blooey."

"We'll stick around and see if she gets out safely."

"She a mess though, real talk – all wounded and shit. Prolly pretty good she jus' go up in flames wit' dis bitch at end o' da day."

"I agree. It would be a mercy for her to peg out like that – a mercy she doesn't deserve."

"So, you almos' kill her ass and now you wanna save it?"

"I do. I think it would be best if she survives. So, I'm pulling for her to get out before, as you said, Bethlehem goes blooey."

Riley's heart was pounding so hard he was almost certain it would pop right out of his chest as the bus idled jerkily, sputtering with mini-explosions every few minutes as the rain bombarded its roof in such clobbering bursts that it could have easily been mistaken for hail.

"Breathe, Riley," sighed Null.

Riley opened his mouth to speak, steadying himself against the coin box of the purloined bus when the first thermite charge belched out its exploding orange glow. He made a little gulping sound as he was about to speak, but the next charge went off before he could do it. Null put a finger to his lips to signify quiet and all that could be heard after that was the habitual struggling antics of the children and the sharp crackling of the brightly glowing mansion under the incessant rain.

"We gotta bounce, cuz," Jo-Jo said firmly.

"We do," Null admitted. "Maybe a couple of minutes more then I can assume Auntie has gone to her undeserved reward."

Riley was sweating and did a little jerk when the next charge blew and the mansion now wore a great aureole of orange. Null let out a sigh and started to lift his arm to give Jo-Jo the signal to put the bus in gear and stopped when he saw it, which was after Riley saw it first and blurted out, "That bitch a right monstah now!"

Auntie was barely ahead of the flames and the hem of her dress of rags was aflame.

"She was one of those for a long time before this, Riley. Now she's finally caught up to herself and looks the part."

It was a reasonable statement made by an unreasonable man. It was also the truest of understatements.

What lumbered through the entrance and out into the rain from the burning mansion wasn't recognizable as the former sexworker known as the Rubber Nun and the buxom donor roper and child broker known as Auntie Nonie Fomites. It wasn't even identifiable as a human being – or, at least, a whole one. And there was nothing womanly about it. The face was absent a nose, the head was absent the ears – but the eyes blazed wildly even in the angry downpour of rain and against the blossoming orange of the flames that were steadily, ineluctably consuming Bethlehem.

There were no obvious breasts, per se, but a darkness that could only have been blood that spread from the chest down looked like an oil slick even under the punishing rain. The face was bleeding badly from deep cuts in it that could be seen despite their blood being quickly washed away. It was obvious that the blood kept coming, stubbornly renewing its presence.

Then came the dull moaning from the open mouth from which blood was pouring out in gouts, further flooding the blood-slicked front of the garment that seemed to have once been a dress, but had been reduced to uneven ragged strips that flapped in the storm. The sound was loud yet muffled, smooth yet anguished.

Riley couldn't help but speak it, so he just let it out.

"Shit. You cut out dat thing's tongue."

"Not exactly, Riley."

"No?" That was all he dared to ask."

"No. I only cut out half of it."

It flickered to a fast clarity in Riley's mind that the Shot Caller wanted her to be able to speak but wanted her to be unintelligible – wanted her to sound pathetic, desperate, incoherent. Just like her little former charges.

Null withdrew the dagger from his coat pocket, pinwheeled it neatly in the air twice, then pocketed it again.

Riley flinched.

"Don't worry, Riley. I have much better plans for you than anything that would have to involve Auntie's dagger."

As Auntie Nonie screamed in the rain that seemed to refuse to swallow her up even as the lapping flames were close behind her, Jo-Jo gunned the bus and took it down Herrick Road toward Center Street, the white minibus behind it following suit a long minute later while she waved angry little sharp-nailed fists in the air – and promptly fell over.

TWENTY-FOUR

His Eminence, Cardinal Isidore Cromulent, was fighting hard with sleep for it to just take him already and give him the blessed respite of at least a few hours before his customary arousal, hot shower with sauna, big breakfast of eggs, smoked salmon, croissants, fresh-squeezed orange juice and the lovely vice of his double cappuccino – all of which led him to the depressing bringdown of the grim duties that being cardinal for the Archdiocese of Boston entailed.

The child-abuse suits and litigations seemed endless, tedious, and the more he dickered them down in settlements—'Jewed them down,' would have been his preferred expression for it in the years before he pursued his calling—the more they seemed to pop up. It wasn't that they weren't just like whack-a-mole (they were), but it was as if the whack-a-mole phenomenon were being played out in a huge dreamy meadow and the moles were dandelions and they sprang up no matter what you did, how many of them you cut and rooted out, how many of them you burned.

And all the billions in the Holy Mother Church's purse were unable to stanch the constant bleeding, and the painful attrition of her approximate billion complicit believers threatened the very power of the church that had enabled their getting away with such peccadilloes for centuries.

His stomach was sour, and his disposition was worse.

He closed his eyes and dreamed of his whack-a-mole field of dandelions shifting into a cloying array of bright red poppies sprouting all about him as he lay there begging secretly to be soothed, but not uttering a word, not even in prayer, which he had privately determined for himself before accepting higher office within the church was as much good as a fart in a natural gas explosion. Oh, but prayer was the best means of sucking money into the church from all sorts of sources – not just from the penurious parishioners, but from the secular business realm itself, ecstatic to wrap itself in approved hosannas to Jesus Christ at a price that Holy Mother Church received gratefully with beneficent aplomb, always ready to confer sacrosanctity onto socially acceptable pimps, human traffickers, usurers and despoilers of the earth, only in corporate form, of course. Respectable beyond reproach. He gloried to himself as usual how lustrous, generous and protective of him Holy Mother Church was in allowing him, her humble servant, to share in her power as he so piously yet with a cunning worldliness pursued her plans and aims.

That last part usually drowsed him off to the deep, blank, untroubled slumber he felt was his special right and that wantonly and capriciously eluded him. Him, a Prince of the Church, on track to be elected the first American pope, having more times than he could count, being reduced to having to beg pagan Morpheus for relief like a homeless person—like the scum bums that mistook his baroque, lush—and continually scaffolded residence of the Basilica of Our Lady of Perpetual Sorrow on A Street for some sort of sanctuary. Well, sure, it's in Southie, so what does he expect? Well, sure the Basilica was his sanctuary and no one else's.

Okay. The yet-to-be-gelded *Defensores Fidei de Puero* took sanctuary there. But not for long. He had them dormed-out at Auntie's so that Sam and Dr. Saladin could finish what little was left of the now disastrous-seeming papal solution to stemming the tide of sexual abuse suits and the thing that was at the crux of the whole thing—evading criminal charges against priests before they could be credibly defrocked, or before the statute of limitations ran out and the little tykes had become adult enough to make coherent, credible formal complaints.

And this single fact gnawed at him that was bigger, blacker, and more threatening than all the worries that rested on top of it: Telling His Holiness that the *Defensores Fidei de Puero* choir program was a flat-out bust. A failure. It would be tough to avoid using the term that the probing papal mind would hit on squarely if he didn't have a counter for it. Disaster.

Disaster.

And when His Holiness used that word, that meant legal trouble, which would place his head on the metaphorical chopping block, which meant that he would be charged with a special mission that would likely leave him freezing to death somewhere in the Aleutian Islands. That very real probability put the kibosh on any further drowsing. And where the hell was Sam? For a scholar, the cardinal pretty well made him for a bumpkin, possibly even on the spectrum. Likely that was it. Autism spectrum disorder. Sam Bricolage in all his dialectical theological expertise, his always superb and irrefragable disputations of atheism, was in the final analysis incapable of reading emotion and social cues. Where the cardinal was nearly always certain what an opponent or ally was thinking, Father Bricolage hadn't the first clue about any of it, and in fact was an obvious reading-between-the-lines kind of illiterate. Without the cardinal backing him, he was a first-rate blunderer, a damn klutz careening and caroming his way through a desultory career in the church with no other significant opportunities.

Damn him, Sam.

Why hadn't he called to give the cardinal the all-clear on the clean ending of the *Defensores Fidei de Puero* program, with all loose ends neatly and finally all tied up? Dead and buried. What was taking so goddamn long?

The cardinal shuddered and sat bolt upright in bed, discomfited and feeling a chill. Before he could get up and put on his robe, the answer to his question came in the form of an explosion. In a panic, he threw on his L.L. Bean plush forest-green robe and went into his study, sat down at his 18th century mahogany desk in the dark, grabbed the receiver from its cradle on the landline console and hit one button for a number he had on speed-dial.

"Derrick, you were wrong. What I was warned would happen is happening."

"Guy, you have my Sat phone. Do you even know who you're talking to? I'm at a secure, undisclosed location doing work for the United States military—"

"You think I don't know that, Derrick? You think I'd dial the emergency number if it wasn't a goddamned emergency?"

"Who the fuck is this?"

"Who the fuck do you think it is? It's the fucking cardinal is who the fuck you're speaking with, you buffoon."

"Oh, Izzy. Hey, I'm sorry. I should have known it'd be you—recognized your whiny, candy ass little voice immediately. And this is a pretty good connect for a sat. Listen, I'm a bit distracted at the moment. Maybe I can hit you up later. We're in the middle of a significant rendition here at present. Um. At this undisclosed place. A secure location. We're getting down to the real nitty-gritty. Blood, sweat and tears type stuff here. Just about to crack this walnut wide open. So, tell me, Izzy, quick—what can I do ya for?"

The cardinal hunkered down with most of his body under the desk but his elbows and chin resting at the top of it. He lowered his voice and spoke in a raspy *sotto voce*. "There were gunshots outside. I counted three, so it's not a car backfiring or some prankster's fireworks."

"Listen up, Padre. I gave you an attachment of three of the best former Navy Seals I had in my outfit and I sure as shit wish they were here with me now instead of twiddling their thumbs protecting your boney ass."

"Derrick, this is no time to fuck around. You remember about the guy I told you about? The one who put it out on the street that he was coming for me. You remember

that?"

"Well, shit-fire, Padre. How does a hoity-toity Prince of the Church get close enough to the street to find out some punk's gunning for him?"

"I told you before. I got it from the Order—"

"Yeah, well, weren't they supposed to be takin' care of that little piece of business for you?"

"Well, you know what happened there."

"All too well, your Eminence. You and them and your whole church are nothing but FUBAR. Y'know what that means, Izzy?"

"I can guess."

"Oh, I'm certain you know. I'm bettin' you're gettin' more intimate with the meaning of that with every passing minute."

"Spit it out, why don't you, Derrick? What do you know that I don't?"

"I think Betty was looped out of her mind on too much cocaine and too many Manhattans to try and make a profit while getting us in good graces with your fucked-up cult, but you really can't go around advancing God's kingdom on earth when you're bombed out of your friggin' mind."

"Never mind that."

"Oh, you're already putting the once-upon-a-time-it-was-never-us-oh-so-clever-deniability of your catamite boys' choir into high gear, now ain't you, Izzy?"

"What's done is done, Derrick."

"I told you before, there's no such man coming to get you. It's a legend among the idiotic scum and low-level criminal mopes of the gutter. Now, are you really sure you heard gunshots?"

"I know what gunshots sound like. Even with a silencer, they're damn loud."

"Suppressor, you mean. Right. Well, kudos to you, Padre. I'm sure it was just one of the boys firing off a practice round at some imbecilic jamoke who was gettin' a might too close to your doorstep. Scared him or her or whatever off. Navy Seals are no joke. Even if this guy existed and was actually coming for you, he'd never get past them. They'd stitch him up in a body bag before you could say Donald Trump. Go drink yourself some hot milk and go back to bed. With the attachment of three Navy Seals, we got your security handled. You heard them shots a while back by now, yes?"

"Yes, that's so."

"You hearin' anythin' more? Shots? Sounds of a scuffle?"

"No, it's all gone quiet."

"Well, doncha think if it were him and he somehow got past my seals, he'd be bearin' down upon you about now?"

"I suppose that would prove to be a common-sense conclusion."

"You're in one piece, yammerin' to me on the sat phone, so we both may further conclude that you're alright—all in one piece?"

The cardinal didn't answer, just hung up the phone, stood up slowly from his position of being three-quarters stuck under his antique desk, rising regally, shaking his head and chuckling softly to himself. He wiped his brow with the back of his hand and flicked the master switch under the long lip of the desk, which turned on all the lights of his study. The quick flash of light hurt his eyes for a moment, so he shielded them with his hand. When he took away his hand, his heart stopped.

"They're all dead, if you must know, Eminence."

Null was sitting in a slouch on the pink, silk-cushioned settee, a look of resolute tedium and indifference on his scarred face.

"Do you want to tell me a story, Eminence, or do I get to tell you one? I forget how these things are supposed to go."

Calm descended on the cardinal like a shadow. He seemed somehow sepulchral even in renewed light. What was before him was a light, ugly little man half-swallowed by an overcoat, his scarred and carbuncled face shaded by a porkpie hat. There was a big gun resting in his lap, but a closer look revealed that it was the barrel of the gun that made it big. The silencer those in the know called a suppressor. Maybe the shots he had heard didn't come from it, but rather from Derrick's Navy Seals, whose shots must have gone wild. They were probably hiding themselves in shame, having let this little, funny-looking man get the better of them. Figured. Derrick was all talk and posturing. The security men he had detailed to the basilica to protect no less a personage than a cardinal were virtually worthless—all show and no go.

"You chased them away, didn't you? The three supposed Navy Seals. Well, you've done me a service, sir, obviously, which I appreciate greatly. Come, let me sit right back down and write you a check – you don't mind if it's personal, do you? Checks written on behalf of the Archdiocese are with our comptroller. I assure you it's good. I'm in a profession where lying and writing bad checks is a pretty severe disqualification."

Null angled the gun lazily so that its barrel indicated a bullet trajectory that would have hit the cardinal center chest. "I'd prefer it if you stayed right where you are, if you don't mind. Our business together is a quantum leap from being solved with a check at this point."

"What business could we possibly have together other than your demonstrating to me the incompetence of my security detail?"

"I wouldn't be too hard on them, Eminence. They hadn't seen or dealt with one like me before."

"One? Like you?"

"Yes, Eminence, one like me. I walk with a limp you know. I'm not a very big- or threatening-looking person. And you know how this damp New England cold permeates everything. Anyway, they made me for a drunk, lost and in the wrong neck of the woods for this time of night. So it wasn't all that hard to dispatch them."

"Dis-*patch*?"

"That's right. Dispatch."

"But they each got a shot off. I heard them."

"No, they weren't able to do that. But I can see how you would think that. You'd think the suppressor would dampen the noise to a more discreet, non-intrusive level. But no, even this one makes quite a bang."

"You're saying those three shots were yours, then?"

"That's exactly what I'm saying."

"Those dolts!"

"They thought they were ready for me, but they weren't. They wanted to help the poor drunken schnook up off the sidewalk, help him get an Uber. Meanwhile, in the last year or so, I've gotten quite good at shooting with a semi-automatic pistol. It's pretty easy once you get the hang of it. And I've had lots of practice."

"I'll just bet you had."

"Don't go for the phone, Eminence. You'll never make it before I drop you. And we have so much work ahead of us tonight."

"Fine. Speak your piece then."

The cardinal made a show of standing quite still and rigid in one place. He didn't know just how far this cretin's mental illness extended, but the main thing was to keep him talking. He took a deep breath and then filled the momentary silence.

"You know, my son, that I'm well-positioned to petition the lord with prayer as your intercessor for you to be granted pardon and forgiveness by our lord and savior Jesus Christ."

"Too late, Eminence. And I don't recognize a lord above me of any kind, including your God."

"All you need to do is ask, my son."

"I won't be doing that. But as I was telling you, those men didn't get off a single shot, hit or miss, at all. I took care of each one of them with a bullet to the brain—headshots all. I know that's a difficult thing to do, but it came to me pretty easily. I didn't even have to think about it. You know, when you do a thing often enough, you tend to get good at it. A neat trick some have said—not that I'll be starting a career as a trick shooter anytime soon."

"You're here to kill me then. You're a paid assassin then."

"Oh, no, Eminence. I would never do that."

"Well, I suppose that's a relief."

"I wouldn't know. I just intend on doing it for free."

"You're my judge, jury and executioner, is that it?"

"Not at all."

"You're not?"

"Just your executioner."

"Pray with me, my son."

"I'm certain you're about to do a great deal of praying, Eminence. I hope you won't be offended if I don't."

"I've alerted the police so you'd better get out of here while you still can, my son."

"I'd better hurry then, if you're right. But let's say I'll call your bluff and just proceed at my own pace. Should they come when I'm busy with you, then I'll hold court with them and, either way, you won't be excluded."

Cardinal Cromulent clicked his tongue, cast his eyes to the ceiling.

"So the street was right after all. You *are* the monster coming to get me. Well, monster, you don't look like much to me. Scrawny and sickly. A wisp of hair and bone. No wonder my security detail underestimated you. You're nothing without that gun." His blood was up, and he was already feeling like his old self. "Why not face me like a man, if you can, and stop beating around the bush?"

"It's not the worst suggestion I've heard. Let me think about that for a few minutes."

Then the cardinal snarled, having lost his celestial appearance of patient discernment above all petty squabbling. He intoned: "What gives you the right to judge me. *Me*—a Prince of the Church? And this is about some pathetic little rodents who barely qualify as children? Repellently scurrying little things with no humanity in them—godless, unloved and unwanted. I was giving them a life, a purpose—an esteemed place within Holy Mother Church, who was ready to accept them and hold them close to her bosom as she would no others. I was on a mission, a *sanctified* mission having been charged me by His Holiness The pope himself. Who are you to even *try* and interfere with that, you useless common hoodlum? You godless degenerate!"

Null was serene.

"You think kidnapping and castrating young boys to then assign each to a priest to be their personal catamites all to avoid the bad press and lawsuits, if not prosecutions, for child rape is really in line with the espoused values of the criminal enterprise you like to call Holy Mother Church?"

"The values of Holy Mother Church ride the tides and vicissitudes of modernity to prove ever refreshing to all those morally confused and transgressing parishioners who wish to cling to her in these horrid, morally situational, morally transactional and far too worldly times. She sees to the fulfillment of the spirit and to the means of conducting the most wretched into heaven, even you—"

"Me? I'm just a drug supplier and distributor. And I use unwanted children to conduct meth heads to their own brand of heaven, if that's what they want. My values aren't for castration and lifelong sexual slavery. And they age out of my system and some even matriculate to colleges and universities. What future would your *Defensores Fidei de Puero* have?"

"Abiding love within and always a place within Holy Mother Church."

"Somehow, I just can't reconcile abiding love with castration and sex slavery, even regular plain old slavery. But I understand the concept of agreeing to disagree, which is where we'll probably have to let it rest."

"So, that's it?" the cardinal asked with tentative incredulity.

"That's it," answered Null as he stood and placed the Heckler and Koch P7 with its long suppressor gently on the settee.

"You're, um, maybe leaving?"

"Of course, Eminence. But first we have a bit of business to attend to."

"And what praytell might that be?"

"Your execution."

"Don't be waggish."

"I'm not. This is it for you, Cardinal. But still, I heard you were a Golden Gloves boxer at one time. True?"

"That was a long time ago. So what?"

"So, this, Eminence," Null said, reaching into his coat for something, found it then threw it down on the rug between them— Auntie's dagger. "Box me."

With a subhuman growl of rage, the cardinal dove for the knife, but instead was met by Null, who got there first. Null was fast, driven in his work but, fast as he was, he took his time with the cardinal, who, after a very short while, had absolutely nothing to say about it. He never had the chance to say his pet prayer as he would do every morning and every evening, *"O my God, my only good, the author of my being and my last end, I give You my heart. Praise, honor, and glory be to You forever and ever. Amen."* It wasn't that he lacked the supreme will to do it—far from it—but his tongue had been cut out.

Null left in silence like a passing shadow two hours before the cardinal's usual morning mass.

EPILOGUE

Spring in the Dallas Fort-Worth region of arid Texas is like midsummer in New England. Bright, hot and sweaty – but with a fine dryness that New England could never lay claim to, which allowed a lax kind of comfort to be enjoyed on such days. Midsummer in New England was an oppressive condition, with its perma-fog of deep humidity which remained the same, whether the weather was a deep freeze or a scorching kiln. The cloud was always there to make either condition that much worse. But Spring in Texas? Where better to spend some of it than at the Rough Creek Lodge and Resort? And there are few resorts as beautiful and varied in their features and diversions than that, plus, a special dimension to the place was its deluxe shooting range, which catered to all forms of shooting sports, whether sporting clays, five stand (similar to sporting clays in that a wide variety of targets are thrown), wobble trap (which has a more extreme target flight path than in shooting standard trap) and shooting complex which provides a 50-yard handgun Range and a 100-yard multi-purpose range, for whatever semi-automatic pistols and rifles you cared to fire.

On the face of things, it seems that Rough Creek Lodge and Resort Shooting Range is one of the finest of its kind anywhere in the United States. It also holds the unfortunate place in history as being the last stand for vaunted American Sniper, Chris Kyle, a US Navy Seal who had boisterously claimed to have killed more than 255 people during his deployment in the Iraq War. He was gunned down at Rough Creek in 2013 by yet another Iraq War veteran, Eddie Ray Routh, who was suffering from combat-induced PTSD. Kyle died while packing a loaded .45-caliber military-style handgun —a Springfield Armory 1911 TRP Operator pistol—that was stuck snug in his waist holster. He wasn't able to remove the retaining strap and unholster his weapon in time to save himself. The same was true of his companion at the time, Chad Littlefield, who was also shot dead in the same instant by Routh, his 1911 TRP also stuck snug in its holster.

In his eponymous memoir "American Sniper," Kyle described killing as "fun", something he "loved."

Killed by a "good guy with a gun," as any astute Republican might say. (Wasn't Iraq-war vet Eddie Ray Routh at least that? A good guy with a gun?)

Irony aside, though, Rough Creek was an ideal place for Derrick DeVille to sharpen up his shooting skills. Hone his technique. Pure fun in Derrick's book. Sweaty and grimy, but happy as he usually was, he hefted his 33-inch-large-gun-range tactical duffel bag onto the back of his Dodge Ram 1500 4-door pickup. He had just come from a long and satisfying multi-rifle shooting session at the Rough Creek shooting complex. Smiling smugly, Derrick got in behind the wheel of the Ram and froze.

There in the rear-view mirror was the scarred, carbuncled face of Null.

His eyes were the eyes of a dead animal. Taxidermy-glass-like. Derrick thought at first that someone had placed a grotesque horror dummy in the backseat for a laugh. But although its eyes were unblinking, the thing moved and stuck a gun barrel at the base of his skull. His mouth was suddenly dry, and he found it hard to swallow.

Okay. He had been trained for this. He was a Navy Seal, able to remain calm in the gnarliest of intense situations.

The dummy wasn't talking, and he knew why.

He was leaving the first move for him to make.

So Derrick moved to play for time.

He abruptly laughed an affected laugh and spoke boldly with all the forced good humor he could muster, "Ho-ho-ho! What have we here? The famous meth kingpin himself?"

"To put it succinctly."

"I don't suppose I could offer you a job, could I?"

"You just did and no, I don't really need the money. All my obsessions are cheap and often boil down to one thing. Just one thing."

"Too bad. I'm a billionaire a few times over. I could pay you a million-a-week and not break a sweat. Y'know – for that 'just one thing' you do?"

"Tempting, but no."

"What can you do with someone who just refuses to be bought? It flies in the face of human nature."

"You'd think I'd know better."

"I don't know what to think anymore."

"You know why I'm here."

"I know why. And not for nothin', it wasn't really my idea to do anything with those kids. I don't even like kids—they're damn enervating. That's why I never bothered to have any. I don't know what Betty's deal is on that score – she's like a dried-up old spinster, yet she just adores the little soul-sucking vampires. Never had any intention to marry though—actually having sex with someone even for procreation was always something beneath her."

"That's something I think Wynona Fomites once said about children, right? Soul-sucking vampires?"

"Why not? The Rubber Nun was chock full of amusing little pet phrases."

"Was Cardinal Cromulent chock full of amusing phrases too?"

"Now, y'see, that's something else that can be pinned on Betty.

She was all hot and bothered to get in bed with the little wimp in any possible way – except, you know, the dirty way. The celibacy thing really floated her boat."

"Even though she was facilitating the means of the sacerdotal violation of celibacy."

"They say irony's dead, buddy, but I think it's still alive and kicking us both right in the teeth."

"I think you may have a point there, Derrick."

And before the Navy Seal could say anything more, Null blew his brains out right through his eye sockets, which made a bright red Rorschach of gore all over the windshield.

———

A curious thing: Betty Deville had mysteriously disappeared from her mansion in Corpus Christi, Texas for three months until she was finally located at Ben Gurion Airport in Jerusalem, packed up in a box awaiting clearance through customs. An autopsy revealed that she had been heavily drugged with propofol, etomidate and ketamine and folded neatly into a reinforced corrugated cardboard shipping box. No one could be sure if she was awake when she died of extreme dehydration or if she merely had slept through it.

The investigation into her murder remains open.

———

The following short squib appeared as a bulleted news item in the *International Times*:

"Suspected arch-criminal and drug lord Joseph Xavier Null of Boston had been spotted by several operatives of Interpol in Rome just after an assassination attempt had been made on the pope two days before at his residence in Casa Santa Marta—*Domus Sanctae Marthae*—a building adjacent to St. Peter's Basilica in Vatican City. There being no outstanding warrants against Mr. Null, he could not be apprehended by Interpol, even though as many as eleven members of the 134-man contingent of Pontifical Swiss Guards were reportedly gunned down by an intruder dressed in a black overcoat wearing a porkpie hat and carrying several kinds of illegal automatic weapons. The intruder was said to have been Mr. Null, though the only surviving witnesses to corroborate this were members of the Pontifical Swiss Guard who couldn't be certain of the fact.

"Prior to the shooting, when stopped by the guardsmen and warned there was no possible way he could obtain access to the pope even if the Pontifical Swiss Guard were somehow removed, the unidentified assailant was heard to announce:

"The journey of a thousand miles begins with a single step."

———

Don't miss out on your next favorite book!
Join the Melange Books mailing list at
www.melange-books.com/mail.html

ACKNOWLEDGMENTS

The author hereby wishes to acknowledge his small band of supporters:

Nancy Pepin, née Durocher, who's with me in all things and in everything that matters.

Scott Oddo, for his friendship and keen intellect.

Link Yaco, for his weird science art; Curtis Kolovson for his unwavering support; Susan Mears for her wonderful literary expertise; Marc Songini, for his wit and his literary japing; Huntley Dent, for all his support moral and otherwise; Matt Bon for his startling artistry; Steve Dooner, for his astonishing breadth of cultural literacy, abstruse and not; Kate Nicholas, for her sharp wit, bordering on slight insanity; Susan Gambrell Reinhardt, whose sweetly acid commentary is always inspiring; Glen Dansker for being a mensch; Brett Hicks for his promotional savvy and Joe Schatzle for always knowing how to crack me up.

This parvum opus is for you all.

THANK YOU FOR READING

Did you enjoy this book?

We invite you to leave a review at the website of your choice, such as Goodreads, Amazon, Barnes & Noble, etc.

DID YOU KNOW THAT LEAVING A REVIEW...

- Helps other readers find books they may enjoy.
- Gives you a chance to let your voice be heard.
- Gives authors recognition for their hard work.
- Doesn't have to be long. A sentence or two about why you liked the book will do.

ABOUT THE AUTHOR

Gary S. Kadet has been a journalist, covering various beats for the Boston Herald, Globe and even Playboy Magazine, which also published his fiction. He was a contributing editor for the nationally-read Boston Book Review where he covered crime fiction in his "Trouble is Their Business" column. In the 90s, he was a trailblazer on the Internet, running the 10th largest adult website in the world, appearing on MSNBC commenting on the future of adult material on the web. His novel "D/s - an Anti-Love Story" was the first novel to portray the real-world BDSM scene without prurience or sentimentality and was a Book Of The Month Club main selection.

GarySKadet@protonmail.com

facebook.com/CleverNovels
x.com/GaryScottKadet

ALSO BY GARY S. KADET

WITH MELANGE BOOKS

<u>Null and Boyd Noir</u>

Condition Zero

Violent Mind Candy

High Body Count

The Ravening Wolves